THE ONES BEFORE

Book One of the Discovery Trilogy

F. D. Brant

F. D. Brant

GRESHAM, OREGON

Books Written by F. D. Brant

Science Fiction Adventure

Of Gods Strangers and Messengers

Survival Trilogy

Time of Isolation

Desperate to Survive

A Taste of history Past

The Harsh Lands

Post-Apocalyptic

Unexpected Unplanned and into the Unknown

Discovery Trilogy

The Ones Before

Discovery

An Ancient Fire

Contemporary Christian Fiction

The Woman in the Snow

History! Who'd have thought that this would be my life direction? Not me, but somewhere it became my passion, intrigued me, sucked me in. And now I'm the head Keeper of the Past. Jllon thought, as he sat at his desk, *So much history, so much chaos, so much unknown, and with those mapping teams out, maybe some answers.* Yet he didn't hold out much hope. It had taken a long time just to reach this point where they would be mapping all the major trails – well as many as they could find. This still left vast areas unmapped and unknown. He hoped to be able to solve some of those conflicting points in their history, to see if the myths were real or would remain myths. But with the costs involved, with this push to map the trails, the chances were slim to none. Still one could hope. After all, there might be something gleaned from the notes of these cartographers that would point to the answers to the too many questions that he personally had.

Questions, for example; why did the myths of the *ones before* persist? There nothing had been found, nothing written, not even a hint that these ancients had ever existed, yet the myths about them were strong, and wouldn't die a natural death. While not a believer in the myths, he had to admit that what was being said about them was consistent, and had remained so for as long as the records had existed. Shrugging, there was a good chance that he would work his entire career and never leave this township. Too bad really, because he, and he had to admit, his mate, loved the fieldwork. But finances being what they were and he knew that there wouldn't be much improvement in the near future, anything he suggested would probably be nixed anyway.

He'd been researching records that went back to the time of chaos and destruction. There had been so little of that time that was written, or known. And what was written many times conflicted with other writings. So how did one reconcile the differences? After all, there was no way to return to that time, to observe, to understand what was happening to their world. Sighing, he thought, *if only*. But that was a reality that none of them could bring about. And because of the scarceness of what they had it was impossible to know what the truth was, and where the fiction began. And there was never any mention that he could find, of those elusive *ones before*. Giving strength to his convictions that they had to be a fictional people – something to keep the whelps in line, something to scare one on those stormy nights, but not real, and as such had never existed at all.

Yet . . . yet, there appeared to be a consistency that seemed almost to exist within the consciousness of all of them. It whispered that these elusive ones were real, had lived, had existed, and demanded to be recognized for who and what they were. He had to admit that he and the rest had to come from somewhere. So how did one go and either prove or disprove such a thing? How did fact become myth or myth become fact? He had no answers to these questions or even how to tackle or solve them. Any of the digs that had been performed had only revealed their past ancestors, and nothing, literally nothing had ever been discovered to point in these unknown ancient's direction. And anything presented as proof of the *ones before*, even from the learned, had eventually been shown to be fakes, to have been created by their own people destroying some of those past learned careers forever. Would there ever be proof one way or the other? *Ah now isn't that the question*, and would he live to see the answer?

Pausing a moment, looking out the window and really seeing nothing, he sat deep in thought. Yet, his subconscious picked up the movement of people, as they proceeded down the dirt pathways. He saw the heat waves dancing off the ground as the pulse of the township continued around him. While he couldn't be sure that what he was writing or thinking at this moment in time would ever become public, knowing how things worked, it very well could. *Again, just what is it that keeps this myth alive?* In a sense, the changes to society that now existed could be traced back to certain times in the written, known history. And when one actually researched what was there, the tradition or method they used today became obvious. He knew that they had far to go before the world they lived would be filled with people. There were vast unexplored stretches and primitive areas that were controlled by bandits or the nomads, and the small villages, and the ones that had grown larger to become townships were more recent developments – within the last 100 to 200 turns. Somehow, and known throughout the written history, contact had been maintained between the 5 continents, and while there was a small difference in the languages, all of them spoke the same language. It was an accepted fact, and it made it easier for all that existed, helping keep things somewhat peaceful except for the occasional attacks from the raiders and bandits. And with all the lands available it was doubtful there would be such problems in the future.

Fortunately such attacks from the raiders and such were rare, and if one did enter the wild lands, the outback where no one lived, the risk became greater that one could become a victim of the bandits. After all, there wasn't any way to enforce any laws upon them, and if these bandits tried to attack the villages, it would be then that they would be hunted down and eliminated. So most of the lawless remained in the areas where, other than themselves, no one lived. It forced the ones who traveled, to travel in large groups for protection, but he felt that someday that even this life style would change, and the bandits would be no more – well, at least one hoped. One thing for sure these thoughts weren't getting this report done, or the research completed. He needed to get back to task and at least finish the report before returning home and to spend some quality time with his mate, Nouma. Thinking of her immediately brought a smile. After all, she was the most important person in his life and couldn't see life without her. *Enough! Back to reality, this isn't getting the work accomplished.*

When those thoughts of the *ones before* entered his mind, he found that it would take a while before he could eradicate them and bring himself to task. What was it about them that kept drawing him back? After all, he would be only one in a long line of learned that had tried to either prove or disprove their existence. And, as far as he could tell, nothing, absolutely nothing had ever come out of all their research, all their field work, all of their dedication to that very subject. So why would it be such a draw to him and by contemplating the *ones before*, was it truly a waste of time, or could he finally put the myth to rest? A good question for sure, but one that had already been asked . . .

So, where would he go from here . . . yeah that is the question isn't it?

CHAPTER ONE

Desert! Fauul thought as he shook his head. *Damn him! Weren't we warned to remain on the existing trails? Yet our fearless, and worthless, if I want to be honest, leader decided to leave the trails and pursue that salt depression. And so here we are . . . lost and off the mark with little to no water. Some cartographers we've shown ourselves to be.*

The desert sun was still hot even though it was setting – heading shortly to be behind those western mountains – mountains that blocked their route out of this hell of heat and cold. They had been in the backcountry for more than a turn of the planet around the sun, and in this desert longer than he wanted, and he was getting tired of the whole business. He had joined this expedition on a lark, a dare, and if he knew who was going to lead the team he would have backed out. Yet here he was with this mapping team, trapped in this desert – not that he wasn't good at what he did, he just got tired of hearing, over and over again, how great a leader the one in charge was. The constant complaining from him about, "How I was never recognized for my abilities and that is why I took this assignment, just to show those ungrateful ones that I'm exactly who I said". It ground on one's mind, and kept everybody on edge.

Well, at least it appeared that maybe, just maybe, they were nearing the end of the assignment, and again if he wanted to be truthful, he couldn't wait. He had overheard a conversation stating that their mapping assignment was almost complete – not that he was unaware of the fact. Of course this had been said too much lately. They were to tie in with some locals in a remote village somewhere over those barren – well barren on the east side anyway –

western mountains, and gather the information that these locals had on the surrounding countryside. Beyond this village was one of the largest oceans of this world. Again, if the information was correct, once they were done in that village, all the hard preliminary surveying and fieldwork would be complete. They would stay there for a short period of time, organizing all the information gathered, and hopefully head back. Of course all they were doing this time around was the mapping of the major trails through the outback. He truly couldn't wait for it to end – this adventure had definitely grown old and tedious. Well, at least within a moon cycle they would be in that remote village, and getting the last of the necessary data – if they ever got out of this desert that is. *And,* Fauul thought, *of course, there may just be a little female companionship there, and that would be a nice change after living with this all male group.*

Fauul didn't think of himself as any more than ordinary. Yet, nature had given him a little more height and girth than his fellow males, and the females, who were his friends back in the township that he called home, had said he was very good looking. But he figured they were just trying to get on his good side, since if one of them could land him as a mate, they would be the envy of their friends. From the female's point of view, after all, he earned a very, very good living, and being high in the cartographer department, had some importance – something that many of the township females, who had mates, liked to brag to their friends about. It was something he would never understand. *Still . . . oh well. Guess I'll never understand the female mind.*

He was second in charge here, but supposedly the majority of the planning and such was to be covered by mister ego, Joellie, the one who claimed to be in charge – at least that was the way, he, Joellie saw it. But if the truth were told, Joellie did more complaining than actual work, which meant, of course, that it fell to him personally. Well, not much could be helped right now. He hoped that the small outlying village had a hostel. He needed a bath, and a real bed instead of the ground, and to be honest that or any bed would be a real luxury right now.

He stood outside of camp, within hearing distance so if any would be looking for him he'd hear. He had to admit the solitude first was something he'd prefer to miss, but right now the quiet, as night approached, and the breezes that rose and fell, still holding heat, but holding a promise of cooling, relaxed him. Staring out into the distance he found his mind drifting, which was no surprise. After all, here it was all the familiar faces, and no entertainment other than what they provided for themselves.

Thinking back, he knew that they had come through what seemed like hundreds of townships, small villages, and too much wilderness. At times, it just seemed like this mapping project would never end, or . . . end in tragedy. There were more than a few times when someone had slipped and almost fallen off a cliff, or had been bitten by some unknown crawler, ending up with some swelling or redness. Then there was that one day, with all were returning to camp extremely tired – it had been a very trying day. It had been one of those days where the camp was behind them and they would need to backtrack, meaning they'd cover the same area twice. The area had vegetation two to three body lengths high and no easy way to go through or see anything. Supposedly there was one of the major trails in the area, but for the life of any of them they had yet to locate it. One of the underlings was working his way through a portion of that brush that seemed to be thicker than the rest. He needed to get atop a large boulder so that they could continue to confirm the mapping or maybe actually see that undiscovered trail. What looked like solid ground turned out instead, to be a hole that he fell into. Fortunately he was not hurt. But it appeared that runoff from rains had formed that hole, and there were no handholds. The rocks that were on the sides of the hole were smooth and slick. It was deep enough that one could not reach down and help him out, which meant someone had to go back to camp and get a rope. Unfortunately, it was a two-hour hike back to camp and a two-hour return. This delay would mean another day in this tough area, but nothing could be done about it. Remembering the incident he almost smiled. It was almost funny, the expression on the trapped one's face, when he realized he would be there for at least four hours. Knowing this one, Fauul knew his imagination would start working and he would place all sort of nasty beasts coming down into that hole to bother him. You could almost see his mind start working in that direction.

As the image sharpened in his mind it did bring a quick smile to Fauul. Still their crew of twelve had managed to stay together with very little arguing and fighting, and the injuries had been very minor – he was thankful for that. Even though they were a little behind, well a lot if he wanted to be honest, the schedule that was originally set up, it had, overall, been a good project, if, maybe a little too long. Others, he recalled, had not been so lucky. There had been injuries, some even life threatening, and one party had been completely wiped out during a rainstorm, that had unleashed a landslide on them. He had been on the team that had investigated the site of the accident, and could see that the slide had happened without warning. It had taken a cycle to dig out the bodies and return them to their loved ones. This, of course, had happened before the beginnings of this major push to map the major trails.

Again, they had their own close call when a herd of wild herd beasts stampeded through their camp. Fortunately they were just setting up and no one was hurt, and very little of the equipment was damaged or destroyed. Although they hadn't gotten off scot-free as one of the pack beasts had been swept along with the stampede and it took quite a while to find and recover him. They had the good fortune that one of the members was a tracker, and was able to track, locate, and recover the beast and the equipment that was still on his back. He shuddered at the thought of how close they had come to death and injury; still overall, luck appeared to favor them.

Like the time when hot and tired and with no apparent relief in sight, they came around a small hill, and there before them, like an oasis, was a small waterfall, pond, with a small stream running out of that pond. The whole thing surrounded by a meadow with a number of shade trees. This scene was just too inviting, and with one mind the team – they picketed the animals – stripped down and jumped into the water. It was great, and close by they discovered a hot spring. One surely could not ask for more, although some females with them would have made it almost perfect – well, maybe not since they would still be stuck with Joellie.

At least, he thought once again, *the journey will be coming to an end soon.* After it's complete, and everything was put together back home, there would be plenty of time to remember – although, he and the team had better not relax too much, yet. Letting down could be such a big mistake. It seemed that when one started to relax, taking one's mind off of what was important that was when some serious mishap would overtake them.

With that in mind he decided that he needed to talk with Joellie, and remind him about that possibility. Besides they needed to get together and plan out the last quarter cycle of surveying and data gathering. That would happen tonight after the evening meal. He also knew that the sketch artist that was part of the team might want to be in on the meeting, well, again, maybe not. So far it had taken two pack beasts to handle just what he had sketched and written in their journals. It appeared they would need to purchase another pack beast or two in one of the remote villages. He had hoped that they would reach the planned village in time for one of the gathers, but now suspected that it would not be so – even though they had informed a runner that this had been their plan and goal.

As his mind wandered a little he started thinking about how important names were, other than identifying one from another. And because of this why had the two of them, Joellie and he, end up on the same team, which had been a mistake. It made him wonder how it actually all started – this naming thing. Considering tradition, if the name contained two letters that were the same and they were consecutive, then he or she was the oldest of his or her siblings, which obviously applied to him, and Joellie. If a name naturally had two letters then the first would be replaced with an "h", unless of course the person was an oldest. This was one of the too many reasons why he and Joellie had problems. Both, because of where they were within their families, were used to leading. This naming style or tradition came into use sometime in the distant past – as to when nobody knew. Probably it had been at a time when there were very large families and it made it easier for outsiders to know who was the oldest, and probably the next leader of the family or clan.

Thinking about it, assigning the two of them this way probably was not a great idea by the organizers of this project. Still with ten teams out, and theirs one of the last to be formed, there probably wasn't much choice. Not that this team was *the bottom of the barrel* as far as team members, it was just that none had ever worked together before. It was an unknown, and if there were problems with the differences in personalities, it could either destroy a team or maybe make it stronger. Most of the other teams had been loosely established over the turns. Until this last great push to map the rest of the land, these established teams were enough. So they were one of the two last teams put together, and it took about a cycle on the trail for each to learn his place and to begin to trust each other's abilities. *Ten teams, someone high up must have wanted this very badly, since it will cost much to fund this size of project, and this is just the fieldwork. Heck when all the teams returned there would be turns of research to make the data available for use.* He was glad that the project wasn't coming directly out of his pocket. Still when he returned, there should be a substantial amount of marks in his account, since he would get his normal income plus the fieldwork bonus, and having no way to spend it here, there would be at least a complete turn's amount there.

Getting back to the problem at hand, he went over to both the scout and camp manager and asked if they wanted to join the up and coming planned meeting. (He had received word the time have been changed and he needed to be there now.) Both bowed out muttering something about Joellie being long winded, and he could just fill them in afterwards. Shrugging, he left and headed over to the main portable shelter so he could join the meeting, which, as he suspected, would be he and Joellie. There was much that needed to be discussed, but he doubted if he would be given the chance to speak. At least he could try, and as usual the evening meal, after this waste of time should be excellent. He only wished he could say the same for this meeting, looking at the history of the past ones.

CHAPTER TWO

It had been exciting when the runners, who delivered messages to the widespread communities, stated that in the near future cartographers would arrive in the village and they should arrive in time for the next minor gather. The elders spoke of the larger townships and specifically the one where the council and learned resided, but their village was so isolated, that they were no more real than the myths like the *ones before*. Yet, this was followed by disappointment, as the minor gather came and went, and with only the locals had attending leaving no chance for a sale. Especially for Lauut and his sister, since they were the local herders who supplied the pack beasts for the entire region, which, unfortunately for them, had little need overall. Still, with the two major gathers they had each turn, they had a chance to see others from many of the distant places, and have a chance to barter, sell, or trade. But even then it was more the traveling merchants and runners then ones who lived in these other places. Still, many times, the traveling merchants did bring orders for their stock.

On a different subject, when Lauut thought about it, he knew that sometime in the unknown past, the area they lived, had a volcanic eruption, and major earth shakes. These past events had changed the area tremendously, and what may have been here before was gone. Yet from the evidence of the earth the last of these eruptions and earth shakes had happened thousands of turns earlier, and the area had remained quiet ever since. Yet recently, a few small earth shakes had returned, and the elders were wondering if maybe the old volcano was starting to come alive again. These shakes could make one nervous.

Yet, if the earth shakes had not begun Lauut would have never found the entrance to what appeared to be a cave or tunnel. These earth shakes had displaced a large boulder, dislodging a lot of debris, much dust, and a small crack had appeared that looked very deep. He was out tending their herd beasts when the shake happened and he heard the crashing of the boulder and the following landslide with a large cloud of dust rising into the air. Since he was close by and curious, he went to investigate. Once arriving, there appeared to be a lot of dust hanging in the air, choking him briefly, and obscuring the site where it happened. After an hour or so of searching for the source of the sound, which of course was long gone, he almost gave up, when something caught his eye. At first he thought. *It must be an illusion*, since it was a calm day allowing the fine dust particles to hang in the air making it difficult to see anything clearly. He had to cover his mouth and nose to keep from breathing the particles in. Eventually as he honed in on the area and found where the small landslide had taken place, he then spied the narrow crack. Looking into it, he could see that it was very deep, and appeared to be running downward. But because of the darkness inside he could only see a short distance. Marking the location in his mind, and thankful it was on the family lands – lands that had been in the family for generations – he returned to his chores, and set up plans to return and explore this new discovery. Who knows, in the end it might be important.

And while on that subject, it was important to keep it to himself – knowing the laws, which stated: If one owned something that could benefit the community and the world, then it would become the property of the world, at least until the benefit was gone. Then once that benefit was gone, would be returned to the rightful owner, and if the benefit was something that would be of a very long lasting thing, then the owner would be compensated in like. Anyway, that was what the law said, but one rarely got equal out of a long-term situation. This land, after all, had been in his family for at least ten generations, and now was not the time to lose it. It was all he and his sister had. Their sires had died in a freak accident when the herd beasts were spooked by thunder and lightning, which had come out of nowhere. It happened on a day when the skies appeared to be clear, with no threat in sight. The herding dogs that had been with them that day, had desperately tried to turn the crazed herd beasts away from where their sires were, but were unsuccessful. They had been left orphaned, and with very little financial stability because of many past poor turns – to chance a loss now would be too great a burden. Besides, where could they go? *It's all they know.*

With the day ending, he returned to their shelter and found his sister Lauma finishing the cleaning of their shelter, and preparing to make a meal – something they shared in doing, as she assisted him in the fields, watching and caring for the herd beasts. After all, it was only fair to share each other's burdens to help lighten the load. Of course he had to get around one of the herd dogs that had decided that Lauma was her personal owner. This particular female dog would protect Lauma with her life. She barely tolerated him, which he found somewhat amusing. Yet, to have this additional protection for her was great relief.

Still he was distracted and excited with the prospect of exploring what he had found, he knew that if he let Lauma know that she might possibly want others to know – for his protection of course, and would not necessarily want him to do what he planned, and at this moment, this was the last thing he wanted to hear or to argue about. Before letting her in on his discovery, he wanted to explore that crack, and find out if it was important or just a waste of time. If it turned out to be nothing, then there would be no problem of informing her. Feeling a little guilty about deceiving her, he covered it with conversation about the land and the herd beasts, and then nervously stated, "Sis, I need to head back out tonight, not that it's something I necessarily want to do, but in the area where that rumbling took place I heard what sounded like a landslide, and there was much dust raised into the air. With the scarcity of water and as soon as possible I need to see if there was any damage done to the land, especially the watering holes in the area, or there's a possibility that one of our herd beasts might have been injured. If we could have afforded to hire someone, then we'd send them, but there's only the two of us. So I'll need to head out after our meal. And because of the distance will probably be gone longer than usual, and it could easily be far into the morrow before I will return." He could see she was about to say something and he held up his hand saying; "Let me finish please. I'll take our camp supplies with me, adding some torches so once it's dark I can see. I plan to be back by the morn on the morrow, but until I can see what damage has been done it might be at least the zenith. Of course," he interjected, as he could tell Lauma was unhappy, "I could be back rather quick if I find nothing. I know this will put an additional burden on you since I won't be here to help take care of the young ones from the herd beasts we have in one of the out shelters, and I will, of course, assist you when I return."

Lauma looked at him with suspicion, deep concern and love thought, *now what? He's up to something, that's obvious. Come on now, what's really going on? There's too much excitement in his eyes.* Inwardly she shrugged. She knew she'd get nothing from him as to the real reason. Pausing a moment as she thought about her response, she finally said, "You be careful out there. You know we still face those wild beasts or predators that can and do attack in the night. And because they have no fear of us, or of our herding dogs, by the way – not that you don't know this – and as you know, our herd beasts seems to be one of their favorite foods." She paused a moment as a thought crossed her mind, and she inwardly shook her head. "Oh, by the way", she was trying to keep the sarcasm out of her voice, "you do remember that we haven't' restocked our night torches, so we only have a few, not enough even to last out a night."

Darn, he thought, *she's right. There might not even be enough to do as much exploring, as I want to do.* Well, it could not be helped. It just meant that he would have to be careful and plan well before he entered the crack and hope what they had on hand would be enough. "That's right . . ." He replied, ". . . still where I'm going should be somewhat protected. So I should be okay, and if I find it takes less time than I've planned then I will return quickly – even if it's before sunrise." Those night torches were critical since they also produced a sound that kept these particular predators at bay. The simple problem lay in the fact they could only be used once, and required replacement four or five times during the night. These predators relied heavily on sound to locate their prey because of their poor eyesight, not quite blind, but very close to it. And the sounds the torches produced masked the natural sounds making them a good defense against these predators. Plus, for whatever the reason it seemed to make the predators uncomfortable also. Fortunately they seemed to be rare in this area, yet they did show up often enough that when one spent time out at night, that one had better have the torches.

Eager to be away he helped his sister finish preparing the meal, and sat down with her and ate an uneasy silent meal, both apparently lost in their own thoughts. Lauma, looking across to her brother, finally said. "You can always go on the morrow instead of now. We could go over to the neighbor and borrow more torches, if they would lend some to us, and then you would have enough to last out the night if it really became necessary. Besides, in the daylight you wouldn't need them anyway."

Lost in his own thoughts it took a moment for him to realize that she had spoken to him. He looked up and said. "What? Did you just say something; sorry I was in deep thought and just realized you probably had said something."

She shook her head, while concerned, she also knew him too well, and with much difficulty kept the sarcasm out of her voice. Besides she really hated repeating herself. "Is it really necessary that you go this evening, night isn't that far off, and there is always the morrow, *and* we could probably borrow those additional torches. It would sure make me feel a lot better about you out there alone. I know we really have little choice since there's only the two of us, but I wouldn't want to lose you like we did our sires." It always worried her when Lauut would these things – stupid things in her mind, and more times than not heading into these unknown situations not fully prepared.

Smiling, Lauut trying to put more confidence in his voice than he felt, said, "It'll be okay. Where I have to go does not appear to be a great distance, and it is close to a place I've been before. And remember, I'm just trying to make sure that we lost nothing, and the earth shake seemed to come from an area where we have water for our herd beasts. We really cannot afford any losses." This was partially true, so he felt he was not really lying, "I want to make sure that there's no damage to the watering hole or the source that keeps it full. And the faster I can check out the conditions the better it will be for us in the end, especially if I need to make repairs. Remember we have that old . . . yes I know, very old, out-shelter there. So, if it becomes necessary, I could use it for shelter in the night." He shrugged, "Anyway I hope to be home before the zenith on the morrow."

She could tell there would be no way to change his mind, so hoped for the best. After all, what else could she do? Again, she worried about the possibility of him getting injured or worse, and by being out there somewhere and alone, there would be no one to know he needed help. Maybe she could convince him to at least fill her in as to the general area, so if he didn't show up she could go look for him, and provide a helping hand, if necessary. Still she held out little hope since he appeared to be somewhat secretive on this on. As strong willed as she knew she was she also knew he could just as hard headed. After all, they were from the same stock – sister and brother.

After the evening meal, he helped his sister with the cleanup, and then hurried out to the supply shelter to put together what he thought he could use. Knowing that he would have to carry everything, he would have to think it through. Another thought that he had not considered at the time, he really didn't know how big the crack really was, so if he took too much it might be too tight of a fit. Yet, the excitement of adventure was pushing him on. "Darn!" He said quietly, "This isn't easy." Thinking back, he tried to remember what he had heard from his learning days, since part of what had been covered in their *past* lessons were some of the underground explorations that their ancestors did, and the equipment they used.

He knew that light was critical, and, oh yes, rope . . . but what else? Heck he had never been underground, even though when he was a whelp he and his friends would build small tunnels. No more than digging a ditch that they could fit into, then cover it with wood, and adding sand on top, pretending to be on a great adventure. Except there was that one time when he and his friends put wood on top that was much too thin to support the sand they had placed there. Of, course they did not know any different at their age, and while they were having their "great adventure" the roof collapsed on them, pinning them under the debris. Yes, they had only been buried for a short time, but ever since then tight places made him nervous – very nervous. This was of course, before they lost their sires, and with that loss their lives changed forever. Those sure were carefree days, the time before the accident – *why did it have to happen?*

Thinking back, he knew when their sires had been killed, that a large empty dark spot seemed to develop in his chest, and his sister had cried and cried. He had felt like doing the same, but thought because he was the male that he had to be brave for his sister. It was hard, even now, to remember much of that time since he had felt so much hurt, and everything seemed to blend into each other. Still he knew that there was nothing that could be said, let alone done, to change that awful time. He remembered the funeral, and the placing of the ashes of his sires – followed by the ritual of taking a small portion of those same ashes and throwing them to the four directions, showing that in spirit they would be everywhere, and would also be a part of the family lands forever. Yet, he had only gone through the motions, barely succeeding, since he was too choked up with emotion, and was desperately holding back the tears that were coming unbidden.

Why was he thinking about this now? He truly had no answer. Maybe it was because he was going underground for the first time since that accident, and just thinking about it still left him sweating. And to add to the memories, it had only been a short time after that incident with their play tunnel that their sires were killed, so it seemed all tied together. *Well, that's all in the past,* he thought. Maybe if he found something of value down in that crack, then he could take the pressure off the family and for once not be in a bind . . . *anyway enough of that*. It was time to really think through what to take. He needed to remember that not only did he need the equipment for his exploring, but he did need camping gear, since the plan, as it was forming in his head, was not to spend all his time in the underground. He needed a base camp to work from, and that would not be underground.

"Let's see . . ." He said quietly, ". . . I must remember to pack food and water, and a way to carry some with me, and, oh yes, a med kit."

Thinking back he remembered some of the lessons about the ancestors who had both explored and worked underground, they had taken a ball of string and a marking device. These items helped them in retracing their steps, so they would not get lost there underground. After all if the lights failed you would be in total darkness. With that thought he shuddered, still remembering that incident so many turns in the past. "Darn!" He whispered, "Can I never get over that cave in?"

He spent about an hour gathering everything he thought he might need, and found that his pack was now pretty substantial. It would be very heavy, but once he arrived at his destination, and unpacked, setting up his camp, it would be much lighter and smaller. He truly hoped that he had thought of everything. It was going to be at least an hour of hiking, and there would be no way of returning to get something, if he forgot. Lastly, he remembered that he should bring his belt knife and their shock weapon, since, if one of those beasts did show up, he would have some protection. It was no more than a springy piece of wood that one bent, and then with a piece of leather, one attached it to a latch so it remained under tension. Then with a quick release it would spring back with some force, slapping whatever had been targeted, with the end and stinging the one it hit with a flying strap of leather and if lucky the wood. Hopefully, with the result of startling or scaring the beast and making it retreat.

Leaving his pack there he went back into the shelter to tell Lauma he was leaving and the plan was to be back by, well, no later than the next after-zenith, or early evening the next day. This, of course, was later than he had first told her. But not being sure of how long it would take he wanted her not to worry.

With a worried expression all Lauma quietly said was, "Be careful and come back." He nodded and headed out the door, picked up his pack and started the trek back to the location of the newly discovered cave or tunnel. Presently it was still light, but dusk wasn't far off. He hated seeing his sister this way, since they only had each other. Yes, Lauma had received some offers to become a mate, but those who had offered were of no interest to her. After all, it was her right to choose, and all he wanted for her was to see her happy. Too much sadness had already been a part of their lives. He hoped that this adventure – his adventure, would change their lives for the better.

Lauut means well, Lauma thought as she again shook her head. But she had been too long with her brother not to know that there was much more going on than what he had told her. She could see the fire in his eyes, but as usual, he appeared to be trying to hide whatever it was from her. No doubt because he probably thought he was protecting her from something, and by doing so she would worry less. Maybe one day he would realize that she knew more of what was happening in their lives, and how close they were to losing the family property. The herd and pack beasts were their only real means of support, and if they even lost a couple, it could be enough for them to finally lose the struggle and lose all that they knew – in other words – everything. *If only our sires had survived that terrible accident, then things would be so different.* After all, and at the time, Lauut was just beginning to learn the trades of the family. Since, in tradition, the lead male and female were responsible for the passing on of all the knowledge and skills that each family group held important and special. Certain families and clans only knew these skills, and they were protected, and never to be passed on to outsiders.

The problem with this tradition became very clear. When the keepers of this knowledge died before they passed it on, then it could be lost forever or at least until it was rediscovered, sad to think that this had almost happened here. Fortunately most of the knowledge and skills had been passed on to both of them, but the difficulty lay in the fact that it usually took much practice and mentoring to really understand and make it work. They never got much of the mentoring, since that accident took away their mentors.

Why is it that the males here feel that they are to run things, and believe that the females can't help in all areas? With some frustration because of her brother, her thoughts continued. *Well, it's their loss.* She found she had placed her hands on her hips as she took that defiant stance her brother was quite familiar with. Hopefully Lauut was not going to do something dangerous or stupid . . . if she lost her brother too – well she wasn't going to go there. "He will be back on the morrow towards the late zenith", she said under her breath while feeling a deep dread in her soul, "He just has to."

Thinking about their family property, she realized that many generations ago, when the first of their clan picked this land, that they knew exactly what they were looking for, and so the family always had been prosperous throughout the generations. It was just now, in this generation, with this tragedy, and pain, that much of that prosperity had disappeared, and if they weren't careful it would be gone from them forever. They, being the last of the clan, and her brother being the leader meant if he died without leaving a new generation, that she, by law and tradition, would not be able to keep this family land. If this had happened after she had a mate, and from that union a male whelp, then that male whelp could claim it, but she never could. Some things seemed so unfair. In truth she knew that she could control this property as well as any male, probably even better.

CHAPTER THREE

Jllon, thinking over what lay ahead, was hoping for something positive. Since much of the field project portion of the mapping was complete, it would be many cycles of the moon, or even turns before all the data would be put together in a workable form. This was understandable since it involved ten teams and took at least a full turn of the planet around the sun for the fieldwork to be almost at a conclusion. The two final teams had yet to return, and once all the data was in it would take many turns to compile it into something that would be useful. This type of project, of course, turned out to be very expensive, which meant, unfortunately, their department, Keepers of the Past, would not have the normal funding for any of their field research. It would probably take at least five turns for the council to

recoup the cost. So most projects would be funded lightly, or put on hold. He knew that similar projects – the mapping –
had been put into motion all across the lands, and while the work here dealt with the west it was happening just about everywhere.

So much could come out of the mapping work that it was worth both the risk and the investment in time, money, and labor. What little he saw of the work showed how rich and diverse the lands were. Still, when there was a great possibility of finding a site where the *ones before* might have lived . . . well, he felt it was as important as the mapping – just bad timing for him and the department. Again, he knew that without the research being conducted by the cartographers there would be no opportunity for any possible discovery, major field research, let alone minor. It seemed to always be that way. Yet, he learned that knowledge gained often came from the most unexpected direction. He could hardly wait to see if any of the information that the last two teams brought back would be positive. Thinking ahead and anticipating that a dig might be a possibility, he laughed. *Once the days and moon cycles have passed, I will be wondering just why I had been so eager to get started.* Shaking his head his thoughts continued, *and most of the time with little to nothing to show for all that effort.* It really was hard and dirty work. Plus one had to be so careful not destroy something that could be "the proof". In the field one never knew if what was found was anything of value until later – just like the mapping, the fieldwork was just the beginning. There would be much work and research to follow in the department and learning centers, cataloging and attempting to date these finds. Then, of course, either tying the artifacts to their existing culture, or maybe to those elusive *ones before*, which, in the end, could be more time consuming than the actual field work. And even with the work done they couldn't necessarily say that how they judged what they found was actually correct. After all, there could easily be other explanations for what had been uncovered.

Still, by not having the proper funding hurt. It meant that they would have to rely on more volunteers from the higher learning centers and less on their team of experts to guide and do the work. By being spread this thin, and having inexperienced team members, this could lead to something being missed, destroyed, overlooked, and, of course, so many things that could and would go wrong. Yet sometimes having those young new eyes and their enthusiasm helped. Oh the questions that would be asked kind of took him back to those early days in the field when he was a volunteer. He thought back while shaking his head and smiling about his own ignorance then. So much time had passed, so much personal knowledge gained. Did those past seasons ever really happen?

In his mind he began to go over what was required when forming one of their field teams. Like the mapping teams, the team would consist of a scout, a number of camp managers, beast handlers, and the assistants to them – but no historian, since they covered that niche, a scribe, a field artist or two, and a language expert. The second team would consist mostly of the volunteers, the diggers, and field researchers. Overall the group would number around twenty or so . . . *a lot of logistics for a group that size.* Again the lack of financing made it just that more difficult. Of course, it could just by a wild flyer chase, and they would come up with little or nothing. That had happened a number of times in the past . . . a promising site, only to find nothing. It really appeared, if the *ones before* had existed that very little of what and who they were survived time. Still that made sense, since it was postulated that if they had existed, it was in the dawn of pre-history, and because very few build to last, dealing with the day-to-day and such, all that they built would have, most likely, wasted away to dust. A second line of reasoning that had been postulated was that something had caused their civilization to collapse and the remnants of that society then lived off what had still existed, like scavengers on a carcass. Until there was nothing recognizable left.

Then, as their time waned, they themselves would begin to believe that anything that had really been there would be fiction – a myth. Since, even for them, the creators of what had been, all or most would have been destroyed, used up, so there would be no proof that they had ever existed – this mythological civilization in its entire splendor. He had to admit that any thoughts on the subject were conjecture, since absolutely nothing solid had ever been found. As he, Jllon continued going over the subject in his mind, he thought. *We then came to the beginning of our written history after that, or so the stories go.* Still they were only stories, and as such were considered old female tales, something to keep the whelps in line, not something to really believe in.

Shaking his head as his mind continued in these circles, he asked, "So why the continuing belief in the *ones before*, and why would the belief in this unknown people from the past not just go away and die a natural death?" He shrugged. *Why care anyway?* Answering his own question he said, "I guess it is the idea that even in myth, there appears to be a small kernel of truth, and it is that small kernel that keeps us going." *And, of course, there are those rare, small unexplainable finds – always, those unexplainable objects that we are incapable of duplicating with our present technology.* It was known that if these *ones before* had habitations to live in, which only made sense that most likely these habitations would have returned to the earth by now.

After all, we can see the same thing happening with our own habitations or shelters, when, for whatever the reasons, one is abandoned. Without care, over a short period of time, it would just disappear like it had never existed at all. It is this kind of evidence that has convinced us that we would be very fortunate if we found anything at all, let alone a shelter from the "ones before". Enough on this circle of thought, it is something we debate almost every day. So it will be nice, in a sense, to break out of this day-to-day routine and look forward to the possibility that we might head out into the field to, once more, to pursue these elusive ones from the past.

Still it was hard not to speculate, overall with so little collected, and even with what had been collected so far, most had been proved as fake, and what hadn't – couldn't be confirmed. So one could not even begin to even make a hypothesis about anything, from the way they possibly lived, to the way they did anything, or even the way they lived their daily lives. Everything, up until now, had just been a big guessing game. Sites, from the past, that had been excavated, believing them to be *ones before*, turned out instead to be our own distant ancestors. Again, who was to say that we ourselves are not the *ones before*, and the items found are of some process or processes that had been lost or forgotten over time.

Well enough on this, the day was over and it was time to head home. Fortunately, for him, it was only a short walk to their apartment. He still had to run the gamut of the underlings and learners who wanted to take some of his time or to be seen with him to impress friends or some female they were trying to prove their worth to. Shaking his head and sighing, he glanced out the door and beyond to the hallway. At the moment it was empty. If he hurried he could go down that hallway then to the left through where the cleaners had an entrance and probably sneak out that way. With the upcoming anticipation of the last two returning teams on his mind, and all the work, both in the logistics and the politics, he did not want to be either distracted or delayed. He was tired, and he and his mate still had an evening meal meeting with one of those politicians who wanted to get him and his name possibly tied to the department for some unknown and impossible project.

It seemed that his position was becoming more and more a political one. Instead of being able to continue research, which was his favorite thing to do, he was forever going to meetings, impressing some unknown dignitary, or trying to get funding for their department. The thought of getting back out and into the field and doing some real research would be a wonderful change, and would probably help clear his head.

"Well here goes." He said quietly, as he let himself out of the office. *So far so good, still no one in sight.* He quickly made his way through the cleaners section and headed out unseen, and then traveled down a couple of back trails, up the stairs and into their apartment. It had only been recently that they had begun building two level shelters. While a little harder to move things in and out he found he preferred it to the ground floor. For about an hour he and his mate would have some quiet time to themselves. That would be something special. After that they would have to prepare for the meeting that was two hours away. *What I wouldn't give to be back in simpler times where I could just do what I love to do, and not be more administrator than researcher.*

It appeared that he had beaten his mate home so he headed for the necessary and bathing space and prepared a hot bath that both of them could share. *Yes, hot water, something only the rich had, but now thanks to a few advances most could enjoy such a luxury.* He looked forward to the few intimate moments he and his mate could share together which were precious. When in the worker-space all things had to be kept on a professional level, which at times almost made them both laugh. When one were mates it just seemed funny to have to communicate in the formal way during introductions, etcetera. Sure she did not work directly with him – that was not allowed, but the intra-departments worked closely together anyway, so their paths crossed more often than not. Laughing to himself, he pictured the meeting from another's point of view. It would have gone something like this. "Good day Head Keeper of the Past, I bow to your authority." Nodding his head he would respond, "And good day to you underling leader of research, I acknowledge your work." . . . or something to that effect. It just seemed out of place when talking with one's mate. He could imagine that Nouma had to giggling to herself. This formality was just beyond them. They both had come from the small villages in outback where such formality was not wanted, needed, or tolerated. Yet, here in one of the larger townships it seemed to be the way of things.

CHAPTER FOUR

Lauma, after her brother left, went to her sleeping space, and finished cleaning the area, then proceeded out to care for both the recent additions to their herds, and the pack beasts. She and her brother were proud of what they had accomplished. Their small herd of pack beasts was considered the best in the region. Still without the base to sell what they had there were no resources to grow larger, and as a result, theirs was a small operation. It had taken many turns and mistakes to learn or relearn what they needed, to continue in the family business and tradition. As she walked toward the out-shelter across the hard packed soil she could hear one of the young beasts making sounds of complaint. Smiling, and shrugging, she thought. *It will be a long evening without the help of my brother Lauut.* Still these hungry younglings had to be fed and then the fodder for the pack beasts needed to be placed into their enclosure – followed by making sure that both clean water and the salty rock they loved to lick were available, and whether any of it required replacement. *One thing for sure the work never ends.*

It was well after dark when the needs of the beasts were taken care of, and she headed back inside to take a needed bath – a luxury that she really looked forward to. It had only been a couple of cycles since they were able to repair the water heating device, and not having to heat water on the fire either in the cooking stove or outside, for a bath, after one was exhausted from the day's work, meant that there had been too many cold baths. She went to her room got her clean nightclothes and retired to the bathing space and drew her bath. Laying out her clean clothes and the soft drying cloth, she undressed and with a sigh of contentment climbed into the warm water, and soaked up the heat that felt wonderful to her tired, aching body. Closing her eyes, she thought. *It would be so easy to fall asleep here.* But she knew that once finished here she would still have a few chores to do to set up for the morrow's work.

Thinking back on the conversation with her brother, she idly wondered what he was really up to. He really should have known, by now, that she could read him quite well. For some reason he seemed to feel that he still needed to protect her. While she appreciated the sentiment, she felt it would be better if he would be honest and up front with her. Shaking her head and sighing, she thought, *Yeah, like that's ever going to happen.*

After the bath and feeling somewhat refreshed, she finished her final chores of the evening and headed out on the porch in her nightclothes to sit and relax a little before going to bed. She loved the quiet solitude of the evenings, and the clear nighttime views of both the surrounding hills, and the stars in the sky – the subtle breezes that would touch her, so softly that they were barely felt. Again, shaking her head, she knew that someday, most likely, she would have to leave all of this, and that was a very sad thought indeed. It was easy to sit there and remember the good days in the past, and all those fun and all the carefree times she had while growing up. Such things as running out with friends to play in the fields, watching the clouds go by in the sky and making different things from their shapes. The secrets that meant nothing they had between each other, of her best friend Sooma, who was a turn older than she, and then there was Traylu, who was younger and a shy person at the time. Yet through that shyness there was a strength that would show through now and then.

Thinking of them made her wonder what they were doing now, and of course, she knew she had no answer. Once that terrible accident happened, the one that had taken her sires away, the small group kind of drifted away. As her brother, she had withdrawn for a long period of time, and when the time of sorrow was finished, so was the innocence of youth. Her friends could continue in that innocence, but for her, it was gone forever. Probably if she reached out and contacted them again, the friendships would be renewed. A wonderful thought really. Sitting there on the porch with her thoughts she drifted lightly into sleep, and moments later realized what had happened, and decided she had better get into bed. On the morrow without her sibling here to assist with the morn chores, would make for a long and tiring beginning to the day. She got up from her chair went back inside and hung the latch on the door, dropped the pin so it could not be opened from outside, then went to her sleeping space and climbed into bed and drifted off to sleep, still thinking nostalgically of her friends from the past.

* * *

He was three quarters of an hour from their home when he realized that he had left the string behind. In his eagerness to be away he did not double-check his mental list. Now with just the markers he was carrying it made this first trip more difficult, and probably much more dangerous. It was too late to retrace his steps and go back to get it now. Shaking his head he said, "That was really stupid of me, now I need to figure out some way to let myself know that each mark I make is different. Otherwise I could end up going in circles in the underground and never even know that's what I am doing."

He was coming up on the site of the split, so he searched for a place to set up camp, an area that would be close by, yet at the same time, provide both protection, and be hidden from view. Looking around he found an area that was a bit farther away than he liked, but it provided what was necessary. Like the location of crack he was going to tackle, the spot he chose for camp was not visible until anyone came around the corner of a boulder – only then would one see it. Yet from the area around his chosen site there was nothing but rocks and more rocks, and because of this it would normally be ignored as an unlikely stopping or camping point – not that many came this way anyway.

Since he had forgotten that string, he had to think of a way to be able to make the trip into the crack and still have it be safe. *Right, safe, sure, as if I have a clue.* Because the crack had never been entered by anyone, and as far as he knew he was the only one who knew of it, if he got hurt or lost, no one would ever find him, or know where to search. He remembered, from his learning time, that backup was important, and letting others know of your intentions and location was critical. Yet, here he was with none of that and it had been a conscious choice. He hoped that it would not turn out to be a bad decision on his part. The last thing he wanted to do was to leave his sister alone, by knowing that he was the last male, the property would then be lost, until a male from the family line was produced. And her with no mate, she would be in for a very rough time of it; with no place to live and very little means to support herself. He knew the value of the land and he figured there were many who would love to claim it as their own.

With those thoughts he began to realize how foolish this adventure was. Yet, he felt the rewards could be worth the risk. *Who knows what this opportunity could give us,* he thought. Again it could turn out to be nothing, and within many body lengths or less down into that crack, it could just dead end or it might continue but be impassible. "Oh well enough speculating," he said quietly. It was getting quite dark, and he planned to take the food he had brought into the crack where it would be out of the reach of those wild beasts – should one be in the area. With nothing to draw them to the camp he could leave it unprotected.

"Well times a wastin' and . . . well . . . ahhh quit procrastinating," he said out loud, "I was a whelp when that cave-in happened." Somehow he needed to relieve the nervousness and tension he was feeling. And with the pack considerably lightened, and too few torches in hand he hiked carefully towards the hidden entrance. He did not want to light his torch until he was close since he was painfully aware of how short he really was. He really should have had at least three times the amount for this exploration – another reason showing him that his sister had a point and maybe he should have waited. *No, better, right now, to find out if this is worth the time and effort.*

It would normally take about ten minutes in the daylight to hike the distance to the entrance from where his camp was set up, but by not having any light it took closer to thirty to reach the area. Even though he had marked the location in his mind, in the darkness the landmarks looked different, requiring a bit of searching locating the entrance. Standing there, sweating a little, and of course, he had to admit that he was somewhat nervous, he thought. *This almost looks like the mouth of one of those carnivorous plants.* In his imagination he could see himself being the victim, as he walked, unsuspecting, into those jaws.

Gosh my imagination sure can play tricks on me here in the darkness. With the torches he now had he had a maximum time of 4 hours. So that meant 2 hours or less in, and when that First of the 2 torches started its sputtering, which happens about 15 minutes before it burned out, he would possibly want to start back at that very moment – whether he found anything or not. Yet, if it looked promising he could continue for a short period of time on that second torch. Well, next time, if there was to be a next time, he would bring his sister along and have spare torches.

He lit the torch and proceeded into the crack and into total darkness. He saw that the torch extended his ability to see by only a body length or two. The reflected shadows made weird images on the walls. He had decided to bring 2 different color marking sticks, that way if the color of the walls changed he would be covered. He had thought long and hard on how he was going to mark the walls, and also the length between markings. He decided that he would make the arrows he drew point to the way out. Also not knowing if there were branches and places where he could end up going in circles, he would add a letter. He figured he would not run out of letters, but if he did, then he would change to numbers.

At the beginning he placed an "X" with his name. That way he would know that he was at the beginning, the point where he had entered. One lesson he had learned in life was that things looked very different according to the direction one entered into a known area. What was once familiar would completely change when approached from another direction, and appear to be completely unknown, until you would orientate yourself to the familiar direction. He also decided that after an approximate time he would draw a circle on the wall followed by an X on the inside, followed by 2 X's, etc. This would give him a second system to check location and time. The torches had a tendency, at regular intervals, to flare brighter for a few seconds. When that would happen he would then place the *circle-X* combination. This way with the arrows, and circles he thought he would have both time and distance covered. "Well, at least it sounds good in theory," he told himself.

As he entered, the first thing he noticed was a lot of debris lying around with the floor of the newly opened passageway being very uneven. Somehow he thought that the floor would be flat and easy to traverse. Instead, he saw that with the fallen rock and uneven terrain that it was not going to be as easy a journey as he had envisioned. He turned and made his beginning mark on the wall, and then went only a few feet and placed his first arrow with the letter above it, and started working his way down deeper into the tunnel. The air smelled old and stagnant, like it had not been exposed to the outside for a very long time. He wondered if the air would continue to be breathable – again, something he had not considered. "I guess there is a lot I don't know about exploring. It sure does look easier in those books I read as a whelp." He laughed as he thought about it. *After all isn't always easier in those stories?*

Another thought occurred to him, he had better keep the distance between his arrow systems within the light. With nothing familiar around him, even with his system of checks, it would be easy to get lost. As he continued along his way, the tunnel seemed to go downward. At the present he was still in what appeared to be the result of the recent earth shake.

The exploring was taking much longer than he anticipated, since he had to work around and over large boulders, and loose soils. With those soils that he was seeing, he felt that there could be no bottom and like quicksand he could fall through and be hurt or killed. It was almost unbearably hot and sticky. He had brought water with him, but now knew that it would not be near enough. "Well I've gone thirsty before." Still it was a major consideration. It appeared one could sweat out rapidly down here.

I always thought it would be cool underground, he thought, *oh boy I surely can see I have a lot to learn.* He looked back and it was comforting that his marks were still visible. The torch had brightened 3 times which meant he had approximately an hour before he would need to turn around and head out. He hoped that the trip back out would be faster. So far it had been a very tiring and dirty experience. He was gaining an appreciation for those who explored these underworlds as their life pursuits. The excitement of exploring, which had overcome his fear of tight places, was becoming one of determination and apprehension, since he was much less prepared than he should have been. Still, this was an initial look, and really, he had no idea what he would find. At places, the walls would narrow and he could barely fit through – other places, the roof area was either, so high up as not to be visible, or so low he had to crawl. In those areas where he had to crawl, he decided to put marks on both sides. The air still seemed to be old, and at times he could see his torch dimming from lack of breathable air. Yet, it never died down enough to make him worry that he might be running out of air.

Finally after crawling through a rather large section he was able to stand again. For the past quarter of an hour he had to stoop as the roof had continued to drop in height. He had to admit that it really felt great to be able to stand again. He stretched, took a small drink from his dwindling supply of water, noticing at the same time that his water supply was almost exhausted. That was very bad news; since for most of hike, he could sense that he had been heading downhill. That meant it would take more energy to head out, and his need of water would be much greater.

He was down to his last quarter of an hour of this first torch when he came up to a wall, which appeared to be a dead end. After all that work and energy it appeared that this was as far as the tunnel went. He searched in both directions, but only ran into the sidewalls. *Well,* he thought, *here I thought I would find something of value to help our family and it just dead ends here.* Shaking his head and somewhat discouraged, he turned to head back up the passageway, when he noticed in the flickering light that something didn't look right. He looked again, and thought. *This must be an illusion. That must be just a jut in the wall . . . or is it?* Walking back towards where he came in, it appeared that the tunnel took a 180 degree turn here, and because of the way the wall turned, it first would appear to be solid, a dead end with no further direction to go. Yet, as he approached he could see the light reflecting off of something deeper in, again confirming that it indeed continued. A closer inspection revealed that somewhere in the past a sheet of shale or something similar had slid to rest here. Wondering what force could have broken such a large piece of stone into slabs, he carefully worked his way past into what appeared to be a large cavern.

This area appeared to have been open for a long time. He could see the work of nature here with both stalactites and stalagmites all around. While these were quite small, it showed that at least this had been here a few thousand turns, if not longer. He could also see, in a couple areas visible in the light, that there had been an ancient lava flow. *Is that water over there?* Well, before investigating any further he had better mark this entrance really well – it appeared to be just as hidden on this side, and he was almost out of time for this first trip, and there would no time to search for this exit. At least so far nothing serious had happened to him, and he had learned much since starting this first journey into the underworld. Many of the ideas he had had fallen away as false. It gave him a new respect for those who worked underground. For example, he had expected it to be cool, and in this case it wasn't. He was sure that many were, but you couldn't expect that to be true of all. After all here was the proof.

He suspected that there might be some hot springs down here that had an influence on the temperature and humidity. At least he had his water test kit with him – something he always carried since he traveled the hills and outback most of the time. He was always searching for new water sources for their herd and pack beasts. So carrying the kit was just an everyday thing, an unconscious habit, for him. Attempting to get his bearings, he walked towards where he thought he saw the light reflect off of what he hoped was a small pool of water.

Again he found the floor uneven, although, at least in this section of the cave complex, there appeared to be more of the floor that was . . . He came to a quick halt, for right in front of him was a drop off of at least 5 body lengths. He had almost stepped right over the edge. Thinking of what would have happened if he fell into that hole brought additional fear, causing him to sweat. As he peered into the hole, from the edge where he was standing, he saw that the sides were basically smooth and if he had fallen into that trap, he would have died a slow death, with no water, no way out, and none the wiser.

Carefully skirting the hole, he continued on to where he thought he had seen the water. Yet, when he was close, he found that it was just a reflection off of one of the stalagmites whose surface was damp. Disappointed he turned to head back towards the hidden entrance when indeed to his right was water – quite a bit really. It looked like a small tank holding probably a couple of hundred gallons of water. Still, as inviting as the water looked, he knew that it could turn out to be undrinkable. So far, he had learned a lot about exploring caves and tunnels, yet he was smart enough to know that he really had only scratched the surface.

After having the close call with that one unseen hole, he carefully proceeded towards the small tank of water. Shaking and weighing his container of water, it felt and sounded almost empty. *I surely didn't plan as well as I thought. Guess I was too impatient and too excited to really think this through.* This brought a silent laugh to his lips when he realized that his sister had always warned him about his impatience. So far, there had been a couple of close calls, but he was still able to continue, and he found that the pressure he felt when closed in like this had lessened. *I guess when you go into an area that your fears control, eventually either they or you win out.* So far he believed that he was winning this battle. It took about 5 minutes of careful hiking to reach the edge of the tank. He noticed, as he approached the water, the air seemed cooler, and he realized that since coming into this portion of the system, the air seemed better, and this cavern overall seemed to be much cooler. And even though it might be his imagination, he thought he could feel a slight movement in the air.

Taking out the test kit he proceeded to test the water. The process would take a short period of time, but he knew from the torch's warning that he was almost out of that precious time. The quarter of an hour warning of this torch burning out had begun about 5 minutes ago, and he should be heading back. While waiting for the results he was idly looking around and next to a wall close by was a pile of debris, and something kept reflecting the light back to him. At first he thought it was his imagination, or maybe one of those damp rocks he had already mistaken for water, but the reflection appeared to be coming from some kind of metallic object. *Now what would metal be doing down here?* "Well, I've about 2 minutes before the test is completed, so if I want to see whatever that is, I had better go look. After all, my time here is more than up!" He said aloud trying to sound confident, but still could hear a bit of doubt in his own voice.

He went over to the debris pile and found broken, strange looking stone, sand, and a curious small square object that indeed was made of metal. He really had no time to look at it, so he quickly placed it into his backpack. Looking at his test sample he found that the results were in, he was more than late leaving, and he really needed to head back. The water was drinkable, but just barely. It had a high mineral content, and would not taste good at all. Still it would give him something to drink on the way out, which he knew that he would desperately need. Starting to become nervous, he realized that this torch was finished and that put him well behind his planned time schedule. He should have been on his way back out minutes ago. His first torch was sputtering its final dying flame when he lit the second and final torch; refilling his water container he started his trek back toward the surface.

He hurried toward where he thought the entrance to the cavern was located, and realized he had headed in the opposite direction. Because time was becoming short he almost panicked. He did not have time for these mistakes. If the torch died before he reached the entrance he would be in total darkness, and be lost. This adventure could still end up as a tragedy with him never finding the exit to the surface leaving him to die down here – futilely searching until totally exhausted and eventually giving up. These thoughts brought back those fears from that accident in his youth. His imagination started playing games with him, and he knew that if he did not get a grip on himself that he would be the cause of his failure and ultimate death.

Taking a couple of deep breaths that he let out slowly, he forced himself to relax. By correcting his direction he located the entrance and exit to the cavern by the marks he left, and began his trek back to the surface. He knew that he had a long way to go, and from this direction everything would again appear new and strange. "Why is that?" He asked again. "Why do things look so different when you come in from a different direction? After all, is it not the same place, or area, or whatever, that I know and have been to before? It doesn't make any sense." Oh well, he wasn't going to find any answers down here. He'd better concentrate on the job at hand and by letting his mind wander; he again, could lose his way. He realized suddenly that he was very fatigued, and that was also starting to affect the way he was thinking. Another factor he had not taken into account. "Stupid on my part," he commented, "I really didn't plan this as well as I should have." Thinking about it now, he realized he had been very rash in his decision to do this exploring. He had let excitement and adventuring cloud his judgement on this endeavor, and if he got out of here safely, he would not repeat that mistake again – at least he hoped not – if there was to be a next time. Yet, he had a long ways to go and most of it rough and uphill.

After leaving the cavern, he ran into the wall, and then remembered that it was a 180-degree turn to get him heading in the right direction – it was too easy to get turned around down here. He was doubly glad that he decided to use the marking system that he used. Without that second mark it would have been impossible to know if he was correct in his direction of travel or just going in circles. Another issue presented itself. He realized that it appeared that torch was burning brighter and consuming itself faster than the other. *Great! What else can go wrong?* He hoped that this was just his imagination, but it was something he could not count on. Hurrying up the passageway he came upon the area where the passage had narrowed requiring him to crawl. Yet on this end the entrance was higher up, and all the rock surfaces were slick. Almost panicking again, he desperately looked around for some kind of foothold that would allow him to climb up and into the narrow opening. Time was running out and he really needed to hurry now. Yet, it appeared that with every turn he was being delayed. It was like this underground world did not want him to leave and was insuring that he remain.

Desperately looking around in his narrow field of light, he saw a possible way. It required climbing a small ledge that was to the left of passage and then taking a small leap to the lip. "Times a wasten'" He whispered. The torch had flared at least twice, and again that just seemed too soon. He worked his way up onto the small ledge, and made the leap . . . when he landed the lip gave way under his weight, and he started to fall back down. Reaching out desperately, he found a tenuous grip, which took all of his strength to hold on. Carefully he pulled himself into the passageway, collapsing with his lungs burning; he sucked in great gasping breaths of air. He found that he was sweating profusely. Still, since it was again hot and humid, he did not know whether to attribute it to the heat or to his close call and subsequent straining of his muscles and his near panic. *More time lost! Just can't afford this.*

That fight to get into that crawl space worked deep into his energy reserves, and he could feel the weariness starting to invade his body and mind. He was realizing in hindsight, how wrong it had been to do this exploration the way he did. Yet, there was nothing he could do about it now. He knew he had to get out somehow. If for no other reason, he didn't want to leave his sister alone, and have to face another family tragedy, followed by the loss of the lands, since she, by law and tradition, could not hold them – *Too much sadness in our lives.*

Had the torch flared again? If it had he should have been farther along than he was. From the weariness that was flooding his body, he was starting to have a lot of trouble concentrating, and finding that he was beginning to lose his balance and stumble – *Can't afford mistakes now.* Taking a large swig of water, he pushed his weary body up the tunnel.

Indeed this torch did appear to be burning more rapidly than the other one. Not that each was precisely timed – since they were made of a special wood that was dense, and full of flammable sap. Careful nurturing over time had produced a consistent product. Again, one protected by the family who had the knowledge. They knew their trees very well. They knew when to harvest, to skip the harvest, all the care, techniques, how to cure and grade. Since this was something that all who farmed and raised the domestic beasts needed they always had a market for their product. They had become financially well off as a result of this. At times, as his family had suffered reverses, to see them continue to grow and prosper, made him envious. *How can so much go wrong for us and everything seem to go right for them?* It was something he would never understand.

Still thinking about that was not solving the most pressing problem – getting out of this passageway and into the fresh air. Picking up his pace, and at the same time hoping he was not becoming careless for doing so, he continued up the tunnel. By looking at his marks he knew he had a long way to go. Yet, it felt like he was so much farther along than he really was.

Then the area was hit by an aftershock of the earth shake. He could both feel and hear it coming. Panic again set in as he realized that the tunnel he was in could collapse around him, trapping him with no possibility of escape. This gave him an adrenaline rush and a small amount of additional energy. Yet, again he knew that it would be temporary, and this would dangerously tap into his dwindling supply of the same. Dust and some debris flew up from the shaking, but other than that everything seemed to remain stable. "At least that's a relief," he said softly.

It was getting harder to concentrate as fatigue clouded his mind and his body ached in every joint and muscle. He could tell that he was coming to the end of his reserves of strength and stamina. He reached for his water bottle, but it wasn't there. Had he dropped it or set it down? He didn't know. He knew by not having water he increased his chances of never leaving this forsaken underworld. Subconsciously he followed his marks, but it was not registering with his conscious mind. It was, put one foot in front of the other and do not stop for anything. He was afraid that if he did stop, that he would give up, and with the torch burning out would be lost forever. His mind drifted from one subject to another never staying in one place too long. One time it was he as a whelp, another the climbing of a mountain in the area a few turns ago.

It was the sputtering of the torch that brought him back to reality. It was the sign that he had dreaded, there was only about 15 minutes before it burned out. He found his next mark, and it looked like he had only 3 more marks before he would be close to the opening where he started his adventure. If the torch held true, he would have just about enough time to exit before it died. He could tell he was getting close because the air was freshening, and he could smell and almost taste the cool dampness that hung in the air.

* * *

She awoke from a deep sleep, and groggily, wondered why she had awakened. It was not time to get up for the morn work. Then she remembered she was having a bad dream. What was it about? It seemed to be something about her brother. What was it? Something about him being stuck underground somewhere, with no light, and no escape – but that was ridiculous, and when she thought about it, of course it was. With a sigh, she turned over and went back to sleep. The morn and all the work would be coming soon enough.

* * *

Lauut stumbled forward, toward what he hoped was the opening when without warning the torch just quit. He stood there looking at the useless dying embers. *It should have lasted at least another 10 minutes or so. Of course I would have had to find one of the few defective torches.* He was left in total blackness. Standing there waiting for his eyes to adjust, he hoped that he was close. Fortunately he was facing forward when the torch quit. So, at least he knew if he went forward carefully using his hands on the walls he should be able to find his way out of the final section of this tunnel. Carefully walking forward he immediately hit his shin on a rock, which made him yell out in pain. That really hurt, and probably would be black and blue and bruised for a long time. Now being more careful and limping somewhat from the pain he continued, only to slice his hand on a sharp rock. He was beginning to truly regret this whole adventure. He thought he had planned so well, and found in truth, that he had fallen short in so many areas. He felt lucky at this moment, even with the minor cut and bruised shin, to have come away with only these injuries. He could have died down there so easily. *Well, lesson learned. I had better do better research in the future, when I decide to do something I'm unfamiliar with.* It just seemed so easy and what real danger could there be anyway?

As these thoughts went through his head his hand suddenly felt no wall. He reached out with the other thinking the shaft had taken a turn, but again felt nothing. *Did I miss something?* Standing still because he did not want to get turned around and find he had headed back down the shaft he felt helpless. Suddenly he realized that he felt, just slightly, moisture touching his skin. The kind you would get from a damp fog. He strained with his eyes to see anything, and then realized that yes to his relief he was outside, and there was a heavy fog drifting through the area. It had made the area appear almost as dark as being in that tunnel, but he could just discern some of the vegetation that lay close to the entrance.

Now completely exhausted he had to find his camp. He found that he was shaking from the cold damp air. The temperature difference from inside the tunnel to outside was huge. It had been so warm in the underground that his clothes were soaked with sweat. Now being in wet clothes, with the temperature change, plus the exhaustion, he worried he could end up getting sick. He stumbled into his hidden camp, too tired to make a fire for warmth; he got out of his wet clothes, changing into something dry, shivering and chilled to the bone. Finding his water supply he took a large drink. It was the best tasting thing he had had for a long time. *Funny how that works,* he thought. After quenching his thirst, he climbed into his sleep sack and as he warmed, fell into a dreamless deep exhausted sleep.

* * *

She awoke, as was her custom, just before the dawn light. It was time to start another day. It would be so much more difficult, since her brother would not be here to help. Yet, it had happened before. She knew that he had done the same when she wasn't here. She lit the lamp sitting on the small table next to her bedding and with light in hand went to take care of her needs in the bathing space. *It's funny,* she thought, *how sometimes nature can get you up in the*

*middle of the night, and other times just before having
to rise.*

In the bathing or necessary space she took care of
those needs, and proceeded to dress for the day's
work. While dressing she remembered her bad dream
about her brother. Thinking about it, she remembered
that in the past when her brother had gotten into some
bind where he could have or had been hurt, she knew
of it. She did not know why she could sense it, but the
only thing that came to mind, was her closeness to
him. Maybe it was something the females of her line
could sense. She remembered something vaguely that
her mother had mentioned, more to herself than to
anyone around, that she could sense when her mate,
whom she loved deeply, had injured himself –
something about the bonding she guessed.

So had Lauut gone underground, as the dream
seemed to indicate? That seemed impossible. Since all
the turns of living here, with all of their youthful
explorations, and generations of the family mapping
of the property had shown none to exist. So what had
led to this dream? What was he up to anyway? He had
been so secretive about his intended destination, even
though he had stated generally where he was heading.
She knew she could not help him if he had gotten
injured. She wasn't even sure which way he went.
*Guess there is no need to worry yet. He isn't due back
until this after-zenith or early evening. If he doesn't
show by then . . . oh stop it. He's fine, and I'll see him*

soon. She chided herself for thinking the worst. But as a youth he kept getting himself into trouble with some of his half-baked schemes and adventures. Yet, much of that should be behind him by now. Shaking her head she said, "Males and their adventures. They sure seem to like putting themselves into dangerous situations . . . stupid really." Lauut was no different. He really seemed to never think things completely through. Although since the loss of their sires he had calmed down considerably and appeared to take on the responsibility of operating, with her, their family property.

Thinking about the family property and all that had transpired here in the past, it would be sad to lose it. The shelter had served many generations of Ktroves, and she hoped it would serve many generations more. Her past sires had planned well. This shelter was a good example. It had been built to take advantage of both the surrounding terrain, and of the rising and setting sun. The food preparation and eating area faced the morn sun to conserve on lighting. The rest and meeting area, a single space, was placed so that it received light all day. There had been areas in the roof that had been designed to let in light also. From the eating space you could look across the hard packed dirt yard to the working pens and out-shelters. This meant that those important areas could be monitored while one was in repast. *Yes,* she thought, *they had planned well.* Since she was alone she prepared her morn meal and hot beverage that always seemed to set the tempo for the day ahead. Then taking both the food and drink back to her sleeping space, she finished her dressing for the day. Other than the fact she had to do the work for both of them, it appeared it was to be an ordinary day.

Once dressed, she decided to take the remainder of her meal and drink, and sit on the porch to enjoy the morn coolness. The morn fog was breaking up, and the sun was starting to peek through. As in the evening, she loved sitting here in the coolness of the morn before the heat of the day encroached. As usual, her constant companion Sadie, one of the herd dogs, came over looking for some attention from her, then lay on the porch beside her. It would be so easy just to sit here and watch the morn pass, but unfortunately nothing would get done. Stretching she got up and headed back inside to clean up the morn dishes, and once finished headed out to begin the day's work. She loved being here – the views that seemed to go on forever – the smells, sounds, the flyers and their songs, all seemed to make it peaceful. It seemed like one just soaked it in, like a hot bath, easing tired muscles after a particularly hard day.

In comparison, being in the village and the one time she had been in a township, there seemed to be nothing but noise and chaos, followed by a hidden pressure that seemed to invade one's spirit. She was always glad when she returned to the family property, and let that village air slide away as the soapy residue would leave you after rinsing. Yet, she knew that someday this place would only be a memory for her to covet, and that was a sad thought, a very sad though indeed. And she really didn't want that day or time to arrive even though it was inevitable as the rising and setting of the sun.

As she approached the pens, the beasts came to the railing anticipating their morn feed. She had a great rapport with the beasts, and they always seemed to be eager to get close to her. Of course it could be her imagination since, like her brother, she cared for them. Going to the supply shelter she pulled out the feed, which were compressed grasses. When the beasts could see that they were going to eat they ran over towards the feeding area, which, until she released the bar, they could not enter. By using this arrangement, it gave the two of them time to place all the necessary food and do any cleanup before the beasts could come in. It was safer that way. It was not that these beasts wanted to hurt anyone; it was just that when it came to food they had a one-track mind. *You know kind of like the males when it came to finding a mate,* she thought. Shaking her head she remembered some of her encounters with some of the males who were very interested in her, even though she wanted nothing to do with them.

Having made sure that all was ready she released the bars to let the beasts in, and once in replaced the bar so she could work cleaning up the rest of the pens. Once finished here she needed to move on to the young ones, and then from there on to the food garden. It was going to be a long and very busy day.

* * *

The sun was well past the zenith when he woke up. For a few seconds he not sure where he was or why it was so late in the day, and why hadn't his sister awakened him. Then it all came flooding back into him mind, the trip down into the cavern and the harrowing return where he almost failed to find the way out. He found that it was nature that had wakened him and he got up to go relieve himself away from camp. Once finished he returned to camp realizing he was still very thirsty, and at the same time quite hungry. *Guess that adventure took more out of me than I thought.* Looking up he realized that there would only be a few hours before the sun would be setting. So emptying his water bottle that he had left in camp he refilled it with fresh water, he drank his fill, and then set about preparing a quick meal. He never remembered bringing the food back from the cave, but since it was here he must have. He needed to get back to the shelter. He found as he moved around his small camp that he ached all over. *Heck, my muscles hadn't been this sore in turns.* Not that he was that old, just in his mid-twenties – Still being stiff like an old male didn't set well with him. He considered himself in pretty good shape – after all the property demanded it. There was no time to be lazy, or things would get run down and out of control pretty quickly.

Once he had finished putting together a quick camp meal, he extinguished his small fire, thinking of the fire dangers here, packed up, and headed home. He knew it would take longer heading back because of his bruised shin and the soreness in his muscles. He started the hike back, limping and very stiff. Yet, he found, as he warmed to the task, that his sore muscles loosened up, and if he favored the bruised leg, he could almost make his normal hiking speed. It was really wonderful to be out in this fresh air, and to be able to see the distances when he crested a small incline or hill, unlike the enclosed confines of that tunnel and cavern. Although each had its own attraction, he knew that the normal life of his was what he preferred. Funny how different adventuring was compared to a book verses what happens to one in real life. In a book the hero seemed always to find a way out of trouble, and somehow something conveniently would appear to assist him if necessary. He found, looking back on his own adventure that he could have been severely injured or worse killed. He had come close more than once. Here he knew there would be no magic solution, or someone coming to rescue him. He had foolishly let no one know where he had been. "Stupid . . . stupid, stupid, stupid!" He said as he shook his head. This had been a tough lesson, and one he was thankful that it had a good outcome for him.

* * *

It was late after-zenith, and her brother had yet to return. Still she wasn't worried as of yet, it was still within the time he said that he would return. She continued her day's work and was presently working the food garden. The after-zenith work with the beasts was complete and this was the final outdoor chore left to complete before returning indoors and finishing up. As she finished watering the food garden she noticed, off in the distance, someone approaching the shelter. Whoever it was, was still too far away to be recognizable. Well, maybe some company, something that hadn't happened for a long time – which was understood, since for most, this was a busy time of the turn – most of the visiting came in the cold and wet season when there was much less to accomplish. It was during that time that all the relationships were renewed, a traditional time for pairings also. It was a good time for new couples that had paired. The nights were long and cool, making intimacy and romance much easier – and nicer to tell the truth. It was during this time that the formal announcements of pursuit would be put forth, and then the plans for the upcoming mating ceremonies at the major gathers were announced or performed.

Watching the individual approach, she noticed whoever it was had a limp, but again he was still too far away to be identified, but she had a feeling it was her brother. Something in the way he moved reminded her of him. Still she would have to wait until the person got closer before she could be sure of the identity. She finished weeding the small plot and checked to see if the fence was still in good shape, something vital if one wanted to get anything out of the garden. If one were careless, the small beasts would, overnight, completely devour and destroy the garden, making all the hard work a loss. As a whelp she had sneaked into the garden with a female friend, and was playing. Then, like whelps, when they left the area, they left the gate wide open. Fortunately, she had been observed leaving and the carelessness of that open the gate, so the breach was caught. Yet, the lesson from her mother which followed, was so severe in her mind that she never forgot to close that gate after that. So, with a quick and thorough inspection to make sure the small beasts hadn't found some unchecked opening in the fence; she left, and closed the gate behind her. She was now sure that the traveler in question was her brother, even though he was still too far out to see his features. She wondered what he had done to himself that left him limping like that. But, on that subject, she knew she would find out soon enough. Shaking her head she said, "Just Like him to show up after all the work is done."

* * *

That bruised leg was really hurting, and it slowed him down even more as he continued his trek back to the shelter. In the distance, up by the food garden, he could see his sister finishing the work there and looking in his direction. He would be there soon enough. He found that even though he had slept well, he just did not seem to have any stamina and his flagging energy was almost gone. Again, he hoped that he wasn't coming down with some sickness. Still he knew it was a possibility, since when he left that shaft it had been very cool, and he was soaked with sweat from the heat within the passageways. So by the time he had reached his camp he was chilled to the bone. Sometimes he knew that the combination of chill, stress, and fatigue could cause the body's natural resistance to drop and allow some sickness to get the upper hand, even if it was brief, like a cold or the flu.

A good hot bath and a better sleep just might get me over the hurdle, and, of course, a good meal would surely help also. Smiling to himself through the pain of his leg, he was glad that this adventure was just about over. Still, he knew he would be going back there, back to that never ending darkness. He felt that he had not enough time to truly explore that one cavern since he had to turn around and leave because of his impatience and poor planning. But, this time he would bring his sister along and do a much better job of planning . . . a very much better job of planning and outfitting.

As he approached their home, he could see that his sister had already entered the shelter, and he would have to be ready to answer questions he was sure he would get from her. Of course, he would probably have done the same thing, still it appeared that the females had a desire to know more, and would ask more, than the males. They, the males would just wait until the person was ready to tell his story, and then ask questions that would help bring out the details. While, on the other hand, the females would immediately begin asking, and continue to ask, until they felt that they got the answers they wanted or were looking for.

I don't know which is going to be more uncomfortable, Lauma asking questions, or this bruised leg. Then shaking his head, he answered his own question, *Lauma of course.* Her scrutiny could be worse than that of their mother when she was alive. Shaking his head and with a nervous smile thought, *Must be something in the blood of females that can make us feel so uncomfortable when they confront us – might as well get this over with.* Then speaking out loud to strengthen his resolve he said, "And why should I be nervous, we are siblings, sister and brother – equals so to speak." Yet he knew that he would feel like a whelp under the gaze of some unhappy sire. He prepared himself for the upcoming confrontation, opened the door and entered the shelter.

As he expected, she was standing there waiting for him with her hands on her hips. *Trouble,* he thought. When she had looked him over she had a shocked look on her face. "Where have you been? You are just covered in dirt and filth. And those are not the clothes you left in and look at your hair and skin. It looks like you were out rolling in a dust wallow. How in the heck did you get so dirty?"

"Woowa sis slow down, I am not even in the shelter and you're hitting me with a thousand questions here. Give me a chance to at least get inside and close the door. I obviously need to clean up, and need to look after my injury to see if I did more than I thought I did. Then while I am doing that, I'm hopeful that you could fix us a meal, and then over the food I'll try to give you a rundown of where I was and what I was doing. I *do* think you'll find it interesting. But, please let me go, and get cleaned and changed. The clothes I am wearing are little uncomfortable and the ones I was wearing are soaked with sweat, I need to . . ."

"Yes you sure do!" she said wrinkling her nose as the stench reached her nose. "Okay, go ahead to your sleeping space, and while you are cleaning up I *will* go ahead and *fix* our meal, but don't expect me to do this alone all the time. This is a shared chore." Flustered a little because he wouldn't tell her much yet, she let him go and went into the cooking area and started to prepare their meal. "So how did you hurt your leg?" She yelled, so he could hear her.

He mumbled something back that seemed unintelligible. "What did you say, I couldn't hear you." She responded.

"Can't you wait?" He asked exasperated.

Stamping her foot, she said, "Oh all right. At least let me know that you okay."

"Other than this bruise and being very tired, I think I'm in good shape . . . will be out of here in a few, then I promise I will fill you in on everything."

"Promise," she asked somewhat mollified. "Sorry, but I do really care for you, and I had a bad dream about you last evening and . . ." She trailed off and just let it end there. She knew that he would tell his story. She really hoped that her dream was just that, a dream and nothing more. She then put her energies into fixing the food, and from the sounds in the back of the house she knew he would be out soon, and hopefully he would answer her concerns.

CHAPTER FIVE

As the camp manager Bayleh, and scout Doube had predicted, it was a long-winded meeting as Joellie had to nit-pick every last detail. As in most of these meetings, he saw that once again, Joellie was considering his team as a bunch of worthless, lazy bums who could not get anything right. Fauul really did not know where Joellie was coming from, since the team had worked well throughout most of this project. Shaking his head he thought. *There's just no pleasing some people. Especially ones like him who thinks they are better on all levels than everyone.*

Shaking his head inwardly as he listened, he reviewed where they were and what still needed to be accomplished. They found themselves at the base of a small range of mountains. They were on the edge of a desert, and rumor had it there was a trail over these rugged mountains. Once on top, it was supposed to be an easy run into that final village and then on to the ocean. That was where this final quarter of a cycle of surveying was to end. Yet, as they progressed down the range, the path had not manifested itself. This had been one of the pet peeves of Joellie. He ranted that even the mountains were against him.

Of course, by being in the desert, water for both the beasts and them were an issue. So far the few wandering locals had given them directions to hidden springs, and some tanks. Yet, the last contact had been days in the past. Still these tanks usually could be counted on, since it was runoff and rainwater that filled them, their availability was never a sure thing. The last tank, which was really needed, turned out to be dry, and from all appearances had been for a while. Of course through Joellie's eyes it was the team's fault, and once again the desert was scheming against him. Where he came up with some of these off the floor notions was beyond Fauul. Usually after the meetings Fauul would have to smooth many ruffled feathers from the imagined slights that were thrown at different members of the team by Joellie. By no choice of his own Fauul had become both a mediator and the camp counselor. And in the end it was why he, unless demanded by Joellie, was the only one to report to these meetings.

Water was the big problem. They still had some left but not nearly enough to tackle the mountain range or their remaining time in the desert. So on the morrow in the morn as they continued to search for the trail, the scout Doube, would need to spend most of his day trying to locate a water source. Most of this would have to be done on foot, since working the beasts would require a larger amount of water than was available presently. This meant, of course, they would not be able to cover as much of an area as they could if the beasts were available for riding, even though riding of the beasts were rarely performed. That also meant that the camp would not be broken down, and Bayleh, with the assistant, would stay in camp to keep it safe and to keep the beasts in their rope corral.

Graze, so far, had not been a problem, as these beasts would devour just about anything green – a tough breed that could survive in any terrain that they had been introduced. While they had been domesticated for a few generations, the original stock had survived in the wild on the edge of deserts. With careful breeding of the wanted traits they had ended up with a beast of strength, and endurance, with a personality that was easy to work with – unlike some of the members of the team. That was not to say that at times, with these beasts, that you would not get throwbacks. Ones who had that original ornery personality that was necessary to survive the living conditions they had to contend with in the wilds. When that happened you could really see how tough and dangerous they were. It made one wonder how the first of this breed had ever been captured and then domesticated; one had to give it to their ancestors. To accomplish this feat alone meant they had to be tough individuals – something that as a civilization grows, begins to disappear.

After the meeting, and shaking off the tension that these meetings always produced, Fauul went back to the ones who refused to attend and laid out the morrow's work and hoped, as he looked towards the day, they would be successful in both finding the trail over the mountains, and finding the water that was desperately needed. The problems one faced in the desert were universal; heat during the day and cold during the night, lack of water, and sparse vegetation with wicked defenses. Those barbed thorns and needles that all the vegetation seemed to have would be very painful if one were to make contact. Well, the morrow would bring its own troubles and discoveries. He was tired and so retired to the portable sleeping shelter, where all the team could sleep if they so chose.

* * *

The sunrise in the desert can be a spectacular sight. The sky starts to gray imperceptibly, then the desert starts to become visible, followed by an orange glow in the area of the sunrise. It seems that the air is still with the anticipation of the rising sun, except for an almost imperceptible breeze, and then the sun breaks the horizon and within minutes the whole desert comes alive. Fauul had been in some deserts where the surrounding countryside shared in the beauty of both the sunrise and the sunset. The colors in the sky seem to be reflected in the surrounding desert lands adding its beauty to the whole scene. It was breathtaking, and distracting. One can also see so many of them that one begin to take them for granted, which in itself is a very sad fact. Each is unique and deserves more than a passing glance. Yet, life being what it is, this beauty can easily take a back seat to the more immediate needs and concerns – and rightly so. So balance was required. Enjoy the beauty of the natural world, but approach with a heavy dose of caution.

Enough of this, it was time to finish the morn camp chores and head out. They had to find that trail up and over this small range of mountains, and make sure, once located; the trail would be well marked on the maps and in the team's logs. So, by leaving just after sunrise when it was still cool, they could do a lot of searching by the time it became too hot – at which point the team would need to find shade – and good luck on that one. They would wait out the heat of the day, and after that continue the search. Of course this time of waiting was not wasted either. Great discussions happened, as well as the updating of notes and sketches of the surrounding areas the team had just hiked through. Fauul surely hoped, as the rest, that Doube would find a water source today, while they were not in any danger yet, still, if water wasn't found soon then the situation would change rapidly, becoming life threatening. And the danger wasn't far off at all. Fauul went to ask Doube what he planned on doing, but realized, as he had worked the camp, he was nowhere around. He found that strange since Doube usually let one of them know when he was heading out. Fauul headed over to the food prep area and asked the assistant if he had seen Doube, with the assistant replying that the scout had picked up something quick this morn and had left before dawn.

* * *

Looking at the situation that previous night Doube decided to head out before dawn. There were many advantages to doing this. He had been one of the few of this team who had grown up in the outback. Doube had thought about their situation and knew he would need all his skill to get them out of this tight spot, and that was why the decision to leave when he did.

The desert, in itself, was a large chunk of land, and it was easy for one to get lost in it. Yet, it was water, and only water that determined where one was to cross and live in this barren land. The water locations shrank the size down, since going where there was none could and would lead to death. Knowing this he used his knowledge that trails, over time, would develop, leading to water sources. These trails were not always obvious or necessarily visible, still finding them was critical. Looking back, in his mind, he realized that he thrived out here. He had tried to become a learned but was unsuccessful. It wasn't that the learning was difficult. He had been a top learner. There appeared to be a bright future for him, still for some unknown reason he just felt uncomfortable in the townships. It wasn't until returning home for a short time the answer came to him. After a day or two there he felt a great pressure slide away – he hadn't even realized it was there. Yet, when it was gone he felt at peace, whole again. He could feel the quiet, could see the natural world, and could sense a flow of what, well, he did not know, but without it he seemed to be missing something.

It then came to him that being in that artificial world of the townships; a silent pressure had built inside of him, and continued to press down on him during all the time he was there. It took getting back to the rural and natural areas for him to discover this. While there was nothing wrong with the townships, he knew of many whom could never be comfortable here in the outback, it was something that would not work for him. So, with that revelation he changed career directions, finding that scouting was more to his liking. As time went on, he found that he had a natural ability for doing this. While the pay was not as good as the original career path, he felt much healthier and definitely happier. It had let him remain in the outback with the infinite views, the soft breezes, and yes, even the terrible storms and problems that this life threw at you. Still he would want and have it no other way. This style of life kept him healthy, and his mind active. Yes especially his mind, since this wild world would throw problems his way that would require deep thinking and quick reactions. Sometimes you only had seconds to act, while others could be solved at your leisure.

While, at the beginning, he had the basic skills to scout, learned from where he had grown up, it was a number of turns and a lot of study and work before he actually became one of the better scouts. He originally was going to be heading out with one of the first teams, but an illness in the family delayed his arrival, and when he did arrive it was to this team he was assigned. Looking over the names of the team, most he did not know, but he knew the two leaders. Thinking about it, he felt that Joellie would be a poor leader, and most likely he got this position through some political pressure or means. So, far his doubts about him had been accurate. In fact this situation they were presently in was Joellie's fault. Even when cautioned against doing it, and repeatedly warned, he left the trail and moved the team closer to the mountain range, figuring to save time. In the desert, this was one of the fastest ways to disaster . . . yet, all of the proof and advice given rolled off him like water off a water flyer's back.

While a desert could be large, and if one were unfamiliar with the ways of the desert, one would feel that there would be no way to track someone down. Yet, even though that had some truth, especially if the one was someone who knew nothing of the desert, water still was the determining factor. So almost all that knew the ways of the desert could be found, since they did not or would not detour far from the known trails and sources of water. In this case Joellie proved himself twice the fool. He put the team in danger by leaving the known trails, and by doing so had taken them away from known water sources, and he refused all advice to the contrary.

Fauul, on the other hand, was very conscientious of his team, and willing to listen to suggestions. He was stuck in the position of having to correct the bad decisions made by Joellie, and try to be the go between. Those meetings of Joellie's were worthless. Something that should only take a very short time would extend on for endless periods of time, while he would complain about how he was overlooked for this or that, and this project would remedy that situation very quickly. *Right! But not in the way he expects.* This brought an inner chuckle. Then Joellie would go into how he would do things when he got his just due – mostly stating unimportant things that had nothing to do with the immediate concerns of the team, or the planning of the next day's duties – not a true leader at all. That fell to Fauul to get it all working and planned out. So by this time he and most of the team just stayed away, and let Fauul explain afterwards. He felt sorry for Fauul, since he had no choice. He had to be there, being second in charge.

Enough of this line of thought, Doube thought. *I've got to find water so we may continue safely to the end of this, and at this point we are so close to finishing.* Thinking about it, he looked forward to the trip back. Since they were to go the known coast route, and it would be a much easier trek. The reason for leaving before dawn was simple. Yet, if you were from the townships, it was something you wouldn't think about or know. Once one's eyes became adjusted to the night, then any trail, even a rarely used one would become visible. Many times, in the daylight, a rarely traveled trail would be almost impossible to see, to find, let alone follow. Yet, at night the trail would show as a lighter area and be relatively easy to follow. So, with this in mind, he left the camp, went out a certain distance so that none of the camp lights would be visible, circled the camp looking for the tale tell signs of a trail, and possibly some of the signs that he was not far from water.

He had also talked with some locals a few days earlier about the trail out of the desert, and knew that even though the range of mountains were not very high, the route would not be easy to travel, let alone find. *First things first,* he reminded himself. He hoped the other party would be successful in locating the trail out of the desert and over those mountains. If he was unsuccessful in his search, then they would need to leave the desert as quickly as possible and find water on top. As usual, when Joellie would do something, to save time, or to explore an area, it ended up costing them more, adding unnecessary problems and delays.

It wouldn't be long before dawn was upon him, and if he did not at least find the beginnings of a path, then it would become much more difficult. He had gotten enough food from the camp manager to cover himself through the zenith meal, and had included enough water for the day. He had also taken an additional water test kit; just in case he found multiple sources of water, which was unlikely, but he felt that it was better to be prepared, just in case he was that lucky.

Plants, while normally a good indicator of water, were not necessarily so in the desert. The vegetation had learned over time how to adapt, and many had root systems that seemed to spread over large portions of the land. The vegetation would remain dormant until a certain level of moisture would arrive, and then come alive with new growth. Once the moisture was gone, they would return to dormancy. While not an expert on the deserts, his conversations with the people who were gave him a rough idea of what type of vegetation he should be looking for. Again most beasts small and large that had adapted to the desert did not require much water. Because of this one could not count on tracks of beasts to lead one to water as would be possible in the hills.

As he continued his ever-widening circles around camp, he established landmarks from many different directions so when he returned he would be able to locate the campsite. They had set up camp in a small depression, and as such from a distance, unless one was higher up, the camp was invisible. He also placed some rock markers to reinforce the camp location. "Always have a backup plan," he said quietly.

Dawn was coming and with the dawn he could confirm his landmarks. In the desert, nights with a full moon, dusk, and dawn were his favorite times. It seemed on those full moon nights the desert took on an eerie quiet beauty. The night air, cooling quickly from the heat of the day, and the breezes becoming soft and cool touching one's skin and almost immediately disappearing – leaving one to wonder where breezes and heat went. It was a time for quiet reflection, a time to be away from camp, to be alone, and to listen and feel the desert. He was raised in the hills, but as he spent more time, because of this project, in the desert, and he found himself being drawn to it. As one spent time here, one began to appreciate the desert's stark beauty, and harsh rules. Which Joellie, of course, had broken, and had placed them in this dangerous predicament. As the sky grayed from the coming dawn he sat on a large rock to await the sun. From the feel in the air he could tell that it was promising to be a scorcher of a day – funny how one could tell just from the feel of the air, even though daylight was still a short time away. Yet, in the desert once the skies started graying, it would only be a short time before the sun rose and the heat would begin to build.

So far any trail had been elusive, so with a sigh he rose and continued his outward spirals. He knew the signs of water were subtle and he would have to really observe, otherwise he would miss the few signs that would show. Of course if the water was in one of the hidden tanks, which usually were depressions in rocks, and sheltered from the sun by other rocks, the only sign would be the water loving crawlers such as the honey-makers. They required much water to produce their honey.

Looking for a high spot where he could observe the surrounding desert he watched the sun rise above the horizon. At this point he looked around carefully. The rising sun would reveal much of the landscape he was in. The early morning shadows would reveal areas that were depressions or ravines or even entrances to small canyons. As the day progressed these hints would disappear with the shortening and disappearing of the shadows that had been produced by the low sun. Taking a small swig of water from his water container, he continued to study the land, finally seeing a possible promising direction he headed out. With careful observation he sensed more than saw a slight downhill run and a possible draw. He hoped that a low depression would also be a collecting area for the precious liquid. There seemed to be much volcanic debris scattered everywhere. Somewhere in the unknown past the area gave the appearance that a large volcano had let go. Even though, so far, other than the rock, there had been no sign of any. Any way he looked at it, today was going to be one of the most important days since the start of this the mapping. There had been other major problems and dangers they had run into along the way, but none posed the threat to the team that this one did.

Looking towards the mountains he could see clouds forming on top, a promise of rain later in the day in the form of thunderstorms. If it did end up with rain up there, then water, again, would become a problem here in the desert, but for the opposite reason, too much water. It would come roaring out of the mountains and create a number of flash floods across the desert floor, making the ravines and gully raging torrents of death and destruction, then the sands would absorb the water and it would be gone as if it never was. At the same time high in the sky he saw a flyer of prey riding the air currents – always an awesome sight. *If I could be up there with him it would be much easier to find water. Just think of all I would see from there,* smiling slightly, as he thought about it, followed by shaking his head. *This isn't gettin' water found.* Still this early morn beauty and solitude was becoming a deep part of him, and it would be easy just to sit, observe, and appreciate where he was.

Looking back to camp, which by now was in the distance, he marked another part of the terrain. With this newest landmark, he could find the camp if, for some reason, he got himself misplaced. With that he headed towards the areas he decided to search first.

* * *

Fauul, after the morn meal, brought together the other members who were to go with him to find the trail out of the desert, or at least a trail that could lead them to the way out. One consolation was that Joellie would remain in camp, and that by itself would ease tensions in the group. The search party would consist of himself, one other cartographer, and the artist. He would have loved to have Doube along, but in truth what the scout was doing was much more important. He had wished to talk with him this morn, to get some ideas on what he should be looking for and possibly where. That did not happen since Doube left before he was even out of the sleep sack. Nothing he could do about that now, probably should have talked with him the night before. *Oh well,* He thought, *guess I can do without the advice; still it would have been nice to have his input.* Yet, he had to admit, by being out in the field as long as they had; he had become pretty proficient in following the lay of the land. He knew even with this added skill, he was not close to the abilities that Doube demonstrated. He felt most fortunate to have him on this team. Most likely, with his skill, he would have been on one of the first teams. Yet, some type of personal problem led to a delay and landed him with them. Doube was a private person, and did more listening than conversing. So when he did speak one had a tendency to listen.

Anyway, their group had approached this area from the Northeast, and was heading southwest when they encountered the range of mountains. If Joellie had not taken them off the main trail three days before, most likely they would have been on top by now, and possibly well on the way to that final village, but here they were. So with these thoughts he talked with the other two members of his small group to get their ideas and suggestions. It was decided that they would head south paralleling the mountains that still lay in the distance. By staying on higher ground, and setting landmarks both in the distance and close to camp so they would not end up going in circles, they hoped that the trail would eventually show itself. The danger would come as the sun neared the zenith; once it did the sun could not be used to confirm their direction making it easier to become lost.

He thought the artist was a good selection to bring with him, since he had an excellent eye for catching the small details that could easily be missed by one who was untrained. In this type of land it would be those types of details that could lead to success or failure. The subtlety of desert could lead one to believe it never changed, and everywhere one looked it was the same. This of course was not true. Again he cursed Joellie for taking them, once again, on one of his shortcuts. This delay would probably overall cost at least an extra couple of days . . . if not up to a half a cycle. Of course the consequences could be much worse.

The sun had been up for a short period of time when they headed south to find the main trail, and if not the main one, any trail to get them back on track. As the sun progressed in the sky it continued to warm. He could tell, once again, that it was going to be hot. He hoped they had brought enough water along for the three of them. While a packed zenith meal was important, it was the water that was critical. He knew they could sweat it out quicker than they could take it in. Then, as their bodies dehydrated, one's mind would start wandering, and concentration would be difficult, leading eventually to irrational thinking, etcetera. And while on that subject he knew that heat stroke and heat prostration were ever-present dangers. All three of them had better be alert to each other for symptoms.

At least in most places in the desert one could see far. There was little to block one's view. Yet, even that could be deceiving by it apparent flatness. It really was anything but. And, when one looked at it from a small hill one could imagine you were walking on the bottom of a large lake or seabed, with the surrounding hills and mountains one could imagine that these to be islands. With all the sand present, it really might have been that way sometime in the past. Still the area was strewn with large boulders giving the appearance of having been tossed about by giants or maybe the legendary gods or the *ones before* that the elders spoke of to keep the whelps in line, or to weave tall tales. Overall the desert appeared to have little life in it; again this was deceiving as there is much life here. You just needed to know where and how to look for it. Most of the beast life did not move during the day being smart enough to stay out of the sun and its dangers. This meant that they probably were not as smart as the beasts, since here they were out in the middle of desert in the daytime. Yet, they had little choice, as their senses were built to function better in the daylight then in the dim light of the night.

Looking back over the last few days of their trip, they had come across a lot of desert. Overall they had stayed on established trails. That was until Joellie saw a great depression off to the south. He decided it needed to be investigated. Joellie and he – and Doube – had argued about it for a short time, but Joellie stated simply he was the leader and the final decision was his. Initially they followed a minor trail down to the edge of the depression. Here it appeared others had come to collect salt. As they continued into the depression and at the same time losing altitude it became obvious that somewhere back in time this had been an Inland Sea.

As they continued south they kept a small desert mountain range southwest of them as a landmark. It took them about half a day to traverse a portion of this dry seabed. It made Fauul wonder if this could have covered the whole desert at one point. Yet, there was no proof of that, as the salt flats were isolated to this one large area. Still it was a worrisome thing, since they were in an area without trails. Once they went far enough south to put the hills west of them, they changed direction going more to the north, then proceeded west. The day was coming to a close, and they needed to find a campsite for the night, and really did not want to camp in the middle of these salt flats, so they pushed on and even by doing so, it was dark before they finally exited the salt depression. Grumbling they made a dry camp, and bedded down for the evening just outside of the dry seabed on a very flat area that appeared that could have been used to build a shelter. It was as if sometime in the past this area had been a village or something, which was impossible. After all, why would anyone do such a thing? No water, no trails, no reason to live here.

The next morn as they were heading west they kept the range of Desert Mountains on their right side, northwest of them. The area they were in appeared to have been a delta in the past, not necessarily a large one, but you could see where water had run and spread out. With no trail to follow they had to be careful. Even though they could see a great distance, they could still easily end up going down a small canyon or ravine, find out it was a dead end, and then have to backtrack and start over. While distances could be deceiving, it appeared they were only about two days from leaving the desert. As Fauul thought about it, yes, there was something about the desert that stayed with you, yet he would be glad when they were out of it.

As they continued that next day they eventually came upon an area that was torn up considerably. They had been warned about such an area that was called badlands by the locals, and this appeared to be that area. From the brief descriptions they had received it was best to avoid such areas. This area forced them closer to the Desert Mountains as they attempted to find a way around them. Here they found a large wash and decided to follow it to see if it might go completely through the badlands. They could see that there were many dry tributaries coming into the wash. It was decided they should stay with the main bed as it was rather large and appeared to cut through the surrounding badlands – all they could hope was this went completely through. The wash had steep sides while cutting through a large area, and once they started down this path there appeared to be very few spots where one could leave. So they were committed to their direction until the wash either ended, forcing them to retreat, or would run all the way through, allowing them a way out of this rugged torn land.

As they continued down, or up, according how you wanted to look at it, the wash and the desert hills were growing in size, and closing in on them. They realized the wash was heading into the badland area. So as they came to the many forks in the wash they had to stop and decide whether to continue in what appeared to be the main wash, or to follow one of these forks. With the limited water supply and not knowing where the next water was, these delays might, in the long run, turn out to be dangerous. Heat was also the enemy. As they progressed up the wash, the badlands started to close in around them, the hillsides, having absorbed heat from the sun, was reflecting it back at them like they were in an oven. These hills that rose above them blocked what little breeze there was intensifying the feeling of the radiating heat. Because it was a dry heat it felt as if, through their sweat, the heat was sucking the moisture right out of them, making the team more aware of how dangerous their situation truly was.

With this loss of moisture they became susceptible to the dangers of heat, heat stroke or heat prostration or both – one was from lack of moisture the other from the body core overheating – both were deadly, and would kill. One fork that had a larger wash area than the one they were following headed north towards the mountains they had just hiked around. Plus the soil that remained after the runoff had been absorbed was darker, giving the appearance of having come out of some volcanic area. There was a possibility it would circle around and avoid both the mountains and the badlands, but there was no proof. So after some arguments they continued up the original wash. After continuing past this second larger wash, the one they were following began to narrow rapidly. Then, as they came up to a sharp curve in the wash, they could see that ahead of them and next to where the team was standing, the wash branched several times, on their immediate right and again ahead of them, approximate sixty five body lengths in the distance. When they first saw the area ahead, it first appeared to dead end. Yet with a closer inspection they could see where two branches of the wash came into that apparent dead end. All three of these washes were much smaller than the one there were presently in.

The wash on their immediate right and one ahead on the right ahead appeared to be the largest of the three branches. So, they eliminated the third that came in from the left, thinking that it could easily lead them back the way they had just traveled. Quickly it was decided that they split the team into two teams. Each would go a short distance up the two washes and see which was more promising. As expected, everyone's temper was becoming short as the heat and fatigue started taking its toll. He was on the team that went ahead to explore the lower right branch, while Joellie explored the other. Doube was assigned to go with Joellie while the camp manager Bayleh and his assistant remained with the pack beasts and the supplies.

As his team worked down this branch of the wash, they found the going becoming more difficult, plus the wash was narrowing rapidly. It really looked as if this branch was heading deeper into the badlands, which was not a good sign. Fauul could see ahead only a little way, and after going through what was similar to a switchback another branch appeared to be just ahead of this one – no, not a good sign at all.

As had been agreed upon before they broke down into teams, Fauul sent a member of the team back down the wash to meet up with the pack beasts and wait for a member of the other team to see which branch was more promising. No sooner had the one he sent back to the meeting point left, he returned. Fauul commented on his speed trying to keep things light. The one he had sent stated he had actually run into Doube coming up to see them. Doube thought, from what he could determine, the other branch was the way out of here. Fauul was very happy to hear that. He surely did not want to have to backtrack out of the area and attempt to find another way around. The day was moving much too quick as it was.

He was told that Bayleh and his assistant Mealoh had already led the pack beasts up the wash, and that they were to proceed until all of them met up towards the end, where the other wash possibly came out of the badland area. As hot and tired as the team was Fauul was hoping that Joellie would call it a day once out of this mess, and at which point they would set up camp. There had been enough problems with all these unplanned detours they had taken.

As they proceeded back up the wash and headed down the other he asked Doube what he thought about the area and what may have caused such a torn up piece of land. Part of Doube's background was geology and even though they were not stopping to study the surrounding rock Fauul thought that Doube had a pretty good idea and opinion. Doube replied saying that he thought that at one time there had been a lot of volcanic activity in the area, and probably some pretty good earth shakes also. The rocks looked ancient, so there was time for rain, wind, and earth shakes, to break up this piece of land into this barren broken land. Yet there easily could have been much more going on to create it and other explanations as to why it was this way.

It probably took another hour before they finally cleared the badlands completely. Thankfully, even though they had yet to find the main trail or water,

Joellie did call it for the day. On the morrow they would break into teams to locate both a trail out and a water source. So they put up the portable shelters and set up camp, trying to catch what shade and breeze they could. Ahead, in the distance, they could see the mountain range that they had to traverse, and knew from the ruggedness of these mountains, they could run into difficulties in finding a way out of this desert and over those mountains. This break also gave time for the artist to work and for the rest of the map team to work the area they had just passed through into the rough map they had been creating. Of course this mapping they were doing would not be complete until some future time. Still it would connect the areas together. There would still be blanks, unexplored or unmapped areas that over time, other teams and locals would fill in to make the maps complete, but when, was anybody's guess.

* * *

Of course that was yesterday and they were now searching for that trail that they had left behind at Joellie's bidding – and headed out of camp in a southerly direction keeping the badlands on their left. As the day progressed the promised heat, from the feel of the morn, started to make its presence known. Where they were, there was no shade, no surprise since this was a desert after all, and the area was wide open with the vegetation being very sparse. Fauul hoped that soon they would come upon a trail that could lead them on and out of there. Yet, as they searched, nothing had materialized. No one familiar with the desert would do what Jollie had required of them and expect to survive. Time and time again they'd been warned to stay on the known trails, and they were paying that price now.

It was pushing the zenith when off to the southwest the soil color changed and at the same time the land appeared to be absolutely flat. Curious, they headed towards the area. It looked similar to the salt sink they had went through a couple of days earlier, except this one was not a sink. It was at the same level they were standing when they approached. The surface soils were very fine in grain also. When they arrived at the area they noticed that there was some sparse vegetation growing in amongst this white soil. In those patches of vegetation the soil was closer to what they had observed in the desert. It was also a good time to break for a meal before continuing. It would also give them some time to investigate this stuff. It did appear to cover a large area. It really was a mystery since there seemed to be no source – no flow into or out of the area – it was just there.

As they were eating their meal they again noticed off to the west the soil changed color once again but the land still remained flat. This whole area looked as if someone had come in and leveled it for some type of project. Yet, there was no consistency to the way of it. They proceeded to the color change and noticed it continued to the West further. So before continuing they finished their meal. And with that meal finished they decided to follow this flat area to its edge on the west side since that was more or less the direction they were heading anyway.

When they reached the edge there seemed to be an old trail heading in the general direction they were going. Because this was the first they had found since leaving the main trail they decided to follow it, nothing ventured, nothing gained. After about ten minutes they saw ahead of them what looked like an oasis. It appeared to be surrounded by some mounds of sand, and yet at the same time gave the appearance of having been occupied in the past. This probably had been a stopping point sometime in that past. Yet, from what they could observe it looked abandoned, and if not, then sparsely populated. Even though hot, the possibility of finding anything sparked their excitement and interest. They picked up their pace and headed directly to the mounds of sand and possible water. One of the promising signs of water was the trees. Since most species of trees required a lot of water it, in itself, was a good sign. Still, if nothing else, the trees would at least provide shade and probably a better location for their campsite.

* * *

After circling the camp a number of times Doube headed in a west-northwest direction. Ahead he used a desert mountain as his landmark. It was something easily seen and would provide a landmark he could use for quite a while. As he hiked towards the mountain he turned around looking back to establish a return landmark. He turned back around and noticed, to his left, the hillsides and soils were of a much darker color. This change seemed to be isolated to this region. He knew the campsite was to the right of the color change, so with that knowledge he now had both an outgoing and a return landmark. As he continued in that direction the land changed becoming somewhat flat. Off to north he could see three major washes coming from the hillside off in the distance, and could see he was going to have to cross all three. From appearances it should be easy. Unlike the wash they had followed to their present campsite the day before, there were no badlands or rising hills. From his brief observations this area had been geologically very active sometime in the distant past – funny how he couldn't keep his passion out of his thoughts. When he thought about it, it was one of the reasons he had for becoming a scout. This allowed him access to all sorts of geology. Something that would have been completely unavailable to him had he went in the direction of the other career.

As he cleared the third wash off to the north there appeared to be a major trail. He headed toward it and when arriving, looked back to the east. Smiling and shaking his head, he thought. *Heck! We missed this one. It looks like its north of where we came through the badlands. Well, guess I'll just follow this and see where it goes. This could be our ticket out of here.* With that he headed down the trail. It appeared to be heading generally in the same direction he was going to travel anyway. This didn't appear to be the trail discussed by locals a few days earlier, but a completely different one, albeit one that showed much travel. As he approached his major landmark the trail turned due south. This was not quite the direction he needed to go but curiosity drove him on, after all, this was not a minor pathway. It had to go somewhere, so he decided to stick with it. As he continued down the pathway he found an area, which must have been slightly lower than the surrounding land. Water, at some point, had puddled there, then had disappeared leaving behind large mud cracks in the soil. Of course it wasn't mud but dry earth.

He stopped briefly thinking about the area they were in. It was turning out to be very interesting geologically. Who'd of thought in such a small area that there could be so many different soils and rocks? He had been in ancient mudflats, which became part of the badlands, as well as volcanic soils, now fine silts were needed to form this type of surface. He saw layered rock, the result of silt being laid down over a great period of time and then turning into stone or sandstone. Apparently, even though this area was desert, it had not always so. Too much of what he had seen pointed to an area abundant in water and probably vegetation sometime in the past.

From the dry mudflats he looked southwest and saw an area that was different again. With so many changes already seen, he was naturally drawn to it to see what it may have been. "What happened in this area?" he asked. "It seems like there are just too many changes to make any sense. Wish I had the time to study this, it has really piqued my curiosity." Shaking his head he went ahead and over to this next soil change.

This looked as if someone in the past had created a large path, no, that would not be a good description. It was much too large, and it had a beginning and an end. It appeared to be laid in an east-west direction. From the short time he had been in the area, he guessed this was in the general direction of the prevailing winds. While cracked and broken into what could only be described as large grey-black stone, the surface looked like it had been made or created and not part of the natural world. Just to the south were some mounds and larger sand hills that paralleled this area and with one's imagination, might have been some type of shelter or shelters, but probably were just sand dunes. Still there was not enough of anything here to be sure. This was not his expertise anyway, so he could only guess. He decided this was a good place to break for his zenith meal. It would give him a bit of time to wander here and see if he could possibly solve the many puzzles before him. He wished now he had one of the "keepers of the past", with him. They could probably give him better answers than he would find himself. Such answers as: If indeed this had been a settlement, possibly how long ago it was here, and if it had been active sometime in the deep past. And was it during the time when this area was wet, or after? Still it could be some fluke of the natural world. There have been many rock formations that appear to have been produced by a civilization only to be proven as completely natural. Yet geology was his passion, and he had never seen anything quite like this in the natural world. That of course, was not to say he had seen it all. Still, this just had the feeling, to him that someone had created it.

While looking over this area he noticed to the south that the vegetation was increasing, a possible sign of water. He looked back to the northeast and saw that both the landmarks were still visible, and from here, if need be, he could cut across the desert to get back to their campsite. Not being able to find any answers to his mental questions and his meal finished, he crossed the trail and headed south. Water was critical and he hoped this sign was a good one. Yet, he knew that much of the vegetation had adjusted to the extremes of the desert and could survive on little water. But, logic told him, if there was an increase in the density it should mean a better chance of finding water. The winds had picked up as the day progressed. When they had started that morn, they were cool, but as the day moved on the winds had warmed considerably. These winds were also dry, assisting the sun in pulling moisture from the body. While they were close to leaving the desert, he knew that they were not out of the danger yet.

Thinking about it he knew that sometimes one would relax a bit when a tough section of a trail was almost over. It was usually where something major would happen. After keeping alert for dangers, one would drop their guard because of the proximity of leaving the dangerous portion, only to be injured or killed. Even at times, the safer portions had turned out to be deadly. He remembered reading a couple of reports where part of a team had been wiped out in what was considered one of the safest areas they were researching. *When in the natural world it paid never to be casual,* he thought – *especially if you want to come home!*

He noticed, once again, a change in the ground – it was becoming lighter in color. He found the existing vegetation, he had originally thought as a possible sign for water, to be native vegetation. Unfortunately, it was a type that took advantage of what little moisture was present and in reality, not a sign of water at all. Still ahead he saw trees, not necessarily many. Among them were many that had died leaving their skeletons pointing to the sky. Yet, when he looked at the pattern of the trees it appeared unnatural. As if someone in the past, being positive of mind, had planted them here, hoping that maybe this area would become a stopping point on the routes through the desert. It did not happen that way, since one of the major routes through the desert ended up going further south or well to the north. As he explored this area where the trees were he was hoping for water but all he found was an area that gave the appearance of a pond at one time. It was empty, dry, and had been for a very long time – probably the reason so many of the trees here were dead or dying. Their once source of water had vanished, as whoever had planted them here in the first place. Off to the south-southeast he observed an area where again the soil changed color again. From where he was it appeared to be almost white, plus it appeared to have very sparse vegetation, and seemed utterly flat.

Again curious, he headed to what he had observed. As he got closer he thought he had heard voices. It was subtle, and had taken time to reach his conscious mind. Stopping and holding his breath he strained to hear them again. With the wind blowing as hard as it was, it could have been something else. Still the sounds or voices he thought he had heard appeared to have come from the southwest. He headed in that direction, and was rewarded with some additional snatches of sound thrown at him by the wind. It definitely sounded like voices. Yet they were too soft and distant to be identifiable. As he worked towards the source of the sound, he saw another grove of trees. From a distance these appeared to be healthy. Maybe this was the source of the voices. The trees were of a type that required water, and as such, maybe there were some locals living there.

As he got closer, the voices were no longer being broken by the wind, yet he was still too far away to recognize any or to discern any words or dialect. From the tone it sounded as if a heated argument was taking place. Not wanting to simply show up where the voices were coming from and surprise whoever was arguing, he approached carefully. As he came closer, he could see the trees were definitely healthy. Apparently they both received care and had a good source of water. With a confirmation, because of the trees, that water was present he needed to go there and investigate.

Still, it was better, initially, to listen to the conversation, to get a feel for what the argument was about, and then determine if it was safe to approach. He thought he recognized one of the voices, but with the wind blowing as hard as it was, it was difficult to be sure. He moved a bit closer and yes, one of the voices belonged to Fauul, but the other was unknown, and seemed to have some kind of accent. Yet, Fauul and his team should have been heading south to find that major trail. Even though the situation was sizing up to be some kind of trouble, he smiled to himself realizing he went out to find water and instead found a viable trail, while the team Fauul was leading went out to find the trail and had located water instead. Now if only both finds could be used – that was the question. As he approached the trees, he noticed what appeared to be very old shelters that were partially buried within the compound. Apparently whoever had originally planted these trees had done so to provide a wind block.

After listening a bit longer he decided to scout around the compound to see if there were any more individuals. It was always important, in these remote areas, to know who or what you were up against. Carefully he proceeded to circle the compound. The size of the compound surprised him. Heck, it could have been a small village at some time in the past. He counted what appeared to be at least fifteen ruins of shelters and mounds that might have been buried shelters within the trees. For something this large to be here in the desert would have required much water to support it. With this discovery some questions came to mind. Where did the food come from? He had not seen any evidence of crops – not that something like that would still be around. Yet, again there had to be some kind of food production to have supported a compound of this size, let alone the amounts of water necessary to grow the food. This was a desert for heaven sake. This was not a lush valley where it would be easy, because of weather, to grow what one would have been needed. Why then was the reason for this to be here?

All the evidence in the countryside suggested that this had been a desert for a very long time, yet what he was seeing suggested that in the recent past, as far a geologic time was concerned, this was a lush green area. Was his knowledge and eyes deceiving him? Another thought came unbidden to him. *Hmmm, maybe whoever had built this place had knowledge and abilities we know nothing about. Could it be they had a way to get what they needed, something such as water without needing the rain?* There was a lot to think about here. Yet, he had better get back to the problem at hand.

Listening he heard the bleating of some small herd beasts, and realized they were probably facing some nomads, and this was probably a stopping point in their travels. If so, once an understanding could be reached, they, the nomads, could provide them with the additional information needed to get out of this desert. A fortuitous meeting, maybe . . . he knew these nomads were fiercely loyal and secretive about keeping their stopping places secret within their clans. He did not know if the linguist was with Fauul.

As he approached the enclosure from the west side he could see the small herd beasts in a makeshift corral. This truly must be a stopping point. Yet, other than the trees there was very little fodder for the beasts. With this insight he felt this was simply a watering hole used by the nomads before they continued to a grazing area. Keeping his hunting weapon out of sight, but still accessible, he approached the group who seemed completely engaged in conversation, and not paying attention to anything around them. He was now close enough to recognize his own people, and saw the linguist was not with them. "Of course not," he said softly. "That would have been too easy. Oh well let's see what I can do about this." Coming within voice range he yelled, "Hey Fauul."

Surprised, Fauul turned toward the voice and recognized Doube, and took a second look. The last person he expected to see was the scout. "What the heck are you doing here? Weren't you trying to find water?" Then smiling, he stated. "We beat you to it, that's if we can convince this group of nomads to share."

"Let me try," Doube responded. "Oh right, and you were looking for a trail out of here. Guess what, I found that for you."

"A trail you say, hmmm, well it may be a good day after all . . ."

While this conversation was progressing the nomad leader stood in silence. *Another one?* The nomad leader thought. *How many are there?* He was holding one of the hunting weapons although he had not threatened anyone with it yet. Still it was obvious he kept it visible to make its meaning clear to the team. It was accessible and it could or would be used if the leader felt it necessary.

Here in the desert, as well as other areas where the nomads roamed, they were famous for the skill in using their hunting weapons. Their skills were developed from protecting their herds. Since their groups were small, a necessity do to water and food scarcity in the desert, it was a requirement for survival. Doube turned to the leader and bowed, "Most honorable one." Having dealt with other tribes of nomads in the past, and knowing a little about their hierarchy, Doube hoped this was the best approach. "We being poor travelers in this parched land, and not knowing the sacred places, ask for the right to use this secret place. So we too may water our pack beasts and refill our dwindling supply."

From past experience with other nomadic tribes he knew a hierarchy existed. It was a necessary part of life. Since disaster followed continually in their footsteps, they had built an elaborate system, and yet at the same time simple. When he had approached the camp he noticed that there were at least 3 family groups. If what he had experienced in the past held true here, then there would be an overall leader for this group, and most likely the desert area was divided into sections with an overseer for each section, followed, at the top, by the nomadic clan leader. He knew, in general, they would all come together in some secret place once a turn to renew old contacts, make mating contracts, and exchange information. Of course there were always celebrations. It was considered a rare privilege when an outsider attended these gatherings.

He had that fortunate privilege in the past among mountain nomads. It had come about all by accident. He had been scouting an area in anticipation of an upcoming assignment, and had run into a small group whose leader had been injured. The males of the group were out hunting and the leader, at the time, was with these hunters. The camp was unprotected and unknown to them they had camped near the lair of one of the wild beasts. Hearing the noise, this beast came out to investigate and discovered the small herd beasts just waiting for him to make a meal of them.

He saw a couple of the older whelps, the younglings were watching the herd when the wild beast attacked – causing the herd beasts to panic and stampede. Being in a position to witness the scene he saw immediately the younglings were in danger and ran to knock them out of the way of the panicked herd. Being successful with that he turned around and faced the wild beast. Because of the size, all he could do was to distract it until additional help arrived. Fortunately the males were returning and heard the commotion and came over to investigate. When they saw what was happening they charged into the fray.

Circling the beast and with his help they began to worry the beast. It was quick, and on one of the feints made by the circling males the leader made to attack the beast from the rear. But hearing was supreme in these beasts. It heard the attempt, spun around, and then struck the leader, knocking him head over heels and once he quit rolling the leader did not move. The fight was a desperate one and no one had time to see if the leader was seriously hurt. This fight continued for the next twenty minutes before they were successful in dispatching the beast. Doube then ran over to see the condition of the leader, and found he had a broken leg and was bleeding profusely from wounds caused by the claws of the beast. This was a serious problem. When one was scratched by those claws infection set in rapidly, and if not treated with a med kit, the chances of him surviving were small.

The nomads normally would try, with their knowledge of plants, to treat these wounds, but were rarely successful with something this severe. Once he had the bleeding stopped, and with care he had the rest of the males carry their leader back to camp, and once the leader was comfortable he set the broken leg, splinted it, and went to work on those wounds. The leader would have some scars when they healed, but at least he would survive. Doube remained there to continue the aid, until all the infection was gone. This took about half a cycle. In this time he succeeded in saving the leader's life, and was accepted into the clan. As such he later had the rare opportunity and privilege to go, with his adopted group, to one of these secret turn gatherings.

It was at this gathering he learned much of the nomad's life and lifestyle. Since he was adopted into this particular branch the whole mountain nomad clan accepted him. Yet, he remained on the fringes observing how it all worked. He knew he had a very rare opportunity here and felt blessed for the privilege. It was the experience gained at the gathering that allowed him to be able to approach this particular group. Again, while not of the same clan, probably much of the same methods of living existed here – and this was what he was counting on. Remaining bowed; he awaited the response of this one, which Doube had considered to be the leader of the group here.

"You may rise," responded the leader. "How is it you know of our ways? Not many outsiders are allowed into our society, and yet you approach with proper respect."

"I am an adopted one of the hills clan, and have had the privilege of attending turn gatherings in the most of sacred places. I was given a name, which cannot be spoken but in private. It was given to me by the wise one, and can only be spoken to the honored one or healer of the clan."

"Yes, the hills clan is a distant member of the overall society of the nomads – even though we rarely meet. They and their branch have plenty while ours is one of constant struggle. Are these others with you? Are you the leader among them? We will speak of these things and of your request later. First I must confirm in private your secret name and the secret name of the hills clan. Then I can either grant or deny what you have asked."

"Honored one, this is as it should be. I will converse with the others who are with me and let them know what is to transpire." Doube bowed again and stepped back. At this point, he signaled the others in his group to follow him outside the compound so he could explain the situation to them.

"There's water here." Fauul stated. "What was that all about, the bowing and low conversation?"

Doube remained silent and once outside of the compound, Doube explained the situation to Fauul and the rest of the team members who were with him. Then he added that he had found a possible route out of the area, but with his clan status, he might be able to have the chief give him a better one. "Most likely I'm going to have to spend the night with them. I'll see if I can at least get permission for some water to hold our beasts overnight. I'm really glad that Joellie was not here. It would have become a real mess with him and his ways. Anyway, I'll lay out what I found and the landmarks . . . leave one of the team with me and the rest head back to camp, and prepare one of the beasts with the water skins. Since they prize their beasts I should have no problem there. You will need to talk with Joellie, and have him produce some type of small gift for the leader. This is a secret place and the nomads have killed in the past to protect places such as this. It is good you did not show any hostile intentions or I may not have been able to do anything to stop what could have come."

"Okay, but be careful. This could have easily gotten out of hand here. By the way", Fauul asked, "didn't know you were friends to the nomads? Are you sure it is safe for you to remain? We might be able to find water somewhere else, and avoid this place all together."

"No, probably one of the few sources here, that's why it is protected by the nomads. You only have a few more hours of sunlight. It should give you more time to explore those areas I was just in, and to see if that trail I found will lead us out of here, especially if I cannot find out from this clan, the trail out."

"True, it would be best to have a backup just in case. Okay, I'll leave the artist with you. He can take advantage of the time here and sketch the nomads, yeah I know, but not the area. After all it is a secret."

"Now you're catching on. Just remember not to come back here unless Jahmes comes back. That will be confirmation that the nomads will allow us to get the water for the beasts. Then, and only then can we come back as a group on the morrow, when I show up in our camp."

"You mean you truly are going to spend the night here in their camp? I'm not sure Joellie is going to go for that. You know how he feels about separating the team. While during the day, at times, it's necessary, still, he wants everyone back in camp at night."

"True, but you are second in charge, and while I understand his need for this, I also know if we are to get the water we need to finish our trip out of here, and possibly learn the best route, I will have to stay with them tonight." Seeing the concern on Fauul's face, he continued. "Come on now, I will let you on a little secret that must be kept between us." He went on to explain how he had become an adopted member of another nomadic clan, and he had a chance here to forge a friendly relationship between their group and this nomadic clan.

Fauul shook his head, and then called the rest of the team to him. They headed out towards where Doube had suggested they look for the trail he had found, and to continue on to the west to see, if it would lead them in the proper direction and out of the desert. The trail was due north of their present location. Fortunately while not the hot time of the year, the days were still longer, giving them additional time to search before returning to the camp. Where, once back at camp, Fauul would have to explain to Joellie what had transpired, and still not reveal what Doube had said to him in secret.

As they proceeded north, they could see, off to the east, the flat white area where they had eaten their zenith meal, and off in the distance the desert mountain that Doube stated they should use as a landmark. Continuing their trek, they approached the area where Doube again stated the ground material just did not look natural to him. They had to agree. But what this cracked and broken substance was, they had no idea. At least by finding this feature they knew they were in the same area Doube had been in earlier. Finding the trail, they followed it as it headed due west. It seemed to be almost perfectly straight, at least as far as they could see. From their vantage point the trail looked like it was heading into another mountain range, but until they hiked it, they could not tell if it just dead-ended at the foot of the mountains or continued on through.

Once they got half way down this straight trail, a whole series of mounds started showing up on both sides, pushing into the trail. It almost looked like a settlement was here at some time in the past. Yet, who would have been crazy enough to have such a thing on the edge of a desert, it made no sense. Yet, if this had been a settlement, it had been rather large. Large enough to qualify as a township and if it was such, what happened to cause it to be abandoned like this? Well, it wasn't their problem right now. Leave those questions to the "Keepers of the Past". Yet it left one curious. As large as it appeared to be, it would have taken a lot of water to sustain the number of people who would have been here, let alone food to feed them.

As they approached the mountains to west, the trail made a sharp turn towards the south. There it entered the desert mountain range and continued in a southwesterly direction. It was a good candidate for a way out of the desert. So with this information, they headed, using the landmarks laid down by Doube, back to camp.

When finally back at camp they found the artist there, and the beasts had been watered, plus all the skins had been filled. So Fauul would not have to explain to Joellie what had transpired since, while they had been scouting the trail, the artist had returned and with the beasts picked up water from the nomad's water source. Doube had not returned yet, but presently that was not a worry since he had previously stated he would probably be spending the night there. That situation had been a sticky one. Once again they had been lucky that Doube was their scout. If he hadn't, well it was something to think about.

Fauul reported to Joellie and brought him up to date on what they had discovered so far. The leader was unhappy with the arrangement the scout had made, but there was little he could do about it. Yet, he made it plain to Fauul that if anything happened to the scout it would be on his head, since he was the one in charge while they were out exploring. So it would reflect negatively for future such assignments. Then Joellie, once again, started complaining about the unfairness of being looked over for promotions. All Fauul could do was shake his head and roll his eyes. How many times were he and the rest of the team going to hear about this person's imagined slights?

Finally able to take his leave and glad to be away from the leader, Fauul returned to his own shelter that he shared with other members of the team. With the evening meal just a short time a way it was time to relax and reflect on the day's accomplishments, failures, and successes.

CHAPTER SIX

After bathing Lauut went to his dressing area close to his sleeping space and put on fresh clothes. Looking a little closer at his leg, he could see that he had bruised it severely. Most likely, from the looks of it, it would include the bone in that bruise. It was going to take a while for this to heal, and he knew, from previous experience, it would be tender for at least a cycle. Taking a deep breath, he steeled himself to face the accusing eyes of his sibling, and got ready to go over the past day and night. Looking back on it now made it seem less a danger than what it really was.

After dressing he entered the eating area and prepared to face his sister. The meal started out in an uncomfortable silence, as she waited for him to say something. Finally with nothing coming forthwith, she asked with emotion in her voice, "Okay bro, so what happened? You obviously did not do what you said you would do." There was a touch of anger in her voice that she tried to minimize, "Out with it brother!"

With a sigh, he went ahead and told her what he had done, but attempted to down play the danger he had placed himself in, since, in the end, he had come back. A little worse for wear, but he could have had the same outcome had he been doing what he had originally told her.

She asked a couple of questions just to clarify some points he seemed to gloss over, then shaking her head she said, "You don't know this, but I dreamed of you in that tunnel or cave or whatever. I thought it was just a bad dream, but apparently it wasn't so. I guess our family's gift going through the females still holds true. We still have the gift of sight towards the ones we love, even though we cannot control it. Why did you lie to me anyway? You know, after all this time together I can read you. Did you feel . . . oh I don't know?"

Feeling a bit sheepish Lauut said, "Look, I didn't want you to worry, especially . . . even though it was a long time ago now, since we lost our sires in that accident. We have enough worry just trying to keep this property." Trailing off, before continuing he quietly said, "I just didn't want to put any added burden upon you. After all I love you, and I do worry about you a lot."

With her arms crossed she leaned forward and asked, "Well, do you not think that it goes both ways? Why is it that you males think that we cannot accept the dangers, even foolish ones – as was your adventure – without falling apart?" She was feeling her anger rise again. "When will you ever learn, that even though we are brother and sister that working and communicating to each other gives us a united strength – one that makes us better together than our individual strengths. You males can be so stupid!"

"Hey wait a minute here, I just . . . well, I didn't want to hurt you, and with everything going on here, right now, you did not need another worry. I thought it was mine to carry, not you." At this point, like her he leaned forward saying, "After all, I'm sure you have things that concern both of us that you do not tell me." Putting forth a sad smile but one that reflected that this went both ways he asked, "Now isn't that true?"

She paused for a short time realizing the truth. "Yeah, I guess it's true. But, you must promise me that you won't pull this kind of stunt again. Losing our sires like we did has been tough, and you doing something like this could have added another."

He had to admit it was true. By looking back on his adventure he saw many times how close he came to not leaving the cave or tunnel. Then he remembered he had found an object, but had not even looked at it. "Wait a minute sis; I just remembered I found something down there. It's small and I really haven't had time to really look at it." Getting up quickly, he almost fell back down. He had momentarily forgotten about his injury. It reminded him quickly. Smiling across at his sister he waved her off, and limped off to his sleeping space, dug out the object, and returned to the table. Once back sitting, he could see the curiosity in Lauma's eyes, and passed it over to her to look at. Because he had not really looked closely at the object he was almost impatient to get it back, but steeled himself to wait until she finished her examination.

"Such a small thing," she said, "It fits in the palm of your hand. It seems to be some kind of metal, but at the same time is so light, but at the same time heavier than you'd expect. None of our metals are nearly this light, and look at those hinges, I've never seen any so small."

Getting up and going over and standing behind his sister he studied the object. "Here let me see that a sec."

She handed it to him, and he rubbed the surface clean since it was covered in dirt. As he did an engraved image appeared on the surface of one side. Again this engraving was beyond anything they could make today. "What is this thing?"

"I don't know." She answered truthfully. "Do you think this thing could have come from the *ones before*?"

It was something he hadn't considered, but after her question, it seemed the only plausible answer. "You may be right. You know because I ran out of time down there, I was unable to really look through that pile of rubble. I think that earth shake, which opened the way into the cavern, may have caused that pile of rubble. It would be worthwhile to go back and do a proper job of searching that main cavern and see if there is anything else there."

Handing it back to her, she took it and ran her fingers over it. "I wonder if those hinges still work, or, are they just decoration?"

As she turned it over the light in the room caught what looked like script on the bottom of the object. "What's this?" She asked.

"Don't know . . . hmmm, let me see that."

"If you found this thing that far underground, and it really is from the *ones before*, do you think," she asked in idle speculation, "they may have lived underground?"

"Good question. But this is only one item. Who knows how it got there, heck it could have been washed down there from some dried up stream or something."

"I don't think so. Its condition is too good. Except for the dirt you wiped off it looks as if it just came from one of the merchants in the village."

Looking closer at the bottom he could see that there was something there. Yet, it did not look like anything he recognized. "Well, I am at a loss . . . Any ideas, sis?"

Handing it back to her, she then ran her fingers up the side opposite the hinges. When she reached the point where the crease circumvented the object, the top portion felt as it had moved ever so slightly. "I wonder if this was a way to carry something of value, although if that is so, then whatever it was had to be very small. Look, when I ran my finger up the side the top moved – not much, but it did move. So I don't think the hinges are there for decoration."

"Okay, let's put it away for a little while. I'll get some lubricant on those hinges, soak the whole thing, and maybe later we can open the top and see what's inside. I surely don't want to break it. It looks so delicate."

Shaking her head and sighing at little Lauma asked. "Okay, so if I am reading you right, you want to go back down there?"

"Yup, sure do, but this time we will work together on it. I learned my lesson last time. Before you object, I know we have much to do around here, and it takes priority over this adventure. I agree anyway. It's going to take some time to get things together to go back anyway."

"At least you're being sensible about it this time. I sure could have used your help today, not that anything special happened, other than your adventure." With that he took the object out to the work area and placed in a small container and then put a liberal amount of lubricant on the hinges, letting the whole object sit in the lubricant, afterwards returning to help Lauma clean up after the meal.

As he entered the shelter Lauma turned to him and said, "While you were out there I got to wondering if, maybe, this thing you found is from the *ones before*. With you finding it that far underground, do you think they lived underground? I know I just asked that but . . . well maybe that's why nothing has ever been found."

"You know that's a good question, but it doesn't seem likely. Yet, who knows, as far as I know they are nothing more than myth, a rumor, you know something that makes a good tale or story, and like I said we could be the ones who made this thing."

Stopping what she had been doing she asked, "Now what are we going to do? After all finding that thing could mean trouble."

"Yes, it could, but who knows, we may be able to sell it and get us stable again. I bet something like that would be worth much, especially to the researchers from the 'Keepers of the Past'. You know the ones we read about in the learning centers."

"Why would a bunch of old hot air bag learned want to come here? I can't see them leaving their dusty tomes that they study, somewhere deep in their repositories with those robes flowing."

Laughing at the image Lauma created, Lauut asked. "Now sis where ever did you come up with that image?"

"Well, how else do you see them? I look back on our learned, and they, at times, appear to be nothing else but hot bags of wind . . . kind of self-righteous, self-centered, and all knowing. You know, as if only they know it all."

"Sis, come on, they weren't that bad. Yeah, I know one or two were pretty bad, but overall without what they taught us where would we be? I heard it said that if a leadership wants to completely control their people they use religion and keep the people illiterate."

"That's probably true, but some of what we were taught was just a waste. We'll never use it. So why learn it?"

"It must be important to somebody."

With mirth she said, "Yeah, the ones who teach it, since they get their livelihood from it." And with that statement they both laughed. Finishing up with the nighttime chores, they grabbed their hot beverages and retired to the porch to enjoy the last moments of daylight as the sun settled behind the hills and twilight approached.

"I love this time of the day." Lauma sighed in contentment. "After a hard day of work, to sit here and relax and enjoy the quiet, and the cooling air from the heat of the day is just wonderful."

"Yes, you won't get me to disagree. At times I like to go up on top of the hill behind the shelter and watch the shadows enter the valleys. Still there are many nights that it is just great to sit here and let the quiet soak into me."

"My feelings exactly. I really don't understand how one can prefer the village or township life with all that chaos, and noise, to this." With that said they were quiet and enjoyed the coming of the evening as the sun set over the hills and the shadows became deeper and with the surrounding hills fading from sight. Soon the stars began to fill the night sky.

"Much to think about," Lauut said quietly, as if talking normally would break the spell. "What I found, the stuff we have to do around here, what your future will be, and the family's land, and on and on."

"I know what you mean, and what you are not saying. This discovery could mean loss to both of us, and that's really scary."

"Very true, but what I've found is only known by both of us at this point, but enough of that now, I 'm tired and still hurt, so I'm going to bed. See yah in the morning sis, and whatever it brings."

"Okay, but I think I am going to stay out here a little longer. I do so love this time of day. Good night to you bro, and watch out for those bad dreams."

Smiling at his sister Lauut wondered what their future would truly be. He didn't say anything but kept it to himself; he got up and retired to his sleeping area. As he prepared to sleep a stray thought entered his mind about his find, and if it really meant anything anyway, but it didn't stay long. With that final thought he drifted off into a deep sleep, being exhausted from his adventures.

When Lauut retired she was left with her own thoughts, and knew in her heart that things would never be the same again. Still she could hope for a good outcome. Staying outside until the moon rose over the hills; she went inside to her own sleeping area, took care of her nightly needs and went to bed herself. The next few days promised to be busier than usual, and she would need all the rest she could get. While probably not as tired as her brother, she was asleep as soon as her head hit the pillow.

He was underground again, but this time as he looked around he found there were many passageways within his vision. He noticed, in his hands, he had no marking tool, and the torch in his hand was sputtering its last before burning out. He reached into his pack and found it empty. Almost panicking he searched the cavern floor for his tracks and saw that it was solid rock and would leave none. *What I am to do, how can I get out of here?* Time was definitely against him, and he started running. Without any light he would be lost forever in these passageways never to see the light of day again.

Sweat starting breaking out on his brow, and he picked one of the tunnels and started following it. Immediately it narrowed and the roof lowered. He could see that this had been a bad choice. When he turned around to head back he found he was looking on some additional passages and again did not know which he had used to get where he was. He was in serious trouble. Then the torch sputtered its last and died out. Now he was in total darkness with no idea of where he was. Fear was rapidly rising in him. Yet, if he allowed it to control him he was finished. Still it clawed at him and seemed to overwhelm him. Then he awoke and then realized it had been a dream. Yet, it had seemed so real. He found that he was sweating. So with the dream fading, with his breath returning to normal he immediately fell back into a deep exhausted sleep.

* * *

The next couple of days were busy as they caught up on the work around the property. They were planning a trip to the village to renew their dwindling supplies – items they could not provide for themselves. Plus he had been compiling a list of items he felt he would need when they returned to the underground. Yet again, because of their tight financial situation, even that list had to be pared down. Finances always seemed tight, always the restricting factor.

In the evening of the second day back from his adventure he went out to the work shelter and brought in the object he had found so they could check it out in much greater detail. If those hinges were real, then after a couple of days of soaking in the lubricant, it should make them workable. Using a rag he wiped it down completely. Then setting it on the table, with something under it to absorb any lube that he may have missed, it was time for a complete inspection. Looking closer at the engravings that were on one side, again above the unknown image appeared to be script, but it was unknown to them. "Look at the amount of lube still coming off it," he said, "I wiped it down better than that." Picking it up, he wrapped the rag loosely around it and shook it rapidly up and down. He had been holding it by what he thought was the top when he felt it shift and heard a click. "Now what? Oh no! I think I may have broken it."

With a feeling of dread, he unwrapped it from the cloth, and found, instead of breaking it, the top had pivoted back and was now open. Yet, with it open the mystery only deepened. There was definitely something inside.

"What kind of device is this thing?" she asked. She took it from him, and looked closely, but could see no use for something like this. It obviously was not used to carry anything as it was filled with some other metal, and the lubricant was all over the inside. "Here," She said, "let me wipe this down." As she did she examined it closer, and as she wiped more of the lube off, she noticed in the center of a perforated oblong piece of metal there was something that could pass as a wick. "Look at this; it reminds me of the wicks we use in our candles."

"Here let me look," he responded.

Looking closely he said, "You're right; I think that's exactly what that is. So what does this small circular thing do? I kind of looks like a wheel. Hmm, I wonder if it turns at all."

Putting his thumb on the wheel, he put a small amount of downward pressure on it. He could tell from that initial contact that the wheel would move.

"Ah, I felt a little movement on the wheel, but there seems to be a lot of resistance."

"Be careful! You don't want to break it," she responded. "Remember you thought you already broke it, and we don't want it to become a fact."

"Right! The surface of the wheel is rough. It makes it easy to keep my thumb on it." Looking closer at the wheel he stated. "Hey, look at this, there appears to be groves cut into it. If this was made today, and I'm not saying it was, but if it had, it'd be very expensive. It would have taken an artisan much time to create the wheel."

Handing it back to his sister, she noticed that the lube was still flowing out of it. Grabbing the rag again, and then holding it upside down, she shook it to remove some additional lube. With a careful grip on what they had figured was the inside top of the object she pulled down with her fingers as she held the outside with her other hand, and was surprised when the whole top appeared to move. "Whoa, what did I just do?"

"What do you mean sis?"

"Look!" she exclaimed. "The top of this thing just moved. See?" She handed it back to him.

"You're right. Boy this sure is a mystery. Do you think this could have been made by a passing artisan who lost it?" Again handing it back to Lauma he stated, "Well, you got it started, why don't you continue to pull it apart and see what we have."

"Why, so you can blame me if it breaks?"

Shaking his head as he smiled he stated, "No, no but you know the pressure you used, and I figure you could use the same to make it continue to slide out."

"Yeah, right – convince me," She said teasingly. "After all, when we were growing up, this was one of the ways you used to get me in trouble with our sires."

Smiling at the past memories her statement invoked, he said. "Yep, and it was always fun to set you up, and you usually fell for it too."

Pouting a little she said, "And what did you expect? I trusted my big brother to keep me out of trouble, not to get me into it."

They both laughed, and he said, "I may have got you in to trouble now and then, but you always were able to return the favor."

"Yeah, we females can be sneaky like that. While you guys are pretty straight forward, we prefer to be devious."

"And what do you mean by that?"

"Well . . . when you guys would pull some kind of stunt, it would be in the open where anyone could see, if they really wanted to. While we would wait for the most opportune moment when we knew the grownups' backs were turned before we would do anything, and then afterwards just look innocent. Most of the time it'd work too."

"Tell you what sis, it's getting late here. I think it's time we put this away for a little while, and look at it again later. The morrow is going to be busier than normal. Since we need to go into the village and re-supply at the upcoming minor gather. Plus, I need to check with the beast-master on whether he is going to want those pack beasts for this upcoming major gather or not. Actually we should have a couple there anyway. And that means, as if you did not know, we only have a short time in which to get our chores done."

"True, true, I really love making that trip. It is just too bad it is such a great distance. Otherwise I would probably visit more often. There is definitely stuff I need to do, and I must remember to pack some of the garden food to sell in the square." Then more to herself than Lauut she said, "Yeah, much to do and some old friendships to renew . . . well maybe."

He got up and put away the object. They had learned many things about it, but still had no idea when it was made or even what it was. "Hey sis, I will let you in the necessary and bathing area ahead of me. I'll go out and do a final check. Then when I come back you can let me know if it is open for me. Sound good to you?"

Yawning she said, "Sounds wonderful. See you shortly."

With that she retired to her sleeping space, and he went outside to check on the beasts, and to make sure the area was secure. The first thing he did was to return the object to the work shelter, and then walk to the corrals. Leaning on them for a couple of minutes, he thought. *What a beautiful and quiet evening. I feel like I could walk to the top of that hill and enjoy this peace. It sure has a tendency to make one relax.* "This type of night sure could make one introspective," he said quietly, as he finished his rounds. *Well, the future isn't written for any of us, and its time I get back anyway. It is really going to be a crazy day on the morrow, and staying out here is not going to get it here any faster anyway.* Taking one final look around, checking on the beasts, and seeing all was secure; he headed back to the family's shelter.

When he left, she, after retiring to her sleep space, sat there a few moments longer just relaxing, and thinking about what they had talked about. *Yup, those sure were carefree days before we lost our sires. It sure would have been nice had the accident never happened. Yet I can't change the past. Too bad, I would love to look upon mother's face again, and see that look of concern and her wonderful smile. Oh well, this sure isn't getting anything done.* With those thoughts she got up and headed to the necessary space, and started getting ready for the night's rest. She decided a quick bath would be great, even though she knew she would be taking another before they left on the morrow. Yet, it felt nice to feel fresh and clean before she climbed into her bed – especially after working the beasts all day. Later, as she got into her nightclothes, she heard her brother return and asked, "How's everything outside tonight?"

"Oh, quiet, peaceful, one of those nights to go walking, if you know what I mean."

"Sure do. Had one of those the other night when you were gone. It sure makes it hard to come back inside."

"True, true, it reminds me when we were young how, when the moon was full and the learning time was over, we would run out and play for such a long time – enjoying those nights so much. Are you finished so I can get ready for the night?"

Sighing and smiling she said nostalgically, "Those were fun carefree times. And yes, I'm finished so it's all yours."

"Thanks sis, see you in the morn." He headed into the necessary space and got himself ready for sleeping. The next day would be coming soon enough.

Once again he found himself back in that center cavern surrounded by those many passages. Once again his torch was sputtering. This time he knew he was in a dream, but why was he continuing to dream the same one? He knew from the past images from the dream that he had only a short time before the one torch he had would extinguish itself. So why was he here? What did it mean? After all when he had been in the real cavern and the passage to it, there appeared to be only one entrance – not that he had time to explore, since his time had been short. He thought maybe he should tell his sister about the dream . . . she might have some insight into it. Before he could explore it further, the dream faded, and he fell into a deeper sleep.

Morn-rise came early as usual, before the sun made its appearance. But, it would be busier than a normal day, since they had to leave for the village by the late morn. If they did not then there would not be enough time left in the day to accomplish all they needed to do in the village. After a quick meal they headed out to do the morn work. He would do all that was necessary with the beasts while she detoured and handled getting the garden food prepared to go with them. They had a small cart they used when they went to the village, and after the beasts were secure he would hitch up one and have the cart ready for his sister and the items she had available to sell in the square at the minor gather.

Besides the main family business of the beasts, they supplemented their income by selling the garden food and some clothing items that Lauma made. She was very good at making clothes, and had no difficulty in selling all she produced. He was good as a handyman, and had hired out a number of times in that capacity. When one lived in the outback one learned to make do.

As they passed each other, while preparing for the trip, she, with a harried look on her face asked, "Everything on schedule?"

Deep in thought as he passed her, he looked up. "What? Oh, ah, I think so, how about you?"

She smiled, shrugged, and said, "I think so. How soon will you have the cart up by the shelter so I can start loading what I need to?"

"That's next after I finish checking on the young beasts, probably half an hour. That okay with you?"

"That's just about perfect. I do wish there was a better way of doing this. If we could have afforded help, we probably would have left at the first light and been there when some of the other sellers were setting up in the square instead of coming in around the zenith. By then all the good selling spots will have been taken."

"Know what you mean, but you usually have no problem selling your stuff."

"True, but if I had a better location, I would probably be able to sell out quicker, and then with your business completed, which is usually ahead of me, then we could head back earlier. Of course I'm planning on staying over this time."

"I know, but I don't mind coming over to help you finish. It gives me some time to talk with others in the village and allows us to find out what's happening, which can be important for us. Plus it lets me see which of the local males have an interest in my sister."

Blushing a little, she said jokingly, "Now that none of your business."

"Sure it is. I have to watch out for my little sister and protect her from those big bad males."

Laughing she said, "Right, and I'm there to protect you from those females who only look at the status they would gain by becoming mates to the family."

Smiling at her he replied, "Okay, okay, so we protect each other. Now let's finish this or we'll never get done." While the selling that happened at the minor gathers, which were between the major gathers, would be small in comparison, it was one of the ways to find out what would be needed at those major gathers, making it easier to be prepared and not necessarily have something there that would be a waste of time and effort. With that said they continued on their original paths to finish their assigned chores. It wasn't much longer until he brought the cart up close to the shelter so they could finish loading. He remembered to face it out so when he brought up the beast to hitch to the cart it would be easier.

Once done, and the cart loaded, they returned to the shelter to clean up and put on their better clothes. The work clothes would not be good for a visit to the village. Especially since they had goods to sell, and he'd be contacting the beast-master on needs of the surrounding area for their beasts. As expected, in all cases where auctions and contracts were involved, the beast-master took a part of the funds earned; he would need his best negotiating skills to reduce that price. Still it was an old game between the two of them after all.

Progress this morning had gone well, and they were ahead of the schedule. He hooked up the beast and they headed west from the shelter. While they would be on their land for a period of time, eventually they would catch the main trail that headed out to the village. The trail, once they were off the property, would continue west into the grasslands, but as it approached the foothills, would head down a narrow gorge. While nothing serious had ever been reported to happen in that particular area, it still appeared to be somewhat dangerous, an area with the possibility of flash floods and such.

Sometime in the unknown past much water had flowed through here. Looking at the canyon walls one could see the high marks left by past floods, and if water flowed again, anyone caught here would be killed. Unfortunately most of their time spent on the main trail went through this area, and it always made him nervous. Oh well, there really wasn't anything he could do about it. All their business was conducted in Rancho, and there were no other villages, let alone townships anywhere within many days hike – so it was Rancho or it would be nothing.

Legend stated that the village was named Rancho because of a marker that was found in the area when the village had been established. Like many small villages it was established in the area of many converging trails, and the area was relatively flat, plus it had a good water source – so critical in this area. While building one of the shelters, the marker was dug up, and while not complete it had that name on it. So the original settlers decided that probably the area had that name in the past, and if it was good enough then, it surely was good enough now.

Once through the narrow section of the trail, it opened up into the area close to the village, and a short distance later you would actually enter the village. When one looked at the village the first impression was are you sure? To say it was small was an understatement. While it was located in a good area – the rest of the surrounding area water was scarce – with the rainfall each turn being little, as a result there was a very small population to help support Rancho. While the climate provided sun for most of the year, and a beautiful mild weather, it wouldn't support a large population.

Once you understood the reasons, the small size really made sense. The village consisted of a mercantile, the beast-master pens and out-shelters, a healer, plus it had some other trades to fill out the needs of the locals and surrounding ranches, herders, and farms. So the main shelters that surrounded the square consisted of only five. Then as you radiated out from the square, which wasn't square at all, you found the minor businesses followed by the shelters where the village folks lived. There were four pathways between the structures, and like spokes of a wheel, led one either to the center of the village, or out to a final circular path that was on the outskirts. This final circular path, which connected the different trails leading into the village, made it simple for anyone coming from any direction to get to the square.

The square was large enough to hold fifteen to twenty sellers' booths, and to accommodate the crowds coming to shop. It was also the gathering place for social events, political meetings, and a place for all in the area to meet for emergencies, such as wildfires, or some other large catastrophe, or accident. It literally was the center of the life for all the surrounding area. For it was here business was conducted. Even all the mating ceremonies during the two major gathers were conducted here.

The sellers' booths were portable and were broken down and put into storage after each cycle gather. This allowed the flexibility for the many uses of the square. Of course, this arrangement was not unique to this village alone. It had proved to be a very efficient design, and was the general method or layout used in most villages and townships.

This cycle it would be a minor gather, and as such, the outsiders would not be coming in to show off their wares, or purchase what they needed, so it would be the locals – not that it posed a problem. It actually meant, while buyers would be less, space would be easier to come by, and there was a greater chance for one to sell or trade all one had brought with them. This of course, put money in the village's coffers, since there was a charge for selling in the square, as all were taxed on what was sold or traded. Fortunately it was small, and being so, allowed even the poorest members to be able to use the square and the booths. Of course, within the village were permanent structures for ones' that lived, worked and sold in the village. Yet, these portable booths gave the outsiders and the ones who lived outside the community a way to present and sell their wares. It was also an excuse for the surrounding area to have a small celebration each cycle. All villages and townships had hostels or something similar for accommodations.

The baker would have sweet rolls and breads available, and for the adults, beer, ale, and wine were available. Many festive flags and clothes would be shown, and the people would have social gatherings in the late afternoon with food prepared and offered. The local musicians would play, and there would be dancing, and general fun. It was a time for games of chance, and of foot racing, and other sporting events. It was a time of speeches, which any one could participate, public forums, and even on the serious side, meetings to deal with problems the village and outlying lands faced. It was also a time to announce future matings.

Even though they had business to conduct while there, both Lauma and Lauut were looking forward to the festivities, something to help relieve the stress of the day-to-day work needed to maintain the land. Both loved and enjoyed the music and dancing. It was a time, even though short, to let down and relax, to enjoy, and forget, even briefly, one's responsibilities. So with anticipation, when they saw the outskirts of the village, they picked up their pace. Lauut knew that he would not get a chance at these festivities this time, as he would need to return to the property before they began. Their herd beasts would need to be taken care of.

Before the evening, there was much they had to do. Even so, she could not help but smile in anticipation of what the night would bring. And while it was still close to the zenith, as they approached the square it was obvious, even for a minor gather, things were hopping. Lauut went over to the proprietor and paid the fee, and then helped Lauma set up the booth, and the wares they had brought. It was slowed somewhat as the whelps ran excitedly around wanting to see what all had brought to the gather. Laughing at their antics and excitement, he just shook his head. Had he ever been that carefree? He could hear his sister tell them to slow down and be careful. The very same words he remembered their mother saying to them. *Funny how such things carry over from one generation to the next,* he thought. He found himself almost ready to repeat word for word what his father would have said, and had to bite his tongue and almost started laughing when he realized it. "Careful what you say Lauma. You are starting to sound like our sires."

She stopped for a second, laughed, and said, "You know what, you're right. I didn't even think about it. When did we change from being carefree like these whelps, to being the ones who bark out the orders?"

"Good question. I can still remember the first time one of the whelps called me an adult. It was such a surprise, and until then I hadn't even thought about it, let alone considered it so. Anyway, you're pretty well set up here, and I need to see Aurto for his order next cycle. You know it's the turn's largest gather. He usually wants to have much on hand for the auction and contracts."

"Yeah, and I'm sure he will have some ale there too, and the two of you will start drinking a little, and telling each other tales with the others who will already be there. So . . . I guess I will see you later . . . much later then."

"Now Lauma, it's not that bad, and you know when you and those females of the community get together, well I don't think we males can match you for all the talking and gossiping that will be going on."

Stomping her foot in mock anger and with her hands on her hips she said, "Now that just not true. Besides where else am I to know what's happening around here? Those beasts of ours surely can't tell me."

Laughing a little he turned and headed to the auction and pen area, as some of the village folk approached her booth, and Lauma prepared to talk with them. *These gathers are sure nice and it raises one's spirits.*

"Oh yes," he said, "I must remember to take the cart with me and leave it with the beast-master so that I can retrieve it before I leave to return back tonight. Lauma will be staying overnight, but I must return to take care of the beasts. Then in the morn I'll head out and meet her on the trail." Sighing he thought, *Might as well get to it now.* Turning around and heading back he stated, "Excuse me for interrupting, but I must collect our cart and beast, and then all of you can continue without me being in the way." Smiling, he then bowed in mock levity, walked to the cart and then led the beast and cart away. In the background, as he left, he could hear the laughter from the females. *All in fun*, he thought, *all in fun.*

For one of the minor gathers it sure looked like it was going to be lively, which was great. Maybe there would be a need for some of their beasts. Yet, so far during this turn, it had been disappointing – not even a normal request. Yet, he didn't hold his breath since most of the needs were for locals this time, none from the surrounding areas or villages would be here. Yet, one can hope. Yes, one can only hope.

Rounding the corner he came upon the familiar sight of the pens and yards of the beast-master. Off in the distance he could see Aurto conversing with someone. At this point he didn't recognize who it was as his back was turned to him. Looking up from his conversation Aurto recognized him and waved a greeting, which Lauut immediately returned. As he approached the two in conversation Lauut realized the other was the present elder of the village. This position was rotated every turn so that all members of the village would serve – of course this excluded the females. They had their own things to do and it did not include the running of the village. At least that was the views presently held. He knew from working with his sibling, they, the females, were quite able of doing anything any male could; yet such an idea just didn't fit here. There probably would be a time somewhere in the future where such wouldn't matter anymore.

He caught Aurto's attention and looked questionably at him as to where to place his beast and cart. Aurto pointed to one of the far enclosures. He nodded in acknowledgment and went in that direction to put the beast away and to store the cart, and once finished, he returned to see Aurto was alone, although he knew that this situation wasn't going to last. Even though this was a minor gather, he knew that the beast yards were always busy – even if it was just to rent storage space for personal beasts.

Unfortunately, he reminded himself, this time his time would be short, since he had to return back to the property to take care of their beasts there. Because this was a minor gather they had not hired a youngling to come feed and water the beasts so he and Lauma could remain throughout the gathering. They couldn't afford to spend what little they earned to pay wages for even a youngling. Both he and Aurto gripped each other's arms in the traditional greeting of friendship. He asked, "Has there been any requests for my beasts, and do you want any for the upcoming major gather for auctioning?"

Aurto responded by saying, "Nothing of consequence as far as requests. It seems to me there is little need for them right now, but I'm sure later it will not be the case . . . as far as the major gather goes, of course. You have the best around, and that alone helps business, helps spark interest in the auction or in contracting." Aurto shrugged, "Sorry about now, I do know it has been a difficult time for you. Tell you what, let's go over to the shade over there, have ale sitting in the cold water just begging to be drank, and you can let me know how things are going out there, and I will do the same about what's been happening here in the village."

Smiling, Lauut replied, "Thought you would never ask . . . Lead on."

Later, and as soon as he could gracefully leave, Lauut left and headed back to where Lauma's booth was set up. Since the shadows were lengthening, *that's what happens when one arrives late,* he was reminded that he needed to start his return to the property soon, and he needed to let her know where the cart and beast were located in the enclosures at the yard. He regretted the fact he would miss the meeting that night, as well as the entertainment, since shortly the gather would move into its next phase, but there was nothing he could do about it.

* * *

Lauma smiled as her brother retreated towards the pens and enclosures. *He sure would be a fine catch for some female someday. Not bad looking either – and a sensitive side too, that rarely shows itself in public. Of course he still has that wild streak, and takes chances when he shouldn't, but he usually learns from his follies. Yes, someday some female will be very lucky to mate with my brother.*

"Oh, I'm sorry," she said to one of the female villagers who had been talking with her. "Could you repeat that, I was just thinking of Lauut."

"Lauut? You should be thinking of finding a mate for yourself. After all in many ways you are past the turns when most of us have mated."

"True, true . . . But, you see, there just isn't anyone here that even interests me. Plus moving to the village, truthfully, isn't something I want to do. I love the outback too much."

"Oh, excuses are all that is. We all learn to adjust to our new lives."

Sadly, she thought, *what she says is probably true. Yet I cannot see myself anywhere else but in the outback.* She replied, saying, "You're probably right, but still there has been no one who even interests me here. Not that the choices are that great – after all this is a small village, and we who live outside of the village on our properties are even less numerous than here."

"Oh come on now, the choices aren't that bad." Changing the subject the female villager asked. "Are you staying the night at the commons?"

"Yes, I will be going to the celebration and dancing also. Lauut has to return to care for our beasts. He will meet me on the trail on the morrow."

"Good! Then I will see you tonight at the celebration. Can't wait really, these celebrations can be so much fun. Too bad this one's only a minor gather. I do so enjoy the two major gathers we have each turn." With that the villager left and continued her shopping among the many booths to see what was available.

It seemed only a short while when her brother showed up at her stall. "Any good news?" She asked.

Shaking his head, "No, not any need for our beasts this time. I hope you're having better luck."

"Of course I am. You know the garden food always sells well, and I have many of the village females who love the stuff I make."

"Good, good, anything will help us right now. At least it is only a short time until one of the major gathers. Well, I must depart and head back, otherwise it will be dark before I get to the property." He followed this by explaining where both the beast and cart were located.

"Okay, may the trails be smooth." She stated from an old traveling poem.

"Thanks, and enjoy yourself tonight. At times you take yourself too seriously, so relax. Tomorrow it will be back to the hard work. Speaking of that, I need to pick up those torches so we can continue exploring what I found. Anyway sis got to go, and please enjoy yourself." With that he left and headed to the stall where torches would be available, picked up a new supply, placed them in his pack and headed back home.

The sun was setting with long shadows stretching far into the distance when he reached the yard. All appeared to be the same as when they had left earlier in the day. He did hope Lauma would enjoy herself. *Who knows*, he thought, *maybe she will find a male she really likes.* Shaking his head and smiling he thought. *Right, like that's going to happen.* Knowing how much Lauma loved the outback, he knew that someone from any of the villages probably would not be of any interest to her. "Well, to the chores," he sighed. He knew that when he worked with the beasts and the necessary things that had to be completed, that it gave him time to think. So far, with the lower than usual demand for their beasts, things had continued to be very tight. He had remembered to pick up a box-meal before leaving the village, which meant he would not have to prepare anything for himself. After all, it was a great distance to the village, and when one does a round trip in one day it tends to leave one tired.

* * *

They had been back a few days, and had caught up all the work. It always took additional time to catch up after attending a gather. Once one decided to go, many other things got pushed back to make time to prepare, and of course these things that were ignored did not take care of themselves. It was now time to return to that tunnel. Except this time he would be better prepared. He had really learned his lesson last trip and had no desire to repeat the previous experience.

The next morn, with supplies in hand, he and Lauma headed out early – just before sunrise. It was about an hour or so of a hike, and he wanted to spend more time in that lower cavern. She appeared to be excited and at the same time, a little nervous, since she had only heard his description and the danger he had put himself into. He knew that one's imagination could blow things out of proportion like that recurring dream he kept having about the cavern. At least having been down there before, and having the foresight to mark out the path he had taken, made this trip easier. Again, luck had been with him, since there appeared to be only one path down to the one main cavern he had found. With that torch failing earlier than expected he could have easily ended in a side tunnel had one existed. "I guess I was luckier than I deserve." He said quietly.

"Lauut, did you say something?" She asked

"No, no, not really just talking to myself. Was thinking about my last trip down the tunnel, which if you think about it, only makes sense."

"I guess so; do you still have those fears of being closed in?"

"Those fears are still there. I think that is why I keep having this dream about being lost down underground."

"Dream? What dream? You haven't mentioned anything to me about it, or if you did, I don't recall."

"Didn't figure it was necessary, since I felt it was just tied to my fear, from when that play tunnel collapsed on me, years ago, so it's my problem, and nothing to bother you with."

"Really, you know sometimes talking it out can help find a solution."

"Now that's our sires talking, and you know we said we would never repeat what they said to us when we had whelps or mates right?"

Laughing she responded, "True, but it just seems to be the right thing to say. I guess we are just locked into what happened to us good or bad."

"True, it's funny how that works. You find yourself, without realizing it, saying something exactly like they did . . . well here we are . . . at least the place to store this extra stuff. I camped here, and the entrance is only a length or so away from here." After placing their extra supplies, and putting up a shelter, they continued on towards the entrance of the tunnel where Lauut commented, "It looks like nothing has been here since I was. Look, you can see my tracks leading out in the soft soil. Can you see the heat waves coming out from the entrance?"

"Yeah, like you, I always thought caves would be cool. After all they are underground and away from the heat of the sun."

"The only thing I can think of is there must be a hot spring or something similar close to the crack or in the larger cavern. When you get down to the actual cavern it is cooler. You have that twine with you? I definitely want to use it this trip when we reach the large cavern. Let's double check what we have, I don't want to go down this time lacking, like I did last time." Smiling he continued, "If it taught me anything it taught me to be doubly careful, and to try and anticipate the unexpected. Remember how dirty I was. I am sure it will be the same. Now once we go inside, let's put those coats just inside the entrance where they can't be seen from the outside but are easy for us to get to."

He pointed to the entrance to the tunnel, which was only a short distance away, but quite visible. Once the details became visible she asked, after eyeing the entrance dubiously, "You went in there? You are either braver than I thought or more foolish.

What made you think this was something you could go into and not be into trouble?"

He shrugged, "Didn't really look at it that way. I thought maybe I could find something to get us out of our current problems. Instead, from both my ignorance and sense of adventure, I went into the tunnel blindly and with a false confidence. We both know the result."

"I guess," she asked nervously, "since you have been down there, it is safe . . . right?"

"Hey, as I've just said, I'm better prepared this time, and know what is ahead of us."

Thinking about it, especially after seeing the opening, she almost decided to renege on her promise to go down with him, but she had promised to help. So with a shrug she said, "Okay brother, I agreed to go down there with you, but, to be honest, this looks anything but safe to me."

"You know, while nothing is completely safe, we'll be fine. Remember I marked the path . . . okay, here we are, and I *have* been all the way down, so if we go slow and careful, other than some skinned knees and dirt, we should be fine."

Before entering they sat down and pulled their backpacks apart one more time to confirm they had everything. They would be underground much longer this time. She would carry the torches and he would carry the water since water was much heavier. She, of course, also carried some food. They both had water bottles attached to their waist belts and, of course, the necessary tools of the trade. He had made sure they had double the torches necessary, so if something did happen to delay them they still would have plenty of light.

Lighting the first torch he asked, "Are you ready?"

"No not really, but go ahead and I'll follow." With that they entered deeper into the crack and headed downward into the tunnel. The first thing she noticed while being close to the entrance it was still light and she did not need the light from the torch to see. Yet, as she looked down beyond the torch it was pitch black. "Well, at least when we come back up I will know when we are close to leaving, and believe you me I will really love seeing that daylight again. You said you went down here the first time in the night time, why?"

"Isn't it obvious? Down here day and night doesn't exist, only place it does is on the surface. Here, it is always night, and only the light we bring changes it. So, when I first went down time of day meant nothing."

A little chagrined from not seeing that she said, "Oh I see. It really isn't something I would have even considered, no not at all."

"Look!" He exclaimed. "See there are the markings I told you about. If we get separated for any reason, just use them and they will bring you back out. Of course, I can't see us getting separated, but you never know."

"No we are not going to get separated, even if I have to tie myself to you." Lauma responded nervously, she had to admit that this was becoming more than she had bargained.

The trip down this time took less time, and when they had reached the place where he had to climb the ledge and jump to get where they were standing he attached a rope ladder so it would not pose the same problem when they returned. He made sure it was attached solidly and also put another spike in the ground and attached a rope for a backup, if for some reason, the anchors he had placed in the rope ladder failed.

"I can see what you mean, about the floor of this tunnel being uneven. Heck there's debris everywhere, and it's uncomfortably hot down here. Definitely not something I would have thought of when I was dreaming of my childhood adventures." Lauma briefly fanned her face trying to cool off.

"It was a surprise to me also. I expected the floor to be flat, and because it was underground, I expected the air to be cool – at least when we get down to the cavern it will cool off. This heat and moisture is why I wanted us to bring lots of water this time. I didn't last trip and ran out. At least it appears to be the same as I remember it, oh look there is another one of my marks."

"Where? I don't see it."

Pointing, he replied, "Over there by that boulder, see?"

Nodding, once she spotted it, they continued their downward trek. "How much further – it seems like we have been down here forever. Hey, let's take a break; I'm getting a little winded here."

"We're a little over half way, as I remember it, and yes let's take a few before we continue. Going down is easier and will take us less time."

"Less time than what?" Then it dawned on her. "Don't answer that, I figured it out. It's all up hill when we go back right?"

"Exactly, and it will be worse because we have burned all this energy getting down here and will have less reserves when we head out."

"Thanks for letting me know," she responded sarcastically. "I don't know now why I let you talk me into this or that I agreed to join you on this adventure." After a few minutes taking a deep breath and letting it out slowly she said, "I guess I'm ready to continue, shall we go?"

As they continued the downward trek, she followed as he led. He continued to point out the markings he had made on that first journey so she would know where to look for them and to be familiar with his method. It had been fortunate that there had only been the one tunnel. Suddenly he stopped. "Here is that wall that appears to be the end. It was just by luck that I saw the switchback." Turning around he pointed to the shadows. "See, if you look carefully you can see something just doesn't look right."

She stared hard but initially couldn't see what he was talking about. It looked like just another wall in the shadows to her. "I don't see it. Maybe I'm not looking at the right place."

Pointing again he said. "There, can't you see it." He then proceeded to walk toward the shadows. Once in the shadows he disappeared into what appeared to be a solid wall, and when he did all of a sudden she could see it. "Wow, it took you going through the opening for me to see it. However did you find it in the first place? It wasn't easy to see at all."

"Don't know really, just didn't look right to me, that's all."

Looking at her clothes she realized that not only were they soaked from her sweat but quite dirty too. It surely was hot and sticky and quite uncomfortable.

"Now," he said, "follow me here, and be prepared for something you've never seen before." Also when we get around the corner here, I want to light another torch and leave it right there. Once we're inside the cavern the exit is almost as hard to find from the other side. I want to make sure that it is well lit and will remain that way while we are exploring the cavern. I really didn't have much time last time." Thinking back at the moment gave him a shiver knowing how close it had come to him not leaving.

She followed him through the opening, stopped instantly and caught her breath. She didn't know what to expect, but it wasn't this. As the torch, she was carrying, reflected off the near walls of the cavern, she began to see the stalactites and stalagmites. In awe of the beauty she said softly, "Your words really didn't do it justice, it's so beautiful!"

"Truer words were never spoken. Light one of those torches and set it here so we can come directly back to the exit when we leave. As you can see this place is pretty large. Straight-ahead is an area that looks like water but isn't, and off to the left in the distance . . ." Looking closely he was trying to point to the place where he did get water, "There it is, that's the place where I got my water from, and then over there is that pile of rubble where I found that object."

"Yes, I see. I wonder how long this place has been here, just waiting to be discovered." Then realizing that there was no way for either of them to know she continued, "Of course I'm sure you wouldn't know."

"True, before we do some additional exploring here, let's eat. Oh by the way, be careful. I almost fell into a hole when I first came here. I'm sure there are others, so before we eat I will show you the one I did find so you have an idea what they may look like."

"Sounds good to me," she replied.

After taking her over to the hole and explaining he had almost fallen into it because he had been running out of time, they went back to the exit and sat down to have a quick meal.

"Do you want to look around together, or separately?" She asked still taken in by the beauty surrounding her.

"Not really sure. This cavern is pretty large, and would probably be safer if we did go together, but we would explore more by going separately. Hmm, just had a thought – we can do both."

"Both? I don't understand."

"Simple really, we go together, but spread out where we can always see each other, and if something interesting, or dangerous shows up, then either you or I can call the other over to see it."

"Not a bad idea really, hmm, you know, as we find these dangers we should probably mark them in some way to warn us, so if we do come back here we won't have to find them again."

"Great idea sis, do you have any suggestions?"

Shaking her head she said, "No, I thought maybe piling rocks or something, but that wouldn't look any different than any other pile around here."

"True, and I don't have many stakes left that I might have used, and we didn't bring that much twine or rope either."

"Maybe we can mark it now with the markers we have, and include a rock pile. The two in combination would help us and maybe there's a way to hang some of the twine. Then if we return, maybe we can come up with a better idea. Like roping them off or something."

"That would probably work temporarily for us, so let's do it, but let's make at least two to three piles and run some of the twine between those piles so it would look less natural."

Once they finished their meal, they headed out to explore the cavern. They continued straight across from the exit area past the point where he had discovered what he thought was water but wasn't, during his last visit. "The colors and formations sure are beautiful," she said. "Look there, it looks like the end of the cavern in this direction. Whoa there, it's not," she exclaimed as she stopped instantly. "There's a large drop off here that, from what light gets through, appears that the cavern goes on down to a much lower level."

Coming over to where she was he looked. "Whew, you're right about that. I wonder how large this cave complex truly is." Looking closer he stated, "Doesn't look like any way down from here to get to the next level."

"Are you thinking of going down there? I surely hope not." She said with emotion.

Shaking his head, "No, no not really, but if one was to fall into one of those holes, from there they might lead out to the lower level we can see from here. You just never know. Well, let's head over to that pond where I was able to get water for my return to the surface last time."

"Which direction is that?" She asked

He pointed saying, "Over there on our left, see the reflection of our torches . . . there . . . see, it looks wet." They headed in that direction and fortunately ran into no obstacles that blocked or holes to fall into. As they approached the water they could see that the cavern extended beyond their lights, and to the left of the pond was the wall where the debris pile was located. So before exploring the area behind the small tank they decided to go over to the pile and see if any other objects like the one he found could be in the pile.

"Boy, this is a pretty large pile of debris, how in the heck did you find that object?"

"I actually saw the light from the torch reflect off of it. I wonder how this debris pile got here in the first place."

Both looked up, and saw the ceiling of the cavern was at least five or six body lengths over their heads, and directly above the debris pile was a hole where the ceiling had collapsed. Thinking about that they wondered if the whole thing could come down on them. Yet, the evidence said otherwise. It probably was caused by that earth shake – the same one that had opened the tunnel into this cavern in the first place.

"I think on this trip this is as far as we go. By the time we reach the surface the day will be close to done. Let's go ahead and work this pile and see if what I found was the only thing here."

"Fine with me, I'm starting to feel a little tired anyway. This has been enough of an adventure for me for now." She then giggled with her eyes twinkling said, "You know, as whelps, we always created adventures for ourselves. Little did we know that once grown we would be in one that was better than any I imagined."

Smiling, and thinking back he responded, "Probably in your case, but I was always thinking of adventures of saving people and villages, you know being a hero. I'm not denying that this was more than I thought I would be involved with after growing up. Still reality sure can meet fantasy that's for sure." They got down to the serious business of working the rather large pile of rubble. For a while it didn't appear that there was anything else, and when they were about to give up, due to the time limitation and exhaustion, it was then when another of the strange objects surfaced. This renewed their energy and they continued for a while longer – in the end they came up with 3 additional objects, and it was really time to go.

They retraced to the exit, loaded their gear and started the return trip. Immediately, as they started climbing heading towards the entrance, she realized it was going to be more of an ordeal than she first thought – period. She hadn't taken into account the energy spent getting here. Now starting out tired meant it was going to be difficult, but what choice did she have? *Wow, I've always considered myself in good shape. This sure is proving me wrong.* After what seemed and very long time she could finally see dim daylight streaming into the tunnel entrance, and began noticing a cooling to the air, and speaking of the air, it never smelled so sweet. She wondered how those ones who chose to work underground ever did it. With this adventure almost over she knew she couldn't.

When they finally stepped outside the sun was setting. She found herself shivering uncontrollably, and realized again that her clothing was soaked from sweat, and the late after-zenith air was cooling down. With it the breeze was evaporating the moisture on her clothes and making them cold. Quickly grabbing her coat she placed inside the tunnel, she put it on but it just did not seem to help. "Let's hurry back to that temporary shelter; even with this coat I'm freezing. Also looking at myself I look like I just rolled in the mud somewhere."

Looking at her he started to laugh, "I must admit," he said, "You do look like that sorry little beast that had just been dragged out of the mud. I know I probably look no better myself. Well, you know where it is, so go ahead and change. I will follow shortly. I want to clean up what was left by the entrance, to at least make it less obvious anyone has been here. Not that anyone would be looking, since it is on our property, but I found it by accident and someone cutting across the countryside could do the same."

Looking carefully he picked up around the area while she hurried to the shelter to remove the wet, cold, filthy clothes. Smiling, she had to admit his description was probably pretty accurate. Even her hair was soaked. It was hard to believe that it had been that warm down there. Even after he had told her of the heat she really didn't believe it. Reaching the portable shelter she went inside, glad to be out of the breeze that even with the coat had penetrated all the way through. Quickly undressing and even feeling colder she climbed into her clean dry clothes. She found the blanket he had brought and wrapped it around her. Outside she heard her brother approach and then called out to him. "I'm dressed so you can come in and change."

"Shortly," He replied. "I want to get a fire going and make us a hot drink before we return to the shelter."

Shortly she heard the crackling of a fire and a pot being placed on it. He then opened the portable shelter and entered. "There's a good fire going, and it won't take long for the water to heat."

She went outside to sit by the fire for the warmth. She could hear him as he changed out of his wet and dirty clothes and once finished, he came out to join her. "Was it anything like what you expected?" He asked.

"No, I had some images, but the reality of it is vastly different. I can't believe how beautiful it is. Just to think that has been down there for a long, long time and nobody ever to see it. Not that it is something I would want to do a lot but I'm glad I went. Now a lot of rest would be nice." She could feel herself relaxing as she warmed up. It was even difficult to hold a cup. She felt comfortable and started to drift into sleep. Since she was sitting up, her head would start to fall which would awake her.

"Know how you feel sis. I could barely stay awake after my first trip down, but we do need to get back tonight."

Smiling, with a distant stare she responded. "Right, but I am so relaxed. It almost seems impossible to move." The next thing she remembered was hearing her brother's voice calling out to her. At that point she realized she had fallen asleep. Looking around she saw that while sleeping her brother had packed everything, and had awakened her when it was all ready. "Sorry, I didn't know I was that tired."

"It's alright. On the morrow you will find yourself with sore muscles anyway. For some reason we end using different ones here. Anyway, shall we go, once we're back you can clean up. I will do the outside chores, and when you finish you can fix us some food while I take my turn in the bathing space."

"Sounds like a plan to me." Shouldering her pack they headed back to the shelter.

CHAPTER SEVEN

As the gray of the morn started showing in the eastern sky Fauul climbed out of his portable shelter. There before him sat Doube with his back to him, talking with Bayleh and Mealoh. Stretching and rubbing the sleep from his eyes he approached the group. As he did Mealoh handed him a cup of the hot beverage that they all drank. Thanking the camp assistant he sat down with the group and turned to Doube. "So how'd it go? Obviously, since you're here and you're unharmed the worst didn't happen." Yawning he awaited Doube's response.

Smiling, Doube thought maybe he would drag it out and make a story of it, but thought better of it when he considered the taciturn Joellie, "Some good and some bad. I was able to get permission for us to fill our water containers for the rest of the trip out of the desert. But I couldn't convince the honored one to reveal the trail out. Hope you checked the one I found."

"Well, at least we will have water, and yes we did . . . funny how this turned out."

"What do you mean by that?" Doube asked.

"If you think about it, you were sent out to find water and we went out to find a way out of the desert. We found the water and you found a possible way out."

"True, you just never know how things will work out. At least we now have a probable route."

Fauul, turning around found they had been left alone as the other two had risen and started preparing the morn feed. As the smells of cooking food started permeating the air they found their mouths watering in anticipation.

"Think I'm going to get another cup of this. Do you need a refill?"

"Sure," Doube responded, "Mine has hit bottom, and a second, or maybe it's a third one . . . whatever, anyway its sounds great."

"Here I'll get it for you. So just sit a bit longer, and we can get into the logistics of how we are to get the water." He left to refill the cups and in a short time returned. "Here's yours, now what's up?"

"I had to work pretty hard on just getting permission even to get the necessary water we need to get out of here. They definitely were not going to give up any of their special trails. Maybe if it had only been me, but with so many outsiders . . ."

"They're a pretty closed society aren't they?"

"That's putting it mildly, for sure. If it wasn't for my past experience with the nomads, even though they are a different clan, we may have not been able to talk our way out of the situation. This is a very important water hole for them. In all the time they have been coming for water at that location it has never failed them. In the desert to find such a thing is rare."

As they talked Mealoh showed up with a plate of food for both of them, which he handed them – eating was serious business so while they attacked their food they were quiet. After finishing Doube said, "One of the conditions of us using this watering place is we are to leave it off any of the mapping we do."

"Hmmm, I guess we can. Joellie really doesn't know where it is, and probably could care less. I'm sure about this time he just wants to finish and get back – not that it isn't on my mind also. What's your guess, as far as days go, for us to reach that village?"

"If things go well, from here out, probably no more than half a cycle or so, but it could be much shorter. These mountains have to be the back side of the same that can be seen from the ocean."

"By the way, didn't you mention you had seen smoke up on top the other day?"

"True, I did, but I think that thunderstorm put it out. Hey Bayleh, the food's great as usual."

"Thanks, you're the only one who usually compliments me on the cooking. All I get is complaints from the rest of these louts."

"You could always make them fix their own, you know."

"True, and what satisfaction I could get out of that watching these idiots fumble with food preparation," Bayleh laughed, "It would be fun that's for sure, but we don't have the food to waste. We, being close to the end here, are running low on too many things. Hope we can barter some fresh meat when we get into those mountains."

"Well, you don't have to worry about me on that account. I'm not very good at it and am always glad when I don't have to eat my own cooking . . . 'fraid that I might poison myself." With that Doube rose and put his empty plate and cup over in the area where the camp assistant would take care of it. "Time's a wastin', I'll get the beasts together, if you will get the additional water containers ready, I'll pack them. Oh, by the way, I can only bring back the artist, so if you will get him up and fed, we can then go get the water. You can talk with Joellie and get camp broke down, and ready, so we can get out of this desert."

"Sounds great to me", while nodding in the agreement Fauul continued, "Actually it sounds wonderful, I surely am getting tired of this desert, and am quite fed up with our leader."

Tipping his head to the side and shrugging, Doube replied. "Know what you mean there." At this point Doube left to get the beasts ready, with Fauul heading to get the artist up, and prepare the water containers. It was time to leave the heat and sand.

* * *

With full water containers they headed west towards where the Desert Mountains jutted out. From there they would pick up the trail that had been located by Doube, and subsequently explored by Fauul and his team. The day had broken warm and clear – no surprise there. With the prospect of finally leaving the desert, spirits were high. Still an exact trail up into the mountains to the west had yet to be located. It was hoped that the trail they were following would provide a solution. Still, if appearances were correct, they would be spending at least one more night on the edge of the desert before possibly climbing out.

As they followed the trail to the west it ran in an almost perfectly straight line towards the small range of Desert Mountains that existed here. Approaching another finger in the range the trail made an abrupt change in direction to the south. Yet ahead they could see where water had flowed down canyon when it had rained. That led to a brief discussion as to which way to go. Joellie was reminded that by going off trail before had placed them in danger and to this delay. So it was decided to stay on the trail. The trail twisted and turned throughout the foothills they were in, but continued in a general westward direction. Eventually it came out in an old abandoned village. The village gave the appearance of being abandoned for a very long time. From what could be determined, it looked like their source of water had dried up. Without it there was no way for those villagers to survive. They broke for the zenith meal here quite thankful they had water with them. It really showed all of them the importance of water to the area and how fragile a resource water could be.

After finishing the meal they continued to the west only to see the trail break and go north and south paralleling the mountain range. Originally they had searched to the south, and had been told the main trail was in that direction. Still by coming upon this split they were left with the question as whether this was a portion of that trail, or maybe just a detour. With no one to ask they decided to go south. Even though they were unaware of it at the time this decision led them to go the more difficult way. Had they gone the other way they would have avoided the range and the necessity of climbing out of the desert, and in the end, save time. They would have arrived at the targeted village at the end of the minor gather as originally planned. The necessary beasts would have been bartered or purchased, they would have been on their way and none would have been the wiser. The trade would have never take place, and the possibility of finding a site of the *ones before* would have been missed, changing the future, leaving the past still in doubt. So fate played a hand in the game and the future was rewritten. As such, the direction they took delayed them by enough to come into the village between gathers. And the timeline and the two possible futures settled into one erasing the other forever. Such are the fates, and as later discovered, when they looked back in hindsight, and speculation.

The southern trail skirted the edge of the desert and ran down a narrow canyon that seemed to wind and twist in a general southerly direction. The trail they were following appeared to be quite old, and while not heavily traveled, was at least traveled enough to show recent usage. While not as tall as other mountains they had encountered or would encounter, these rose up on their right or the west with no obvious way to scale them. This had been one of the reasons this area had not been officially mapped. Access to and thru these mountains did not seem to exist.

As they continued in a general southerly direction, the canyon opened up and once again they were back in the desert. The eastern side of the trail hugged the Desert Mountains they had gone through earlier, and the western side opened up into a small plain. It really appeared that they were going to be led back into the desert instead of out of it. So they decided to stop to allow Doube to scout ahead and see if the chosen direction had been a good decision. They really had no desire to backtrack. Yet, if it became necessary, then they would do it. As Doube left and headed down the trail, they set up for a brief stop until he returned and reported on what was ahead of them. "Don't be long," Joellie stated as Doube prepared to leave.

With a small bit of sarcasm in his voice, Doube responded, "Only as long as necessary." Then smiling he continued, "Who knows it could be a couple of days." With that he turned his back on them and headed down the trail. Shaking his head to himself he thought. *After all this time he really has no idea. As if I would just dilly dally about, and waste time. It's like we are on a time schedule that only he knows. Oh well what is one going to do, after all he is the one in charge – more or less.*

The trail they were following and he was scouting continued to go back deeper into the desert hugging the Desert Mountains. On the right a ravine opened up. At some time in the past a lot of water had ran through it. There were a few trees growing next to it, yet, no visible water. The trail started bending to the east and away from the range they needed to climb. He began to wonder if indeed this just led back into the desert. Then somewhere ahead just beyond his eyesight he sensed more than saw a possibly that it intersected another trail. Continuing on he would know shortly. As he approached the intersection, which he could see clearly, the trail he was on continued on into the desert going south, while a second trail ran east and west. Obviously the eastern direction of this intersecting trail ran back into the desert and could have been the trail they were to remain on originally when the deviation through the salt depression had caused them to lose it and trek across the open desert. Although from the descriptions they had received it did not appear so.

He decided to explore the western direction of the intersecting trail and to see if it would lead them out of the desert and up to the top of these mountains. *Funny*, he thought, *if I were in the air like a flyer then this crossing would look like a large "X", even though a little off center.* With the western leg more promising, but again knowing that even this could be deceiving he started down it.   It became more promising as he traveled, as it almost immediately headed uphill. Again, in the distance, it seemed to continue in the proper direction. Before going back to the waiting team, he decided to continue far enough up it to at least confirm that the trail went into the mountains. At the same time he needed to locate a place to camp for the night. Since it was obvious to him, that by the time he returned and then all came forward the day would pretty much be finished. As he continued the gentle climb he saw the trail turn to the left, a bit south. Once he reached that point and just ahead he could see an area that had been used in the past for resting and camping overnight. He went to the area and inspected it and saw that it was a great place to stop.

Looking both back in the direction he came, and across the countryside, he saw that there was a chance he could cut across the area back to where the team was waiting. Being on foot allowed him some flexibility that wasn't available when you had pack beasts. He decided to cut across for the time saving aspect. That way when they returned to the area he had chosen, it would still be daylight and much easier to set up for the night. And once he had crossed this area, it might turn out to be an easy route for the pack beasts, saving both time and distance. By keeping the mountain range on his left he headed back. Then off to his right he noticed a small dim trail that had been little used. Curious, he went to it and saw it was going in the same general direction he was. Usually these trails went somewhere and even if it dead-ended; it still was generally in the direction he needed to go anyway.

Half way down the dim trail he came to an abandoned shelter, with a number of out-shelters. It seemed to have suffered the same fate as the abandoned village they had passed earlier. Their water source had dried up and without it, any chance of survival. In the desert things can remain standing much longer and it was hard to determine how long the place had been abandoned. Still the shelters had an ancient look to them. Plus, from appearances, it looked like a good strong wind would topple them. This had been a pretty big operation sometime in the past. Now all that remained were the ghosts of the past, dust, and vacant shelters, with the only occupants being the small beasts. While keeping his eyes open for camps, he felt it would be better to travel on to the one he had found earlier. With that he passed the shelters, picked up the trail on the other side and continued on his way. He thought he could see where this dim trail intersected the main one, and as he approached the area could see that it actually did. "This will save us some time that's for sure," he said quietly. "And how'd I miss this when I was headed south?"

In camp at the end of the day, and with both the abandoned village, and property behind them, they talked about what they had seen and guessed about whom these people were who had been forced to leave. Where were they now, were they able to recover, and was there any tragedy other than the obvious? Yet, from the condition of the shelters it could have been a generation ago or longer when this event had taken place. It was hard to believe, for most of them, that such a thing could happen, since they had spent most of their lives in townships. Yet, if nothing else, this assignment had opened their eyes to other hardships. While much was understood about the world, it did not mean that it would be easy to live everywhere. Some places, like that village, which had existed on the edge of the desert, had, from the brief study, survived there for many generations. Then without warning, or maybe just a few seasons of warning, the life force water had left. Then there was nothing they could do, but leave. This brought them back to the beginning of the discussion of where did these people go, which finished that train of thought for now. Next, came the anticipation of actually leaving the desert and getting into these mountains, which led them, in anticipation, of finding a surviving village and talk to the locals about an area the villagers would know.

One thing that Doube stated seemed to hang with them. He had stated that there probably was no area anywhere that someone hadn't already been, and traveled over sometime. These new discoveries were in fact re-discoveries. The information on these areas had been lost or destroyed, or even forgotten. The abandoned village was a prime example. Most likely these people had worked and traded with the people who live or probably had lived in these mountains. To them it was all familiar, and it would seem strange to those villagers to hear the team talk about these areas as something undiscovered. Still, the thought of having to abandon all you had ever known put a somber mood on the group, and they grew silent, drifting back to their portable shelters, quite content to be introspective. The morrow would bring its own challenges.

* * *

Fauul Saelor left his shelter quite early the next morn, and as usual, found the camp manager Bayleh Pands and his assistant Mealoh Forsby quite busy preparing the morn food. There was a chill in the air and yet a promise of heat in the feel of the air at the same time. It seemed funny that one could really tell such a thing. The smell of the hot beverage drew his attention and he went over to where they were preparing the food and asked if the beverage was ready. Bayleh replied saying that it had been for a while. After all it was one of the first things he did after getting a cooking fire going in the morn. Besides Doube had already been up and was gone, as usual.

Grabbing a cup of the hot beverage and putting his hands to the warmth of the fire, he thought. *I really thought I had beaten the rest of the team up, except the manager here.* As he found a place to sit his thoughts continued. *Doube, now I'm doubly glad that we were able to get such a qualified scout.* Thinking back to a couple of incidents that had happened to them, it had been Doube who had found a way out of those situations. Yes, they were very lucky.

The rest of the camp started to stir, and pretty soon it would be busy with the preparations of the day. He knew, from past experience, that Doube would be back in camp just before they pulled out to let them know the conditions ahead and also to get the information from the team leader as to the goals of the day.

Jahmes Landow, the artist, was busy with his sketching. Everything he had done was a rough out. Later, as time allowed, he would fill in the sketches and missing details therein. Between the notes he wrote and the drawings he would be able to fill the missing parts easily. He was looking forward to the village towards the coast, where they were heading, because his supplies had definitely run low, and it would also give him time to add details before they faded from his memory. His work, added to their field notes and ground work, would paint a complete picture of the areas they had traveled and were mapping.

Yet, they were probably at least three to four days away from their destination. If the trail they were on took them into the mountains, great – if not then it might be much longer before they arrived. It would have been nice to have run into a local traveler from a village to help them. Yet, the abandoned village had shown them that other villages out here, other than the nomads, would be difficult to find – well, at least in the desert. There was more promise in the mountains. After all, the mountains offered more since; from their present location they could see trees and vegetation in abundance above them. Yet, there had been no sound of running water, something that seemed common in other areas with similar vegetation. Heck trees required lots of water, so there had to be a source somewhere. Still, if they wanted to be honest, that source could be deep underground, leaving them with no way to refill their water containers when they emptied.

The next three days ran pretty much without incident. When they finally reached the top coming out of the desert it had been a relief. The temperatures were much cooler, and here they could feel the breezes that blew off the ocean – even though it was still a great distance away. Here too they found a village, but like the last one it was abandoned. Yet, this time it was not for lack of water. In the recent past a wildfire had swept through the area and destroyed it. Looking around they could see that at one time it had been a mining community. But, from all indications, whatever they had been mining had played out a long time ago. So if the fire hadn't destroyed it, most likely, it would have died, since the reason for its existence was gone. The area around the village had burned hot, and even the trees had been consumed. The fire appeared to have happened earlier in the summer, and in places there was smoke coming out of the ground. Wondering how that could be they did a small investigation and found that the roots of some of the burned trees were carrying fire down through their system.

At least they were able to refill their water containers here before continuing. And finally after a half day walk on the trail leading out of the area they left the burned area. And that was a relief as they were tired of smelling the burned vegetation, and walking through the ashes, which were extremely fine in consistency. With each step in these ashes one would form a small cloud of black and gray dust, which could lead one to choke if inhaled. Finding the beasts that had perished in the fire was of no liking either. The predators had yet to return to the area, and the carcasses were bloating in the heat – those that hadn't been consumed by the fire – leaving a horrible stench that permeated the surrounding area where the burned bodies laid. It also turned out to be a strange silent world where small dust devils roamed, and small breezes picked up the ash. There was no sound of flyers or of the crawlers, just the sound of the wind. At times they found themselves holding their collective breaths trying to hear something other than themselves. It was a dead alien world. So much destruction – how long would it take for it to recover? What would winter rains and probably snow do to the area? Questions they had no answers for, and as they continued through the burned area they found themselves somewhat depressed. Unconsciously, they had picked up the pace just to get out of this silent dead world.

After leaving the burned village and the large burned area the terrain trended downhill towards the coast. Eventually they would end up there, pick up a water-craft, head back north, then follow the main route back to the township beyond the gorge where they had begun over a turn ago. As they continued their trek the land changed again and became quite flat with local grasses covering the soil. This made travel much easier yet, from the views ahead, they could tell that they still had to go through some additional hills and canyons before they would reach the village that would mark the end of their official duties. After picking up what was needed, getting a much needed break, they would continue on to the coast, head north for a few days to the known port and finally head back home. The thought of being this close to the end of their task raised the spirits of the team. It would be easy at this point to let down, relax with the end this close in sight.

When they finally came out of the mountains, at the point where the meadowlands started, a trail intersected theirs from the north. From appearances it was as well traveled as the one they were presently using. At the intersection they found a trader there who traded in local foodstuffs and equipment that could be used for replacements during travelers' journeys. His overall inventory was small, yet adequate for the needs. Here, they discussed the upcoming terrain and the surrounding countryside. They found out that the trail that intersected them from the north went to a small village inland, and from that area there was a route into the desert. It left them wondering if they had turned north instead of south, at that intersection, after leaving the abandoned village, that they would have met up with the trail they were now observing. The local thought it was a good possibility. Still, since he himself had never been over that trail, he could not confirm it at this time.

After the brief halt, they continued towards the village of their destination. At least now they had a better idea, with the knowledge gained from the local trader, of what was ahead of them. The days were still long, and this meant with the type of terrain they were presently traveling, they should make good time. From information gathered, they knew they were going to travel, first in a southwesterly direction, away from that village of destination, where the trail would gradually change to a more northwesterly direction. They would continue to drop in altitude, and as they approached the coastal foothills the land would close in on them with a few canyons, before the land would once again open up into meadowlands. With that future last change they would be no more than a half-day from their intended destination. The information provided made it much easier to plan the travel of each day. The weather seemed to cooperating also, which in itself was a relief. After the heat of the desert, the mildness of the area was a nice change. It would be easy at this point to rest a few before continuing. Still, with the village being this close, resting on a real bed instead of what they had, became a bigger draw. Add to it baths, even if they were public baths, sounded like something to be anticipated.

They found, once they inspected their equipment, after hiking through the burned area, the ash had penetrated everything, leaving both stains, and the smells of the burned area on them and their equipment. The trader had commented on it when they approached. Once they arrived in that distant village they had much cleaning and repair work ahead of them.

Following the trail across the meadowlands back into the hills and canyons they finally emerged in the area described by the trader. From here they knew they were within hours of arriving at the village. Joellie sent both Doube and Fauul ahead to make arrangements for their arrival, while the rest of the team stopped for a short period to rest and eat the zenith meal.

After the meal break the rest of the team followed the two into the village. It was pushing dusk when the team arrived, and as planned Doube and Fauul, who had come into the village ahead of them, had the necessary items arranged. Doube led Mealoh and Bayleh to the beast yards where the beasts would be kept, while Fauul led the rest of the team to the local hostel where they would be staying. Close by was a public eating shelter, and the bathing space was next door. Once all the equipment was unloaded and placed into a secure location, all would gather at the hostel before cleaning up. They would all go to the eating shelter together, spend a leisurely evening, then on the morrow do any repairing followed by a thorough cleaning of the equipment. The idea of sleeping in a real bed appealed to all of them. After all, the ground was not the most comfortable place to sleep, and they had been doing this for over a turn. With of course, a few brief breaks in other villages they had passed through. Yet, of all the villages they had stayed, this one was the most important to them. It was the last one before returning home – such a wonderful thought.

Yet, while looking back on the previous turn, it was hard to realize that they were near the end of the journey. While much of it had been tough, they had the opportunity to see a lot of country, some of it harsh, and much of it beautiful. There had been times when things had gone wrong, and some of the team members had been hurt. Still, the injuries overall had been minor where in some cases it should have been severe. Once they left this village, only two days later, they would be on that water-craft heading north, relaxing, reminiscing about what they had seen and done. It would be a small vacation while on that water-craft with nothing to do but relax and watch the ocean and the shoreline. Of course once back on land they had another half cycle or more before they returned to the township. But, that was different. It was on a known major trail, and in comparison to where they had been and what they had traversed it would be easy. This final leg was to the far north and paralleled a large river.

It could be seen in all their faces, the eagerness to be done. Although once back the real serious work would begin, the re-writing of the notes, the improvements in the drawings and sketches and an overall reorganization of all the data. Once that was completed it would be turned over to the department to incorporate into the existing map data. Still, that was in the future, and at the present they needed to clean, repair, and organize their equipment, get a message out with the next runner, secure another pack beast or two, and purchase the necessary equipment. Unfortunately they had arrived in mid-cycle, which meant they had missed the gather. This complicated things, but there would probably be a way to work around it. A discussion with the beast-master would be able to answer that one, but again all of this would be on the morrow. Tonight was a time to let down and relax. Let the morrow be what it would be.

* * *

In the morn Joellie called a meeting breaking up the team into different work parties to get all the equipment cleaned, repaired, and organized for the trip back home. He put Doube and Fauul in charge of talking with the beast-master and locating the necessary beasts so they could continue and not leave anything behind. He followed this by putting Bayleh with Mealoh in charge of locating and securing the necessary equipment for the new pack beasts, while the rest of the team proceeded to the actual cleaning and repacking of their gear. Joellie himself went to talk with the local person in charge, thusly staying away from any of the real physical work.

With the assignments made, the meeting broke up and all went to their assigned tasks. Joellie went to negotiate payment and fees for their stay, and confirm the marks he was using for payment would be acceptable here. Many times, in remote villages, trading and bartering was the way, with some minor use of the world currency. The marks were assigned to the different major houses in the lands – These houses representing the different fields, such as mining, manufacturing, learning, entertainment, council, agriculture and the raising of the beasts. The importance of the field became the determining factor for the value of the mark.

This made each area they had been placing different values on the marks according to local needs, and understandings. Joellie needed to determine the value of the marks he carried, and if any additional bartering would be necessary. This would let Doube and Fauul know what they had to work with when they went out to get the needed beasts. It was obvious to them that with what they had to accomplish the team would be in this village for at least a quarter of a cycle. Since a cycle lasted about twenty-eight days that would be seven days of reconditioning and preparation before they were finally on their way home.

Doube commented to Fauul that the beast-master's name was Aurto Satrneze, and he definitely fit the idea of what a beast-master should look like. Plus he was the local brewer and had a "mean" ale. Now, "a good" ale at this time sounded great. They hadn't had spirits in a while, and to tip a couple of bottles sounded like something to look forward to. When they approached the yards, other than the beasts within the enclosures, the place appeared to be empty. Looking around, the owner didn't seem to be about either. They headed towards the shelter, which housed both the beast- master's office, and off to the back side, his living quarters. His mate and their offspring worked the yards also. Since the two of them were here, and the beast-master and his family weren't immediately available, Doube and Fauul decided to check in on the beasts that were in the pens. Walking over to the pens they found that they had been fed, groomed, and watered. It was obvious, from the care they were receiving, that this village beast-master took very good care of his beasts or ones put under his care – that was a very good sign. Looking around they also noticed the yards were kept in excellent condition. Even though nothing was new, and showed great use, the grounds were clean, and the beast-master had even brought in fresh soil to keep the odors down.

Continuing their tour of the yards they eventually headed towards the shelter where business was carried out. The door was open, so they went inside. Yet, again, even this was vacant. Looking around the office area and still not finding anyone they shrugged, and proceeded back outside. Suddenly they heard what sounded like banging going off in the distance. It sounded as if someone was using a hammer. Using the sound as a guide they attempted to find the source. Sure enough off in the distance they could see the beast-master working on something. He had his back to them and with the noise he was making, probably would not hear them approach.

Instead of startling Aurto, they called his name out. Initially he didn't hear them as he continued his project, but as they approached closer, he suddenly realized someone had been calling him, stopping what he was doing; he turned around to find out who had been yelling at him. They realized, from his perplexed look that he did not recognize their voices. This was understandable, since they were not from this area, and Doube had only talked with Aurto once. Then he recognized Doube and said. "It's you, and who is this with you? I'm sorry, where are my manners, I am Aurto Satrneze. My family and I have been in this business for generations, and you are?"

"Aurto," Doube replied," This is Fauul Saelor, one of the people in charge of our project – a great one to work with for sure. Oh by the way I heard you are the local brewer also. Is this also true?"

Looking at Fauul and pointing at Doube, Aurto responded with a smile, "He doesn't waste time does he? Before our introductions are complete he is already trying to find out about something else." Then looking at Doube he continued, "Yes, yes I am that also."

Doube with a sad look on his face stated, "I do hope you have some of your ale around. As it has been much too long since I saw one let alone drank one."

Shaking his head and smiling once again, "Yes, and I have found a way to keep the ale cool also. It does seem to improve the flavor somewhat."

"Then why are we standing here and talking, I surely could use one while we discuss our needs with you. Of course Fauul will be paying for them."

Fauul responded, "I knew there would be a catch in this, so he's buying and I'm paying is that it?"

"I think you got the gist of it."

Smiling and shaking his head he said, "I knew there was a reason you wanted me along, but who can turn down 'good ale', and as you said it has been a long time. Shall we go?"

As they headed for the shelter where the business was conducted, he remembered that on the porch, where chairs were sitting, there was some weird container hanging from the roof. It had been wrapped in some type of wicking material, and was wet. Curiously he had touched it and found it to be cold.

Looking at Aurto, Doube stated. "I seem to remember, while we tried to find you, we saw that wet thing hanging from your porch. Is this what you use to keep your ale cool?"

"Yes, yes it works very well. I accidentally discovered it, or should I say my mate did. She commented on the fact that when she hung her clothing out to dry after cleaning them, they became cool from the breeze before the sun warmed them up. I didn't think much about it until one day when the wind was blowing pretty strongly, I went out to help her take down the wet clothes so they wouldn't be blown away. It had been right after she had put them up. They were still wet, and quite cold. So I experimented and come up with this container. It has water in it, and I put the ale in that water, then by keeping the wicking wet the air cools it. It really works well." By the time he had finished his explanation they had reached the porch. He lowered his modified bucket and pulled out a bottle for each one of them.

"You're right," Fauul stated. "This stuff is cold. Most of what I have drunk has always been warm so this will be a treat. The only time I usually get my ale cold is when the winter is upon us. But, in truth I don't have a lot of ale that time of the turn. Personally, I prefer it in the warmth of summer."

"Yeah, yeah," Arturo responded, "pretty much the same for me. But here there is only two seasons – the wet season, and the dry season, and the wet only last for about three to four cycles."

"Wow, paradise. But I guess even with paradise there's a bad side. When we were heading towards your village here we went through two abandoned villages. The first had lost their water source, and the second had been burned out by a wild fire."

"True, it has always been a fight to keep water supplied. To find a good source can make one rich here. Not financially, so to speak, but as long as the water holds you can conduct your life and business with fewer problems. On that subject what brings you to me at this time of the cycle?"

"Before I answer that one, I would like another of your ales. They are very good, or maybe it's because been so long since I had one that it could be the worst in the world and still taste great."

Smiling, so not to have his guests' mistake his intention, Aurto stated in mock anger. "You think my ale is the worst in the world?"

Laughing Doube stated. "I've had pretty bad ale; even flat ale . . . no this is probably one of the best in my opinion. Of course I've been wrong before."

"Are you sure? After all you just insulted my ale, or is it that you want to get one for free?" Smiling Arturo continued, "Now, now I am just joking. But with those kinds of insults maybe I charge you twice the going rate."

"With this weather, peace, and gentle breeze here on your porch, I might stay here all day and soak it in and probably not notice that double rate. It sure is beautiful here. Of course I'm sure you ordered it, the weather that is, then you can demand whatever you want for your ale." They all laughed and Doube stated, "We really need to pick up a couple of pack beasts. Now I know it's between gathers, but there must be some source here where we could find some."

"Maybe it is of good fortune you came here. One of the members of our village area whose family has been here for many generations, and who has property a few hours from here raises the best of both herd and pack beasts in the region. There has been tragedy in the family a long time ago, and the brother and sister now own and operate the property. At this moment in time, there has been little demand for their beasts, and it has been hard for them to keep it operating. The sister makes and sells clothing and such at the gathers, and some of the garden items they bring in, has been the only things that has kept them from going broke."

"If they have the best you would think there would be no problem in finding buyers."

"Normally that would be a true statement, but these surrounding areas are sparsely populated, and the demand isn't what it should be. As you have seen, on your journey here, water is not plentiful. This has limited our growth – even though it is a beautiful place to live. Yet, in the last ten turns we have been in a drought. It was one of the reasons for that fire that destroyed the mountain village."

"How so?" Fauul asked.

"It isn't unusual for that area to have thunderstorms, and small lightning fires. Most of the storms put out the fires the lightning starts. But more of the storms in the last couple of seasons have been dry storms, and with the vegetation being as dry as it has been, it would be like lighting a fire in a meadow full of grasses after it has cured. Poof! In minutes all would be ablaze." Shaking his head he continued, "While it was a small village, especially since the mining has played out, it was a nice place to visit. I myself am sorry to see it gone."

"What do you mean?"

"Well, in the summer it was a great place to go and visit with my mate and the whelps. They, the whelps love to play and pretend they are on some great adventure. It allowed us a place that was close by, and yet, far enough away, to seem like a change. It gave us a chance to relax and forget about what we had to do in the daily grind."

"I see kind of a change of pace, sort of something different."

"Yeah, that's it. All I know is, even though we didn't do it very often, when we came back we were refreshed and ready to get back into the daily work here."

"Sounds really nice. I must admit this area can really start growing on you, even though I said that before, it's really true."

"Anyway," Aurto inquired, "do you have something to write on?" He continued when he received the affirmative. "Here are the directions to get you out to the herders . . . The property, which is family owned, is even better situated overall than here in the village. Their ancestors were some of the first in the area."

Paying Aurto for the ale, and thanking him for directions, both Doube and Fauul headed outside of the village to get a feel for the trail that they were to travel. The information from Aurto had been detailed, and they felt they should have no problem in locating the property. Once satisfied that they could follow those directions they headed back to the hostel to let Joellie know what they found out, and to pick up some harnesses for the pack beasts, if they found any that would work. While knowing Aurto worked hard and kept his yards in great shape, he was only a local. As such, his praise of the pack beasts these local herders owned and trained, well they had to just wait and see. In truth, because of the time of day, they would have to delay the trip out there until the morn. Leaving now would put them there at dusk, and leave them little light in which to judge the beasts. Plus, once the decision had been made, they still had the return trip to consider. While the remaining travel was short overall, these beasts still had to carry much, and had be of good temperament.

So they put together a daypack and went out to locate the team members, who were purchasing the additional equipment for the new beasts. They needed a minimum of two, but hopefully could find three. With a little free time at the moment it also gave the two of them some time to explore the village and surrounding countryside close by, plus assist where necessary. After all, the sooner finished, the sooner they would be on the trails home.

CHAPTER EIGHT

In a short time it would be time for the zenith meal. Lauut would not be back until the evening meal, so she planned on only something light, something that wouldn't take very long to fix. Since returning from her adventure in the cavern, she and Lauut had cleaned up the small treasures they had found. Two had no designs or markings on them. One was a dull silver color, while the other of the plain looking ones was sort of a burnished gold. The third was inscribed and had what appeared to be two words below the engraved picture. It wasn't a scene, but appeared to be some kind of crest. Again what they were and who had constructed them was beyond both.

After the meal she was working in the garden area, which overlooked the lower areas around the main shelter, she was able to see the entrance to the property along with all the young beasts they had in the pens. There was also a great view of much of the surrounding area. She didn't realize when she first noticed, but eventually she saw two strangers approaching the entrance. They had to be coming to their property because the direction they were taking would only bring them here. The taller of the two appeared to be the one in charge. He had the look of someone who had lived in a township, yet, from the tan, had spent at least sometime outside. The second had the look and motion of one who spent most of his life in the outback. She didn't know how she knew this; still once they came closer she'd be able to confirm if her initial impressions were accurate. They were still too far away to be recognizable, other than obviously being males.

"Great!" she exclaimed. The herding dogs were out with her brother, all except that female who had attached herself to her, and there had been some rumors of a small gang of thieves working the area – although she couldn't remember anybody locally who had been robbed. Well, she wasn't going to be the first. She went inside and got her throwing knives and belt knife and kept it on her person. If they were those rumored thieves she would let them know stealing from them would not be so easy.

* * *

It had been a pleasant hike from the village out to their destination. The weather had cooperated and it seemed like a lazy spring day. The directions given by

Aurto had been accurate and easy to follow. Up ahead they could see the entrance to the property of the herders, and in the distance the main complex of shelters that served as the headquarters. They had made small talk about nothing in general on the trip out. Some comments on the surrounding countryside, and being glad this assignment was close to being finished. Although, since mapping was his main area of work, he knew that there would be turns of work ahead of them simply putting all the information together. At least it was job security that was for sure. "So what are your plans, once this is finished?" Fauul asked.

"Don't know really. Probably go back to the family farm for a while – haven't seen that place in at least a turn. The advantage I have is that I only have to do this kind of thing when I want to."

"Why, are you independently wealthy or something?"

Doube laughed, "No, but since it's only me, and I have very little needs, I can live off what I have earned for quite a long time. Prefer being in the hills anyway, and that only costs me time."

"You do know, with your skills as both a scout and a geologist, and being as good as you are, you could write your own way into a high position. Doesn't that interest you at all?"

"Interest me, no, not at all. I find myself wanting to return to the outback whenever I spend too much time in small villages let alone townships. Guess I just enjoy being in the natural world and even working on the family farm."

"Each to his own, I guess. I myself feel invigorated by the life in a township. The villages we have been in really move too slowly for me. I love the competition, the press of the people, ah the energy that is there. I don't quite know how to explain it, but it makes me feel alive."

Shaking his head Doube stated, "Not for me, no not for me at all. You mean that even after this project we are completing that this world we have gone through has left no impression on you in any way, shape, or form?"

"Well, if it came down to it, I guess I could adjust to something like this. Still, I would really miss my life in the township." They found themselves approaching the gate at the entrance to the herders' property and stopped briefly at the gate. Doube reached up to unhitch the gate and walk through when he heard a "thwack" and instinctively ducked.

"What the heck was that?" He exclaimed. Looking around he saw a throwing knife sticking out of the gate post, and then heard the growl of a dog off in the distance. With that he quickly closed the gate and waited to see what was to transpire. Looking up the hill towards the main shelters they saw, about half way up the hill, a female standing defiantly, and a large dog sitting next to her with its hair standing up and growling at them. While the distance was great enough not to be able to make out the details of the female, Fauul could see she was about shoulder height to him and slim. She had brown shoulder length hair that was tied back, and was wearing work clothes appropriate for her work. Still they couldn't hide her shape.

"Are you the one who threw that knife, and if so why?" Fauul yelled because of the distance.

"Obviously", she replied, "you don't see anyone else around here do you? And that was just a warning, one to show that I can protect what we have as well as any male."

"Well, if you couldn't, I am sure your companion there could. That dog doesn't appear to like us."

"Really, I would have never guessed", she said sarcastically. She has never cared for males anyway, and I can't say I blame her."

Fauul and Doube looked at each other, Doube whispering to Fauul and said. "Hey you're the one in charge here, you figure it out."

"So, you're putting this on my shoulders huh?"

"Of course, boss." Doube replied smiling.

"Okay . . ." Turning around and looking at the female Fauul asked, "Ah. . . ma'am why the show of force here? We've come to do some business with you and to buy a couple of your pack beasts."

"Then why were you not in the village during the last gather? That's usually when and where this kind of business is handled. It is the way of things."

"True, but our team did not make it to your village in time for the gather, and we are in desperate need of two, possibly three of your pack beasts."

"There are thieves working around here somewhere, how do I know you aren't them, since you being here is, how should I say it, so unusual."

"Okay, what do you need from us to prove we are here for legitimate reasons?"

"You, the one who are talking, you come in nice and easy, and the other one stay where you are at the gate. I will keep Sadie under control, and as long as you don't make any quick moves she *will* leave you alone."

Doube shrugged and whispered to Fauul, "Sounds fair to me. She sure looks like a handful, so I wouldn't argue. After all she and her brother has survived keeping their business going and she has proved she can handle a knife. Suspect she has dressed out beasts too, so I would do as she says – unless you want to be dressed out also."

Shaking his head and smiling at Doube's comment Fauul started opening the gate, the female said something to the dog that immediately lay down at her feet, but remained fully alert. He could tell the dog would be up in a flash if any of his actions were deemed harmful or appeared so to the dog. As he approached he was able to see her better, and saw that she was not a beauty, but still there was something about her that was attractive. He just couldn't quite figure it out. Slowly and carefully he approached the two, rehearsing to himself what he would say. When he was within two body lengths of the two she told him to stop, which he did. He could tell the dog was not one to mess with, and the dog's mistress seemed to be just as tough.

As he approached she sized him up additionally. She had chosen him to come forward for a couple of reasons – the first, being his demeanor, showing him to be from a township, and the second, he seemed to be the one in charge. One thing for sure he definitely was a looker. He probably had females all over him from wherever he came from. She realized as he approached that she only came to just over his shoulders in height, and there appeared to be some strength in those shoulders also. "Do you have any proof of who you say you are and what you represent? Let's be honest here, rarely does one come out to one's property to conduct this kind of business." She wasn't going to let him know at this point that her brother was out attending the herd and she was alone. It was always best to keep others off balance and off guard if possible.

"Yes, that's true, and had we come into the village when we had planned, we would have been there in time for the gather and this would not have been necessary. Anyway, my name's Fauul Saelor, and I'm second in charge of our team. The one at the gate is Doube Mickles our scout."

Looking down at the closed gate and the one standing there she said, "So that's Doube Mickles. His rep precedes him. We deal now and then with the travelers who go into the camps of the nomads, and he is big medicine to those clans."

"So, if you do know of him, is it safe to invite him up and break up this impasse? I myself would like to see this moment end quietly."

"One moment, you did say your name is Fauul right?"

He nodded his head for a yes," then asked, "You didn't give me your name?"

"True", she turned towards the gate and yelled. "Hey you at the gate, give me your name."

"Doube, Doube Mickles ma'am . . ."

Looking closer at the male at the gate, she could see that he could possibly be that Doube. He had the look and movement of one used to being in the wilderness, and it was said he had become a brother to one of the clans. "So what do you know of the nomad tribes?"

"I do know they are all over, fortunately only in small groups and families."

"Is that all?"

"No, that's not all. Who is this one in front of me here?"

"Fauul . . . Fauul Saelor, ma'am."

Fauul broke in and added, "If you want to know if he is tied to a nomad group the answer is yes. He generally does not speak of it at all. Yet, back in our travels to here, we ran into a group of the nomads in the desert. It was he who kept the situation from getting nasty. It seems he is an adopted member of one of the mountain clans."

She knew that this information was not general knowledge, as it was only known to the different nomad clans, the travelers, and a few of the ones that dealt with the clans. These societies were much closed, and to reveal anything about them could lead to dire consequences for the one who gave out the information.

"Doube, why don't you come on up and join your companion here, so I can get a better look at you."

With that he complied and joined Fauul who was still standing a distance from the female.

When he arrived she surveyed both trying to decide how to proceed, since at this moment everything was at an impasse. Then she shrugged, smiled at them and said. "My name is Lauma Ktrove."

When she smiled at them their jaws dropped. It seemed that the smile changed her from someone ordinary into a female of radiant beauty. Stammering at little Fauul bowed and said, "Glad to make your acquaintance Lauma Ktrove. Can you do something about your dog, or are we going to stand here all day?"

"Sorry, we rarely have anyone but friends come by . . ."

"If this is the way you greet them it would be understandable." Fauul replied sarcastically. He was hoping to see that smile again. It seemed so unbelievable that something so simple should make such a transformation.

She called the dog off turned around and said, "Follow me up to the porch, but don't make any fast moves or Sadie here, will be all over you without me saying anything. Somewhere in her past, she was a stray, a pup when we found her. She was abused by a male, so she doesn't trust any of you."

As she led the way to the porch Doube whispered. "I really didn't expect that. She has a real hidden beauty there. I know of a lot of males who will kill to be with her."

"Don't know about that really, she apparently can take care of herself, pretty self-sufficient. It's no wonder she's without a mate. She probably intimidates most here in her village."

Laughing quietly, Doube responded. "You know you're probably right. She's definitely is a force to deal with, that's for sure."

With that said they approached the porch where they noticed a number of chairs sitting there. She motioned for them to sit, and then went inside. "I'll be right back." She said.

While waiting for Lauma to return they surveyed the surrounding property, the out-shelters and pens that was in their sight. They also noticed the view from here, which was spectacular. Adding to it was a cool breeze blowing out of the southwest. It was obvious the location of the main shelter had been carefully chosen. Its location gave a commanding view of all the area, and captured whatever breezes blew to help keep it cool in the summer heat. Looking at the pens and out-shelters it was obvious, while old and worn, all were kept in good shape. This showed pride and care. With only the two of them, brother and sister, this meant they were working hard and kept busy almost all the time. From the size of main area they could see that at one time there was a much larger group who worked and lived here.

About that time Lauma returned to the porch and had something for them to drink. "This is some fruit juice we grow and squeeze right here." She told them.

Thanking her they took the drinks and tasted it. "This is pretty good stuff." Doube stated. "You actually do this here? Where do you find the time? From our view there's more work here than what you two can handle."

"At least we have no problem sleeping at night."

"That's an understatement for sure," Doube replied

Fauul followed by saying. "We were told by Aurto that you have the best pack beasts in the region, and we are in need of about three of them. When will your brother return so we can negotiate for our needs?" With that statement, he noticed a change in her; she appeared to be angry for some reason.

There was definitely a storm brewing in her eyes. Then with some emotion she asked, "What is it with you males? I hear it all the time here in the village. Is it so prevalent all through this world? Do you think that females are there only to look pretty and produce whelps for you males? And by the way how did you know my brother was not here right now?"

Taken back by the fury in her voice and her body language, he knew he had stepped on some dangerous ground here. No doubt about it, whoever mated with this female, had better be strong. She obviously would settle for no one other than her equal. "I'm sorry if I offended you, but normally business, especially in these small villages, is handled by the males, and I was assuming it would be the same here. And if your brother had been here we should have seen him by now. It's not that hard to figure out really."

With that statement she relaxed a little. "Sorry, as you can see it is a touchy subject for me. I see no reason for this status quo where the males must handle all this important business. I and others of my sex that I know can do just as good a job, and in some cases better job than you males. In fact, even though many will not admit it, many males get input from their female mates all the time, and I think they are better for it."

A lot of fire in this one, I had better step softly as she is very strong in her views, Fauul thought. "You're probably right, but I do not have a mate, so I can neither confirm nor deny what you say. Let's drop the subject for now. Can you tell me a little about this area and show me the grounds here. Then you can show us the pack beasts. I'll have Doube here do a close inspection, and he will decide which he wants to add to our pack beasts. Sound fair?"

"Fair enough", was her curt reply.

He could see the anger draining away and thought. *I really wouldn't want this one angry with me. She'd tear up a male and put him in his place quickly. And what defense could one provide, since she would consider herself right.* For next couple of hours they looked over the shelters, and pens. She explained a lot of what was going on and what was happening. They noticed again the age of much of what they were viewing, yet all was in good repair. They definitely had pride in what they did, and it reflected everywhere. If what they had been told back in the village was correct these two were having difficult times. Still looking around one would never guess that it was so.

Finally they went to the area where the pack beasts were kept. Even from a distance they could tell these beasts were of quality. No wonder the beast master had bragged about them. Had this property been closer to an area where there was much demand for such as these, the herders would not be lacking for business. He left Doube to find the three for their needs, and with the female he retired back to the living shelter. It would take Doube some time to narrow the beasts down. Probably once that was accomplished, the brother would or should be here or returning from the herds. It was obvious, at this point; they were going to have to stay the night, and then head out early the next morn.

He found himself comparing this female with the ones who were always after him back in the township. There was a quiet strength here that seemed to be lacking in them. While, he had to admit, that many of the township females were beautiful, he was finding as he was around this one that they were not on the same level. Overall he couldn't quite figure it out. Yet, there was something here he didn't understand – not that any male would ever understand the female mind anyway. He really didn't know why he was thinking this way anyway. After all, in a couple of days, they would be back on the trails and heading towards home with very little chance of ever returning to this area again.

When they came into the shelter she excused herself as needing to take care of nature. So this respite gave him a couple of minutes to explore this part of the shelter. Again, the area was well cared for, neat and tidy, but not overly so. It would be a very comfortable place to relax after a day of hard work. He found overall he liked it. Then he saw the four small objects, obviously made of metal. Curious, he went over to them and immediately liked them. About that time she returned and saw him admiring the objects. "What are these things?" He asked.

With a chill in her voice she said. "First of all, let me say they are my brother's, and you will have to ask him when he gets here. Secondly, I should have put those out of sight. Of course we were not expecting anyone, and thirdly it's none of your business." With that she took the one he had in his hand and placed it with the others, and covered them, anger again showing in every movement she made. "You were here to purchase pack beasts right? If that is so, then our private stuff is off limits, understand?"

He couldn't quite understand the coldness in her voice. After all it had been just an idle question – although those items still intrigued him. Well, nothing he could do about that now. He would have to ask the brother. Then trying to smooth over the moment he stated, "Sorry, while I was waiting I was just looking around and saw how neat and comfortable your place is, then these things just caught my eye."

Who is this guy anyway? He is obviously the one in charge, and Doube obviously respects him. And if that is the case then he would be one to demand respect. Yet, he doesn't show the kind of ego of many who are in charge, and seems willing to admit when he makes an error. Those obvious facts intrigued and confused her, leaving her a little more curious about him than she wanted to admit to herself.

This left an awkward moment when the atmosphere seemed a bit uncomfortable and the silence a bit too loud. Finally to break the silence and to get back on solid ground he asked, "Can I have some more of that fruit juice you served earlier? It really is quite good."

She flushed a little realizing he was attempting to smooth over the incident that just had happened. Then realizing that she had probably over reacted a little, she went into the food prep area and brought out some of fruit juice and refilled his glass returning the container from where she had retrieved it. "It probably won't be long until Lauut will be back." And just like that she heard the herding dogs barking in the distance, and knew her brother was almost home. Having his support here right now would be great. She was afraid to admit, even to herself, that she was very uncomfortable with the situation as it stood. Even if these two were exactly as they stated, she, being by herself, left her at a great disadvantage. Even though these two had been here long enough to ease her fears somewhat, it still was a problem. She being smaller and weaker than the two males left her very vulnerable – left her with a nagging fear in her soul. She really did not know them, and in the short time they had been here the fear hadn't lessened. So hearing the returning dogs was a relief. She excused herself from the company of Fauul, and returned to the porch so she could watch the approach of her brother. She quickly signaled and passed on to him, when he was close enough, that they had two visitors – even though the dogs had raised a racket alerting him to strangers. Her signal let him know how many so he would not come in unprepared.

She left the porch walking towards her brother so she could meet him half way and fill him verbally to what was happening. As she left the porch, Fauul watched through a partially open door to see what was transpiring. He could see the brother, and while about the same height as Doube, his build was much slighter. When the sister came close to him, Fauul could definitely see the family resemblance. They could have never denied they were related to each other. Once one saw one, and then later met the other, you would know they were from the same family.

Quickly, as both of them approached the porch, Lauma filled in Lauut about the situation and what these two males' story had been. Lauut could see some relief in his sister's eyes, and knew from her reaction that this had been a serious incident for her.

They had talked about such situations in the past, and what they would possibly do. Yet, in truth, they had never expected it to happen. Still, happen it did. Whispering to Lauma, Lauut said, "Just introduce me to the one down by the corrals first, and then we will walk up and you can introduce me to this leader. At this point you can temporarily excuse yourself . . . maybe something about taking care of the herd dogs or something. You know just long enough to give me a couple of minutes with the leader and see if I agree to how you feel. Then you can come back in and join us. Does that work for you?"

She thought a minute, and said, "No, that'll put us at a disadvantage. Since even for a short period we would be separated, and that could be a bad thing."

"Possibly, but had they wanted to really do harm to both of us, the opportunity was earlier when we were already separated. They would had taken care of you, and then just waited for me to come home being none the wiser."

"True, but I was aware and when they showed up, between the warnings I gave them, and besides Sadie of course, didn't like them anyway. So that might have changed their plans. You know, take care of both of us when they knew where we both are located. Then again, they could be exactly what they say." With the last of the conversation needing to end as they approached the porch Fauul exited the shelter and joined them immediately. "Hi, I'm Fauul, second in command of the team who is mapping the region." Well, so much for their plans on meeting the other first.

The first thing that Doube saw in the pack beasts was good care. As he inspected the beasts he saw they had been gentled properly. The stock was healthy and well bred. He was impressed; indeed they had the best stock in the region. Again, unfortunately for them, it was sparsely populated and the demand would be small. Had they been closer to some of the larger areas they wouldn't have had any difficulties. It was going to be difficult to narrow it down to just three beasts. He saw, in an area where they had not toured, a pen built for training of these beasts. He saw the shelters where they were groomed and kept in bad weather, and the training pen looked well used and well developed. It was obvious there would be little problem with these beasts whichever ones he chose.

His concentration was broken when off in the distance he became aware of the sound of barking dogs. *The brother must be returning from working the herd beasts.* Suddenly he realized that most likely, being a stranger to the dogs would leave him in danger. Quickly he left the pens where he had been inspecting the beasts and headed back to the main living shelter to avoid a confrontation with those dogs. He was just coming around the corner when he saw the sister talking with her brother and approaching the porch, followed by Fauul emerging from the shelter onto the porch. It appeared he would be just behind them and would also make the porch before the dogs, which presently were interested in Fauul, would probably notice him.

So not to make the meeting awkward, Fauul stepped off the porch and offered the standard greeting of open hands, which displayed no weapons, which Lauut returned. Fauul looked up and saw Doube approaching from the pens, and said to Lauut, "Our team scout is behind you coming in from the pens, Lauut this is Doube."

Turning around and seeing Doube approach made him realize that he and his sister were between the two, and had been outflanked. Had they wanted to harm them they could have done it at that moment. Still looking at Doube he could detect nothing hostile. "Doube, I'm Lauut, and I understand my sister has provided some hospitality since you arrived."

Thinking back to their introduction to the property he smiled and said, "You could say that. Would you introduce us to your dogs so they will leave us alone?"

"Where are my manners? Of course." He introduced the two visitors to the pack, which consisted of about ten dogs. The dogs were curious, and loved the attention they received from the newcomers, but when that ended, and they saw no more was coming headed off and started lying around, as dogs generally do.

"If these herd dogs are as well trained as your pack beasts seem to be," Doube stated, "then you must really appreciate them."

"With only the two of us it would be impossible to control the herds without them. Yes we appreciate them a lot, and yes we do train them similarly to our pack beasts. At least in the methods used. We, of course, have no plans to make the dogs beasts of burden."

"I wouldn't think so. Not while you have such fine beasts anyway."

"Okay, Lauma wasn't able to fill me in on everything, so why are you here? I know you stated you needed some pack beasts, but as she told you, this way of obtaining them is really unusual."

"As I told your sister, we would have been in your village, which was expecting us by the way, during the gather, but we were delayed and did not arrive when planned. We also are in need of continuing before the next gather so this was the only solution."

"As you probably know there's a small gang of bandits working the region, and your method of entrance would be a way to get inside."

"Aurto never mentioned anything about that. Had we known we would have sent an advance runner, or something."

"So you met Aurto huh?"

"How else would we have gotten those fine directions to locate you anyway?" Fauul asked.

"Well, if you had been that bandit gang, you would have known where we are, and probably have scouted us out."

Shaking his head Fauul said, "Boy you have an answer for everything don't yah."

"When you work the land as we do, it kind of forces you to plan and hope what you plan is right – then and if not to adjust quickly."

"I agree with that, since working this project for over the last turn, I have had to make quick adjustments to avoid or solve one problem or another."

"So Doube, what has your inspection shown?"

"These pack beasts are definitely some of the best I've ever seen. The difficulty will be in narrowing it down to three, and, of course, setting a price." The four of them sat in the chairs that were on the covered porch.

"I guess before we go any farther," Fauul asked, "will accept the marks I have for payment? Before you answer they were accepted in your village for payment for the lodging and other services we require – which reminds me, I saw some small objects inside. I think about four, made of metal. Your sister took the one I had in my hand back and then covered them saying they belonged to you."

"Yeah, what about it? They were something I, or we found. I think with a little work I might be able to find more of them."

"Well, I like them. Is there any way I could barter, purchase, or negotiate for one of them? And if not I would at least like to get another look at them if you would let me."

His sister shot him a warning glance, and a non-verbal suggestion that he say no. Yet, they were in a desperate need, and even though knowing they would sell three of their pack beasts for a fair price, it would still be tight. So any additional funds he could bring in would help. Sending a slight shrug to his sister, he turned back to Fauul and said, "Sure, I will at least let you have a closer inspection. Still, I haven't really had these things very long, and hadn't decided what I will do with them to be truthful." Lauut arose from his chair on the porch and entered the shelter, picked up the basket they were in, and returned to the porch. He sat down and handed the basket to Fauul who was sitting next to him, and waved at Fauul to go ahead and look over the objects. "I really don't know what they are. As you can see they are small, and made of some type of metal. Yet, overall, they are light and seem to be well made. While I've spent my whole life in this area, I don't believe we can make anything like them. Since you have seen much more of this world than I, do you agree?"

Before answering Fauul did a close inspection of the objects. Everything Lauut said was true. They were compact and well made, and two had engravings on them with some kind of script. One of the images even looked like a partial map, and he should know, as it was his business. The second with engravings on it, appeared to have some kind of symbol, which he did not recognize. "The workmanship is definitely fine. No, I don't think I've ever seen anything like these."

Taking the one with what appeared to have the engraved map on it Lauut stated. "This was the first one I found. After cleaning it up we found it opened like this." Which he demonstrated, "Inside, and oh, did you notice these fine hinges? Ah, inside is this and then it pulls out to reveal a screw and a packed space – still haven't figured what they were used for. It's definitely a mystery."

Doube was now becoming curious himself, and asked if he could inspect one. Lauut immediately passed one to him. While this was taking place Lauma excused herself, and went inside to start preparing a meal – leaving the males to their discussions and inspections of the unknown objects. She knew this would take some time, and right now she just wasn't interested. She knew her brother was proud of these found objects, but to show them to strangers was beyond her. She still had her suspicions, yet that Fauul intrigued her more than she wanted to admit even to herself. She realized that she had finally met a male who was not set in stone in the ways he viewed things. Still he would be gone in a few days, so it was nothing to get too worked up over that was for sure.

She got a small fire going in the cooking stove and heated water for some hot beverages, and when it was ready, proceeded to take the drinks out to the males. Who, it seemed, were still in deep discussion as to what these objects were and where they may have originated. Looking up from their discussion when she came back out, they took their drinks, thanked her and returned to the discussion. Shaking her head she said, "May I interject something here? You know these things could really be from those mysterious *ones before*. I'm sure you all have considered it, but maybe you haven't got around to saying it."

Fauul looked up at her, and said, "It was a thought since where I come from, even in the large township where I live, there isn't anything to compare to these simple but ingenious devices. Still, things have been found in the past that were believed to have come from them only to have been proved to have been made by us sometime in the past, and really, these items could be no different."

"True, Lauut it's getting late, can you come in and assist me in the fixing of this evening meal, and since we have two guests, you need to show them the shelter where they can spend the night before they head out on the morrow."

"Right, right. Okay you two, let's head over to that one out-shelter as it is used for the times when we can afford to hire workers. After you get settled in you can come back up here to the main shelter and we'll eat. Sound fair? Then after the repast we can discuss the final points of our business deal with the pack beasts."

Later in the evening when both Fauul and Doube were resting in the provided shelter, they looked back on the day and felt that overall it had been successful. The business with the herders was complete and the herders had not taken advantage of them by charging exorbitant prices for their pack beasts. Something they could have easily done knowing the needs of the outsiders, and the chances of them ever returning here, small.

"You know that female is a very interesting person. If I were looking for a mate, she would definitely be on my list," Doube said. "No air head there, real down to earth."

"Yes, but very opinionated and head strong. I must admit she has my interest. After all, I didn't think too much about it until she smiled. It was like lighting a candle in the night, all that inner beauty and health just radiated out. Still, as I've said earlier, it's no doubt she has all these local males cowering. No, never have met a female like her that's for sure."

Smiling at his boss, Doube could tell that this female had bothered Fauul much more than he was willing to admit. Changing the subject he asked, "So you were able to talk him out of one of those objects huh?"

"Yes, but it really wasn't the one I wanted. Being a cartographer I wanted the one that had what appeared to be a map engraved on it, but had to settle for the other engraved one."

At that point they both fell silent, as both were tired. It had been a very busy and profitable day. They felt they had friends here. Both brother and sister were hardworking people, and very honest in their dealings. It had been too bad that disaster had befallen them, and placed them in the present difficult situation. Yet, given time they would probably come out okay.

After the two of them left for the worker's shelter Lauma and Lauut went to the eating area and cleaned up. With the guests leaving in the morn, with their beasts, it would make for a very busy morn. "You know sis, I was watching you all night, while our guests were here, and you could not keep your eyes off of that Fauul. So does he interest you or something?"

"Well you must admit he is easy on the eyes. He's just a mystery to me. I mean he is obviously, from the reaction of Doube, the one in charge. Yet, there is none of the 'I'm in charge' feel about him. It seems that he earns their respect, and doesn't demand it."

"Now sis, I know there is more to it than that. But, I do have to agree. I have never met one in charge who acts the way he does."

"And what do you mean by that?" She said as she put her hands on her hips. "I was just trying to be friendly to our guests. After all they left us a lot of marks behind for our beasts, and you selling him one of your prizes were a surprise."

"If you say so," he answered teasingly. "It's not too late, since you were only being neighborly, to see if they would like another cup of that hot beverage before they retire. I know we do. We especially like to drink it there on the porch before we retire. Maybe they would like to join us . . ." With a smile on his face he asked, "Or maybe just you and him?"

She flushed a little and replied, "And what is that supposed to mean?"

"Oh come on, it was obvious to both Doube and me that you two were eyeing each other all night long. Even though both of you tried to hide it."

"I was not!"

"Were too."

"So what if I was. He's heading back to the village in the morn, and within a couple of days or so will be heading back to his home. I probably won't see him again anyway. Besides, someone with those kinds of looks probably has many females to choose from back in his township. Plus having some position of power seems to attract them like flies to fertilizer anyway."

Laughing Lauut looked at his sister and repeated, "Do you want to invite them out, or shall I?"

"No, I like the time on the porch here at the end of the day with just myself or the two of us. It has been a tradition for us. I remember our sires doing it when we were just whelps. I didn't understand it then, but I really do now."

"True, I didn't understand, back then, when they did it either. It seemed so boring. How can one enjoy, night after night, going out on that porch and just sit there? I have to agree with you, it has become our tradition, so let's keep it private. Let's finish here so we can do that."

"The morrow will come soon enough as it is, bro. So let's call a truce on this teasing about males and females and just finish off the rest of the evening right. I'm finding I'm tired anyway – since the day had its share of tension in it."

"Agreed, truce, and yes it did didn't it?" Lauut knew that while he liked to tease his sister, and what brother didn't, he only wanted the best for her. Even though she had her share of suitors, none had interested her. Then, as if ordained, a male shows up who really piqued her interest. And while he was no expert on the female mind, he felt that it had affected her on all levels. Too bad he would be leaving, and most likely never to return. Still, who knew what the morrow would bring? As he remembered their sires saying, "The future is not ours to know. It really isn't something we can control or are even allowed a peek. We can guess, and yet we get it wrong more than right. So let this time, this day, be all we worry and deal with. The morrow will bring its own problems and needed solutions."

They headed out to the porch and sat down and began unwinding, each within their own thoughts. So much had happened in the last cycle, and things appeared to be moving faster and faster. It was another thing their elders had left them with. "As you age the days appear to be shorter and shorter. Yet, they in themselves do not change. It is you, who have grown older, with more responsibilities, with more knowledge, with the lessons that are given each day, with more having to be accomplished, in those same hours. So the days and cycles and turns start to appear shorter. Then, before you know it you are an elder with whelps grown with their own whelps. You wonder how did you ever get here so fast? After all, it was only yesterday, and you were playing in the yard, dreaming of what your future would be like, and then in a blink of your eye it is all gone, all in the past." Still, here they were now, both without mates, still trying to keep their life of land, and work, alive and afloat. Yes, it was a wonderful time to be able to sit here and just let the quiet evening to soak into their very being and let the worries of the day flow away.

Lauut, looking over to his sister said, "You know while I was teasing you inside, this is the first male you've looked at with more than a passing interest. I know he's leaving on the morrow, so what really are your feelings here?"

"I really don't know truthfully. He intrigues me, leaves me curious. Even when I had challenged him earlier today, there was, even then, something drawing me to him. I really have no answers really. But, does it really matter anyway?"

"And what do you mean by that sis?"

"You know that answer. On the morrow he and Doube will collect their pack beasts and head back to the village. Then after getting the remaining information from there, pack up and head back to where they originated. Then he will never be back here again. Most likely he has some female waiting for him back where he's from anyway. When one has his looks and personality he probably has no lack of female companionship. After all, all I am is a not so pretty outback female, who could probably not compete with those sophisticated females from the township where he lives and works."

"There you go again sis. When will you ever realize that when the right one comes along, whatever was in the past will not matter? I know it sounds trite, but I have been told over and over again that when the right one comes along you will know it. You may have thought others from your past filled that bill, but when it is the right one you feel it right down to your toes. Again, as usual, you are much too hard on yourself. Yes there are much prettier females out there, but many times that's all they have to offer, their beauty. That in itself will never support a relationship for very long. Sophistication is just a view, and your inner beauty and strength alone is worth more than any sophisticate out there."

A little awed at her brother's response, and a little humbled, she replied. "I didn't know that you had really thought this out. I just thought, like in the past, you were carefree and wanting adventure, with little thought of the future, and of relationships, and of life. Yet, what you have just stated shows I was wrong. You are much deeper than I have thought you were, and for that I apologize for thinking so shallow of you."

"Ah, don't worry about it sis. It's a part of me that I've hidden, even from myself. And, I'm really surprised at myself for speaking so much on this subject tonight. Yet, it felt right, and it makes me realize that I, like you, am on the same quest to find someone who can share my life. Not, that you don't do it. Yet, soon, and maybe sooner than you or I have thought, you will leave to fulfill your destiny and leave me alone – which is as it should be. When that day comes I will be extremely happy for you, but sad for me as another part of our lives will have changed with no way to go back, to relive, or to retrace."

They both fell silent for a while, again deep within their own thoughts thinking about what had just been said, enjoying each other's company. Something about sitting here in the evening with that full moon and quiet soft breezes that just left one introspective. "Well sis, it has been a long day in its way, and I for one, am ready to turn it in. The morrow will come soon enough."

"Okay, go ahead; I'm going to stay just a little longer. I have some more thinking to do, and I feel I do my best thinking here in the evenings."

"Know what you mean . . ." With a sigh he got up and went back inside leaving Lauma there thinking, and staring out into the night.

* * *

As Lauut thought, the next morn came around much too soon. Yet, when one had responsibilities, you had to take care of them. With a yawn, he got up, took care of the morning's nature call, and proceeded into the food prep area. He realized he had that dream again about the cavern with many exits, and no apparent way out. Looking around he saw the hot beverage was sitting there, which meant that Lauma was already up, and from the looks of it for quite a while. Curious, he went to the window and looked out towards the beast shelters and pens. Since it was predawn, it was difficult to see anything. Yet, it appeared she was leaning on one of the rails deep in thought.

Grabbing a cup of the beverage, he headed out to see what might be happening. She turned at his approach and smiled at him. "Hey, and good morn brother," she said softly.

With a questioning look in his eyes he said, "Good morn sis, why out here this early? And from the looks of it you've been up for a while."

"They've left," was her sad reply.

"Before sunrise? It's almost impossible to see anything at all right now, so how did you know?"

"You know I'm a light sleeper, and I heard some unusual noises that awoke me. I looked out and saw or rather sensed something going on down here. So I got up and dressed quickly and came out to see what was going on." She paused staring out into the semi darkness.

"Continue please."

"When I came out the door I could hear them talking and preparing for their return to the village. So I came out and talked with them briefly, and suggested that as a host I should at least give them some hot beverage before they left, which they said they would gratefully accept. So I came back in and prepared it. I then called out to them saying it was ready. We spent a short period of time enjoying the drink on the porch, and they thanked me and left."

"Wow, I must have been more tired than I thought. With all that happening I didn't hear it at all. Did they tell you anything at all?"

"Just that they would be in the village area for a few more days, and then return to where they are from, and that they needed to get back early today with so much still to accomplish before they left . . . you know something, even though I've only been around Fauul a short time, I miss him. Can't explain it, but I do."

Not knowing what to say he shrugged, put his arms around her, and just stood there. Quietly he said, "Come on back into the shelter sis, we have a full day ahead of us too. Who knows, your paths may cross again, especially if it is supposed to be that way."

She looked at him and gave him a small sad smile and then followed him back into shelter.

* * *

As they were heading down the trail back to the village Fauul looked over these new additions to the team. These beasts were magnificent, and very gentle. No doubt these herders had some of the best stock he had ever seen. Not that he was an expert, but on this journey he had seen many, and these were superior to any he had an occasion to come across. "So Doube, what's your opinion, at least initially of these beasts?"

"Well, none better, in fact I've not seen any better. They could have asked much more for them than they did – real honest folks, kind of refreshing really. Since so many, when they learned of our project and who was paying for supplies, wanted to charge us way too much."

"True, it sure seems to bring out the greed in many people. I wonder what is going to happen to her."

"Who? Oh her . . . are you going sweet on that poor outback female? You who can have any female you want. I mean I've personally seen how all those females have pined after you."

"True, but it does make it difficult to get past the distractions they throw your way. I don't know . . . she was . . . well different, and even though nothing was really said between us, and she did not even attempt to throw her female wiles my way, I find I miss her. I know it's crazy, I have seen her for what, less than a day. Oh well, enough on this, I guess."

It was close to the zenith when they re-entered the village. From there they went over to the pens, looked up Aurto Satrneze and put the new pack beasts in with the others so they could become aquatinted. It was better for them to work out their differences here than on the trail. They then took the equipment back to the hostel shelter, checked back in, and went to the local public eating shelter as it was now past the zenith. They had taken the trip back slowly to become familiar with the new beasts so there would be no surprises.

As usual, the local female table server was eyeing him, and while in the past it made him smile to himself that he could have this kind of an effect on females, it now only irritated him. Thinking about it he began to wonder what had brought about this change. Before he had time to dwell on it Joellie showed up and sat down at their table, "Heard you had returned. When you are finished here I need you and Doube to swing around the outskirts of this village, and find out some additional local information on the surrounding countryside. I'm sending Jahmes with you so that he can ask any questions you may miss. He'll also do a rough sketch and see if anyone you are talking to can add or change what he interprets."

Fauul looked up from his meal and said, "Come on Joellie, we just got back in, and I haven't had time to even process the paperwork for the transactions from the herders yet."

"Speaking of that how did that go?" I haven't gone down to see what you ended up with – pretty busy really."

Sure you are, Fauul thought, but said, "All went well, and the beasts are some of the best Doube has ever seen."

"Okay, file your paperwork, then pick up the artist and at least get some of it done. I would like to be out of here and on our way back by the seventh day of this fourth." With that Joellie got up and headed back out to wherever he felt he needed to go.

Shaking his head and looking at Doube, he said, "So much for the pleasantness, he sure can ruin a meal."

Laughing Doube said, "True, but at least by being away from here we won't have to deal with him for a little while."

"You know, I like your attitude, and that does kind of lift the clouds off of it doesn't it."

Laughing lightly Doube nodded. "Let's finish our meal, go take care of the paperwork, and get out of here."

"Just take your time; I think I want to go back over to the beast-master's place . . . Another ale would just settle this meal for me."

"And you expect me to argue?"

Laughing out loud he said, "No not really, but it is kind of a tough decision, whether to get out of here away from Joellie, or go get that ale."

"You're kidding right?"

"Yup, I'm kidding, right."

* * *

The next few days went by rapidly as they collected the information from the locals. Once Joellie was satisfied with what they had, he announced that on the morrow they would be leave and be on the final leg of the return trip – that was if the weather would cooperate. They had been hearing and seeing thunderstorms. So far the storms had continued to be isolated remaining close to the mountains. Still each day they had become more severe becoming much larger in size.

They went ahead, the night before departure, and packed everything and confirmed all was ready. They had plans on getting an early start, and make the coast by late morn. From there the trail north should be wide and easy. It was almost a time to relax. Not too much though. Since this was a well-traveled known trail from the coast out, the dangers would be greatly reduced. The only worries at this point were the new beasts, since these had never traveled aboard a watercraft, and even as well trained as they were, there was a chance that they would be very nervous, as any of the beasts that had never been on the water before had a tendency to be.

The next morn as they looked out, it was dark and ominous. The storm clouds had started forming in the night, and by morn promised an uneasy day. It was obvious they were not going to leave today. The rumbling and darkness of the sky promised real danger to any traveler who ventured out in the open. With the initial disappointment, they settled down to wait out the storm. And they didn't have long to wait as the skies opened up with heavy rain, winds and lightning. If one went out in it they would be soaked immediately, and if one, when outside, attempted to talk to another it was not heard. If something was not tied down, it was blown around, as if the winds were playing catch. Even the buildings shook from the force of both the winds and rain. Inside it raised such a din that it was difficult to carry on any conversation.

So they were left mostly to themselves feeling more like trapped wild beasts. It was hoped that once the storm had blown itself out that the trails would still be passable. Secretly both Fauul and Doube were glad they were not in the desert right now. It had to be full of flash floods.

As the team lazed around he thought about that female he had met, and that reminded him of that object he had bartered for. So he dug it out of his personal belongings and did a closer inspection. He had seen many objects, in the township he was from, offered for sale. Yet, none seemed to have such fine detail as this object. What the heck was it anyway? How was it constructed? Just as Lauut had said, those hinges were small well-made and strong. Whenever it was made, because of the fine work in the engraving, it must have been very expensive when new. Even the metals it was constructed of seemed light, strong and unknown to him, a real mystery for sure.

With a thorough inspection he did begin to wonder if this might have been from those mythological *ones before*. As far as he knew there had been nothing ever found that could be attributed to these unknown people. With nothing concrete ever found and just the legends and myths that had been passed down from generation to generation, these *ones before* seemed more fiction than real. Yet here in his hand could be the proof. When he got back he would need to show it to someone to get his or her opinion – well maybe.

The storm continued throughout the day and well into the night, making it uncomfortable and difficult to sleep. Yet, eventually the fury of the storm played out and when they arose the next morn it was gone. They packed up, got everything together, and left. Knowing now, with this storm, which had just passed, that the trails would be dangerous, and at some points impassible, but they all were eager to head out. If the truth be told, they were on the final leg back home. That by itself was a wonderful thought, word, and a valid reason not to delay.

* * *

The next two cycles passed quickly and without incident. It was a time, while on the water-craft, to organize and update all the information they had collected over the past turn plus a couple of cycles. It had been hard work, and yet at the same time rewarding. They all saw country they would never would have had the opportunity if not for the project. It showed them just how large this continent was. Still, at the same time, as a physical map developed within their minds, the land became smaller – a definite paradox for sure. And over the time of being involved with translating other projects into workable maps the same had happened. It seemed that as one filled in the missing pieces that the map in the mind would shrink with each new addition or section being added. In a sense it was like being one of those flyers of prey. All of a sudden it would open up in one's mind and points of entry and exit would connect and a very sharp image would emerge.

It was entering fall when they left the water-craft and headed inland towards the main township. One felt it in the air. In the morn there was a bite to the air, a crispness that said soon the snow and rains would be coming. They knew that with what was left to travel; they would barely beat out the beginning of the coming winter – a good time to be back, in reality. The winter was a great time to work on indoor projects, and here, with all the other teams coming in, would be more work than any one team could handle into the unknown future.

Thinking about it, they knew there would be much story telling between the different teams, and of course, plenty of descriptions of the surrounding country they had traveled. Yet, even with the end coming and the anticipation of this future, Fauul's mind continued to return to that last village and that female . . . *What was her name – yes it's Lauma.* He didn't quite understand why she had left such an impression on him. After all they had only met, and in a not so friendly way, truthfully. Still, her demeanor, and her ability to be self-sufficient had impressed him – so different from any of the females he usually dealt with. He wondered how she was getting on.

Soon they were on familiar ground and in the distance they saw the township. One felt the anticipation of finally being back. It ran like a lightning bolt through them all. Unconsciously they picked up the pace. With the end so close it was unanimously decided to skip the zenith meal and simply push through. Halfway between the zenith and evening they arrived, checked in, had the beasts turned over to the yards, and turned in the initial paperwork. They followed this by putting the paperwork into the storage area that had been set up for the teams. When all had been accomplished it was well after dark, and since none had eaten they went as a group to one of the eateries, had a final meal as a team. On the morrow, they would be together as a team for the last time. Here in the meetings, they'd relate what was found, costs, etcetera. After this, they would meet only when something needed a better explanation, and only then would the team be called in as a team. Still, these meetings were rare, and as time continued, the members would be scattering to other assignments and become unavailable.

Before this assignment had begun he had heard rumors of the personality of Joellie and was quite happy that their paths rarely crossed. He usually put little credence into what one said about another worker, yet after being with him for the past turn, he realized that all those rumors turned out to be quite true. Well, at least here he would never have to work with or for Joellie again. And if assignments came up in the future he would definitely avoid getting assigned with him. Most of the ones he worked with on this project were great, especially Doube, who had a unique gift of becoming part of whoever or whatever group or project he was involved with. Enough on that it was time to get back into the work assignments here.

He found himself carrying that object he had bartered off of Lauut. It fit comfortably in one's pocket. Unconsciously he would find himself handling it, and idly opening and closing it, and listening to its clicking sound. Then one of his bosses saw him handling the object and was curious about it. He had worked for Bihl for many cycles and they had become friends.

"Hey, Fauul," Bihl asked, "what is that thing you have in your hand?"

Fauul had been looking over some of the work they had performed on the assignment and had been unaware he had the object in his hand and was unconsciously opening and closing it. He was in deep concentration, and hadn't realized he had been spoken too. Then all of a sudden he realized someone was looking at him intently, and looked up to see who it was, asking, "Bihl, do you need something?"

"No, just curious that's all. What is that thing you have in your left hand there?"

Realizing that he had the object in his hand he looked up and said. "It's just something I bartered off a local down in that last remote village. He had four of these objects, all the same but all different. I just happened to like them and was able to get one. Not the one I really wanted, but this one isn't bad. Haven't figured out what it is but whatever it is, it's comfortable to carry and easy handle. I find myself doing that, handling it that is, quite often, and not realizing I'm doing it."

"Can I have a look at it, if you don't mind?"

"Sure, no problem . . . From what I have seen it appears to be pretty rugged. And while I'm sure you could break it if you tried, I believe you would have to really try." Tossing it to Bihl he let him have a closer look at it. Fauul got up from where he was working and went over to him and started pointing out the details of the object.

After a while, Bihl commented that the object was too fine to have been constructed by any artisan he knew of. Just the hinges themselves were beyond their ability. Not that they didn't know how to make hinges, after all, it was a well-known process. But, he had never seen so small and finely made hinges. The metal was one piece and light, yet seemed very strong. Again something they couldn't produce. If that wasn't enough, the engraving was something he had never seen before. The lettering, while the same they used, yet the words were unknown. "You know

Fauul, this thing could be the proof the "Keepers of the Past" have been looking for."

"What do you mean?"

"Well from my unpracticed eye, I would say that this object might have come from our legendary *ones before*."

"Oh, come on. It was something I thought about, but these *ones before*, are no more than myth and legend. No more real than the stories our elders and sires told us to keep us in line when we were whelps."

"That may be true, but I think you need to take this over to the 'Keepers of the Past', and at least let them look at it. They can tell you whether it was made by someone in our time, or may be actually something very old."

"Tell you what, I'll think on it. I didn't barter for this thing just to lose it to those record keepers, so someone else could claim it as their own."

"Okay, but think on it, and if you change your mind, I will put you in contact with one of them."

"Sounds fair enough to me." With the completion of the conversation he took the object back, and placed it into his pocket. *I've got to be more careful about showing this thing off,* he thought.

For the next cycle Bihl continued to ask if he would like to have someone who he knew from the other department look at the object. Finally tired of hearing it from his friend he asked, "Why are you so adamant on me showing this thing off? It was only a whim that I got the thing anyway. You make me almost sorry I did."

"Don't take it that way. You know yourself that most of the time discoveries are made by accident, and usually not by the ones who are trying to make the discoveries. Remember that it's our past that points us towards our future. While it is important not to dwell on the past, it is still our history; it's what makes us, well us. What would it hurt to have them look at it, and then one way or the other it would be identified. Isn't that important in itself?"

"Yeah, I guess you're right. Go ahead and set up a meeting, and I will show him this thing . . . then will you forget about it?" Smiling a little he added, "I did consider it as a possibility, but there has been so many things thought to have been from the *ones before*, only to be proven later to be a fake. I figure this, while not presented to me as something from those myths, to have been made by some distant ancestor of ours. Then, whatever skills they had, being lost in the passing of time."

"I know what you mean. We have no idea what our distant ancestors knew or what their skills were. At times, when day dreaming, I have thought that we may have lost some great skills in our past, but really, I don't know what they might have been."

"True, it might have been that way. With the way families and clans protect what they know; it would be easy to lose something or at least to lose methods to make something when some tragedy befalls a group. I think that it makes it more difficult to advance something also. An example of this that I can think of is a sister and brother who are herders. The beasts they create there with their breeding and care is unmatched. Yet, they are the last of their line. Their sires were killed in a tragic accident when they were younglings. It happened before everything was passed on to them. So while they are still doing an excellent job, I'm sure they lost something that had yet to be taught to them."

With a faraway look in his eyes Bihl said, "Hmmm, good example, and I'm sure you have it right. Okay, I'll contact Jehm in the "Keepers of the Past" area. He would be the one to do the inspection anyway."

"Why?"

"He has been the expert, and has uncovered most of the fraud and fakes. So if this is in that category, or maybe just something from our past, he will have a good idea about it."

With the conversation over Fauul started thinking about that female again. For whatever the reason he could not get her out of his mind. Since he had returned he had been out with a number of the local females, but they seemed shallow and completely uninteresting. He had only been around Lauma, what, that one day, yet she seemed more complete in his mind than any of these here. Why her? What was it that kept drawing him back, and did she harbor any feelings for him? The overall time together really had truly been brief. It would be far better to forget about her. Still, he had tried, and so far it had not worked, no, it had not worked at all.

CHAPTER NINE

After Fauul and Doube left Lauut felt elated. While the last turn had been a lean one for them, at least now, with the sale of those three pack beasts to the mapping team, they would have enough to last another turn, especially if they were careful with the funds. Trading one of his objects had been a bonus. It was not planned, and in reality he had not truly thought in that direction. Eventually he knew he would go back down in that cavern and do a more thorough search – Plus there were a number of areas that needed to be roped off for safety. Turning to his sister he said, "That was a fortuitous meeting. I must admit at first, I didn't know what to think. One never does this kind of business in one's shelter. It is always traditionally done at the gathers. What's your overall impression?"

"You're asking me, a female?" she responded angrily.

He knew that this had always been a touchy subject for his sister, yet there seemed more to it than just her view of the injustice of making the female less. For a second at loss for words he asked. "Where did that come from?"

"Oh, just leave me alone for now", was all she said as she left quickly without another word and headed for her sleeping space, closing the door, leaving him standing there.

Not knowing what to do, he stood for a moment and eventually headed outside. Maybe, just maybe she needed some time to herself. He'd go out and do the morn work, and once finished, come back and see how she was doing.

She had no idea what had come over her. She wasn't mad at her brother, even though it must have sounded like it to him. And once in her area, she began to cry, and she didn't even know why. *What's happening with me?* After all, other than that unusual transaction and confrontation, everything was normal. Yet, deep within herself she knew it wasn't. She was going to have to admit to herself that that male Fauul had affected her far more than any male had ever affected her. Yes, he was attractive, and tall. She shook her head, and thought. *Now doesn't this sound like those romantic stories females like to pass around?* She wondered if her mother had had feelings like this when she met her mate and their sire. Unfortunately, with her not being around, she had no one to ask. One thing for sure she couldn't talk to her brother about it. He was a male, and probably wouldn't understand female emotions at all. This brought a smile inwardly because she knew that many times, other females didn't understand them either. It just seemed like her world had just been turned over, and she had to learn to walk all over again.

She thought of her childhood friends, but realized that too much time had passed, and she did not even know if those past friendships still existed. She suddenly realized that after the death of their sires, she and her brother pretty much isolated themselves from the rest of the village. They had buried themselves into the upkeep of the property and the beasts isolating themselves even from their friends. It was something, in the beginning, for which they had little choice. But, as time went on, this life style just kind of took over. Yes, when they went to the village, they both had many casual friends, acquaintances – yet neither had that close friend in which to confide. Now she was regretting it, since having a close female friend to help her sort out what she was feeling and thinking would be exactly what she really needed.

Well, no reason to dwell on it, she thought as she dried her red eyes, *and these feelings, it's probably one way anyway. He's gone, and there's nothing I can do to change it. So get over it female.* Still, looking back, there definitely seemed to be a spark between them, or had she imagined it? Shaking her head she quietly said, "Now stop this. There isn't one thing you can do. Get on with your life." *Yeah, if it was only that simple,* she thought. Yet, why should it be? As a whelp things appeared to be so much easier – simpler. The elders hid so much of what was real from them. So, her early beliefs said that being an elder herself was something she wanted. They appeared to be able to do just what they wanted, and when they wanted. Such freedoms were something, as a whelp, one didn't have.

Then you grew up and found that with those supposed freedoms came many more responsibilities with hard, and at times, impossible decisions. Then you wished you were a whelp again when these things were hidden. So, she thought. *The circle is complete – as a whelp wishing to be an elder, and as an elder wishing for the simple times and hidden truths of a whelp.* She started thinking back on that time and immediately her two friends from the past came to mind. Yes, it had been too many turns since she had seen either of them, but she desperately needed to talk with another female about what was happening to her. Thinking about it she remembered that Traylu had mated with the village healer, and would probably be available there at their shelter. As, she remembered,

Traylu was the shy one, but at the same time saw much or was aware of more than she and Sooma. Sooma, on the other hand, had mated the local merchant and probably would be working at the mercantile with Franc, her mate. With those final thoughts she made up her mind, she was going into the village and see if she, Sooma, and Traylu might renew their lost friendships, and then they would talk. If she didn't get this solved it was going to eat at her for a long, long time.

Lauut could see that something was really bothering his sister but didn't know quite what to do. One thing for sure, he knew that on an emotional basis she would never confide in him. It just seemed that the females needed to talk with each other, and leave the males out of it. In many ways, it seemed to be a big conspiracy, they against the males. Well . . . at least in appearance anyway. He noticed, in mates, that some worked well together. They were united and very much attached to each other. While others it was nothing but one battle to another. Why this was so he didn't know. Again, since he had yet to find a female whom he felt would be the one for him; he probably would not have any answers at all.

He remembered a friend who once said, "You know there are plenty of females out there I probably could love, and I don't mean that in the physical sense – even though that is a wonderful thought – but you cannot build a relationship on that alone. And just because I could deeply love this female or that female, doesn't mean that I could live with them or them with me. You must find that balance where you meet, each of you, on all levels, spirit, physical, mental, and etcetera. Everything is important. Remember it's you and she against the outside world, and if you do not stand together, in the end you both lose."

He thought that the statement had been quite profound and had remembered it. Well, enough on this for now, the work needed to be done, and he had better get at it. Of, course while he worked it gave him additional time to work on problems. *Just as long as I remember to concentrate on what I am doing so I don't hurt myself,* he reminded to himself.

At this point Lauma came back out and joined him in the morn chores. But, he could tell that her mind wasn't on the tasks at hand. One thing for sure, Lauma was quite distracted, and appeared to be just going through the motions. Even to the point, at times, of starting to say something and then stop in the middle. But as the days and time continued, these episodes became briefer, and slowly he had his sister back as she was before the arrival of Fauul and Doube. It appeared that finally she had made some type of decision. Although that trip into the village was a surprise. She told him that she would be going, and when she returned it had been obviously therapeutic.

She was gone a full day, and when she returned she appeared to be more relaxed, and more her old self. "So, who'd you visit there in the village?" He asked. But all she said was, "To see an old friend or two that's all." Then she'd smile slightly, and have a faraway look in her eyes. Well, she looked fine, and overall it wasn't his business anyway. So he just chalked it up to another thing males would never understand about females.

* * *

The trip to the village had been worthwhile that's for sure. When she finally made her decision, she let Lauut know, and then left that next morn. When she arrived in the mid-morn she went to the mercantile and to her surprise found both her old whelp friends inside and talking about something. At first shy about interrupting and undecided she stood and looked longingly at them. Eventually one noticed her, and realized who it was and asked her what she was doing. She had replied she had come in to talk with them if they would permit. The response had been overwhelming. "Permit! What do you mean by that? We were great friends before that terrible accident, and at some point we were hoping you would come back. After all, you know how important it is for us females to stick together. I just figured our friendships would last a life time."

Blushing a little, she thought. *That Sooma has never been afraid to speak her mind; I'll give her that.* Then she responded softly, "It's really more than I had hoped." She looked from face to face, and saw both were smiling at her, and beckoning her over to join them, which she happily did.

For the rest of that day they caught up on the time since they had been separated, and as the day progressed it felt to her like they had never broken that old link from when they were whelps. Why had she waited so long to renew these old friendships? The answer really was simple, truthfully life had a tendency to get into the way, and the day-to-day small emergencies always seemed to push back what one really wanted or needed to do. Then the days turn into cycles, which turn into turns, and before long, too many turns had passed without being aware or seeing it happen. As evening approached she regretfully said her good byes, and knew that she indeed had friends for life with these two. Still with the evening approaching she had a long ways to travel, and if she left right now she would arrive back on the property just before dark.

* * *

Lauut knew when his sister left in the morn she had much on her mind. It had shown itself in the distractions as if she was somewhere else, with a far off and into the distance look in her eyes, at times. He hoped this trip to the village, for whatever the reasons, would help. He knew how much he needed her here to help. Plus, since that accident, they had been very close, and what was happening to her right now, being so out of character, that it left him worried. While she was gone he would be doing double duty, but each had done that for each other in the past. It just stretched the day out a little longer. Still, with her gone, he missed the companionship, and as evening approached he began to worry, since she had yet to make an appearance. As he was finishing up the day's work he found himself continually looking towards the entrance gate, and listening. He really did not like it when she went to the village alone. Even though, overall, it was safe to make the trek alone, there were dangers, and more so for a female alone. Yet, since this was more a spur of the moment thing, he could not go, as it took planning to leave together – it really sounded like she did not want him along anyway.

As dusk approached, and objects were starting to become indistinct, he thought he heard the gate open and close. He strained his eyes trying to make out any movement at the gate, but it was too dark. So, he decided to walk towards the gate, and as he approached he could make out the indistinct figure someone walking towards him. He could tell from the walk that it was Lauma and let out a sigh of relief. "You know that I worry about you when you make those treks to village by yourself."

"Yeah, I know," she said softly. "But, this was one I really needed to do, and I'm glad I really did go. Shall we go up to the shelter, I'm really tired." Then she said nothing else.

"Sure, I just finished up and was getting ready to head that way myself." Curious, he knew better than to ask. If she wanted to let him in on what happened in the village she would do it in her own time.

* * *

Fauul came in for his usual workday only to find that Bihl had made the appointment for him to see Jehm in the Keepers of the Past section. The appointment was after the zenith meal, so once he completed his visit with this Jehm he would consider it a complete workday and head back to his personal shelter, an apartment a short distance from his working place. With all the work they had brought back from their portion of the mapping, the morn went quickly. Before he knew it, it was time to have the zenith meal, and when finished headed, with some nervousness, over to the records section where the Keepers of the Past worked. In truth the place he was heading was not close and would take some time for him to arrive. In fact it would be between zenith and evening before he did. Fortunately, after finishing this meeting it would be a shorter distance to his shelter since he lived in this direction anyway.

He arrived at the facility and was directed by an underling into a research area where this Jehm did his work. At first the space appeared to be empty. Yet, it was hard to tell, as everywhere he looked were stacks and stacks of documents and items – leaving very little open space to be able to place any additional items anywhere. Plus, to add to the confusion, there were only narrow paths among this chaos. To put it politely, it was a disaster waiting to happen. Curiously, he started looking around for anybody, and then called out. "Is anyone here?"

He got a reply from over in one of the far corners, "Over here." Fauul could see that there was no direct path to where the voice had come from and started working his way through the maze. *What a mess*, he thought. As he continued working his way he thought he caught a glimpse of the owner of the voice. He wasn't a big person at all but actually a bit short. Of course, he being tall was used to most being shorter. Finally getting a good look at the male he realized he was just about the height of Lauma. *Now why did I compare this Jehm with her?* He thought.

Jehm turned around as Fauul approached, and spoke in an uppity fashion. "So you're the one with the object from the *Ones Before,* right? Do you know how many of these supposed items I have seen?" Shaking his head, Jehm continued, "No, you wouldn't know. I really doubt that *yours* is any different than any of the many others, which have proved to be a fake. Still, as a favor to Bihl, I said I would look at it. So, is it outside or can you bring this thing in here?"

Jehm appeared to be somewhat animated and jittery, like he had drank too much of the hot beverage, but it appeared to just be his personality. "Slow down there. No it's not outside, and no it is not a large object."

"So I understand that you bartered it off of some local. Did he push the idea that it just had to be something from the *ones before*? I know it's a way to sucker one into paying exorbitant prices for something that usually is worthless."

Fauul was beginning to dislike this Jehm, but as a favor to Jim, decided he would stick it out. "No, no, nothing like that. He didn't even present it to me that way, and it was I who found his items. He had them covered in their shelter, and I was just waiting for he and his sister to come back and was just looking around the sitting space and found them there. It was me who wanted one of them. He had four, and from our conversation he thought that he could get more. He really did not want to part with it. We had a discussion, and thought maybe they might have come from those elusive *ones before*. But it had been a discussion by the three of us, and I did *not* get the thing because it might have been from the *ones before*. I got it because I liked it. I really had to convince him to trade me for one. I think if they were not in the hard times they were, he probably would have refused."

Waving his hands as if the explanation was unimportant Jehm asked, "Okay, if it is not outside where is it? Generally these things have some size to them, and have to be carried in, with help." Jehm was definitely becoming curious now, since everything Fauul had presented to him was different from the usual method of passing a fake.

"Are you telling me," Fauul asked, "that when someone presents something to you for your professional opinion that whatever it is, is large?"

"Yeah, and that's usually the first clue to me that what they are presenting is fake. In the turns I have worked in both the field and in research, very rarely is something found whole, and generally, when located, is in very small pieces. Time has a way of destroying the past."

"Know what you mean there. In one of the areas we were, while mapping, we came across an abandoned village. It appears that the water source had dried up. Still, you can see that slowly it is returning to the earth, the village that is. Probably in a couple of generations there may not be enough left there to show that there was even a village."

"That's true, and if you look at thousands of turns, even less is left. Enough of this, can I look at this object that you have?"

Reaching in his pocket Fauul handed the object to Jehm. "Here, this is it."

First, Jehm was surprised by the object's small size. Then taking the object, the first thing he noticed was it was warm. Probably from the body heat of this Fauul, and it was definitely metal. All of a sudden he was excited. *Can this thing actually be what we've been looking for?* Not one to get ahead of himself, he started doing a close inspection of the object. "You say the discoverer said he might be able to get more of these things?"

"Yeah, why?"

"Can I keep this for a while – I would like to study it closer, since to me, it does look promising. What's this script on it? The letters are familiar, but the words are not . . . hmmm."

"No, I didn't bring it over here just to lose it to you and your department." A little impatient now he asked for it back. "Look, the three of us back at their shelter talked about it possibly being from the *ones before*, but seriously we didn't think it was so."

"Well, from this initial look, I would say there is a great possibility that it is. Just the feel of the object alone says much to me." With a practiced eye he continued his inspection, "You see, we do not have a way of making such fine hinges, and the metal is unknown. Appears to be strong, and yet at the same time light. The two words are unknown, and this design, I've never seen before. So, yes it is a good candidate. If I can't keep it here for a while . . . let me at least get an artist over here to sketch it. Is that okay?"

Again a little impatiently Fauul said, "Sure, but hurry up, I have somewhere I need to be – plus I have to go back to the cartographer department to talk with Bihl."

"Okay, okay, just sit here for a few, and I will go get our artist." Jehm hurried out to find the artist, leaving Fauul alone.

Fauul found a chair, sat down, while thinking. *Now what have I gotten myself into? I really do need to get out of here.* While waiting he came to a decision. *I must take a leave of absence, and head back down to that village. I've got to find out if what I have been feeling is real, and I won't know by staying here.* What is it about attraction anyway? A female should just be a female, yet he was finding it wasn't so. Getting impatient, Fauul got up and started pacing. *How far away is this artist anyway?* Still no one showed and time continued to move slowly. He had almost decided to leave, when a breathless Jehm arrived with the artist. "Sorry for taking so long, but the artist wasn't where I expected him to be, and I had to go find him."

"Okay, just hurry up. I really need to be on my way." He watched as the artist did a thorough sketch of the object. Even with his impatience to be gone, he became interested in the sketching. The artist was definitely very good at what he did. "Here let me show something else about this thing." He then opened the top, and pulled the object apart. This surprised Jehm.

"What the . . . this convinces me even more that this might be our first real proof. Are you sure you won't leave it with me?"

"No, your sketches will have to be enough."

Once the artist was finished, Jehm handed back the object with some reluctance. "If I need to look or present this to someone in the future could you bring it back by? I know the head of the department would really like to see it."

Nodding, Fauul said, "Sure, but with my work schedule being as it is, you would have to get an approval from the head of my area." Still he knew that most likely, he would not be here to give them a second look at the object. He would be gone, and there was a good chance that he and Jehm would not cross paths again – thankfully. The sketches would simply have to do. As quickly as protocol and manners allowed he bowed out and headed to his personal shelter. Now that the decision had been made he couldn't make the arrangements for leaving fast enough. Still, he knew that it would take a couple of days to put it all together. Fortunately with that turn's worth of work and little use for his marks he was relatively well off and could live off what he had for at least half a turn – longer if he was frugal with it.

As the evening progressed a couple of ideas presented themselves to him. The first he dismissed, but the second would allow him to continue in his chosen field, but getting approval would be difficult. Well, at this moment it really didn't matter. He had made his decision, and was going through with it. Yet, it had merit, but again it would be a while before he could possibly put it into effect. In fact, as he thought about it, he knew he would not be able to present it until some time had passed. So, he put it away for a later presentation, and continued putting together what he would need for the journey south. Because it had only been a short time since he had returned from one, he knew exactly what was needed. Fortunately it would not require any expenditure for these items as he had them all. *Save where you can,* he thought. With his position within the cartographers, he knew his request would not be denied. The time lost until he left would be getting the travel arrangements made, and tying up any loose ends here.

It seemed that once the decision had been made to return to that remote village things started falling into place. Where it would have normally taken a couple of days to put his shelter in order, convince his superior, and then arrange the trip, it instead, had happened all in one day. It appeared that this decision was meant to be, and he was supposed to return. With a rising elation he found himself feeling great. Still, he knew that like the final leg of the project, it could take a couple of cycles, even with him being by himself, to reach that remote village. This would give him time to think, and decide what he would possible want to do. Since his finances were finite, he would need to find some secondary means of providing. And if Lauma would accept his offer for each to continue to see each other, well who knew how far it would go? Still he knew, that most likely, he was going too far in his own mind and expected to find her already mated, showing the trip as a waste of time, and making him a fool twice over. Since he was an outsider to this area, and really knew nothing about the village or its residents, maybe just maybe, it would be different and she hadn't found another. And at this moment, the idea of becoming the mate of someone was a surprise even to him.

He knew by tradition that the female was required to leave the properties where she had grown up. Why this tradition had developed was anyone's guess. But, if one thought about it, it probably came from many incidents in the past where the new male would take over the properties, and maybe steal them from the family who had worked and owned them. By making the newly mated, if the family member was female, to move out and on their own, this prevented, at least directly, a confrontation. So it probably was for protection of the family and the family's property.

In that short time there on the property he found that she loved that life. Moving into a village or a township was not something she ever wanted to happen, and while he had always enjoyed the life in the township, he was torn between this life, and the one he thought he was about to establish. Of course he might be assuming too much. There was a great possibility that the feelings he had for Lauma could end up being only one way. Still having made the decision and actually being on his way back he felt great, and at least he was doing something about it.

* * *

Jehm studied the drawings made by the artist, and found no fault from what he remembered when he had handled this small object. It had been a real surprise; he had expected much of the same that was usually passed off for something the *ones before* had made. This one was so very different, and while the original owner did not push the idea of it being made by the *ones before*, it could easily lead one's thinking in that direction. He dropped whatever projects he had going, and in the next two to three days did a thorough study of the drawings. He continued to try to find fault with the object, but there just wasn't anything he could disprove. He wished he still had the object, but there was nothing he could do about that. The present owner of the object was not going to let go of it.

Yet, as he continued his study of the drawings, he continued to become more excited. Finally, something had come forth that might actually belong to the myths. He really thought that that was exactly what they, the *ones before* had to be myths. Still he had in his hands drawings of something concrete that just might prove they were not, and what did those two words, *"Sempher fi"* engraved on the object mean anyway? Let alone the engraved image that was on the case. He had to admit he had never seen either the image or the words before.

At least, to his practiced eye and mind, he could find no fault with the object, and after trying for a few days, gave up and decided it was time to present his finding to the *Head Keeper of the Past*. While not friends with Jllon, he knew he, Jehm, was trusted by him. They worked in different sections and rarely met. He knew, both by personal experience, and from the rumors that normally go through a work area, that Jllon was a great person to work under. So he felt no nervousness when he decided to present his finding to him. Still, one did not walk in on one of such rank. He would have to go through the proper protocol, and he knew this could take a couple of days. This was okay, as it would give him the additional time needed to put his case together. Again, from experience, he knew that Jllon dealt with facts and with the research to back those facts. So he had much work to do before he would present his findings. Yet, to even have a slight possibility of proof was exciting. If the object proved to be false later, then much still would be learned from this exercise, and study, showing that such a small object could be created to look like it was from the past.

It had actually taken longer than just a couple of days to be able to get a confirmed appointment to see Jllon. It had turned out to be a very busy time for the Head Keeper of the Past. It seemed that every official had to have some of his time for what reasons he did not know. Still, he was grateful that it was Jllon and not him that had to deal with these officials. He did not have the patience to deal with these people, and their inflated egos and petty ways. This additional time had given him a chance to study and restudy the sketches in detail and confirm in his own mind that this object was a real candidate for something very ancient. So finally the day arrived for the appointment with Jllon, he gathered the drawings and his thoughts, and headed for the office of the Keeper of the Past, ready to present his findings.

Since he had never really ever met Jllon, he wasn't sure how to present himself. But, Jllon took that awkward moment away by just standing and offering his hands and arms in the traditional greeting of friendship and stating that with any of them from this area informality was the way when behind closed doors. In public the protocols had be observed, but here it was a relief not having to deal with them.

"Okay Jehm, what is it you have for me? Oh, by the way I'm sorry I did not have time for you earlier, but it is the time of the turn for budgets and officials, and truthfully I hate it all. Still what are you going to do anyway?"

"You hate it all? I didn't know that, but then again I guess being just a worker in our area leaves one ignorant on what goes on, on high."

"Believe me, if there were any other way of doing this, I would be the first to try. Anyway, what do you have?"

"Well, I had a visitor about ten days ago. His boss and friend suggested and then set up an interview with me to view something he had gotten from some villager in a remote village. The boss felt it could actually be an artifact from those myths of the elusive *ones before.*" He took a deep breath before continuing, "You know that this is my area of expertise. I have uncovered most of the fraud and fakes that have been presented as being from the *ones before.* I'm afraid I was a little testy and short with him when he arrived. He almost turned around and left. Anyway, I thought, what did he have, and how far would I have to walk to see this supposed artifact? I mentioned that to him, but to my surprise he removed something from his pocket. Immediately I could see that this object was different than any that had been presented to me in the past. I asked, of course, if I might handle it, and he reluctantly handed it over to me."

"Do you have the object with you?" Jllon asked.

"No, wish I did, but the owner wouldn't give it up. In fact he was quite impatient to be on his way. I could see something was really bothering him. I was at least able to convince him to stay long enough to get an artist down there and have it completely sketched. Then he surprised me again as he took the object apart so the artist could get a good sketch of it and all its pieces."

"So, I assume you brought those sketches with you, right?"

"Right and I've had time to research what we know, which of course, is very little. I compared this object to any we had record of that has been presented as being from the *ones before*. None of these drawings and descriptions came close to this one." Taking the drawings out, he spread them so that Jllon could see and study them.

Immediately Jllon saw that this thing was very different from any he had been shown in the past. This immediately gave him hope, if not from the *ones before*, at least from another unknown race from the past. "It's really that small?"

"Yes, you can hold it in the palm of your hand, and it is of some unknown metal. When this Fauul took it apart, I handled the individual pieces and this outer case is extremely light, but at the same time very strong. Before you ask, I really have no idea what it was used for. See the small wheel, which appears to be a different type of metal, and yes, it is grooved. In the bottom of this portion appears to be some kind of fastening device. Whatever it is it's well made."

"Yes, yes I can see that. Have you figured out what the script or the engraving is yet?"

"No, no idea really. I mean it appears to be the same type of lettering that we use, which immediately made me suspicious, but it's only two words and both are none we use today. As far as the engraving goes, it looks like a symbol for something. Again what it may represent I don't have a clue."

"I understand the suspicion, but as small as this appears to be, I don't think we can make it with our present abilities. I'd really like to see this thing in person. Is there any way you can contact this person or his boss again and have it brought around so I may see the real thing?"

"It might take a day or two to accomplish, but other than the fact he was impatient, and was not going to give it up, he had no problem with us examining the object."

"Please do, and keep me informed of the progress. Also, drop whatever you were doing for now and make this your priority. We need to find out as much as we can about this object. Suggestions here . . . Why not bring in one of the metal workers, and have him look at your drawings, then explain the feel of the object to him. Maybe he could give us some insight into what it is made of. One way or the other let me know by the end of this quarter of the cycle."

He saw how Jllon had become the leader here. He was efficient, and would immediately see other possible solutions, and could definitely lead. He was gaining new respect for this leader. "Sure will, when I contact the metal workers should I use your name?"

"Please do, as it may speed things up, and make sure you ask for one of their experts. We don't want an apprentice here."

With that the meeting was over, he felt exhilarated with the contact with Jllon, who obviously knew how to get things moving. Jehm decided he would need to bring in a couple of more to help him. Possibly a couple of learners who could do additional research in the archives to see if anything like this had ever been found in the past. *Yes, much to accomplish before the meeting in seven days.* Still it was the zenith. All this could wait, for now as it was mealtime, and he found he was quite hungry.

The next seven days just flew by as Jehm brought together the researchers and learners in the section. He was fortunate as one turned out to be the mate of Jllon. This had both a good side and a bad side to it. She was known as one of the best researchers out there, but at the same time this meant that Jllon would be informed all along the way. When dealing with the metal specialist it turned out to be more difficult. Without the actual object for him to see, he held his opinion. The only thing he would state was, without it would simply be a guess. But from the description, most likely, it was something they could not produce. This, he said, was an unofficial view since Jehm, who had seen it, was not a metal expert. So there wasn't a way for him to be sure of the accuracy of the description?

So, the only thing he would do was put it down as an unofficial speculation on the metals in the object. The other parts of searching the past records and viewing other fraud items that had been presented were easier, if not time consuming. It had appeared that this practice of attempting to produce something that had come from the *ones before* had been going on for hundreds of turns. They found a whole section just dedicated to these fakes. Yet, as was his experience from his uncovering of fakes, most were large objects – the very thing that probably would not survive time. Most had drawings attached, and one could see the roughness in the work. Still an interesting thing he noticed, or was pointed out by Nouma, that when one went further back in the records, the quality of the fakes improved.

This led him to thinking that maybe they had lost skills over time and that made him wonder why.

Shouldn't it be the other way? Shouldn't we be improving and finding better ways to do things? At least he thought so. Still before him was the evidence that it was not necessarily so. This led him to thinking that maybe this object was still a fake, but one from long ago. It might have been made during the early times when craftsmanship seemed to be better. While it was a possibility, the problem was, all the fakes uncovered from the past, so far, were much larger. Still, being small did not eliminate it as fake.

Not that it was necessary, but after the seven days he presented his data and conclusions to Jllon. Who took the written data and said he would study it and let him know. Jehm knew that this was the way it had to be, but it still left him in a quandary. He'd have to wait for the Head Keeper of the Past to give him his conclusions on the research.

It was another seven days before he was summoned to the Keeper of the Past's office. There he was praised for such a thorough report, and in such a short time. And while, yes he was kept up to date of what was going on, because of his mate being part of the team, he knew he would only be getting a portion of what was truly happening. Jllon thought there was enough evidence to push it forward and to work on getting a team together to go and investigate. He also had found it interesting that fakes had over time become poorer in quality. Still, it was those two things that had made it appear that the object might be real – the small size, and the absolute quality and unknown method of construction.

When Jehm left the office of Jllon, he felt exhilarated. It had been a tough seven days but, to get such praise from one who was known for his thoroughness was a great compliment. He was sure that some time in the future this might lead to him getting higher position, and gaining additional responsibility. But he knew he would not be part of the field team, he hated that kind of work and reveled in pure research. Still unknown to him, his fate had been determined by his grating personality, and his refusal to take field assignments. Here, to be worthy of being a boss, one had to be able to work well with others, be willing to do major field works, and handle the politics of the villages and townships.

Jllon shook his head after Jehm had departed. It really was too bad about that personality quirk. Jehm had an inflated view of himself, and it came out too often when one had to work under him. Jllon had no doubt about his skills and thoroughness in completing a project or assignment. Still, word always got back of how hard it was to work for Jehm. These things would keep him where he was, and Jllon was sure that it would lead to trouble sometime in the future.

Enough on that, it was time to see if he could hold this mysterious object in his hand. Yes, the sketches were nice yet; having the real thing in one's hand let one get a better feel and understanding. It was interesting again, how the evidence showed that things had regressed. It wasn't obvious until researching those fakes, which had shown a definite fall in skills and abilities over time. Wondering he thought. *Does this mean we were much more advanced at some time in the past, or is it just the ones who would want to create and pass on the fakes became less skilled in their chosen line of work over time?* Of course he had no answers to these questions . . . and truly there might never be any way to find those answers anyway.

It had only been a few generations ago when they all worked exclusively for themselves. As villages grew into townships it became necessary to change the way some things were done. It led to the type of council rule and life style they presently had, where all shared in the duties. It led to things becoming more specialized, and as the needs changed, things such as record keeping and a place for knowledge to be stored had to be developed, and here now presently he was the keeper or leader of that known history and of general records. This information was available to all that wanted to research it, but a system was still being developed to make it easier to access. This was becoming a very necessary thing, as the amount of records and history continued to increase. Maybe putting Jehm in charge of figuring out a good system would put his talents to good use, and make him feel important. For sure, it took too long to find anything right now.

On that subject, he felt there had to be a better way to keep the records together also. At the present everything was single sheets piled. Then a series of holes would be drilled through the bundle and then tied together, and placed in different areas that represented different general subjects. Each of these tied bundles was called books. Who would have thought that there would be so much information, and no easy way to protect and access it? Figuring that out might take someone a couple of life times.

"Enough on this", he stated. He looked back into the report that he had just read he found the name of the person who had the object. Jehm had been unable to make any additional contact. Writing a note he had his underling contact a runner. He needed to have a meeting with this Fauul and get the information and object directly from him. Reading a third party translation often lacked accuracy, so direct contact was critical.

Later, that same day, the runner had returned stating that the person he was to deliver the message to was not available or not around anywhere. Was there another place he should deliver it? Knowing from the notes that Fauul was a cartographer, he asked the runner to deliver the message there. He also added that it could be delivered and read by the person whom Fauul worked under. The runner left to take care of the redelivery.

While awaiting a response Jllon had much to accomplish, besides the setting up this field project. Knowing this trip might be coming up was exhilarating. It had been much too long since he and his mate had worked in the field, and frankly he was tired of just being an administrator. He thought he did better work while on a dig or doing a large research project. Still, he knew he had been picked for this position because of his ability to organize and to see almost immediately what was needed to solve some large problem or puzzle.

It was a couple of days later when a runner returned with a response. Curious, since he had expected direct contact, he read the message. It came from Bihl Kaetr, who was Fauul Saelor's boss. He stated that Fauul had asked for a leave of absence, which was granted, and had left at least half a cycle ago. Fauul had stated he had to take care of some personal business back in one of the villages the team had spent time in. And since it was of personal nature nothing was required or had a need to be revealed.

Shaking his head, Jllon wondered. *Now what? We are not even sure where this place is. Our one contact, and of course, one object of interest has left.* With the message read, he decided it was time to go over and visit Fauul's boss. From the tone of the message, it appeared that both Bihl and Fauul were friends. It could be that Fauul passed something to him that would be helpful. He thanked the runner, and told him there would be no return correspondence. He looked at his own schedule and saw that most could be pushed back till later. He contacted the underling who worked with him, and headed out to have that conversation with Bihl. If he hurried he probably could take Bihl out for the zenith meal where neither would be interrupted by the normal day-to-day business of their particular departments.

After returning from the meal with Bihl, Jllon felt a bit frustrated, because the elusive object was now completely out of his reach. This would make it a little more difficult to get the necessary approval to continue the research and the proposed field digs with what has appeared to be a very viable clue which had become unavailable. Still, if he could convince the board to allow it to happen, there was a good possibility of either putting the myths to rest, or proving that the illusive *ones before* were real, thusly ending the controversy once and for all. At least at the meeting with Bihl, he learned about the team, and the leader of that team Joellie Trag. He also found out that Fauul had been the second in charge, and actually had done more of the real work than Joellie. Still, Joellie was here, and he would need to be contacted so more information could be gathered. Since Jehm had done his work well, it was now his turn. He had to take all the data that Jehm had given him, and whatever he could learn from Joellie, then present it, and hope for approval.

Since this major mapping project had just ended, as far as the field research went, finances would be thin. He thought that he would need at least twenty individuals to do this properly. Plus, if any possible sites were discovered, serious digging would have to be done, he would need authority to hire locals, but might have to settle for the team only. Again, since this could be one of the most important finds in their history, he thought that he had better head up the team, and push everything back for a little while. Besides, he had to admit to himself, working in the field was his true passion anyway.

After another quarter of a cycle had passed, he thought that finally he was getting a handle on the information. He had found out from Joellie, who was an egotist that Fauul and Doube had gone out to one of the local herder's property to procure some additional pack beasts. When asked why he had done something like this, which was very unusual, he had stated they had come in between the gathers, and he had decided they wouldn't wait. So he sent the two out to get the necessary beasts.

At least he now knew where and which village it was, and about how long it would take to get there. After that, trying to isolate things down to location, and names should be easier. Still this village was small and isolated. Looking at a round trip there and back it would take between a quarter and half a turn to accomplish. So he had better give this field project a full turn of attention. From the brief description of the weather in that area, it appeared they would be able to work the areas almost anytime.

Well, at this time it was all a guess anyway. Reports might be wrong, and the information may actually apply to a different area, and could easily end up being mixed and tagged to another area completely. Since he was the Head Keeper of the Past, he had access to all the raw data the cartographers had produced. It allowed him access to the field notes, sketches, and initial conclusions made by the field teams. There was definitely a lot of information here. Of course most would not pertain to what he wanted to know. Still it was useful since it let him see what the land was like and how vast it was. Between those sketches and descriptions he was able to put a general picture in his mind. Weather in the area he was looking at intrigued him. Other than a scarcity of water, the area seemed to have a mild climate. Warm comfortable summer and spring days, followed by mild falls and winters . . . very different from here. Here, in the winters, they were covered in heavy snows, and fall warned one of what was coming. And while spring was nice, it was way too short – the summers that followed being hot, humid and miserable. That other area almost seemed like a paradise in comparison.

Still, there were always tradeoffs. Well, at least he thought there might be. Yet, at this moment, other than the area being isolated, it just sounded too good to be true. In fact it sounded like a great place to go to get away from the day-to-day grind. He found that he needed to do some thinking. He knew with this major mapping project just completed he would have to come up with some imaginative ways not only to present this to the ones who had control of the coffers, but find as many ways as possible to keep the costs very low.

He realized, since Fauul was gone, that he might be able to get Doube, who appeared to be free at the moment. Maybe he could convince him to join them on this new endeavor. To be able to have a scout of his reputation with them would be fantastic. Thinking back to what he had read from those final days on the mapping project, he realized that there had been mention of another site that had potential. Not remembering exactly where it was, he grabbed the notes, and spent the after-zenith researching. He found the information he was seeking in the personal side notes and not in the main narration. The side notes dealt with ideas and conclusions of what was viewed by the cartographers and the support staff. Many times the information here gave a better picture than the official data.

Looking closely he found what he was searching for. It was written by a number of the team members. Yes, it was in the desert and they were attempting to find the way out. Water was an issue, and one small team plus the scout had gone out on separate assignments – the scout to locate water and the team led by Fauul to find the trail out. Funny how things work though, it appeared that the opposite happened. Fauul's team found water, and Doube found the trail out. Still the side notes describing the area were most interesting. Both Doube and Fauul had thought that sometime in the past this area had a large population. There was nothing there that they could prove or disprove. Still their gut feeling said this area had once been a township.

He was coming up, after reading the notes, with the same questions in his mind that they had presented. In the desert, where was the water necessary to support something that size? How did they provide themselves with food? And most importantly what was the work there they used to support the township? If this desert area he was planning on researching came up empty, maybe if this other area was close enough, they would send an exploratory team there to do some initial work. He thought that maybe he would work that into the proposal. By doing so he could present a cheaper investigation. Since they would have two sites, and only have to finance one team. *Good thought.*

Looking over the notes and rough maps told him the two areas were only days apart. Even with the rough drawings he saw that the trails to this other area were passable. *Why would someone want to live in the desert?* After all, most of the time the weather while clear, would be uncomfortable. Still while enjoying fieldwork, he had to admit that deep down inside he had become a township type of individual, but not by choice. To work in the field was one thing, but to live in those places without others around him was now beyond his understanding. He had to laugh at those thoughts since both he and his mate were originally from the outback.

Each to his own, after all if there were no individuals who would want to live in the outback, then there would be no foods, or beasts of burden. These could only really exist if raised or grown in the outback. It did sound counter to his present life. But, it was that research, that possible discovery on those digs that drove him. He knew, it truth, he and his mate would find it easy to go back and live that lifestyle again.

He personally knew it was his intense curiosity, the joy of discovery, the solving of puzzles, and the day-to-day problems that were continually presented, and yes even the disappointments when these digs produced nothing that drove him. Yet even then, when nothing showed itself, or was discovered, it, in itself, would correct a legend or tale about an area.

Yes, gaining that new knowledge and of learning was his passion. He knew that in the distant past that there had been wars over the scarce resources. But as time had progressed, the people had changed and instead of fighting, had become somewhat united. He had completed a dig in an area where one of those great battles of the past had been conducted, and was appalled at the amount of slaughter that had happened there. The evidence suggested that thousands had died. How sad, and what did such a great loss of life accomplish?

Still, the past was important if one listened. It'd help one avoid repeating those past mistakes. Yet, each generation seemed to think it was smarter than the last, and continued to repeat the same mistakes over and over again. Enough of this rambling, he needed to finish his proposal, and then get to organizing his team – at least on paper. He knew to make this work that a portion of the work crew would need to be learners from the higher learning centers. He would present an offer to the ones who were learning in his field of a free turn or more of higher learning, and this fieldwork would count favorably towards finishing their area of learning. That would save many marks in cost, and add the experience of these learning ones which would be an advantage later in their lives.

He still needed to talk to Doube, and find out what he knew. Right now he was the only source available, since he had been on that assignment to secure those additional pack beasts. Looking at the personal notes again he saw that Doube had considered the beasts they had purchased to be some of the best he had ever seen. This was good news. It meant another savings. They would only need enough to get to the area in his mind, and then if something was found they would purchase the beasts locally. Yes, the proposal was coming together, and he needed to emphasize the savings in his proposal giving it had a better chance of acceptance. Later, before submitting it he would have Nouma tear it apart. She was very good at the small details.

* * *

It took to the end of the cycle for him to finish his proposal. He made the necessary appointments, discussed with the underlings the proposed plans, got input from Nouma, and finally submitted it to the full council. He then held his breath figuratively; since expenses had been high on the general mapping project, causing the majority of other projects to be refused. At least, until the coffers were full again, there was a good chance this one would also be refused, forcing them to wait. Yet, to his surprise; before the next quarter of a cycle had passed he was summoned to the offices, and was handed an approval. The council had not even called him in to explain the finer points of the proposed fieldwork – that was a shock. Any he had submitted in the past had required a huge investment in his time, going to the township hall and explaining one point or another, and defending the proposal. So to have this one pass so easily really took him off guard. Of course, it was a possibility that they, like he, were interested in solving the myth of the *ones before*.

He found when he went to pick up the approved proposal that they had added a stipulation stating that they would require regular expense and progress reports. The council would review these reports, and if they, at any time, felt the costs of research were either too high or not producing results, they would terminate it and require the team to return. That stipulation definitely put pressure on the team to both be frugal with the funds, and show positive results. He knew that in the past, others had tried to fake the results to be able to continue, and to him, this was downright wrong. Usually when one took this tact, the good work one had done in the past became questioned, when the false data finally surfaced, which it had a tendency to do, and the said individual would be caught in the lies that had been created, destroying forever their reputation and previous good work.

All he could hope, was the board initially would be forgiving, since early on there were rarely good results. Once they arrived, there was much ground work that had to be completed. Then once the site was located, the camp had to be set up, and locations set for the actual work. Of course there would be much scout work to find that good starting location. Still thinking about all the details that had to be worked out once they arrived, let alone the details to be finalized before they even left, left him shaking his head. *Well, guess I better get to it*, he thought. The reason for the first proposed site, he had decided, because of its isolation that they would start at that desert location – less chance of being discovered or observed if they actually found something.

CHAPTER TEN

The days turned into quarter cycles then cycles before all the planning and preparations were complete. He was doing double duty since he still needed to administer his area along with the setting up of the field operation. It left him arriving at their shelter totally exhausted. Many a night he was too tired to eat, or even consider a bath, and at times conversation with his mate seemed impossible. That sleeping space looked better and better as time went on, and he was usually asleep by the time he lay down. Still the time flew by, with work continuing to pile. Then, before he realized it, the team was assembled, and the next morn it would be time to begin their journey. As usual, he worried that something had been forgotten, or the one he left in charge, while away on this project, would prove to be incompetent. Yet he had to admit that this was one of the few ways for one to be evaluated for leadership and promotion.

That night sitting and talking with Nouma, they both realized it would be a long time before they would see this shelter again, so this time became very special to them. Yes to be adventuring together again was a great thing, and they had to admit that not many mates could do this. Yet, it would be more business than pleasure. Still, when one worked in the field it was nice to have someone close to you to discuss what the day's finding were, and in what direction the next day's work should proceed. With this type of situation one felt more comfortable with discussing ideas that normally one wouldn't say out loud. It gave one the freedom to work through ideas and directions with the help of someone else. And because of this, one, at times, found it much easier to bring those ideas to fruition because of this familiarity.

They decided one last bath together and some very close intimacy for the last time in their shelter would be nice. And while that intimacy was wonderful, it was also the conversations they had afterwards that seemed to be just as fulfilling, bringing them oh so much closer.

* * *

The morn came quickly enough, and they locked down the shelter, knowing one of their friends would periodically check in to make sure all was well. This eliminated one worry from the many that they faced, and after a quick morn meal, grabbed their packs and headed for the gathering area for their outgoing team and the projects that waited.

It took a little time to walk the distance, and when they arrived, it was definitely organized chaos. Everything was in full swing, and there was a loud noisy din over the area, as orders and questions, were being passed around. The sounds of the beasts, the noise of equipment being moved, and sundry other unidentified noises – it really was exhilarating to watch. Shortly he knew he would be required to give a small speech to start them on their way, and he knew that is exactly what it would be, short. Looking at his mate he smiled and said, "It sure appears to be in full swing, why don't you go over and join your group. I've got to find both the scout and then the one who is in charge of the camp crew. We can meet later just before we leave. By the way, I'm glad we have a couple of female learners who have decided to join us this trip."

"Okay, see you later," she smiled and nodded, "and yes, I know these young females are my responsibility. Where do you want to meet before we leave?"

"Hmmm, good question." Looking around he saw the beginning of the trail leading out of the township. Pointing he said, "How about over there. Does that work for you?"

"Anything you say boss," she responded teasingly.

He did a double take not sure if she was teasing him or not, but her smile gave it away. Shaking his head he chuckled quietly, "So I guess I'll see you a bit later then." With that he headed in the direction where he thought the camp managers were located. He knew that it would take about one quarter of a cycle on the trail for things to work themselves out, and everyone to become familiar with the trail and routines that go with traveling. For many of the learners this would be their first time away from their shelters and the township for such an extended time. With them, at first, it would seem like an adventure, where everything they'd be doing would be new. Yet, with as long as they were to be away, when these learners returned he knew that this now familiar place would feel strange.

As he continued towards the camp crew he noticed, off to the left, Doube the scout, leaning against one of the rails and watching the chaos. He detoured over to the scout, having a couple of questions for him. Waving and yelling over the din he said, "Doube? Hey, over here!"

At first Doube couldn't place where the voice was coming from. Looking around he saw the Keeper of the Past walking his way, in his mind he asked. *What's his name? He sure seems to have intensity about him. Oh yeah, Jllon.* Doube held out his hands and arms in the friendship gesture and asked, when Jllon arrived, "Is there something I can do for you?"

"Just a couple of quick questions that's all. I mean you really just got out from under your other assignment with the mapping team a few cycles ago. I was really surprised when you agreed to go with us. Why is that?"

"Simple really . . . Since you will be returning to the last area, and I went with Fauul when we picked the pack beasts, I know exactly where we need to go. Plus I was getting tired of hanging around the township anyway, and was trying to come up with some excuse to get away. Was thinking of going back to the farm, but your offer came first."

"Well, I really appreciate it. Your skills alone are worth having you along. Still, by you being with Fauul when he got the object . . . you didn't happen to get one yourself?"

"No, while I thought they were nice, and I know he was more interested in the one that appeared to have a map etched into it, they were something held no interest for me."

"So how many of these things did this herder have?"

"He had four of them. All were identical, but at the same time different. Two were plain with no markings on them, but one was gold in color and the other silver. The other two had the engravings."

Nodding Jllon asked, "He, the herder that is, stated he felt he could possibly find more of these. At least that is what is stated in Fauul's and your notes. Did he mention, even in passing, where he got them?"

"No, not a word on that. I think he thought that if he had found them on their property that the old law would be activated, leaving them with have no place to live or go. You know how often that one has been abused."

Nodding, Jllon agreed, "I do know what you mean. In that way I can't blame him for not saying anything."

"Do you mind if I ask you one?" Doube asked.

"No, go ahead. After all it's only fair."

"What's so important about that small object anyway? I mean, we both looked it over quite a bit, and really never figured what it was for . . . it appeared to be just an artifact, nothing important."

"It may seem that way, but there is too much about it that we, in our current advancements, cannot manufacture or make. It may be the first real evidence pointing to the myths. You know the *ones before*."

"Really, I truly had no idea. We thought so, but it was just idle speculation. Hey it looks like one of the camp managers is trying to get your attention over there."

"Where? Oh I see, guess I better go find out what he needs. Doube, I'd like to continue this conversation later if that's okay with you."

"Of course, any time."

Jllon left and went over to the area where the camp managers were working, finalizing the packing, and making sure all was there. Jahnsyn Lytle was the one in overall charge of this part of the team. While he did not personally know him, he knew from others that this male was great at organization. When he reached Jahnsyn, Jahnsyn asked, "You are the leader are you not?"

"Yup, I'm Jllon, and you are Jahnsyn right?"

"Correct, what I can use from you right now is some help. We are running a little bit behind, and a few more bodies would move this along much more quickly."

"Hmmm, let me think a minute here . . . tell you what, I'll head over to the area where the learners are finalizing, and I will see if I can break a few of them away from what they are doing. I'm sure anything they would learn from you would be invaluable anyway. Does that work?"

"Yes, yes, strong young ones are exactly what I need. Even though they don't have the experience, maybe three or four would make the difference."

"Okay, once you have them how long do you think it will take you to finish?"

"Mid-morn and we should be ready to start down the trail. We are the last to get the final packing, since we have the most."

"Sounds great, didn't plan on us making a great distance today anyway." He took his leave and headed over to the learner's section which was completely on the opposite side of the compound to get the additional help requested. There he ran into his mate who was working on the breakdown with the learners. In truth, she was in charge of them, and the learners were learning, if necessary, she could be a tough taskmaster. "I need your learners to go assist the camp managers on the final packing. Make sure they are willing to work, as this will be physical. I think it would be best to send the males, since there are only four they all should go and assist. This will leave you without any of the males to assist over the final packing here. I can send over a couple of the camp assistants to help you, if necessary, I'm sure they will be good at it. Of course if you want to keep the females assisting you, I have no problem with that."

Laughing a little she responded, "That will work out well, won't need any additional help at this time. All of the learners can get involved with that packing. We were starting to wind down here anyway, and I noticed some were starting to be a little lazy anyway."

"Good, then I must move on and see to the rest. You do know where they're located?" He saw her point in the right direction. "Okay, I know I have left this in good hands – will see you a bit later, thanks." He left knowing it would be handled immediately. They were generally on schedule, and many times in the past they had not been, so he knew that this was a good thing and a great start. His next destination was the dig team. He knew they were traveling light, only taking tools that would not be available locally, to save on the amount of needed pack beasts and finances. The few tools they did not have would be purchased just before arriving. That way the prices would not be increased since there would be no warning of their needs. Human nature being what it was, to take advantage when one could, seemed to be the way of things.

Seeing Payle Evyrs he waved to catch his attention, and saw him wave back. He had known Payle for turns, and worked with him on other digs. He could not ask for a better co-leader for the dig team. He, Celt, and Flar had led their own teams in the past. "Everything on time here?" he asked.

"Actually ahead of schedule, since we are really taking less this time around."

"Really? Do you think you could free up a couple of your team to go over and help the camp managers finish up? The more we can get involved over there, the quicker we will be able to leave."

"No prob' really. Tell you what, I'll send half of the team over there. Is that the last section that is delaying us from leaving?"

"Yes, they have the most to pack and load. I've had some of the learners' go over to help. But, they are inexperienced and may be more of a hindrance than help, while your team has, obviously, much more experience."

"Okay then I'll get them moving – can't wait to be on another dig. It has been a very long time – too long to be truthful."

"Sounds great, much still to do, and you're right, it's been too long. Got to move on and see how the rest is progressing, and then give my short speech to get us on the way. See you later."   He left and continued his rounds, more to encourage the team, and to get a feel for the overall group.

As they approached mid-morn things appeared to be wrapping up and anticipation was high. He knew it was time to give the official kickoff speech and to be on their way. He had to admit all this energy around him had him feeling great. He signaled to the leaders of the different groups to have all their people gather close to where he was. It took a few moments for them to get there and then quiet down. Even here he could feel the energy in the crowd. He looked over all and with a smile, began. "Many know me only by my title, 'Head Keeper of the Past', but when one takes this kind of journey, we all begin to know each other on a personal basis. Since we will work together, eat together, and yes, I know, even sleep together it will be impossible not to learn much about one another. Many of you have been with me on other digs, and for you learners, this will be the first time for you. I know, in truth, you have your private views of what you are embarking on, but most likely you will find out that these ideas will be wrong and not be close to the actual work or travel. This next quarter of a cycle we will be learning the routine of travel. At first you will be clumsy, but that will pass.

"Now to all here, we may be heading to the most significant dig we have ever worked. We have reason to believe, on good evidence that the mythological *ones before* may be real. On this dig we hope to, either finally prove, or disprove their existence – not that others haven't attempted this. While this sounds simple, the actual work will probably take turns to complete – followed, of course, by turns of research. Still, in the end, you may be able to tell your descendants that you were there at the actual site, part of the actual team that discovered that proof. Which means that this team has a chance to both influence and goes down in history . . ." Looking around at the gathered team he paused for effect saying after a moment, "Scout, camp managers, dig managers, learner manager, are we ready?"

"Yes!" they all answered in unison.

"Then I officially state . . . Let's hit that trail!" He got down from what he had been standing on, and joined the team, as they began heading out onto the trail. It always sent chills up his spine to see the beginning of the project head out on the trail, and this time was no different. As was his habit, he initially took up the rear position. This was to make sure that all moved out and there were no problems. If a leader truly wanted to lead, one had to follow as often as be in the front. It was important for him to get a good feel for the team and all who made it up. While many had been on his teams in the past, there were many more that had never been, let alone on a dig such as this. He always understood the need to be available to all. Still, seeing the team leaving the township, full of hope and energy, was something he always remembered. He saw the desire and the eagerness of the members to be on their way, to find new things, to discover previously unknown information. He knew that as the days wore on and became cycles, where it would settle into a routine, much of the energy displayed here would be gone. Even something new eventually became old, dusty, and routine.

When he knew for sure that all were on the trail, he started working his way up to the front – stopping briefly by the different groups, listening to their conversation, and participating when necessary. Eventually he reached the front and joined the scout to get an idea where, because of the time they had started, he would recommend their stop. He reminded him that many of the members of this team were green and would need additional time to set up tonight, and to plan it that way for the next couple of days.

"Agreed", Doube replied, "I kind of figured that. I saw that some of your team, to put it gently, is a bit inexperienced. So, I thought we would only go until mid-after-zenith before stopping. Only figured, truthfully, to put us on the trail for half a day – work for you?"

"Perfect, I know, as you do, the morrow will actually be tougher. I know that many will not sleep well tonight, and their tempers and attention spans will be short once we're back on the trail on the morrow. So I think we will want to push through this second day to really tire them out – but again to set it down well before sunset. I think by the end of this first quarter the routine will be well set, and then we can start pushing for time."

"My thoughts exactly. As you know we are on a familiar good trail, so it is a good time for these new ones to learn before we get into any areas that might be dangerous."

"Okay, I'll leave the campsite locations to you. I know that most of your work is still to come, and this portion is almost a vacation for you. I would like you to observe many of these new ones and bring any problems to my attention. I want the problems to be solved before we hit bad and dangerous trail."

"Fine with me, it makes my job easier if everyone learns and does what they are supposed to do."

"Yeah, mine too. Well, see you down the trail at the chosen site. I'll continue to monitor the people here." Jllon turned around headed back into the groups, again observing and encouraging them on.

Doube headed on down the trail. He had in mind a good area ahead that would make it easy for the new ones in the group, but not so easy that they would not learn a little from the experience. The one thing that Doube knew was that one needed to be constantly on guard. Even in an area that was frequently traveled. In the natural world things were constantly changing, and what was safe yesterday did not mean that today it would still be that way. Travelers who camped overnight rarely used this first area he had chosen. He wanted them to be somewhat isolated so that he could concentrate on his observations – still, it had all the necessary elements, relatively flat, a water source, an area with much dead wood for fires, and a place to be used to take care of nature's call. Right now with new people who had never done anything like this, he was going to have to deal with carelessness, both from the eagerness to do new things, and from ignorance. Unfortunately out here that eagerness and carelessness could kill. So while on the well-traveled portion of the trail, it was time to get those lessons learned.

Again dealing with a new team, and one that was much larger than the last, and not really knowing anyone on the team, meant he would have to learn what level of experience and competence that any of them had, and this included the team leader, and all who were below him. From his contacts with Jllon, he found one who was into the details and one who cared for his team – a great improvement over Joellie, so at least in the beginning; he would have to give this leader a positive view. Still, they had just started out of the gate, so to speak, and he would hold final judgement until later.

His mate Nouma, who was part of the team, was a beautiful female. He wondered how someone, like himself, who was not a really good looking male in a female's eye, could have ever won someone like her. Shaking his head, he thought. *You know you really never know what brings two together as mates.* He hoped that this wouldn't be a problem since his mate was the only mate on the team. The other mates had remained home leaving the two of them unique. Yet, the two of them had their jobs to do and would only see each other when it was either required or at night in camp.

With the late start, he knew they would arrive at the camp area a little later than he would have liked, especially for the first stop. He knew it would almost be comical to watch these, new and inexperienced to the field and trail, try to set up camp. He also knew how frustrated the camp managers were going to be, and how late the evening meal would probably be. Jllon was thankful to have one such as Doube scouting for them. Over the turns he had heard much about him, and there had never been anything negative. With a team as large as this one his skills were needed. Not necessarily here at the beginning, but as they continued on out of the more populated areas into more of the wilderness his skills, both as a learned one, and as a scout, were invaluable.

He knew that right now his team overall had more inexperienced people than any time in the past, and the quicker that changed, the quicker they would be able to move, be more efficient, and show less wasted motion. Both in time spent and materials used, since when one was from a township, it was easy to pick something up. Once on the trail such luxuries rarely existed.

The day continued rather well with only one minor mishap as the load on one of the pack beasts came apart and fell to the ground – the result of a poor packing job by one of the learners who had told the camp managers he had packed before and didn't need any instructions or assistance. Still, nothing was damaged other than someone's pride. So with a quick repack and a double check of the other beasts they were on their way again. As time stretched out on the trail, it was starting to get late in the after-zenith and Jllon was starting to worry, he had yet to see the marker that would be left by the scout for the night camp. Yet, he knew, or thought he knew where the scout would have them set up and that area was still a little ahead of them. Yet, to his surprise, it was not at that location. He saw the sign that told them to continue. *What the heck? Well, the rep of this scout is perfect so he must have something in mind.* Indeed he did, as only a little further down the trail he saw the marker for the night camp pointing off the trail. He laughed to himself when he saw where they were heading and he realized what the scout had done. Once they had arrived, it became apparent that this was a great area to set up, away from any other group that may be on the trail. It had all that was needed, but the location required planning for a proper camp.

Here, on the first stop of many, one would find out where one stood as far as their camping and wilderness skills. So, immediately any weakness would show itself, and as the days continued those weaknesses would be addressed and solved. He turned to the trailing team and gave them the sign for "end of day on the trail" and to set up camp. He would assist where he could but at the same time he and he assumed Doube, would observe.

Sure enough a short time later Doube showed up and smiled at him. "So, what do you think of my choice for the first night?"

"Brilliant, is all I have to say. I can tell you live up to your rep. This wasn't where I thought we were originally heading to set up for the first night, but I have to admit it is perfect."

"My thoughts exactly. I wanted a place out of the way where early on we could determine the weaknesses. On the morrow evening the place I have in mind will be a little tougher. I want the learning to start early, problems discovered and be known, by the time we hit dangerous trail. After all, even though the safety of the team is yours, it's mine also, since I'm responsible for the overall route and the dangers that are out there."

Heading back into the camp area with Doube, Jllon said, "Shall we see how good this team is then." Looking around the area Jllon could appreciate the location. While out of the way, it had many advantages over the regular stopping place. First off he could see the area was surrounded by hills. And some time in the past there had been a collapse or small landslide that had partially blocked the stream that ran through the area. This had created a small lake, which would prevent anyone or anything from approaching, or leaving in that direction. The small lake tied into the hills and there was plenty of grass in the area for the pack beasts. If one put a rope across the area it became a natural enclosure with the only exit closed off by those ropes. Just off of this was an area that was relatively flat and would be an ideal location for the main camp. There were also many trees and plenty of dead wood for the night fires. And off in the distance the main river was visible, and a landmark since the main trail paralleled it.

Looking at Doube he stated, "I've been down this trail at least a dozen times and have never seen this area. I'm impressed, this place is not visible from the main trail, yet is close, and has everything we need. How'd you know about it?"

Smiling, he replied, "Part of the service I provide. As you know my main learnin' is geology, and this area intrigued me. So on one of my times between jobs I came back and studied the rocks. Of course, when I do that kind of thing, I'm also looking at these sites as possible stopping points – kind of doing two things at once. I have many others marked in my memory. It kind of comes in handy now and then."

"Well, one thing for sure, you're already living up to your reputation. Hopefully I can live up to mine. I know when we finally reach where we are going you will have some free time on your hands. Still, you know that we are not going directly into the area where Fauul received that object. One of the reasons I wanted you along was because you were the scout of that team. From reading of the notes it appeared to you and at least Fauul that on the desert's edge there were signs of a past settlement. I want to go there first to confirm your speculation. If you are right this whole area may be rich in finds. So, if this first area turns out to be a bust, at least there is a second area to look at."

"So, the plan is not to take the water-craft down the coast but cut inland. Is that right?"

"Yes, this will give my team, our team, a chance to look over the landscape and maybe on the trip down find other possible sites. I have to take advantage of this opportunity as projects such as these don't happen very often."

"For you maybe, but I never . . ." Suddenly they heard a large crash followed by a sound of chaos reaching their ears. They both looked in the direction of the sounds and saw one of the pack beasts running wildly through camp. "What the heck?" Jllon exclaimed as they looked at each other and ran over to the area. When they arrived they saw one pack beast wide eyed with fear and shaking, still carrying a portion of the supplies on its back, trying to escape. The rest of the supplies it had carried seemed to be spread over a large area. A quick assessment showed that the other beasts were already placed into the makeshift corral, appearing to be calm and unconcerned with this one panicked beast the last. They saw, at the moment that other than pride, that no one was hurt or had any equipment been damaged. One of the camp managers was still on his backside looking both a little angry and embarrassed. Looking back at the beast they could tell it was still trying to escape whatever had frightened it. Fortunately the halter was still attached and unfortunately, one of the learners reached out and grabbed it, but the beast wasn't having anything to do with it and immediately dragged the learner off his feet and into the dirt, then with a quick snap of his head, whipping the line, threw the learner up into the air. The result was unexpected for the beast as well as the learner. As he was falling the learner tried to gain some control but ended up landing on the beast's back and was holding on for dear life. The beast wondering how he ended up with a rider did a 180, followed by a 360 spin. If the situation weren't so dangerous, it would have been hilarious. The look on the face of both the unintended rider and the beast was just down right funny.

Doube stepped in quickly and grabbed the halter, yelling for another person to come in and assist him. At this point one of the camp managers grabbed the other lead, and between the two finally stopped the pack beast. This allowed the learner to get off, doing so carefully, feeling somewhat foolish and shaky. The beast stood there still appearing to be a quite frightened. It was soaked with sweat and continued to shake. Talking softly to the beast Doube finally was able to calm the beast enough to keep it under control, even though the beast continued to roll its eyes. He turned it over to the camp manager who led it away where they finished the unloading and turned it loose with the others. Some of the team members went to help clean up the items the beast had shed during its rampage.

"Okay," Jllon asked, "what or who spooked the beast?" Looking over at Doube, he could see that he was trying hard not to laugh. He knew if he wasn't careful that he would be himself.

One of the camp managers stated that he really wasn't sure, but some of the learners – on their assigned tasks – were assisting the unloading and placing of the beasts in the temporary corral when this one decided to go wild. Now that everything seemed to be back under control, Jllon asked, "Was anyone hurt?" To which he received a negative answer. He then spied Celt Morlen and asked, "Celt, can I have you investigate this thing and get back to me? You know soon as possible, since we can't afford a repeat of this. We were lucky this time since no one was hurt, except maybe their pride."

"Sure", Celt answered, "sure thing boss".

Then raising his voice Jllon stated, "Okay all, let's finish getting this mess cleaned up, and finish getting the camp set up or we will be doing this in the dark, which, if I remember right, is no fun at all."

The team began returning to their assigned tasked that had been interrupted by the incident, and night wasn't far off. Turning around he saw that Doube was still standing next to him, and was continuing to smile. Doube quietly said, "Now that was fun. I can see why you wanted an early end to the first day. Do you always put on this kind of entertainment for ones who have never been on your team?" With that comment they both started laughing. It helped release the tension of the moment. The only thing lost was some time and that learner's pride. Jllon replied, "No, not really, but that look on that learner's face when he involuntarily mounted that pack beast was humorous I will say. Anyway before we were interrupted, I wanted you to know that I was given permission to have a copy of the notes made by the team you were assigned. Of course I have copies of all the notes from all ten teams anyway. But yours are most interesting."

"Why would you want those anyway?"

"It seems of all the mapping teams that went out, yours were the only one to have encountered areas that might be rich in the kind of stuff we are interested in. By studying those notes we can do a better job of researching that area when we arrive. So when we hit the coast from here we are going to trek down it a short distance, cut inland, hitting areas not often traveled, followed by heading over to the locations you found in that desert. Then, after working that area, go on into that remote village where the object was found."

"Okay, that's fine by me. I originally figured you might just take the water-craft down and from there head inland once we were close, but the other works. It just means we will take longer to get there that's all. Just a thought, and again it's your call, but we can head inland earlier and avoid the coast. I know of a little used trail that will tie into the one I believe you want to travel."

"Good, one of the reasons I wanted you as our scout, other than the obvious skills is the fact that you were on that mapping team and are familiar with most of those areas I'm most interested in. Plus, if I understand it, from your notes you were interested in the geology of that desert area. Once there you have my permission to go do some of your own research."

"Hey, that would be great. It definitely left me curious that's for sure."

"Okay. Once we are away from here, I would like nightly meetings so we can plan out the next day's travel, and to get any input that you have as to what we may be facing."

"Works for me. Truthfully this will be the first time on any project that I've been part of to have females along." Doube smiled and shook his head slightly. "Not that it's a bad thing, only it means I have to make allowances. I've scouted for families and wondered how they ever remained together the way the infighting went between the whelps – especially if they were of both sexes. Know this is a different situation. Still having both sexes can lead to problems."

"True. And even with us on these digs we do, at times, have both. Usually family – you know mates. And in this case Nouma has the responsibility of the learners, especially the females."

"Nouma? Is she your mate? A really beautiful female if I do say so myself."

"Yes, she's my mate, and she doesn't see it, the beauty part. She feels it's simply a come on by others to get her attention. And yes I feel fortunate to have her as a mate – especially since we work in the same field and she loves fieldwork like I do." He shrugged, "We just work well together on all levels. Enough of this, let's get this first night's camp set up and see where we need to improve."

They headed off in different directions, Jllon, to see how the portable shelters were coming along and to make sure of the locations, Doube, heading over to see to the beasts and the makeshift corral. Doube also wanted to contact the camp managers to see what needs they had. Looking over the whole scene Doube thought. *Yes this is going to take a few tries before they have it down. I will mention what I see at tonight's meeting, and then we will see how it breaks down in the morn.*

In many ways the morn breakdown and packing was more important than the previous night's set up. They needed to be very efficient so that they'd be on the trail quickly, and be able to cover the distance planned. *Yes, right now things are very sloppy, but that will change.* He found even in this short time he liked Jllon – easy to get along with and very good at organizing. Plus he accepted suggestions readily, a good sign of a true leader. No wonder he had been assigned the "Head Keeper of the Past" position, even as young as he appeared. Still it was obvious to him that Jllon had never wanted the position, but still accepted it anyway, working it to the best of his ability.

* * *

As expected, it took much too long to get back on the trail the next morn. Still, as the days continued, this would change. As everyone learned their tasks and with the rotation of the team members through all the different areas it would eventually produce the efficiency that was required. Jllon had each of the sub-leaders continue to work with the team members to improve their trail skills. By doing this, it also gave him a chance to see who was good at a particular chore or assignment. One of the interesting results came out when it was discovered that one of the females – one who overall was petite – had been raised on a working farm, and had the experience and temperament to work the pack beasts. In fact she had put the experienced team members to shame, all the ones who had worked them in the past. He learned her name was Suzzane Karnes. Watching her work the beasts, when she had her rotation, he could see the confidence and sure handedness she had. She also had a natural ability to anticipate what the beasts were going to do. She also seemed to have a calming effect on them. When asked, she simply said that it was a gift she had, and while she did not mind working them, she had come to learn the skills that only higher learning could provide, including the study of the past. It had always held a great fascination to her.

He also noticed that one of the learners, a Jayson Braylok, appeared to have a crush on one of the other female learners. From conversations with his mate, he learned that the female of interest was Kaern Slopes. Kaern seemed unaware of the interest, but still seemed to have similar thoughts. It was something to watch.

* * *

When they were back on the trail in one of those early days out, Celt Morlan walked up to him as they proceeded down the trail, and gave him a quick update to his investigation of the incident that first night's stop over. His conclusion was that one of the female learners had been sent over to help unload the pack beasts. "She was wearing some type of shiny earrings, which kept picking up the setting sunlight and reflecting it around. It seemed that it kept striking that last pack beast in the eyes, and the beast not knowing what it was, started getting nervous. Finally it just panicked and took off on its run. Jayson Braylok is the male student who thought he could bring it under control, and ended up on the pack beast's back. Jayson's never worked with beasts, nor did he have any idea of their strength, since he's a township whelp. Figuring it would be easy to stop the beast and at the same time impress a fellow learner, and a female besides, he reached out and grabbed the trailing reins from the halter figuring he would just stop the beast and this would look good to her. You know, '*my hero*', type stuff.

"His surprise came when the beast flicked his head and sent him into the air, followed by the second surprise both to him and the beast. That, of course, was when being thrown into the air with him coming down on the back of the beast."

"Thanks Celt on that information. Let's make sure in the future that if someone is to be working with the beasts that anything shiny is kept away. We do not want or need a repeat that's for sure. Fortunately no one was hurt, other than his or her pride. Still I can't help but smile, after all it was kind of funny."

"Okay boss, I'll make sure that we extend it even farther. We really don't need anyone wearing anything reflective during travel, setup, and take down anyway."

Nodding, Jllon replied, "Very true, and that's a better idea. That way we eliminate an accidental source if something changes. Plus things that reflect can be seen a long ways off, which could be a problem when we don't want to advertise our presence."

* * *

As the next few days progressed so did the improvements in camp setup and take down. The group was beginning to work as a team, and it was beginning to show. While not quite to where he wanted them yet, it was a vast improvement over that first stop and next morn start. Still, they were on the main trail, and most of the areas chosen by the scout were chosen for the lessons that would be important later when they began traveling the lesser trails, the ones where teamwork led to being safe and alive. While they could take care of most medical emergencies that arose on such an outing, they were unable to take care of something truly life threatening.

While traveling the major trails team defense was generally unnecessary, but as they left the highly traveled, and moved on to the ones seldom traveled, they could become targets for bandits or worse. In the wild lands there was very little to deter them. With little chance of reprisal they did as they pleased, attacking and wiping out small groups, and then disappearing again. So while not necessary on the main trails, he had them begin the nightly watches. There was a lot of grumbling and joking about such a need, but Jllon had seen the result when one did not take the normal precautions. He hoped they would not have a chance to see what carelessness could produce. He also had the scout start training any who did not know the use of the weapons of the day.

These weapons were used for hunting mostly, but were used for protection if necessary. They consisted of a belt knife, which was a long knife in a sheath that went about half way down one's thigh. The other was a throwing knife for which you usually carried more than one. The amount carried was up to the individual. He always carried three. He really hoped that they would not have to use them for defense. His thought was with the size of this team it should be large enough to deter most small bands from attacking. Still that didn't prevent them from trying to sneak in at night and steal something – not that they really had anything of value. But these thieves and bandits would not know that.

As the cycle moved on, the team continued to improve, and improve to the point where they would be set up for the night by sunset, and be packed and on the road by sunrise. It was early spring and the weather had been cooperating. Half way through the present cycle they headed south, leaving the main trail and heading out on a less traveled trail. By keeping the mountains to their west it would be easy to continue in the direction they wanted to go. This was an opportunity to check out some rumored areas that was supposed to lie close and to the east of these coastal mountains.

* * *

As they neared the end of their first cycle on the trail, the scout returned to the team unexpectedly in afternoon. It was one of those beautiful spring days where the temperature was perfect, with a soft cool breeze blowing and a scent of the blooming vegetation in the air. It was one of those rare days where it would be easy to relax and let the day pass by without doing any work at all. In the distance they had noticed an unusually large flock of flyers, but they were too far in the distance to recognize them.

Doube walked up to Jllon with a serious look on his face, stating, "What we feared has happened, but fortunately not to us. Those flyers are scavengers, and it isn't beasts they are feasting on. I need you to call a halt, and then come with me. Just be prepared that's all."

By the tone of his voice and the seriousness of his look, Jllon just nodded, and didn't even ask any questions. Turning around he signaled to the team for a stop, and then went over to the sub-bosses and gave them a brief message. Afterwards he rejoined Doube and headed out. Following Doube for a period of time they came to a small rise. The wind was blowing in their direction, and Jllon caught the scent of death. Still, when they topped the rise, and peered into the small enclosure below, he was unprepared for the sight. Four or five bodies lay in death. From the smell and appearances it had happened at least two days before. What immediately struck him was the silence of the area. Other than the breeze and scavengers nothing stirred. It was like all the beasts were silent in respect for the dead.

Doube stated, "I scouted the camp and found where the attack had come from. It appears the bandits came out of the setting sun as they were preparing to set up camp. You know how it is after a full day's travel. For a brief period you let down, and are not as alert as you should be. They came in quick, and from what I can see, the battle lasted only a very short time. It appears the surprise was complete."

"Do you know if there were any females with this group? What I am seeing are only males."

"I really hope not, because in comparison the males would have gotten off easy – their deaths came quickly. If there had been any females with them, the bandits would take them alive, use them up, and then kill them. They leave no witnesses."

Shuddering while looking over the scene Jllon replied, "Then I do hope there were none with them. I wish nothing like that on any female."

"Agreed, because of the remoteness of some of these areas, the bandits can pretty much operate and do as they please."

"Okay, I want all of the team to see this, and especially the females. They need to know the seriousness of this. We will set up camp just past here, and then bring a few of the team back and bury the dead. I guess we had better increase our alertness. I do hope that this group of bandits is so involved with what they stole from these dead that they won't find out that we were here until we are well gone."

"You won't get me to argue that, and yes I think it's important for the whole team to see this."

They headed back to the waiting team to inform them of what had been discovered. With this discovery any part of the spring day that was light and easy had disappeared. The harsh reality of death had destroyed it. While Jllon and Doube were returning they confirmed that they would head past the slaughter, have the camp managers set up for a quick cold meal and then go back to bury the dead. This additional delay would not be a problem for the dead. Once the dead had been buried so that the flyers and other scavengers couldn't get to the bodies, and if anything could be found on the bodies to identify them, they would continue into the early evening before setting up camp. It again would be a cold camp, with just a few hours sleep. Fortunately the moon would be rising late, and once it was up they would again head on down the trail, the goal simply to put as much distance between them and the area of ambush.

Once back to the team, they passed the word about what had been discovered. It was as if a black cloud had descended on the team. It had gone from easy conversation and laughter to silence. Many of the learners had never even seen a body, and bodies in this condition would be hard to take. With a hand signal, they headed down the trail quietly, as if to prevent even the beasts from hearing of their passing. The first thing to assail them was the smell of death, which made the pack beasts nervous. They swung wide of the scene to both keep the pack beasts in control, and to avoid leaving too many tracks in the area. They continued down the trail past the site until they found a good place to halt. Jllon left a skeleton crew, members who had seen this before, and headed back to the massacre. He especially wanted the females to witness the bodies, as well as the others who had not experienced death in this way.

Fortunately, from this direction the winds were at their backs, so the smell did not reach them. Again, as they topped the rise from the opposite direction they looked down on that scene of death. It was obvious that it bothered most that were present – and rightly so. He and Doube would look for anything that might identify these people while the rest would dig the graves, and place the bodies into them. While this was happening the females would return to camp and assist there. This was something that needed to be done quickly. They had to be out of the area as fast as possible. They had no desire to confront the bandits or have the bandits know that they were here. As they approached the bodies, and their true condition revealed, a number of the team started retching.

"Nothing to be ashamed of, this kind of thing is never easy", Jllon said. "Just go about your assigned task. After all, these people at least deserve a burial. While we cannot go through our normal methods here, at least we can put them beneath the earth. One last thing, once the job is finished, go over to the stream and wash off. One can become sick from handling bodies."

The bandits had been thorough. There was nothing left to put an identity to any of the victims. It took them to late after-zenith before it was completed, and before they headed back to the temporary camp, Jllon felt it necessary to at least say a few words over the dead.

He began by saying, "We come into this world not by choice and most of the times leave the same way. One can only hope that the journey from the beginning to the end is a good one. Life continually changes, and what one has planned rarely comes to fruition. Does that mean that one should not try? No, since on our journey one does not know whom one will touch or change. For these unknown dead I hope that their journey to here was as they wanted. No one knows when or how the end will arrive. Yet, none of us will ever avoid passing on. We are created in a moment of passion, and may we live our lives with a passion for life, and in the pursuit of our dreams. May these silent dead have found theirs." Finishing his statement the team turned and quietly left. Doube remained behind briefly to wipe out part of their tracks, to at least give the appearance that there were just a couple of individuals who had found the bodies, leaving nothing that would interest the bandits.

As they returned to the camp the whole group was unusually quiet. It was never easy to face death, but to have seen it in all its ugliness usually left a mark. It had a tendency to show one's mortality, and most put that away for some future time – something to ignore until it arrived by its own calling. Still he had seen the turns fly by, and while still young in time, he and his mate were much older than the learners, yet it had only seemed like yesterday and they were the same as the learners. Once back at camp, they ate a quick meal and headed on down the trail needing to put as much distance from this place of death as possible. The team wanted to be sure they were not the next victims of the same or other bandits. They stopped just before dark to give everyone a rest and a quick meal. Everyone was supposed to catch a quick nap, because once the moon rose, they would be moving out again. On the morrow they would look at making it a three-quarter day, and then break. Now distance and the greater the distance from the spot of ambush the better for all concerned.

CHAPTER ELEVEN

Fauul arrived at the port a few days northwest of his chosen destination. The closer he came to returning to that remote village the more nervous he became. While starting this personal journey it had felt right, now he was starting to feel like a fool. He had almost convinced himself to turn around and return to his home a number of times. Yet he had to know, and that was what pushed him onward. Looking back on his decision, he reflected upon the incident that finally pushed him in the direction he was now going. It was after a day at work and because his apartment was stuffy, he had his window open. Outside he could hear one of his neighbors strumming his guitar – an ancient musical instrument. No one ever remembered when they weren't around.

The melody was simple but it had a tendency to stay with you.

He really wasn't paying that close of attention to the melody until he realized he was humming the tune. It was at that point he started listening to the words, although most he could not hear. Yet, part of the chorus slowly became clear. It must have been an old song as the name "John" being used in it was an ancient name, one that was rarely used today. Plus it was mentioning some fictional land that did not exist – at least as far as he knew. And it used other terms to name the two sexes. While it had the correct name for his opposite it still had a different one included, which in his mind meant that the lyrics had been changed a little sometime after it had been originally written. In his mind he started going over the lyrics of the song, or at least the parts that he heard or remembered;

John met a stranger just the other day

Remembering back to the wild lands, and seeing the ladies who

Know the ways of a man, but not that way

Brought John forward
To his female friend he found
She was easy to be around

She liked to dress
In the clothes of a man, but I digress
Not that it could hide

Who she was or what she was inside . . .

From there he couldn't remember it, but it seemed to be going in the direction of this person's discovery of what relationships between females and males were really about. That area beyond attraction and the physical, to the spiritual, and mental, it was at that very moment he realized that until he had met Lauma he had only seen the first two parts. The words had brought home to him that this song might have been written for or about him. As he thought about it, he knew that after that meeting and subsequent contacts she had changed him forever. So here he was possibly wasting his life, and his time, chasing what he had been shown. *Well, such is life I guess.*

His next worry would be finding a group who was heading down the coast. Not knowing a lot about the area, other than the mapping, he was aware that traveling alone wasn't safe or smart for that matter. Not that one got bothered much, but individuals had disappeared, and he did not want to become one of them. Without thinking about it he suddenly realized that he was going to be arriving down there at one of the two major gathers. So there should be a good-sized group of people there. Which meant, and most likely, he would end up meeting Lauma before he was ready. Not that he would have been ready had he went out to the property where the herders lived and worked.

How did one approach someone who has no idea you are coming, and is really not expecting to see you again, and then tell them that you want them to possibly share your life with them? When he truly looked at it, it seemed too ridiculous, even stupid. And for once, he had to admit that the person who had no problem with females, and their ways, felt completely out of place and uncomfortable. *What's that all about anyway?*

"Enough of this", he said quietly, "got to find a group heading in the village's direction." Of course with major gathers going on, even here at this port village, to find a group going in that direction could be a problem. So he started hanging out in the areas where groups gathered before heading out to whatever destinations they were traveling. Yet, so far, any that was traveling was heading in different directions and not the direction he wanted to go.

He had to admit that the energy being created by the anticipation of the major gathers was exhilarating. Walking the center of the small village where the venders were setting up, and listening to the conversations, the hopes of the people made him feel really alive. He really enjoyed this atmosphere. He almost felt like waiting out the gather right here at the port before heading down, but he knew that all he was doing was delaying the reason for taking the leave of absence in the first place. Funny how that worked, while he was looking forward to seeing Lauma again, at the same time, he had a fear building that kept him from wanting to have that meeting. It was a deep down nervousness and a feeling in the pit of his stomach that continued to get bigger the closer he was to returning to that village. It would be so easy at this point to "what if" oneself to death. You know, what if she found a mate, what if she doesn't feel the same, what if, what if. It was almost funny how one built a whole series of scenarios in one's mind as to the outcome of the encounter, and probably none of them would be as he imagined. In fact he knew if he didn't control his imagination he would probably turn around and leave saying, "Forget it". Shaking his head, he thought. *Now come on, you're a full grown male, and it's not like you haven't been around the other sex. Get over it.* While he could come to terms with himself, it did not get him any closer to solving this present dilemma, finding that group and heading out.

One day while idling around a young male, who worked for one of the local merchants, approached him and said that his boss wanted to see him right away. So he followed the young one back to the shop. There the merchant told him that he had just learned of a group heading out in the direction he was going. And yes, the group was trustworthy as they worked many of the smaller villages. They, in fact, were heading to the gather at the very village he wanted to go. Thanking the merchant, he got directions to their camp, and went immediately to their campsite to make contact. He found them right where the merchant said they would be, and it was obvious they were packing to leave.

Approaching with the open hands of peace he walked towards the one who appeared to be in charge of the small group. The leader looking up from the preparations and seeing someone approaching quit what he was doing and waited. Fauul introduced himself saying, "Hi, I'm Fauul Saelor, and I just came from the local merchant here, and he stated that you were heading south. I want to join a group like yours that is heading that way, since it is often unsafe to travel by one's self."

The leader of the small group replied, "Hey, I'm Tomast Levie, this one here is Brihan Smithey, and the one over there finishing up the portable shelter is Larse Fabels. Actually we would be glad to have you with us on this portion of our trip. We ended up being one short anyway, and I had asked the merchant if he knew of anyone heading in our direction. So, you're welcome to join us if he vouches for you."

"Well, he vouched for you and your group, so I guess it works both ways."

"Okay then, I'll confirm with him, and then you're good to go."

"Sounds great, I'll get my pack and be back in time for your leaving. Is there anything I can add to help on the trip?"

"No, not really. This is a trip we make quite often. You see we contract with herders, and farmers for their needs, mostly in the beast area. Then we travel the different gathers looking for the best in both beast and price."

"Well, the village I am trying to get to has some of the best I've ever seen, and the scout that I was with, ah what was his name, yes Doube agreed completely."

"Doube Mickles? Is that who you mean?"

"Yes, why? He was our scout on the last assignment I was a part of. You see I'm a cartographer, and we were mapping the trails and some of the surrounding areas leading up to and around that village I am heading to."

"I've never met him, but his reputation precedes him. He is considered one of the best in that field, and you actually worked with him, wow."

"Actually we ended up being friends, but we haven't stayed in close of contact since finishing the assignment."

"So, what village are you trying to get to anyway?"

"I do believe it's called Rancho. There's a brother and sister herder team there, and it was from them we purchased some additional pack beasts before heading back to the township from where we had started."

"Coincidence I guess, 'cause that's where we are heading. These herders wouldn't be the Ktroves now?"

"Yes, Lauma and Lauut Ktrove, how'd you know?"

"It's where we're heading. We've seen some of their beasts, and were going down under contract to see what could be arranged for both of the beast types they raise. You know herd and pack beast."

"That's really great news. This means I can be with you all the way into Rancho and will not have to find another group in some remote area where that likelihood of finding another group heading towards Rancho probably wouldn't exist."

"Oh I don't know about that. After all, it is one of the two major gathers, and there will be groups moving in and out of all the local villages this quarter cycle. These things run seven days, while the minors only run two. It's just worth going for the festivities even if you have nothing to trade or sell."

"Okay then, you can check with the merchant and I'll go grab my gear and join you. I'm more than ready to be on my way, and, of course, I'll assist however I can on the trip down there."

* * *

Lauut and Lauma had been informed by the runners that a group of traveling merchants would be coming down to this major gather to look at some of their beasts. So ahead of time Lauut made arrangements with Aurto to use some of the corral space to have a few extra beasts on hand for inspection. Then the two of them brought the beasts in the day before the beginning of the gather. Arrangements had been made back on the property to have it covered while they were at the gather. They had contracted with some of their neighbors who had younglings who would rotate in and out to cover for a small fee or favor. By doing it this way it allowed all the families living in the outback some time at the major gather. While overall, it was serious business, there was still time for the music, the gatherings, the dances, and the food . . . yes, all that wonderful food. Plus this was a time for the announcements of future mating's, the mating ceremonies, and the promises for the future that such would bring.

During the day the business was carried out. To include such things as trading, purchases, and contracts for needed work or construction, plus announcements of births, of planned matings, and on the sad note of ones who had passed on. There was definitely high energy in the air for the anticipation of what was to come. The nighttime was the time of festivities and of celebration. These major gathers happened in the spring before plantings and in the fall after the harvest time. The nighttime was the time to show off one's finery, to enjoy the company of the extended family, it was a time to renew old friendships, and make new ones. And while a major gather here would never match one in a township, it was still a joyful time .With so many around it became difficult to move without bumping into someone.

Lauma had her normal booth, and Lauut would come in periodically to assist her as she offered the goods she had produced for this occasion. He would spend most of his time at the beastmaster compound to keep contact with any that would be looking for beasts. Of course, his beasts were only some of the many kept there. It was nice the area was broken into many pens, each with a small booth to allow business to be handled semi-privately. Overall the whole gather was invigorating.

He was there at the corrals when the small contingent of traveling merchants arrived. At first he didn't pay much attention since they had just arrived, and would need time to set up and relax before getting down to any business. In fact he knew that today they would only browse the gather, relax, and get a feel for the atmosphere, spend an evening with the community, and then on the morrow the serious business of the back and forth bartering and bargaining would begin. He turned his back on the group and started to head back to check on the beasts he had housed here, when he heard his name called. The voice sounded strange, yet familiar. He turned back around and looked in the direction he thought the voice was coming from, seeing in the distance someone walking towards him and waving at him. At first he did not recognize who it was, *stranger,* he thought. Still as the stranger approached there was something familiar about him, yet it took a moment for it to register. *Fauul, that's who it has to be* – yet he was the last person he expected to see here. "Fauul, is that you?" Lauut asked questioningly.

Smiling and slapping Lauut on the back he responded, "Yes it is, and it's great to see you too."

"What the heck are you doing down here? I thought that when you left we'd never see you again. Not, that we didn't . . . well you know what I mean."

Teasing he responded in mock seriousness, "Do I now? You figured once I was gone that it was good riddance. Speaking of we, where's that sister of yours?"

Returning in the same mock seriousness, Lauut responded, "And I thought you came back to see me or to bargain for more beasts."

With that they both laughed, with Lauut continuing, "She's at the booth in the middle of the village. You know she hasn't been the same since you left. In a way it has been good. She started up some of her old friendships she had before we lost our sires."

"Oh, now I don't know if that's good news or bad. Does it mean she's picked up with some other male from her past? If that's so I don't want to interfere – since I'm the outsider here."

Laughing by the look on Fauul's face he said, "No, no it's not case. She tied in with her close female friends. I believe they are Sooma and Traylu. After the accident we both just cut off ties from our past. By your arrival last time, followed by your subsequent leaving, soon after she renewed those ties, and it seemed to have helped."

"Helped? I don't quite understand what you mean."

"If you don't know she has never found any male in this village or in the surrounding area to be acceptable to her. But, when you left she seemed to have changed. It was soon after she went into the village and renewed those old friendships."

Concerned Fauul asked, "So, was this change good or bad?"

"On that subject you'll have to ask her yourself. Since like you, I'm male and knowing and understanding the female mind is way beyond me. Still, if I had to guess I would say it was a good change. Hey it's a nice day here; let's go get some ale before we continue."

"Great idea, the trail can make one thirsty. Then you can fill me in on what has been happening, and I'll let you know why I am here, as if you can't guess." Walking over to the main area of the yards they grabbed ale from Aurto's stash and sat down and caught up on the times since he had left. Thinking about the area Fauul wondered how anything could be accomplished down here. The weather always seemed to cooperate. It would be so easy just to let time pass and do nothing. Then Lauut interrupted his thoughts.

"So, you are going to tell me what brought you here. Still, if I had to guess, it would be Lauma – am I wrong?"

"Is it that obvious? And yes, but you don't know how many times I almost turned around and headed back thinking myself the fool. And when you think about it, it makes sense since I was only there at your shelter for a couple of days or less. Yet, in that time she affected me like no other."

"Why the indecision", Lauut asked. "You never hit me as one that would have that problem?"

"In my field and in general I would agree. But come on now, this could still be a wild flyer chase. You know where the flyers are on the ground and you approach them to capture them alive just to have them fly away."

Laughing Lauut replied, "True, I remember when I was a whelp and my sires stated that if you could put seasoning on the tail of a flyer you could catch it. Of course I tried and tried but could never do it." Smiling at the image he could see in his mind Lauut continued, "Still the statement is true, but you don't see it for what it really means."

"Yes, as a whelp we tend to see things one way or the other, and don't understand the subtleties of life yet. And when it comes to females I do not think that we will be able to fully comprehend the subtleties of their minds – thusly, why this could be a wild flyer chase."

"Well, I'm due at the zenith to replace her in our booth so she can take care of eating and the nature calls that one cannot escape. Why not come with me and take her out for the zenith meal, and then you two can get re-acquainted, so to speak. Find out how it has been and whether your trip back here has been the right one. Personally, I think it is. But, that's me, and I would love nothing better than to see my sister happy. And while she has been, I do know that having a mate is something she is looking forward to as much as I do."

"Sounds like a plan to me, when will that be, oh that's right, you said the zenith."

With mock seriousness Lauut looked at Fauul and stated, "Oh, just one more thing, since she is my sister and my sires are not around . . . I would have to approve any union. So you had better be on your best behavior around me." Then not being able to keep a straight face started laughing. After all, it seemed funny to him that he would be in this position.

With the same mock seriousness Fauul responded, "Well, sir can I wipe your feet? Only of course if you haven't stepped in that fresh manure you are spreading." He had to admit that he really did like this brother of Lauma's. It was at the very moment he realized that if his plans went all the way through that indeed Lauut would be his brother.

"Well, it's a little early, but I think she might want to use some additional time away from the booth today. For some reason, other than the gather, this will be a special occasion for her." They fell silent for a few minutes as they finished their ales, both lost in their own thoughts. Other than the energy in the air from the gathering, the day could be one to just watch go by and watch the sun set. "Well, I've finished mine and from the looks of it you have finished yours so let's head on over to the booth. I know you don't know where it is other than in a general way so let me lead on."

"Fine with me," Fauul responded.

* * *

Lauma was dealing with one of the outsiders when in the distance she saw her brother approaching. Still at this moment, it was a bit early for him, so she went on with her discussion. Subconsciously she realized that someone was tagging along with him, but still put no significance to it, since the sale was important. The outsider was looking to purchase some of her needlework for his mate. So she was busy showing him different items either she had available or could contract for a later time. "Now, what I have here in this stack is what you can get during the gather, while this one has other options. These I will produce for you under contract and have them delivered by runner to your location. And of course, take your time looking. I know the importance of finding the right item for your mate."

"All of what you have here is really beautiful. So you make it difficult for me to decide. This is to be a surprise for her . . . she has no idea. I've come to this gather to barter for some additional equipment I need, and this, unknown to her, was the second reason I came."

She glanced quickly over to her approaching brother, and her jaw dropped in surprise. It appeared that the person approaching with her brother was Fauul. But that was impossible, since he lived a very long way from their small village. Plus she was just coming to terms with the idea she may never see him again – yet, here he was. With the surprise came a small bit of anger. *How dare he show up without letting me know he was coming?* Was that fair to her? She definitely was caught off guard and off balance. Then as quickly as was possible the anger was gone, and her emotions rose up, and she then flushed, her face turning red. She found herself unable to control her emotions at all – something she had always prided herself on being able to do. She stood there in silent shock.

Fauul, watching her face could see all sorts of emotions traveling across it, from surprise, to a brief flash of anger, to finally embarrassment. He said, as they reached the booth, "You know in the short time that I've known you I have never seen you with a lack for words. I don't know if that's a good thing or bad."

Still unable to say anything she just stared. Then catching her breath she said, "Fauul, how dare you show up without even allowing anyone to know you were coming! You should have at least let me know."

"Why, as far as I knew this may have been a short trip. I could have found you mated and have a whelp on the way. At the end I almost did turn around and go back without finding out. But, here I am."

Realizing she was ignoring her customer she turned back to him and found him smiling at the whole scene he was just privy to. "What are you smiling at?" She asked flustered.

"Oh, I don't know, you three I guess. Especially you and him, anyway I can see you are busy right now, so I need to think about what you have here and come to a decision. Then I will be back to let you know." The customer smiled and said, "Have fun you two," at which point he left.

Looking over at the two males and stamping her foot with her hands on her hips she stated, "Now see what you did. I probably lost that customer, and you know we need all we can get."

Smiling and shaking his head Lauut said, "I don't think so. I believe he enjoyed every moment of this conversation, and he will be back. It probably reminded him of himself and his mate at their beginnings." Continuing Lauut said, "Now I've come to relieve you early from the booth, so you can take care of nature, and then have a long talk at your zenith meal with your male friend here. And yes I use that term. Anyone who has seen the two of you together earlier could see where this is headed."

Still confused and still off balance from seeing the last person she had expected to see, all she could do was shake her head and leave. She looked over at Fauul and pointedly said, "You wait here, I *will* be right back. Then we have some things to discuss." With that said she fairly skipped out of their sight and headed for the necessary space.

The two males looked at each other shrugged with Lauut saying, "I really think you left her unsure of herself there for a moment. She definitely lost her composure, something I really have never seen before. I know for a fact that no other male around here has ever done that to her."

"Well," Fauul commented, "I have to admit it's the same for me. In all the time I have been around females who were interested, it never was serious – thought so a couple of times, but in the end it wasn't so. You'll know what I mean, when the right one comes along for you. Until then all you will do is think it is so."

"You're probably right, but at this time it hasn't happened. If you and she decide, in the end, to go either way, I'll know it has been good for her. Of course being her brother, older brother even, I want only the best for her, and with everything that has happened to us, she really deserves it."

Lauut entered the booth to taking over for his sister, and Fauul stood beside the booth people watching while he waited for Lauma, thinking. *You never know when things are going to happen to you that is never planned or expected. You go along with your life planning well, when something comes along and completely destroys those plans.* At this point in his thoughts he saw Lauma returning and walked towards her. "Now this is your village and you know the best places to eat, especially during a major gather, so please lead on." He reached out and offered to take her hand.

She stopped for a moment and seeing the gesture, wasn't sure if she wanted to take his hand or not. She was still attempting to get over the shock of his arrival, and at this point things seemed to be moving much too fast for her.

"Come on now," Fauul responded, "we've made no promises one way or the other."

"I know, but . . . well . . . you have . . . darn!" She was so off balance she couldn't even come up with a coherent sentence. Then smiling she said, "Okay, you're right." She reached out and took his hand. "But don't expect to be always right."

"Lead on oh mighty one." As he bowed and smiled, finding himself suddenly full of joy, and the only thing he could attribute it to, was being with Lauma.

She led him through the crowds towards a small food establishment that was off the main area. "This place is one of my favorites, plus there are a couple of tables where we can have at least a little privacy. Still, in a small place like this, everyone will know about you and me before I even return to the booth. I suppose I will be answering questions from the village folk for the rest of the gather."

"Is that a bad thing?"

"It can be. After all they will be making their own conclusions, and the stories will get bigger and move away from the truth, and it will take time away from us, ah my brother and I, from getting the capital we need to keep the property going."

"Well, at least there I can help. I'm here for as long as I want or need to be. I took a leave of absence from my occupation. I left the leave as indefinite."

"Really? Oh look, there's one of the tables I was talking about. If we're quick we can grab it before anyone sees that the ones eating there are about to leave." Still reeling from the surprise, she still did not have her feelings in check. She had hoped that maybe someday he would show up, but in truth, had convinced herself it was not going to happen. Yet it did, and here he was – now what? Was she prepared for the direction this could take? She just didn't know. The people who had been sitting and eating at the table of choice got up to leave. Once they had she immediately claimed the table for them. The owner of the eatery came over personally to clear and clean the table for them, and commented. "Hello Lauma, is this one of your clients for your needlework or just a friend?"

"Hey Jehry, no, not a client . . ."

Fauul then interjected, "I'm hoping to be more than a friend."

"So, if I understand you right, you're going to ask for the right to pursue?"

"Well, we haven't gone that far yet. As you know to ask for that right, you have to get permission from the family and most importantly from the female who is the object of interest. I have done neither yet."

"Yes, yes but that is just a formality. I do see there is a definite attraction between you two. I guess I will have wait and see. So, what is it you would like today?"

"Now that the two of you are finished discussing me and my future, can you let me know what you have available today? Oh I don't know just bring me my usual, and the same for him also." She then looked across at Fauul and blushed again. *Darn,* she thought, *can I not control this blushing in his presence?* While she had hoped that maybe Fauul would come back, she had convinced herself it was not possible, and to just let it be. Yet, right at this moment, here he was sitting across from her. *Damn he's good looking. Why me?* So many things were going through her mind as well as her emotions. She definitely felt completely off balance and out of control.

"You're awfully quiet. It seems that wasn't a problem back on the property when we first met." Thinking back to that day he remembered that confrontation he had with her and that dog. Who would have thought, at that time, he would find this female as the one he wanted to be with?

"If you had at least given me some warning, you know, just a hint that you would be coming down here to see me, something, anything, I don't know. I'm still trying to get over the shock that you are sitting here across from me. I've been talking with my old friends from before the accident and they thought that the distance was too great and just to forget you, but I couldn't. Are you serious about announcing a pursuit? It's really something I haven't even considered."

Smiling he said, "Boy, from silence to so many words I can't even reply. Look, I realized just a short time ago that you, and I mean you, left a very big impression on me. Plus somehow, and I don't know what that is yet, I've changed and you're the one responsible for that change. So I felt it only right to come back and see if it was the same for you. I know that sometimes when one deals with a relationship that it can only go one way, and then there is nothing you can do but just let it die. I was hoping that this would be a two-way relationship, but I wouldn't know that until we got together again. So, here I am." At this point he shrugged.

"Just that simple – right? Oh here comes the food, I do hope you enjoy it. I've always liked this small shop."

After they were served, he asked, "Trying the change the subject here are we?" Then he smiled showing he was only joking.

Still a little flustered she blurted out, "No! No, that's not the case at all, you know that. You sure can take a female's breath away you know."

Quietly he replied, "Yes, I know, and all I can say is that it's a gift of nature. It has made it difficult, at times, to find out if the females who were interested in me just wanted to have someone who made them look good, in our society, in the township, or if they were truly interested in developing a relationship. I admit at times it was fun to have those short flings, but eventually they became two dimensional, and just died a natural death."

Between bites she said, "Know what you mean there. I've found no one, not one male who even interested me beyond being polite and going out for a meal now and then. That is until you showed up, and then something was different. Thinking about it, yes I believe something in me changed also. At least it made me go out and renew those old friendships –

something I should have done a long time ago." She realized that she was eating automatically and didn't, in truth, even taste the food. She had reached down for something else and found her plate empty and was quite surprised having no memory of even grabbing anything from plate. "What the . . . I guess I was hungry I didn't even realize I was eating, which means I am out of time for now and must return to the booth. Will I see you later? I mean after I close down the booth for the evening and head for the evening festivities. And if so where will I be able to find you?"

"Oh most likely I will be with your brother. After all I do have some serious things to talk to him about don't I."

"You mean like pursuit?" She asked innocently as she smiled at him.

"Could be, but I came down here on a leave of absence, so I must figure some things out for myself and your brother would be a good source to bounce things off. Tell you what I'll cover the cost of this meal, and I *will* definitely see you later."

Nodding, she got up and started heading out the door, stopped and turned around to see him again. She felt the emotion of joy starting to overflow as she headed back to the booth. *How is this going to end? Well, one really never knows that's for sure.* Yet, at this one moment, everything appeared to be bright. Still, from personal experience, she knew how that could change in a moment's time – leaving one devastated instead of the anticipated joy. Yet, he was here, and that in itself was the last thing she had expected. She had felt that once he had left that was it and, knowing what she had been told as a whelp knew that in love there are usually no second chances. It was just how it worked. Still being with someone else other than Fauul just did not seem a good fit for her.

Before she knew it she was back to the booth. She saw that her brother was talking with someone, and she signaled him she was going to go the necessary space before taking back the booth. He glanced up from the conversation he was having with the person and saw his sister approaching. She fairly glowed, and it was obvious the time with Fauul had been good. She then signaled him she was going to use the facilities before she returned, and walked away. He returned to his conversation with the individual only to see a few minutes later Fauul approaching the booth. He, on the other hand, was much more difficult to read; still he had to admit that he really liked him.

"Sorry, was distracted there for a moment, so in a couple of minutes my sister will be back and you can then close the deal with the amount of the work you need. She will contract for the product and give you a time for delivery. On that subject would you like it to travel to your location by traveling merchant, the runners, or are you going to be in the area to pick it up yourself?"

"Well, not sure really. It will depend on how long it will take her to produce what I need. I'm on the road a lot myself, so there's a possibility that I will be close to this area when it is completed. If not, I'm in contact with the traveling merchants all the time and that would probably be a good second choice."

"Okay, I'm sure both your mate and your female whelps will love these items. My sister has a wonderful talent for this type of finery."

"You won't get me to argue if these samples are her work. I have seen none better. And believe me since I travel a lot I've had a chance to see many examples of this style of work. In comparison this is very superior to any I have seen, and is much more reasonable in cost. If she can deliver in a reasonable time, with this same quality, then you and she will have a return customer in the future."

Fauul, standing next to the booth, idly followed the conversation as he quietly waited for the transaction to conclude. He watched the crowds as they flowed among the many booths and wares that were being presented. It was a place full of energy and it reminded him of being in the township where he lived. He did so love this, but knew if all came to a conclusion, as he expected, that the only time he would experience it again would be during the major gathers.

All he could think about was Lauma, and was waiting for the magical smile of hers that transformed this ordinary female into one of rare beauty, at least in his eyes. And no, he had not imagined it, because it was still there. It was something he was hoping to do often was to make her genuinely smile. He looked over to Lauut and said, "I'm heading back to the yards. When you are finished here, you can meet me there. But, don't hurry, I think I'm going to wander the crowds for a little while and enjoy the sights."

"Okay, sounds great to me. I think when she arrives here in the next few, I'm going to get something to eat, then will do a little looking myself. I know I do not have any major deals happening with the beasts until the morrow. Still, by hanging around the area, who knows, might be able to move a couple in the meantime."

Fauul took his leave and headed into the crowds to see what this major gather had to offer. Now that he knew that she was still as interested in him, as he was in her, he could at least start looking to his future. Still he knew that it would remain indistinct even if he tried to plan everything. Life didn't work that way. He also knew that the two of them would have to spend more time together to find if that initial spark between them would grow. There would be many get-togethers, and then sometime down the trail of their lives he would make a formal announcement of pursuit. This was the precursor to becoming mates. It was generally an announcement to the world that this female was his exclusive interest, and he was hers. It did not mean that she could not see someone else and it being the same for him. But, it was a sign of the seriousness they felt for each other, and after a set period then they would progress on to the next step, which would be the announcement they were to be mates. A time would be set, traditionally tied in with one of the major gathers, and at that time, they, through the traditional ceremony, would become mates.

Even now he realized what a change in his life this would be. He had never had to be responsible for anyone but himself. Here he was heading down a trail that would forever change that. It was much to absorb. Funny thing he found that he was willingly doing it. He remembered laughing at a couple of friends who had taken these steps, and yet here he was finding himself doing the very same thing. If they saw him now, they would probably be shaking their heads, and smiling a knowing smile, saying "I told you so."

CHAPTER TWELVE

The beasts remained with their packs loaded so that when the moon rose, they'd be back on the trail quickly. On the morrow when they finally stopped he would address the team again. With the graphic evidence they had all seen, he thought that the grumbling and lack of attention, when they set up, followed by the guarding of the camp, would no longer be a problem. He knew that he himself was not going to get any sleep until the following night. With the moonrise he went around and made sure all were awake. Then as quietly as they could they headed down the trail. When they finished the travel the next day would be essentially over, the only stop that would be made was for a quick dry camp for the morn meal, and then they would continue until late past the zenith. Doube had stated that it should put them in an area for a camp that he was familiar with. It was just off the trail and if you did not know it was there you would miss it.

He knew, as they traveled through the moonlit night, it would be more difficult to cover their tracks. Because of this he assigned a couple of the camp assistants to help Doube work on track removal. It would not be perfect, but again if it at least appeared to be something that would not interest the bandits their work would have served its purpose.

As they moved out it seemed that even the beasts were quiet. While it was bright for an evening, with the moon lighting the way, it still was a land of shadows. In the soft light of the moon the trail showed up as a lighter ribbon to the darker surrounding landscape. While they would cover less ground this way, by the time they stopped on the morrow he felt the distance would be great enough to put them out of harm's way, and away from the hunting grounds or claimed territory of this group of thieves and murderers. The night dragged on and every once in a while he would hear someone curse softly because of a misstep or a stumble. But, overall they were silent. As promised, he rotated members of the team out to Doube to keep the ones who were attempting to cover their exit from the area as fresh and alert as possible.

Finally the moon started setting, and looking to the east he thought he saw some graying of the sky. This time of day was always interesting to him, the first false dawn would show where it appeared to be darker, and followed by a hint of gray. Something when you first saw it you were not sure if indeed that it was the dawn. Yet, as the dawn got closer, the sky would begin to lighten, and then you would see the outline of the distant mountains, followed by a touch of blue sky. After that the sky would turn colors – if there were clouds close to the rising sun – making the sunrise as beautiful as many sunsets. As your eyes adjusted to the change, the landscape around you would start to make itself visible. Where the sun would touch the horizon, starting its rise over those distant hills, the sky would be yellow. All this seemed to take a very long time, until the sun did rise above the horizon, and once it showed all of itself to the world, would appear to rise rapidly. Of course, in truth, it was steady and constant. The slowness was just an illusion probably caused by the anticipation of the sun rising. A slight drop in temperature would follow this, as the sun would start to influence the airflow. This made it feel chilly even if one had been moving. It was a time that a morn fire felt good, but this day there would be none. Like last night it would be a dry camp – quickly set up with no fires, a bit of trail food, and back down the trail.

He looked over his team and saw the fatigue on their faces, but there was nothing he could do about it. They still had most of a day ahead of them and he would have to push them to get the distance that he thought was necessary. Ahead, just a little way, he saw an area that appeared to be a good place to make that morn dry camp. Doube and his helpers had joined them, since Doube thought they had enough distance behind them to quit covering their tracks. Knowing the nature of the average bandit, he knew that overall, they were lazy and didn't do more than they had to. Plus the bandits generally stayed within the area they worked. It was familiar to them and they knew all the points to attack, and the numerous escape routes if need be.

He talked with Doube and pointed out the area he was eyeing for the morn break, but Doube stated that just a little further there was a better one. Knowing the scout as one to trust, he agreed to push them on a little further. He also knew, because they were all tired that now they were very vulnerable to surprise attack. So he took some of the younger ones, who would be more observant, and sent them out as flankers, with Doube scouting ahead. He truly would not feel safe until they were completely out of this area. With the younger ones he assigned one of the experienced males. He wanted both the better sight and better experience out for observation. He also placed some of the younger ones in the forward position and had the older ones trail. Besides, he felt that most likely, if any danger was here, it, more than likely, would come from the rear, since this bandit band had attacked from that direction. Yet, that did not mean there would be no danger from the other areas. With Doube scouting ahead he'd cover any lack of experience from that direction. He knew it would be at least a couple of days before they were through the worst of it. They, after that would be heading into some of the more civilized areas where these attacks on unsuspecting travelers were less.

It was mid-morn when Doube returned and pointed out the area he had spoken of earlier. When one first looked at it there wasn't anything that made it look any different than the surrounding terrain. Yet, when one went down a narrow path through brush, which was over their heads, it opened up into an area that dropped down and was surrounded by the same high brush. In the area there was plenty of room for the pack beasts, including a small meadow to allow them some graze time. Looking around he saw a small grove of trees, a small creek, and a pond. Looking over at Doube he asked, "How'd you ever find this place? There really is no sign of its existence at all."

Smiling, Doube replied, "I'm not going to give away all my trade secrets. Let's just say when I was in this area I was curious. Something just didn't look right to me so I did a little exploring and found it. When I find these areas, as I've said, I tuck them away in my mind for future use. You just never know when this knowledge will come in handy. I think you can call in your flankers and post a guard at the entrance. It's the only easy way in and out."

"Okay, I'll take your word on that. But it does make me nervous if there is only one way in and one way out."

"Not quite what I said, no there's another way out, it just isn't easy. I always make sure there are at least two exits out of an area. Just because we are at peace over all on this planet doesn't mean in those areas where civilization doesn't exist as of yet, or is spread out, that we will have peace. There are always those individuals who prefer violence and have no conscience. They seem to think that any and all can and will be their victims. After all, hard work and planning is just for suckers. For them it is easier to steal, murder, etcetera. And they do the worst that they can get away with."

"Truer words were never spoken. It surprises me that we still have to face this type of mentality. Since, in truth, they steal, and accomplish less, by taking the direction in life that they do. The pain and suffering they cause bothers them not the least. I just hope, as our civilization grows, that we can eliminate most of that type of behavior. If not, at least make the penalties so tough or severe that they will think long and hard, before committing such acts – at least one can hope."

"From what I've seen, it will be many turns and generations before our population will fill in the empty lands. It makes me wonder, at times, if these areas were ever filled with people. I know there have been hints of such. But, these few hints might have been ones like me who like these wild lands, who knows?"

"As you know that is what I do. Try to find out if there ever was a greater population than what we have now. Before we continue why not go out and signal the flankers in. We're only going to be here long enough to eat, and then be on our way again." Jllon knew the greatest danger was still just ahead. If the bandits were following them, the bandits would know that as this day progressed the team members would be exhausted from the long time on the trail with little or no sleep. When one is tired it is so easy to become less alert and not recognize a developing situation until it is too late. He walked back into the group and passed on the admonition that they be quiet, eat quickly and be prepared to move out again. He turned around and saw the flankers coming in and going over to their particular areas to grab something to eat. The next half-day would prove to be critical. Again he thought that once they set up camp at the end of this day they would have traveled far enough to be out of any immediate danger.

The camp was strangely quiet, but he did know the reason. Many of the young ones had never faced their own mortality, and it can lead one to think deeply about the direction in life they were taking. Besides, he was sure most were just too tired to converse. After all that took energy and they had burned much of it just getting here and would need more of it for the trail ahead. After a too short of time they continued their flight from the massacre heading down the trail to the south – at least the weather was cooperating. Like the day before, it would have been a wonderful time just to sit and relax and enjoy what nature was providing, the flyers singing, a soft breeze, a smell of nectar from the vegetation, and soft warmth from the sun – a perfect day really.

Fortunately nothing happened and the rest of the day went without incident. Doube came in and said they were making great time and the area he had chosen for them was not far away. Again its location was just off the trail, and not really visible. Plus, if need be, it would be easily defended. There were numerous exits, but all were defensible. From the outside, if one decided to attack, they would find themselves at a disadvantage, since all entrances led through choke points leaving it easy for the defenders.

It was mid-zenith when they reached the planned stopping point. Inside the area was a large meadow for the beasts to graze, water and a large supply of fallen wood from the trees in the area. He had to admit that he was tired, but at this moment he had to put it aside to make sure all members was okay, followed by the setting up the rotation of the guards.

With this last flight from danger he wanted hourly changes to give all a chance to rest, and to make sure the guards remained alert.

Once back on the trail, on the morrow, they would only be approximately two days out from a small village. After that there would only be one to two days between villages. This portion they were presently traveling was the most dangerous, and they were almost through it, and he could almost breathe a sigh of relief. He wanted to get the team together and congratulate them on getting through this portion, and admonish them that they were not quite out of all the danger. So he passed the word that he wanted a group meeting after the meals had been complete.

He wandered the camp making contact with the different members and see how all were faring. He wanted to make sure everything was set up correctly and each area had a plan for defense – if need be. Even though it appeared they had come through the danger area unscathed, he really had no real proof. He followed this by heading out of camp for a little distance to see how visible the site was and how far the camp and beast noise traveled. He found that as he approached the trail they were traveling that the camp was completely invisible and because its location was low and behind a small hill, sound did not travel very far. Again if he did not know there was a large group camping there he would not even have been aware the site was being used.

He again felt doubly thankful and fortunate to have Doube as their scout. His reputation every day was proving to be accurate. This male was very knowledgeable in all aspects of scouting, and had no problem teaching others his skills, if one was interested. It appeared that Doube was of the same mind as he when it came to knowledge. It was best when it was passed on to others. Tradition had set up knowledge as something to be kept to one's family. In his mind this stifled learning and advancement. Only when shared would it grow. Unfortunately much of this world was still stuck in the old ways of keeping knowledge secret. He was sure that originally there had to be a reason but, if by some tragedy, the family group were wiped out, then their particular knowledge or specialty would be lost. It was something that slowed their growth to a better world. It was time to get back to camp, and to eat something himself. He could feel the weariness drag on him, and he knew it would apply to all. Yes, while the field was his life, it could also be his death.

After the meals the team members remained to assist the camp managers and assistants in cleaning the area. Once completed Jllon called for attention. "I wish I could say to all of you that this flight we've just taken was unnecessary, but for our safety it was. I do believe that we are now far enough away to be safe. Yet, not really knowing the territory of this particular bandit clan I cannot be sure. That is why we will run heavier guarding at this camp. And we will change the guarding members hourly. All of us are tired and more vulnerable to missing clues that would alert us of someone approaching this camp.

"I have to say you all did very well on this portion. For many it was the first time you had to face death in this way. It's never easy, period. Now I'm keeping this short because of all of us being tired, so I'll open this up to a very brief question time and then we will break up and head out to our assignments. One last thing we will be pulling out early, just before sunrise. We are just about one to two days out of one of the small villages where we will stop for a quarter of the day or maybe overnight and get information about the surrounding area. With that I will now ask for any questions you may have."

One of the learners, a female rose and asked, "So, how is it that you know about these bandits? It isn't common knowledge in the townships that they even exist, as far as I know."

"Oh, they exist alright. And you saw what they can do. They do not want any witnesses, so usually anyone who is attacked by them does not survive. I have firsthand personal knowledge of what they do. To explain, when I was younger and was on an early dig, a group of bandits raided some properties outside the village we were close to. Normally, the bandits do not do such things sticking instead to the wild lands.

But for some reason this group thought they could raid and get away with it.

"Anyway, they, the bandits were tracked down over a period of time and eliminated. I was on part of the team that went into the bandit's camp after they had been eliminated. It was there we found one of the females the bandits had taken alive. She was barely alive, and actually died while we cared for her. Let's just say it is something I never want to see again, and I wish that kind of treatment on no one." A hush fell over the group as they imagined what it might have been like. He looked over the team then asked, "Any more questions?" Looking around he saw that it appeared that the answer from the previous one was enough and there were no additional questions coming. "Okay, we need to be back on the trail by sunrise with the plan to push on. We hope to reach the village by sunset. Of course, as an incentive, most of the villages have hostels, which would mean real baths and some real beds; something that will allow us a small break from this project. Get as much rest as you can and be alert during your duty time." And with that he announced the short meeting was over and sent them back to what they needed to do.

He again walked the camp, leaving a good word here and there. He, as he always did on these projects, made himself available to all. He had learned that by doing so, he would have a better idea of morale of the camp, and of what rumors or ideas were being passed around. Again, by doing this, he made himself accessible to all – something he encouraged to all of the leaders on the team. He knew of others who had led similar projects, refusing contact with the members and preferred to remain aloof of the team. From his point of view, these teams seemed to be less successful in their endeavor, than teams who worked together from top to bottom and vice a versa.

The following day went without incident, except for the short tempers. He knew it was because most were still tired from the extended run they made from the area where the bodies were discovered. He was also sure that some of it was finding out the world was not as peaceful and protected as they had thought it would be. Still a night at the hostel before they continued on would be a good thing. He truly was looking forward to a good bath, plus the thought of getting a night's sleep in a real bed left him smiling. Again, since they were on a field project, it would be a bed without his mate. *Such are the consequences when one involves oneself in such fieldwork.*

As evening approached they saw the village in the distance, and it was a welcome sight. Up until actually seeing it there had been no signs of a village close by, no out-shelters, farms or herders, and he was beginning to wonder if something had happened to cause the village to be abandoned. Yet, it finally was there ahead of them. He gave a sigh of relief. He had so anticipated the evening in the hostel that it would have been a large disappointment, not only to him, but to the whole team. *Funny how that works,* he thought. *We've been doing nothing but camping, which is fine, but when a bit of change and a good change is anticipated, and then fails to appear, one feels slighted.*

As they approached it was becoming dusk and they saw the lights of the village starting to become visible. Now for sure, they knew it was still occupied, and active. But, until they had confirmed it was safe, only a small contingent would enter and negotiate the overnight stay at the hostel. With the evidence of the attack on that unknown group, they wanted to make sure the bandits hadn't overrun this village and this was actually one of their strongholds. Yet, as they approached, they saw both females and their whelps going about their normal lives. All seemed quite normal – still, additional caution wouldn't hurt. The village was laid out in the traditional wheel, spoke arrangement which meant it would be easy to locate the center of the village and contact the ones' in charge. After getting the approval and once the team was set up he would pass on to the town elders on what they had discovered.

It took a little longer than he figured to get everything set up. It had been close to mealtime and, of course, they were not expected. So no one was at the village offices to greet them. They had to go to some of the local shops and ask around to locate the one in charge for this turn. When finally located, he was quite surprised to find a group coming in, especially one of this size. Yet, this person seemed to be a quiet, strong, and honest individual, and upon learning they were from the one of the major townships and of the council, simply charged them the standard rate. He followed this by putting them in contact with the ones in charge of the hostel. He also handed them a small map of the village identifying the bath shelters, eateries, beast yards, and storage areas.

For this he was thankful. It was also the first time he had seen a village providing such a thing. It was a great idea, and more should be doing it. It simplified things considerably. Since most of the communities were laid out on the same general patterns, things such as maps of the places just didn't enter one's mind or thoughts and thusly were considered unneeded. Still, when you got down to the individual locations within the villages and townships, the locations of the different facilities varied. Before he left the elder he stated that once the team was settled he wanted to talk with him about what they had found back on the trail before coming into their village. And with the contact and paperwork taken care of they headed out of the village back to the team who was waiting for word one way or the other. He informed them all was well, and to head in. He could almost sense a relief running through the team.

Once they were settled, he headed back over to this turn's elder and made contact as promised. Entering the working shelter he found the elder waiting for him. "That's a pretty good sized team you have there." Joehansehn stated.

"Yes, that's true. We're heading down south for a dig. You see I'm the Head Keeper of the Past, and this is one of our rare field projects."

"Really, the actual Head Keeper of the Past. I didn't think the heads of these places ever left the townships where they worked."

"I can understand that. There is usually much to keep me there. But, in truth, fieldwork is my joy, and when one comes along I want to be a part of it. Anyway, that isn't the reason I wanted to come back and see you."

"I figured that. Is there something we can do to be a service to your team?"

"No, not our team but maybe you can help identify some individuals we found while coming down the trail."

"You mean they refused to identify themselves?"

"No, not exactly. They couldn't identify themselves. There were dead."

"Dead? What happened? Where was this?" He asked being shocked by the statement Jllon had just provided.

"Where, almost three days back. From what little we could find, it appears bandits attacked them. The bandits waited until they had stopped for the evening, and just as they were preparing to set up, swept in and wiped them out. Our scout was able to figure it out from the tracks and evidence left. We were the first to show up after it happened."

"Okay, what did you need from me or this village then?"

"The attack happened at least a day before we entered that area, which is probably a good thing for us. It meant the bandits were done and gone, since they normally do not stay around an area where they have attacked. Anyway, the dead were completely stripped of anything that had any value. There was nothing left in the camp to identify who these individuals were. We did a thorough search and came up with nothing.

"I can only hope that no females were along, knowing from past experience, what happens to them, when these bandit bands capture them. Anyway, we were hoping you might be able to at least identify them, and before you ask, no, we did not bring the bodies with us. We buried them at the site where we found them. I'll have our scout give you a location later if you like."

"Okay, how can I help then?"

"The party size, or at least what we found, was four. Other than their general description, I can tell you little more."

"So, it would have been approximately four to five days ago they were attacked. Hmmm, only four members . . . could you tell what direction they were originally heading?"

"It appeared to be north, and it also appeared the bandits shadowed them for at least half a day."

Leaning on the counter he asked. "How were you able to tell that?"

"Once we found the bodies and knew that we were the first to find them, our scout went out and tracked both groups – the victims, and the attackers. We wanted to make sure we were not going to be next. After all, by taking the time to bury the bodies, we left ourselves open for attack from the same band. We wanted to make sure they were far away from there."

"Yeah, that makes sense. It would have been a great time to be attacked since all your attention would have been on the victims and their camp. Hmm . . . we had a small group of traveling merchants here about the time frame you figure this happened. You know they usually contract between villages and properties for goods that cannot be provided locally. The bandits took everything?"

"Yes, even the clothes the victims were wearing. The area of the attack was pretty chewed up from the attack and from the subsequent pillage, but the tracks coming into the point of attack said they had two pack beasts. Does that help?"

"A little, I think that it was them. While they didn't come here very often, if I remember right, they said they had a contract with a village down south, and would be heading up to one of the major townships to fulfill it. We were just an overnight stop on the way."

"Just males in the group then – no females and no whelps right?"

"Yes, that is correct, which is, if this was that group, a good thing." Shaking his head, and speaking almost to himself said, "Yes, a very good thing."

"Agreed – not that I would wish what happened to them, on anybody. Do you have any runners coming through tonight or on the morrow morn?"

"No, why do you ask?"

"I was hoping to get this information out by a runner so we can alert the surrounding villages that this group of bandits is active here and to be especially alert."

"Good idea, I'll do that with the next one when he gets here, which, unfortunately, will not be for five or six days."

"Okay then, as we continue south we will inform the villages we cross, and maybe find out more about the victims. You know things like, if they had mates and whelps, and where they may have been from.

Thanks for the use of the hostel, and that map idea is a great one. I'll see you in the morn just before we head out. Have a good evening."

"Same to you sir, and I will be here early so you can catch me here."

Jllon turned and left the shelter and headed back to the team, and with the new information he had some thinking to do. He at least knew the victims were just male, but still no identities, or knowledge enough to be helpful, and just enough to let the local authorities know about the bandits and the fact that they were ruthless and without mercy.

When he returned to the hostel all was full of activity and a din of conversation and chatter was flowing making it hard for one to hear. It had been quite a while since they had been with civilization. He felt the energy and excitement. The few females had left and were at the public bath areas, and when they returned the males would do the same. Then as a group they'd go to one of the local eateries. He checked with the camp managers to see if there were anything they would need to add to their equipment, or had need of repairs, and the condition of the yards and the overall shape of the beasts. He knew it would be many hours before he'd relax. Logistics and condition of equipment was so important, even at such a brief stop, as they would be making here. He knew with the increase of villages, from this point out, that the trail would become easier. So far, with his practiced eye, he had seen nothing to inspire curiosity to even do a test dig. It appeared, so far, that there was no sign of anything that might be related to their main quest – frustrating to say the least.

In the end it may have been better to travel the main route, but if they had he would never have known if there was anything of value. Only by making this trek could it be determined if there was anything of interest or be worth returning later. It also gave him time to see who would be good at the different tasks that would be needed soon. He was an observer, and a watcher of people. It was these traits that made him good at his main job, the Head Keeper of the Past, and, of course, his passion fieldwork. Plus, he had an uncanny ability to focus on the problem at hand and to work it through until a solution would appear. Anyway, he knew the route they took was a calculated risk. Overall, all it was costing them was time, and a little more of the necessary items, to do it this way. Again, he needed to take advantage of the project, as much as possible. Time in itself was not a consideration, just the results. He really hoped to solve the question, the ongoing puzzle, this time out. Were they myth, or were they real? And if the *ones before* were real, was the way they were perceived by this generation accurate, or were they completely different? Of course, one thing he knew, even words change in their meanings over time. So, most likely, if these elusive people existed, their lifestyle, let alone their speech, would be strange to them today.

* * *

They were back on the trail before sunrise, and as the elder had stated, he was there the next morn to see them off. He could add nothing new to what they had discussed the previous evening, but again confirmed he would get the message out through the next runner.

Jllon thought about the village as they left. He guessed it probably had a population of no more than a hundred or so. And that included any of the outer areas that were serviced by it. What was it that brought people together to form these small villages? He knew many came into existence because of the location of a cross trail, or because the distance was right from a township to make it a logical stopping point – these were obvious. Still others had no such advantage or need, yet still existed. Well, it wasn't his field to study why people did what they did. Yet, as he thought about it, it was something that could help one in the search of ancient artifacts. Why he hadn't thought of it before he did not know, but a cross discipline of what he did and understanding why people did what they did as a society should help tremendously for finding and planning projects and of discoveries in the future.

Talking with Doube as they headed out, Doube informed him that the travel over the next few days would be easy and relatively flat. It would be a little warm though. So make sure all was well supplied with water.

"So it appears you have traveled much in these areas, is that correct?"

"Yeah, you know my discipline is geology, and when I am not performing my work as a scout, I enjoy going out and study the land. Before you ask, no I haven't seen any sign of the *ones before*. After all, if as much time has passed as it seems, then there would be little of theirs that would still be around. That's not to say that some of the places I have been could have been locations for them, but I really wasn't looking. Besides, it's your specialty not mine."

Jllon laughed, "Yes, that's true, but, did you not put in your notes from the last assignment with the mappers that you thought there in the desert that there was a chance that a township was buried there?"

"Yes I did, and for a very good reason. While it may not turn out to be so, there were just too many inconsistencies to be natural. Yet, the one thing I have learned is that nature can fool you."

"Of course you were not the only one who thought that way. Usually if only one note states something like that, I generally ignore it. But when a second independent observation states a similar conclusion, then it has a tendency to make me want to look over the site. Fauul Saelor stated much the same thing. So to have a cartographer and a geologist come to the same conclusion is strong evidence for me."

"That makes sense. Of course there's the object he has also. Even though it's from another place, the locations are only a few days apart."

"My thought exactly. If it had been in two different regions with great distances between, then it may have weakened my request for this fieldwork."

The following days went rapidly. With the continuation of good weather, and the villages' distances being only a day apart, it made travel easy. There were no additional problems from the bandits, and they had learned no more about the victims. Still, what little was learned led them to believe the victims were originally from somewhere north.

It was a common practice to have these traveling merchants. They provided a needed service. While much was provided locally, not everything one needed would be available. Many items or needs was only found outside of their particular areas, and most had not the time or the means to be able to make these journeys to find what it was they needed – so these traveling merchants filled that need. Many of the local merchants used them to pick up and move supplies to other villages. How it started no one really knew, but the service had been around for hundreds of turns. To keep their own cost down they never numbered much more than four. Once they had what they had contracted for they would hire locals to help deliver the product, if it required more than the team to handle the contracted item or product. Of course it, at times, left them vulnerable to attack by bandits because they were such a small group and might carry valuable items with them. Yet, at the same time because they were a small group and a required service, they often were able to pass through most areas unseen and untouched – even bandits had need of their services now and then.

* * *

It would not be long before they would be entering the northern edge of the desert. While it was spring, and desert would be much easier to pass through, water would still be an issue. Doube, thinking back to the last time he passed through the desert, reminded Jllon that the trails were there in the desert for a reason. He spoke with him telling him about Joellie and his wanting to leave the established trail, which he then did. This had come close to leading the mapping team to disaster. Jllon thanked him for the reminder and said that he had no plans to leave the trails. This group was much larger than the mapping team and he wouldn't take those kinds of risks. It was hoped that the winter had been good and all the tanks and springs were full of water. They did not want to have to travel a couple of days without water if they could avoid it.

Before entering the northern edge Jllon called a meeting of the team. The meeting would happen just

after the zenith meal just before they headed into the
desert.

CHAPTER THIRTEEN

The major gather went well, and Lauut had successfully sold beasts to the traveling merchants, and Lauma had sold many of her items, with contracts for additional items. The nightly festivities had been a nice break also. It was now time to pack up and head back, pay off the younglings who had been watching the property, and get back into the routine of daily living.

Thinking back on the gather Lauut thought that it went even better than hoped. It appeared that his sister had finally found a mate, even though nothing was official yet. Still, if anyone had seen them together it was obvious – even if it wasn't to the two of them. Where did that leave him? He truthfully had found no one as of yet, still one never knew when the right one would come around. When he thought about it,

Lauma was not even looking for anyone at the time when Fauul arrived. And it was obvious he wasn't. Yet after all these cycles had passed, here he was and there she was. *Funny how things work*, he thought.

This led him into another train of thought. Now that Fauul was here, what was he going to do? He had held a pretty high position where he came from and was an individual who loved the township style of life. Where was he going to live? Actually that part was pretty easy to solve. They had a workers shelter, which was vacant. He could offer it to him and see if he would accept. Besides, he wanted to be around this person a little longer anyway, to make sure he was all he appeared to be. And only by being with the person would he be sure.

Fauul had enjoyed the major gather, and had stayed at the hostel in the village at night. He found the more he was around Lauma the more he wanted to be around her. Was this how it worked, or did this feeling and need start to fade after time? For this he had no answers. So he just shrugged and thought, *I guess I will just ride this out and see where it takes me.* Lauma's brother was a great person himself, but underneath both of them he could sense a sadness that was from the great tragedy in their lives, and was very much a part of them

He knew that both missed their sires very much even after all this time. For females, once grown, the time they spent with their mothers as equals was very special. Since she, as the daughter, would be both a whelp and grown up. There would be a history that made the bond so much stronger. Yes, mothers and daughters, with most, you could see their strength and connection. Not that it was any different with fathers and sons. Yet, to be honest, it was different, since it was on a different level that males would connect. He felt part of it was that females had a connection with eternity – forever. They were the bearers of the future; they were the ones with the connection to family. It seemed that males were more on the outside of the family, while being a part of the same. While they contributed to the future generations, they never would have the investment in that future as the female would.

Now that the gather was ending the hostel would be closing down for the inevitable clean up. While all that had participated in the gather would be required to assist in the cleaning of the village center, only a few would work the hostel area. This whole process usually only took half a day since there were many to assist. After the zenith meal most would be returning to their properties, and resuming their daily lives until the next minor gather. During the gather Fauul had inquired about lodging, and found, at this time, there was nothing available in the village. It was something he hadn't considered in his decision to come here. He knew, if necessary, for a short period of time, he could camp, as he did when part of the team. Still, he needed a better long-term solution to the problem. While he contemplated his situation, he assisted in the clean-up, crossing paths now and then with Lauut and Lauma, as one had a tendency to do. Finally Lauut approached him and asked. "Have you found a place to stay yet?"

"No, not really . . . It kind of surprises me, since where I'm from there is no problem with lodging."

"In a township, I hope not. But this is a small village and remote. While the gathers bring in many, they as you know, stay in the public shelters or hostels, and after that, these are cleaned, and return to being the hostels for ones that are passing through. We just don't have need of any permanent temporary shelters, which is a contradiction of terms."

"How so? Oh. Ah, that I'm finding out quickly. I even asked about unused space in a private shelter or two, but even that isn't available."

"I've discussed this with Lauma, and she agreed to it . . ."

"Oh planning my life now are we", he said with a smile. "Sorry for interrupting, continue please."

Laughing Lauut said, "Now, I don't know if I want to . . . anyway, we have a workers shelter on the property, back when the operation was much more successful than it is now. You know which one since you and Doube spent the night in it. If you are interested you can live there for a while." Then smiling back at Fauul once again, he said, "Plus I can keep an eye on you and protect my sister from you if necessary."

Looking half serious, Fauul asked, "And who's going to protect me from her? After all when we first met she didn't need any protection at that time. Between those knives and that dog of hers, she could have handled more than just the two of us," he then laughed out loud, which Lauut couldn't help but join in.

Lauma approaching heard them laughing and asked, "Okay you two what's this about? Are you talking behind my back here?"

With an innocent look on his face Lauut asked, "Does it look like it to you Fauul that she has her back turned on us? As far as I can see she's facing us. So how can we be talking behind her back?"

Stamping her foot in mock anger and with her hands on her hips, she said, "You know what I mean, now stop it."

"Okay sis, I was just offering Fauul here the use of the workers shelter, and then mentioned that I was going to watch him to protect you if necessary."

With some sarcasm, Lauma said, "Right, as if you could against someone who's at least a head above you. Plus with his natural build he would just throw you to the ground and sit on you, and that would be that."

Giving her some sad eyes he replied, "Do you think so little of me sis? Anyway he stated that you didn't need any protection, and reminded me of the first time you two met. Then asked who was going to protect him from you."

Fauul broke in saying, "So, I'm standing here listening to you talk about me, as if I'm not here. So if you are going to do this, at least let me leave for a few, then, when its settled, you can signal me and then I'll just come back."

Realizing that was exactly what they were doing they both turned to him and in unison said, "I'm sorry."

Fauul laughed while Lauut rather sheepishly said, I guess we've been together too long."

"Well, I hope so, as you two are siblings after all. Okay look, as you know I've been unsuccessful in locating a place to live, and if you both are willing to rent me the workers shelter I'm fine with that. But if I were to stay on your property it would only be fitting that I work with you. I'm not the type that will just sit around and watch someone else work. Although, I could say, I love work – I could sit and watch it all day."

All three then burst out laughing at the little joke. "Okay, if Lauma approves then the space is available. Are you sure you want to work with the beasts? It's a really dirty job, and definitely different than anything you've ever done – especially since you are a township whelp."

"Now don't rub it in. I can't help it if my sires were from a township and wanted nothing to do with the outback or wild lands. Look I just came off over a turn in the backcountry, and yes while it was nice to be able to return to the township, I can see how this can grow on you. So yeah, in many ways, I'm green from not being a part of this my whole life. Many things you take for granted, because it was always there, are things I will have to learn."

"Yeah I guess that's true of all of us if we went to one of those townships. We would feel both nervous and very much out of place."

"True, you both would probably just stop, once you first entered and just stare, wondering what you should do next. So, I guess it works either way – me here, or you two there."

"Well sis, do you agree? Should we rent this space to Fauul?"

"You're the male here, why ask me?"

"Because I know that even though males supposedly are in charge, that if we did not get the approval from our females that there would be hell to pay for a long, long time. And that applies even if you are my sister."

With a demure look, she asked, "I don't know what you mean dear brother? Are you saying that we females can be a problem for you males?"

Responding to the challenge, Lauut replied, "A problem? No not really. After all you can usually, after a time, find a solution to a problem, and I really don't think we males will ever figure you females out. So, if it is unsolvable it isn't a problem . . . let me think . . . what would be a good word here."

"Be careful bro, your treading on dangerous ground here."

Smiling at the two of them Fauul then stated, "Yes oh fellow male, how are you going to get yourself out of this one?"

Shrugging, Lauut stated, "Have to think about it a while . . ."

"Yes brother, think about for a long while, and think well."

At this point in the conversation someone yelled in their direction, "Hey, you three we're here to finish the clean-up and not talk all day. You can do that afterwards. We all want to head back to our shelters." Guiltily, they looked around and realized that they had been talking among themselves for quite a while, and should have continued with the clean-up. They replied, "Sorry about that." And went back to the duties they were performing before they got together and started talking.

It was towards the zenith when the work was completed, and the workers went for a last communal meal before heading out. They all said their good byes after the meal and broke up heading out to their individual properties. All still had much work to do on their family properties, and it would take some time for all of them to find out how successful the major gather had been. But, from the initial overview it appeared to have been one of the more successful gathers overall.

There had been some announcements of pursuits, and of up and coming matings. Plus a number of contracts and problems that were presented had been either finalized or resolved. Still costs verses income had to be compared, and the results posted. Of course any of the contracts that had been made had to be reviewed and then the work would begin on fulfilling these services. Lauma herself had six new contracts for her goods that would keep her busy for half a turn. Yet, it was important, since full payment would not be received until the items were delivered.

The trip back to the property was leisurely, but before they really knew it, they were at the gate and ready to enter. All were tired, but they had a few chores that had to be accomplished before they could call it "finished for the day". Lauut and Lauma had to inspect the work done by the younglings that they had hired to cover the property and chores while they were away at the gather – pay them their due, and send them on their way back to their own shelters. Fauul needed to get set up in the workers shelter, followed by assisting the other two in whatever still needed to be done. He knew he was about to get his first introduction to working with these beasts, and in truth looked forward to it – at least for now, anyway. He, being a township person, had never really paid much attention to the beasts. Since, in a township, it was unimportant.

It would also give him a chance to observe Lauma, and he knew she would be doing the same. When one normally spent planned time with a prospective mate, both were usually on their best behavior. So, with both being in such close proximity to each other, the opportunity to see each other in the day-to-day light would allow them to see each other more realistically.

He had to admit it was definitely quiet here. You could hear the winds, the bawling of the beasts, and creaking of the floor as he walked on it and that was just about all. After putting his personal items away he headed out across the yard to the porch and sat in one of the chairs waiting for one of the two of them to let him know more about what he was going to do here. Looking around he saw Lauut walking with one of the younglings, who had covered the property, while they were gone. It was obvious he was inspecting his work, and commenting to him about something. Lauma had yet to leave the shelter so was probably inspecting it, or something to that effect. He thought that until the hired ones had left to return to their own property that he would stay out of it and just wait. The only problem was that by sitting here in the sun with the cool breeze blowing it was hard to stay awake and found he was dozing off without realizing it. The first hint he had that he had been asleep was when Lauut approached and knocking his leg down from its crossed position.

"Sleeping are you?"

Stretching Fauul stated, "Well, I figured I'd wait until you were finished with the ones you had hired to cover, and then join you. So, I sat here, as you could see, relaxing while you finished up. The next thing I know is that you came over and I am asleep – must admit it's comfortable here in the sun."

"Yeah that's true, but unlike a township when you leave your job you are finished, here there's always something that needs to be done. Anyway, the younglings are gone and heading back to their properties, so it's time to head inside briefly before we work the evening chores. Once they are completed, then we can relax. Oh, by the way, we all assist each other in food prep, as well as the work involving the beasts."

"Sounds fair to me", Fauul said smiling, "but once I fix a meal you may change your mind. Shall we head in then?"

"That bad?"

"You have no idea. I learned from my mother who to be kind didn't win her mate from her cooking skills."

CHAPTER FOURTEEN

With the zenith meal completed Jllon called to order the brief meeting. "Okay all, so far it has been an interesting journey to this point. I know many of you have seen more than you ever expected, and probably at the same time figured that some of what you have traveled has been some of the most difficult traveling you've ever done. We're just about to head into the desert. Actually, for most part, we will be traveling on the western edge. But nonetheless, it is still the desert. Most deserts cover large areas, and one assumes because of that vastness there are many places to travel, and many places to go. In the desert, while that may seem to be true, it in fact is not. Almost all beasts and creatures require water. It is the true limiting factor. So the size shrinks to locations of water. Some of these locations are seasonal, and others are permanent. Yet, even the permanent ones cannot always be counted on. Another phenomena in the desert is mirages, a reflection caused by the sun that makes it appear there is water, usually a lake out ahead of you. But, like the rainbow, as you attempt to approach it continues to recede. It is an illusion. So as we head into the desert do not separate yourself from the team, and stay on the main trails as these have been established by water locations. One last thing, there are poisonous creatures out here, so watch where you step, and in the morns shake out your footwear as some like to climb into them at night.

"Our destination or first real stop is towards the southern end of this desert, and we will do some major research there. Eventually we will leave a small team at this location, before we move onto where the object was found, whether we truly find anything at this first site or not. Thank you all for the efforts you have put forth so far, and know that possible discovery is just ahead of us. Okay let's pack it up and head on down the trail." He didn't leave it open for questions at this time. He figured that he could talk with individuals who had specific questions as they progressed. He wanted to make sure they made the first water source before dark. Because the next day and one half they would be traveling dry with no known water sources. Because of this, he had purchased a couple of additional pack beasts and additional water containers in the last village. He wanted to make sure they were covered if any of the seasonal water holes were dry.

As the day progressed it was obvious to all that the area they were in was very dry. For many of the team it was the first time they had ever seen a desert. To them it appeared to be stark, ugly and with little life. Hearing these comments Doube replied, "Give it time, the desert will grow on yah. And there is much life here; you just need to know where to look. Plus the beasts and such are not stupid. They stay out of the sun during the heat of the day, unlike us. I do believe that after a while you will start to see the secret beauty that the desert holds. So, yes just give it time.

"After all if you think about it, we will be spending much time in it. Part of the area you will be doing your work is desert. While it is only a day or two to get out of it from there, it might as well be across an impassable canyon since you will not be traveling to there for quite a while. So learn from the desert. She can be a harsh learned. Here, not learning the lessons can mean death." With that he smiled and continued, "Okay, just obey the rules of the desert, and be careful and you should be fine."

Even though it was spring they could feel the heat building as they continued south. There were no trees to speak of, just vegetation that had dangerous looking thorns – definitely something to stay away from. What vegetation there was, was widely scattered. Much looking dead, but on closer inspection seemed to be alive but in a state of suspension. It was like this vegetation was waiting for something – whatever that something was. Then there were areas of rocky soil followed by sand and rock, just like it was a large beach on the ocean, but lacking the ocean, of course. Every once in a while they would see something scurrying across the sand hills, but whatever it was moved too fast to be identified. Yes, this was definitely a new world to most of them. The other surprising thing was how vast the distances were. When one had been raised in a township, or a village, and one did not travel you thought the whole world was your little corner, not really realizing how narrow a view this really was. Also the area that they were from had trees which had a tendency to block views.

Again when someone described a trip or a tale about something, or began talking of travel, one had a tendency to put into it what one knew, and not what was really out there. They had been on the trails now for well over a cycle, or maybe it was two, who really knew? Another thing they found, these new to the trails, was time seemed to just blend from one day to the next. It was so easy to lose track of it without any of their past routines. Here the routine was up in the morn, eat, pack, and head down the trail, observe possible dig sites, break for a quick zenith meal, and continue on until evening when they would set up for the night. Then repeat, repeat, and repeat. With the only changes being the terrain, or a remote village or two, and even at times even these changes would be subtle.

That evening they stopped in an area that appeared to have been a mining site. They could see the tailings from the digs everywhere, and from the appearances it had been in operation for quite a while before the operations finally shut down. It was obvious that the site was very old. Any shelters that may have been here were long gone, and there was not even a sign of where they may have been. Still knowing that the site had been occupied for a period of time meant that somewhere they had been getting water. Of course since this was a regular stopping point on the desert trail that source had been located and was used regularly by travelers. Jllon decided to have the team spend the next day here to inspect the mines and to see if there was anything that they could use to identify when these mines may have been worked. He suspected that anything of value would have been removed long ago – especially since it was a known stopping point. Still, one could get lucky, and he was not one for passing up any opportunity.

Looking around the area he found, as the sun set that the rocks in the area were of many colors. Yet vegetation was extremely sparse, and shade non-existent. Even though summer was still a long ways off it was warm here. While traveling down to this point he had noticed that over time the desert itself had grown. He had seen signs of vegetation that only survived in a wetter climate. It made him think that there was a great possibility there were people living in the area sometime in the distant past, other than the miners who had worked here.

But studying the area they were presently in, there was no sign of a recent change in climate. This had been desert at the time the mines were in operation. With the summer heat it must have been unbearable to work these mines. Still whatever it was they had mined, it had drawn them here and the discomfort did not matter, since it was an opportunity for a few to become wealthy. You know, a little discomfort now, so that sometime in the future, you could live comfortably. Again, he knew, from the history of strikes, that few really ever came out ahead on these ventures. But it was the dream that pushed so many of these early miners on. More times than not it was tragedy that answered those dreams and many times the ones they left behind never knew what happened to them. Most of the time it would end up as a double tragedy since many of these families that were left behind were poor. With part of the support of the family missing, and most likely never to return, it left failure at home. So what little they had would be taken because of past debts, and they themselves would be out on the pathways and trails with no place to live.

That evening as he was wondering through their camp he overheard one of the members, one of the females actually, mention that the colors here reminded her of calico. When he heard this he thought about it and yes in a general way it did. He, later that evening, contacted Doube, who was a geologist, and see what his idea was. He found the scout just outside the camp looking at the surrounding area in the dark. Not wanting to appear to be sneaking up on him he made some noise. Doube turned saying, "Heard you coming a ways back, sure is a pretty night. The stars are really bright here and the breeze is very light. The heat of the day hasn't left the desert yet, so it's still comfortable. But, later on it will have a definite chill."

Coming over to sit next to him Jllon said, "True, this surely is a stark area, even for a desert. One of the females said that the colors of the hills here reminded her of calico. I hadn't thought about it, but it kind of does."

"Hadn't thought about it, really . . . It's a bit barren, but it does expose the rock and my guess is at one time they were pulling precious metals out of this area."

"Really?" Then being silent for a short period of time absorbing what he had been told, and enjoying the quiet here he asked, "So what would your guess be? I know you haven't had a chance to really look, so it's just idle speculation on my part."

"First off this area has been picked over pretty heavily so I doubt that we would find any raw ore. Still if I had to guess I think it was silver."

"Silver, I guess that would have been enough to pull miners into this area and put up with the harsh conditions. It's really funny how we are when it comes to such things as this."

"How so?"

"If you think about it, most of us are looking for a comfortable life style. Yet, for some to try to accomplish this they endure some of the most extreme hardships. And most of the time, end up with nothing to show for it, but the scars and being a little older, and hopefully wiser."

"Yeah, but 'the dream' was there wasn't it? I guess when you think about it, it has always been 'the dream' that pushes all of us on. For me, it's the freedom of the wild places. I feel more at home here, than in the townships and villages."

"True, in my case, it's being in the field, discovering the past and how it relates to us now. You know that one big find that would either finally prove the existence of the *ones before* or disprove them and leave them as myths. Yet, I'm a realist enough to know that I'm no one special, and as such I may never find any of that."

"Yeah, hundred turns from now who's going to even know we were around, let alone care."

"Yeah, very true. The only ones who might would be ones we are related to and then only as a name and that would be that."

"Makes you kind of sad doesn't it. After all, you work hard throughout your life, and try to do something that will put you in the history books, but in the end it seems that most end up completely unknown – just as if they never lived." Shaking his head Doube continued, "Now that we've gotten melancholy, let's get on to a more positive conversation here."

Laughing a little Jllon said, "You know you're right, okay what would you like to talk about?"

"Nothing much really, but what is your plan for the morrow?"

"Overall it's simple. Will send the team out as groups of three, one experienced and one who is on this journey for the first time will be included. Of course with three it also makes it a bit safer. Then spend the day just searching the site and see if anything remains that would give us a hint as to when this area was mined. Part of this is where your expertise comes in. With your geology you may be able to help in dating this site. Still, since it is on the main North-South inland route, I really don't expect to find much at all."

"Nothing made by us anyway. Like you I figure anything here would have been taken long ago."

For a short period of time both were silent enjoying the night air and sounds. "You know it is quite peaceful here," Jllon stated, "It's good for the mind and spirit just to sit and do this now and then."

"One of the reasons I do this, but I'm sure you already knew that."

Getting up and preparing to head back to camp Jllon said, "I'll leave you to your enjoyment. See you in the morn."

"Yeah, I'll be here for a while and probably will work around the perimeter of the camp, and then turn in myself."

He watched as Jllon retreated back into the camp area and disappeared from sight. He thought about the illusion of quiet that surrounded them at night. *You know,* he thought, *that out there in the night is a life and death struggle to survive.* In the natural world it is the prey and the predators. This did not only apply to the wild beasts out there. Even the vegetation was in a fight for survival. If one listened carefully one could hear the scurrying of the small ones and the silent flapping of the wings of the ones who search these out. So in truth, yes it's an illusion – the quiet, the peace. Still being on top of these struggles did not make one immune to becoming a meal for one of the larger wild beasts. If these large wild beasts were really hungry and one was careless . . . well the answer was probably death and you the meal. No one was immune from that part of life. No one is given a special place – even though in ones' youth it is thought that one is special and can cheat death. He had seen it come in so many different ways. Shaking his head, *enough of this*, he thought.

Getting up from the rock he was sitting on, he started hiking the perimeter of the camp, to check on the ones who were guarding, and to get an overall feel for the lay of the camp at night. Once he had completed this circuit he would turn in himself. He wanted to be up before sunrise to watch the shadows develop as the sun rose over the barren hills.

Jllon headed for the center of camp when he left Doube. He wanted to check on the schedule of guards for the night and to talk to the camp manager who had the night shift. Since this was the general gathering place for the team it was here the assignments were posted. He was also curious how those two who had a secret crush on each other were faring. He needed to make a quick contact with his mate who was observing the whole affair. But she was not around the camp center. Asking Metchy, who was the night manager, if he had seen her, he stated that he had not.

Oh well, it was something that could be put off until he saw her again. He walked the inner camp acknowledging each as he passed by them, and then headed off for the night rest. His head was full of plans for the next day and a quick and general search of the old mining site.

* * *

A couple of shifts of guards had come and gone and it was deep into the night when one of the present guards, who were up on a high point overlooking the camp, felt a brief strong wind out of the south. It was gone as fast as it had arrived. It was followed by a deep silence. Listening carefully he thought he could hear thunder in the far distance, but wasn't sure. The second guard approached and asked, "What the heck was that?" They both looked in the direction the wind had come from and it appeared that again, in the distance, there were some flashes. They looked at each other with the first guard saying, "Looks like one of those rare thunderstorms that happens every once in a while in the early spring – more likely to happen in the summer. It's still quite far away, so maybe it will miss us, and play itself out soon."

"Really hope so. I really have no desire right now to get wet, and cold."

"Know what you mean, but if it does get this far that will not be the worse of it."

"How so?"

"Well, if it does reach us there will be a lot of wind, and being that we are in portable shelters, I suspect that a few may be blown down. Then the lightning and thunder might spook the pack beasts and we could have them panic and run off. You know maybe I should head on down into the camp and warn the night camp manager of the danger. They may not have been able to feel the wind, and since the storm is way out yet, probably haven't seen or heard it either. Tell you what, you stay here and monitor it and I'll go down and inform him, then be right back."

"Okay, but don't be gone too long, as you seem to know more about this stuff than me."

"Understood, I'll hurry." He quickly headed down the hill towards the center of the camp to find the camp manager. About half way down the hill the winds hit again and this time with some additional force. He looked to the south and saw that the storm was much closer. Obviously it was fast moving, which meant, if it did hit them it would be with fury. He picked up the pace and entered the camp and found the camp manager standing peering to the south trying to find out what was happening. The camp manager hearing the footsteps looked around to see the guard approaching, "What's going on?" He asked.

"Looks like we may be hit by a thunderstorm," the guard replied. It's really fast moving, and in the time that it has taken me to get here the winds have picked up and the flashes have become more visible."

"Just what we need", Metchy replied. "Okay, you let me know, head back up and keep me informed as you can, I'll go wake up Jllon and see what his plans might be. Thanks, by the way."

"No problem." With that the guard turned around and headed back to where he had left the other one.

Metchy sprang immediately into action and headed to wake Jllon. This could definitely become an emergency and much had to be done before the storm struck. Of course they might be lucky and it would pass by and miss them, but the winds just didn't feel right for that. It most likely would hit them. Besides, it was better to be prepared than not. If it missed them then they would only lose a little sleep.

Jllon was in a deep sleep when Metchy awoke him. It took a little time for him to come out of it. "What's going on?" He asked in a stupor.

"Storm approaching boss – looks to be a mean one."

"Okay, give me a minute here to come awake." Sitting up he tried to shake off the cobwebs that seemed to be in his head. His mouth tasted of metal, and was dry. He picked up his water container and took a deep drink, and got up trying to shake the buzzing in his head. He then headed outside, and could feel the wind picking up. In the distance he both heard and saw the approaching storm. "Let's get the camp up," he exclaimed, "this looks like it will be on us very quickly, and there is much to do before it hits."

The camp manager left heading back to the center of camp and rang the alarm to bring the camp alive. People started pouring out of their temporary shelters looking confused, tired and still asleep. They proceeded to the camp center to find out what was happening where they were informed of the approaching storm. Although it was becoming obvious as the winds were increasing rapidly.

"Okay," Jllon yelled, "first we need the pack beasts brought in and cinched down so when the thunder and lightning starts booming and flashing around us the beasts cannot stampede. I need at least three of you to stay with them to help quiet them. The rest of you go around and pick up anything that can blow away, and then go back and check your shelters to make sure they are tied down. We're also going to have to make sure that everyone stays out of the gullies. With as much water as this storm is going to dump on us we'll be dealing with flash floods. Let's hope we've set this camp up far enough above the ravines that the floodwaters cannot reach us. Oh and by the way, as if you didn't know, everything is going to get wet. Okay let's do it!"

Everyone left the center of camp and started working their assigned tasks as fast as they could. The winds were now whipping and it was starting to sprinkle. It would be a race to get everything tied down before the storm hit. It was definitely a fast mover. Jllon knew that once the storm was over them that the winds were going to get very erratic, and when it left, the winds would change direction and be from the north – such was the nature of thunderstorms. Just before it struck in its full fury Jllon thought, *I really wasn't expecting one of these now. It's just too early in the season for them, but there's nothing I can do about it now as it has arrived.* And it had, as the fury of the storm dropped down upon them. The night sky lit up with lightning as it danced between clouds and struck the ground. The sounds of the thunder went crashing around them, and then the downpour hit with huge drops of rain that battered at them like the rain wanted to destroy them. In minutes everything was soaked and because of the erratic strong winds a few of the shelters were torn from the ground and were blown away.

The beasts were definitely in a panic, and additional people were needed to go assist in keeping them under control. To be heard one had to yell as the din created by both the wind and rain made it almost impossible to hear. When it appeared that it couldn't get any worse the rains starting falling even heavier than before, while the winds picked up to even a higher velocity, which caused more of the shelters to collapse and leave the area. The downpour put out their campfire and the only light they had presently was from the flashes of lightning, creating dancing shadows and light as it flashed. The camp was utter chaos as they tried to keep it together. Then they heard the roaring of the water in gullies, which was even louder than the combination of wind, rain and the storm. "Flash flood!" someone yelled.

Then, the volume between the rushing water, and the storm drowned out all conversation. Nothing could be heard but the fury that was surrounding them. He noticed that the people working the beasts were having problems controlling them. He signaled to a couple of the team members who were in sight to come to him. He quickly headed in their direction. When they met, even at close range he had to yell to be heard. "Get a couple of more and get over and help the ones controlling the beasts. We can't afford to lose them. Also when you get over there cover the beasts' eyes with something so they cannot see – it will help."

"Gotcha," was their response, they headed out to grab a couple more of the team and head over to the beast pen. Jllon started walking the camp, fighting both erratic winds and the whipping rain. He wanted to try and account for everyone, but the chaos, at this moment, was too great. He saw camp gear spread everywhere. AS he watched, he thought. *This is going to be a mess to clean up when this is over. Probably a good idea to have stopped for an extra day, but not for the reason I had originally planned.*

Then as quickly as it had arrived, the storm passed over them, and continued on its northward path. The winds now were out of the north and rapidly dying. The only sounds being heard were the distant thunder and the roar of the floodwaters as they crashed down the streambeds and gullies. The next sound to assault his ears was voices and the sound of fear from the pack beasts. Surveying the campsite he saw that every temporary shelter had been knocked over by the wind, everything was scattered and soaked. It was obvious that no one was going to get any more sleep this night. Looking around he saw the camp managers attempting to get a fire going. He knew as wet as everything was, even that would be a difficult task.

Jllon yelled for attention, and asked for everyone, other than the ones who were tending the beasts, to come to the center of the camp. He realized he was shivering. While the desert wasn't necessarily cold this particular night, with the normal breezes returning, he found as they touched him he got cold. As everyone came to the center he asked, "Do you know if the two guards came down or are they still out there?" No one had an answer for him, as they were not sure who was supposed to be out. "It's quite obvious we will not get any more sleep tonight, so I want you all to work together and find and recover the temporary shelters as you can. The camp managers are working to get a fire going, and then will provide some hot beverages for us. Most of what we will need to do cannot be done until the sunrise, so as the shelters is found, and put back up, come back in and go to the fire, get a cup of the hot beverage, and then try to dry out. I also need a head count to make sure we've lost no one in that flash flood. Probably in a couple of hours or longer, the water will recede and then somewhere around the zenith you will never know that it even rained or there was water in the ravines."

He followed this by confirming the head count to make sure everyone was here. Minus the two guards he was missing three others. "Okay, who are we missing?" Looking around at the group he had he realized one of the missing was Doube. The sound of the floodwater just east of their camp was deafening, and made it difficult for anyone to hear. Not wanting to lose anyone else, and not knowing where the missing individuals were he organized a search party to look for the missing persons. "I want these groups to be no less than three. That way if one of you gets into some kind of trouble, there will two others to help you out of it, and if they cannot that would leave one to stay with the one in trouble and one to come back for help." He looked at the camp managers and said, "I'm putting you in charge of the teams and the setting up of the search areas for each team. Make sure you place a reasonable time for each team to check back in so we know that all is okay with them. It won't be light for a few hours yet, so be very careful. I'm heading up the hill to where the guards are supposed to be. I want everyone who is here to be back by no later than sunrise. Good luck all and let's hope that the missing did not get caught in that floodwater."

He turned and left the weak firelight as the fire tried to burn the soaked wood and headed up the hill towards the guard positions to see how they had fared in the storm and if they had seen any of the missing individuals. He took his time hiking up the hill that overlooked the camp. With it being a moonless night it was not easy to see the ground and it was easy to trip on the unseen rocks and the uneven ground as he climbed – the mud didn't help either. One thing for sure it wasn't a quiet trip. He thought with the noise he was making that someone who was deaf would hear him approach. Stumbling once again and almost falling, he thought. *Better to slow this down. Wouldn't be wise to have an accident here and slow down our trek southward.* At least there was no way for him to fall into the floodwaters if he did fall. Eventually, he reached the crest and saw three people standing there conversing. He could see their silhouettes outlined by the night sky. Still, with the roar of the floodwaters, he was unable to hear them at all. He was sure they knew he was approaching, since some of the rocks had let loose when he had stepped on them making a lot of noise as they rolled down the hillside.

Once he reached the small group, he found that Doube was with them, and to his surprise sitting down where they were not immediately visible were two of the missing individuals. Doube turned around as he approached and said, "That was a surprise. Not too often is there one of these types of storms this time of year. Yet, when they do strike it's just like this. Hard fast and I'm really glad we were not out on the desert floor. Had we been, we could have been washed away by the flash flood."

"That I have to agree. We were definitely lucky this time. No one died, but I'm sure there were some minor injuries, and the camp is a shambles. I feel we will be here a couple of days, with the morrow now being a cleanup, and a dry out day." Turning to face the two who were sitting down he said, "I need you two to head back down to the camp and let them know you are okay. We've organized a search party to find you, and when you do let them know that Doube is up here also. How'd you end up here anyway?"

One of the two responded saying, "When the storm hit and the rain was as heavy it was, we heard someone yell flash flood. The only thing we could think of was *get to higher ground*. So we both headed up here and ran into the guards, then a short time later Doube showed up. He suggested we stay here until the chaos settled then return."

"Makes sense to me. Anyway there's a fire going down there, plus something hot to drink, and if not now there will be shortly. The sunrise is still a couple of hours away. So I need everyone who can get some rest, to do so. Yes, I know the camp was leveled by the winds and rain, but as uncomfortable as it is, a little dozing will help." He saw them the get up and carefully head back down the slope in the direction of the camp. Turning back towards Doube he asked, "So why did you come up here?"

Shrugging he said, "I knew that there wasn't much that could be done down there at the camp site. As long as everyone stayed away from the dry beds where the water runs when it does rain here in the desert, then other than some minor scrapes from falling on the slippery soil and rocks everyone should survive. I felt I needed to come up here and see how the two guards were faring. On that subject, I really don't think we need anyone out any longer tonight. This storm will discourage anyone or anything from bothering us."

"You know, as usual, you're right. Okay let's all head back down to the camp and see if we can attempt to dry out by the fire, and at least try to get warm. A hot drink sounds great just about now."

"You're not going to get me to disagree."

"Okay, the two of you who have been on guard shift, let's head down to that fire and get warm." He could see when they were silhouetted by the night sky that they were cold and shivering. A short time later they all entered the camp, and saw that everyone on the team was around the large fire and looking quite miserable. Fortunately with the two of the three who had been missing showing up the search parties were unnecessary, when a second headcount had shown that the third one missing wasn't missing at all.

* * *

It seemed like forever but eventually the sun began rising in the east. It was a very welcome sight. As the sky grayed and the camp became visible, it took the tired team a while before the damage from the storm could be viewed and an assessment made.

"Here is what I want to happen this morn," Jllon said, "First, as the daylight gets bright enough for us to see and walk safely, I need you all to go to your areas and find out the damage and report back. While this is happening, the camp managers will be preparing the morn meal. Once we have an overall assessment of the work ahead of us and after we eat we will start the cleanup. Stay away from the running water there to the east. While it is flowing slower it still is deceiving because it will still sweep you out and probably drown you." Looking around the team he continued, "The sooner we can complete this, the sooner we will be able to relax."

Doube added, "He's right about that water flow. By the early after-zenith it will have stopped, and only then will it be safe to go into the ravine. Then looking at Jllon he said, "You may continue."

"Thanks, I think that most of the damage will be just wetness that in most cases can be dried. So, let's get at it and after the meal we will know more about what needs to be done." He followed by saying, "Its light enough, so the sooner it's accomplished the better for all of us."

The team broke up and headed to the different parts of the camp to see what had really happened. Doube and Jllon headed back uphill to overlook the camp to get a general feel for the devastation. Jllon looking at Doube said, "The whole plan for today is really simple. With the damage brought on by the storm, and the lack of sleep, we are only going to clean up and repair where we can, then take the rest of the day off to recover. You will be free to scout out the area if you so desire. Of, course having you help would be nice also."

"Don't have a problem assisting, you know that. But, you're right; being a geologist this area sure has a draw. I'll have to see how the day goes. I know that the morrow we will be here anyway and we, at that time, will be looking over the area anyway."

They reached the top of the hill and looked back down on the camp. They saw that not one of the portable shelters remained standing, and the wind and rain had played havoc with anything that wasn't tied down. Equipment and personal items were spread everywhere. It was going to take some time to clean it up and assess the damage. The sun felt comfortable as it warmed them and their clothes, which hadn't completely dried, were steaming a little from the sun's warmth. "Hey, that really feels good," Doube commented. "Could just sit here and let it warm me."

"Know what you mean, that's for sure. But, unfortunately it's time to head down and help with the cleanup."

"Right." With that they both headed back down the hill to assist where needed.

What they saw was discouraging, but at the same time encouraging. While almost all of the portable shelters had been knocked down by the combination of wind and rain, with anything that had been inside of the shelters then exposed to the elements, everything appeared to be more wet than damaged. At least by being in the desert things should dry out quickly.

As he studied the camp, he thought. *Now if I was looking at this from a humorous point of view, I would say we all needed a bath anyway, and the portable shelters were looking pretty filthy too. Clothes, with the lack of water, were probably becoming a little ripe. So nature decided it was time to fix that. And nature being what nature was didn't waste any time at all.* This train of thought brought a smile to his face as he joined the clean-up effort.

They strung ropes up to hang the portable shelters on so that they would dry faster, and then put up smaller lines to dry the clothes and other small items. They found many small personal items scattered over the entire campsite and there was much calling back and forth as items were found and identified, waiting for the owner to claim it. By the zenith the campsite appeared to again look more like their camp. It would still be a couple of hours before the portable shelters were dry and would be set back up, but most of the smaller items were dry and had been packed away. True, to the prediction, the flow of water down the channel had almost completely stopped. By evening there would be no sign of it's passing at all.

Once the shelters were finally dry and set back up, it would leave the after-zenith for relaxing and recovering from the storm of the night before. Looking at the team Jllon saw the fatigue. None of them had more than a half a night sleep, and it showed. At least they were on no set schedule where they had to show up somewhere by a certain time. It was one of the reasons for going in this direction. The zenith meal bell rang and he with the rest of the crew headed over to the eating area. When he sat down with his food he found the camp strangely quiet – another sign to him that these members of the team were exhausted. Well, the cleanup was almost done, and other than posting of the guards, most would be able to rest or nap for the remainder of the day.

When he moved to his provided shelter on the property of Lauut and Lauma, and began to assist them in their work, Fauul thought that working with beasts and their general categories would be easy. After all, all that was required was cleaning the stalls, making sure they had clean water and food, when it was time, and added to this list, now and then, a few other minor inconveniences, right? Instead he learned that there were many categories of beasts that they worked, and each requiring a different approach and understanding.

He learned that the herd beasts had a sub-letter attached to them to represent the different breeds. Because he had spent most of his life in the townships it was something he would have never even considered, let alone thought about. And of course, so did the pack beasts they worked – to his surprise they too had sub-letters attached to them also. He asked why this was so, and was told, as the time went by, and as he worked with them, it would all be explained. He learned that most of these beasts he was working had existed for thousands of turns, and went back further than any written record. They also told him that somewhere in the unknown past that the beasts were not called beasts, but had individual names attached to the different breeds. Yet, somewhere in time it had all changed. A kind of shorthand had been developed, and the term beast began to be applied to both the domesticated creatures and wild ones. For whatever reason, it had stuck, and so, to almost everyone, they were simply beasts.

Overall he was finding that this type of work would require almost as much learning as it had when he became a cartographer. This was a real surprise, since the work just did not look that complicated. He found, as they talked to him, trained and showed him the working methods that he was just scratching the surface, and they had much knowledge. Even still, they both would apologize that in some areas they were still lacking since all had not been passed on before their sires had died. So, in some ways they were still learning and re-discovering things that probably were known to their sires and would have been passed on to them.

It was hard work. It ran from sunrise to sunset each day. Then if something unusual happened, which happened more often than not, it could end up being all night. Nature being what nature was, things were always unpredictable and ran on whatever schedule nature decided. So if there was a difficult birth, or there were problems with the herds, or the weather was playing havoc with them, it meant they had to be there to take care of it. One thing about it, at the end of the day he was exhausted. He looked forward to a bath, a hot meal, a little relaxing time, and then bed. He found that while he had considered himself in pretty good physical shape, that initially, he was sore and aching all the time. He was finding muscles he didn't know he had. Still, working here in the country and the fresh air was starting to change him in a positive way.

Since he was a township type of person, ones who preferred to live in the outback, the country was something he truly did not understand. *How can one live without people around?* He thought. *After all, the township style of life is invigorating and full of energy, where it seems just the opposite here in the outback.* He was finding that as he spent more time in the outback that there was another change happening to him. Where he thought he was pretty self-sufficient and confident in his abilities, the challenges that were being thrown at him were new and difficult. As he overcame each one he found that what he had thought was confidence was not at all. The township style of life was structured and really overall predictable. So when something different happened it was rarely on the scale he was dealing with here every day. Being in and around the natural world, left him, in the end, tired, yet, at the same time, feeling more alive than at any time in his life – he really was beginning to appreciate his surroundings. He was also learning how to see instead of just look. Even the time he had spent on the mapping project had not taught him as much as he was learning now. *Probably,* he thought, *because we depended on Doube to take care of the natural things while we performed our tasks.* Yes at times, there had been some dangers and some really stupid things had happened, but overall it still was more of just fieldwork than really living in the outback.

He observed the siblings in their day-to-day existence and saw that they were very close to one another – he, being very protective of his sister, and she, watching over him. He also found that as time continued the two of them – he and she – were becoming even closer. What he thought was relationships in the past were nothing in comparison to this one. He was learning that she made his day, and each day he looked forward to being around her. It was something he looked forward to in the morns to see her and after the day's work to have time to sit and talk about the normal day-to-day things or simply to sit quietly and watch the night approach.

When they were together in such situations he felt they were really only one. It truly was a different and wonderful feeling. He found that she fulfilled his needs on all levels, mental, physical, and spiritual. He had heard that this was the way it was supposed to be, but really never believed it. He had always thought it was some tale told that really held no truth. Like that saying, "When the right one comes along you will know it". What a lie he used to think – *Funny how one's thinking changes over time.* Because he had to admit that he was finding himself in the very situation this statement talked about.

It hadn't been planned, yet here he was in the very last place he thought he would find himself, or would have planned to be. Now he could not see himself anywhere else. Looking into her eyes he could see it was much the same for her. Now he knew what others meant when they had stated that they would feel very lost if their mate would disappear, and that a part of them would be gone forever with no way to recover that missing part. He knew shortly that he was going to ask permission to pursue, and believed that both of them, the brother representing the family, and she would agree. Once accepted, it would only be up to them to decide if they wanted to continue and become mates. He wondered where that term had come from – *pursue*. He knew, for example, that one pursued a beast in hunting until either captured or killed. Yet here it was a formal announcement that the couple was serious and looking to become mates. Once the announcement was made, the people around would be aware, not that they wouldn't be anyway, that the family approved, as well as the ones involved. It did not forbid anyone else from seeing the two, but most of the time these were considered casual and of no consequence. He really suspected that after the next major gather he would no longer be single – and most surprising to him, he looked forward to it.

* * *

The days just flew by, and with Fauul here, it just did not seem real. She had been frustrated for so many turns, never really finding anyone that would fulfill her in every way as he seemed to be doing. It was so difficult to believe that he was here. After all, when he had continued on after their meeting, which she had to admit was a little fiery, she felt that that was that, and she would never see him again. Yet, when she looked back at those first few days she wondered how the relationship had advanced so quickly. She had always thought that when one started a relationship that it would be something that would develop over time. *Not something like this.* It had almost been instant on her part. Of course she had marked it up as just attraction. After all, he was very good to look at, and very easy on her eyes. She determined that once he had left that she would forget him and move on, of course that hadn't worked either. In her unguarded moments thoughts of him would come unbidden into her mind. That was the reason she had sought out her friends from the past. As it turned out that had been a great move for her. They had missed her and really wondered if she would ever come back and they could begin again.

Once she had rejoined them, it was like she had never left. It had been wonderful to have the support of other females – something she had left behind after the loss. Yes, her brother had always been supportive, but he was a male, and they, the males, couldn't understand. So if Fauul had never returned, some good came out of the meeting anyway. She had her childhood female friends back and it was great.

Yet, to her complete surprise, he did return and she was the reason. That left her a little humble to think that someone else considered her so important that he would leave his very career for her. Wow, she never felt that her worth was that much. Still it seemed like a dream and she was afraid that eventually she would wake up and find it was just something she had wished for, but in the light of day or reality, something that did not happen. But, it did happen and he was here . . . he was really here for her. She felt herself overflowing in happiness and joy. She could see that soon he was going to ask for the right to pursue, and while she had thought about teasing him by refusing, she knew that it was something that she probably could not do. How could she refuse him?

The evenings had been unbelievable with him here, as they sat on the porch and relaxed after the day's work behind them. Just having small talk or staring out at the natural world. It was becoming her favorite time all over again. She always did enjoy doing this alone or with her brother, but now this was even better. She wondered if this was how her mother had felt about her father. If so, she was beginning to understand what committing to one person meant. It was not so much a sacrifice, as it seemed to be to her personally at the time. Her mother had come from a higher class and it seemed she had lowered herself to become her father's mate. Yet, if her mother had felt as she did right now it definitely was not that way at all. She saw that each day she was becoming closer and closer to this person who only a short time in the past was a complete stranger. Funny, but at this moment, it seemed almost like he had always been here, and those turns of bad outings and refusals never happened. Still she knew that every one of those things from the past helped her become who she was, her views, and her stand on the rights of the female. Looking over at him now was so reassuring. She just loved to lie in his arms with her head on his shoulder – it seemed so comfortable and so natural.

Watching all this happen Lauut couldn't be happier for them. It was funny how out of nowhere and with no one looking, this relationship took off. He saw that it was very good for his sister as she literally glowed. He wondered if this was how it was when their sires had met. As a child you never think of those types of things – since they, your sires, had always been there when you showed up. You always seemed to put them in the role of mother and father, and not two individuals that had been single at some point and were looking for a mate to live with for the rest of their lives. It was really difficult to realize that at one point their sires had been no different. Smiling at these thoughts of placing their sires as whelps with sires of their own, probably pulling some of the same pranks they had, in a way was a nostalgic thought. That brought another smile to his face as he thought of his father as a whelp, then pulling some prank on someone, only to get caught, as he personally had time and time again. Yes, as a whelp you always thought, at times, you could outthink and outwit your sires. Yet, you would forget that being a whelp you did not have the experience behind you that your sires did. And most likely something you were attempting was something from their past that they had already attempted or done. New to you, and thusly adventurous, but something they had already seen and probably had been caught doing.

This led him to a new thought – new to him he suspected, but probably not to others. While each generation seemed to repeat much as they grew up, he realized that when one's sires watched you make some discovery that was new to you, it gave them a chance to live it again through your eyes. So while much would have been old, to watch a whelp discover it was to see it as new and different.

Had their sires been here he could almost see them secretly enjoying this growing love between Lauma and Fauul. It probably would have taken them back to their own beginnings. Even though theirs would have been somewhat different as each relationship is. Still there would be much that was the same. He was sorry that they would never get the chance to see it. It also made him wonder when his time to find a life mate was to come along. If this relationship was any indication, then it might come along any time and most likely, like his sister, it would be unexpected and from someone he didn't even know as of yet. In a way he was almost jealous, as they grew closer, she was now paying more and closer attention to Fauul than to him. Of course he knew that was as it should be. But he felt sad that some of the closeness they that they always had was slowly being shifted to this male.

Again, it was obvious that they would be mates. It meant, of course, that they would have to come to terms with the tradition of once a female mated they would be required to leave. Unfortunately, in this situation, the help that Fauul had been providing was desperately needed. With the two of them they had been pushed all the time just to keep things close. Fauul had relieved some of that burden and pressure they had been under.

One evening as they all were sitting in the gathering area of the shelter Lauut idly picked up one of those objects he had found in the cavern. He was flicking it open and closed. Then he opened it spun the wheel and some sparks flew off of it igniting what turned out to be a wick. Surprised Fauul said, "Wow a fire starter. That's what those things are. When did you discover it?"

"Oh, actually just like when I found them, it was an accident. You remember the wheels on these things appeared to be frozen in position. Yet I felt they couldn't be there just for decoration. And you knew that I cleaned this thing in that fluid, which of course is flammable. Anyway, I kept just looking at it and it slipped out of my hands dropping it, and while attempting to catch it on the way to the ground, I knocked it pretty hard with the back of my hand. It struck the ground open and it must have hit the wheel. I really thought I had damaged it but when I picked it up the wheel turned. Not easily, so I tried using my thumb in a downward motion and it sparked and lit. It so surprised me I dropped it again." Shrugging he said, "But from all of the abuse you'd think it would have broken, but when you look at it you'd never know."

"Who would have guessed – not me for sure? It would be something nice to have when you travel, and it appears to be very rugged in its construction, and yet so simple."

"True, but I don't light it very often as I found, in one of the others, the screw on the inside does come out and a small cylindrical object fell out. It's what the wheel strikes against. So it will slowly wear out as it is used. I, of course, have only the ones that came with these fire starters. Once they are gone then these things will only become something to look at."

"I guess so, but that was really all I was doing with the one I got from you anyway. Oh, by the way, these things seemed to cause quite a stir in the township where I'm from. The 'Keeper of the Past' was really interested in it, and like us, speculated that it could have been from the *ones before*."

"Really?" Lauut asked, "But for me, ah us, it was just idle speculation. You know, not really figuring it was. Still I know we don't have the ability to make them now. At least I don't think we do."

"I haven't seen anything like them in the travels I've made. Of course, I think I've traveled a little more than you because of my occupation. But, I saw nothing even close. Can I look at the one that appears to have a map engraved on its surface? It always intrigued me, since mapping is my chosen field."

"Sure," he said as he tossed to him. "So how are you feeling about the country or outback life now?"

Lauma, leaning forward before he could answer said, "Yes, I would like to know. While I was always curious about a township life, I knew it was something I really only wanted to visit and not live. You know, too many people around, too noisy, and not enough area between shelters. Very restricting if you ask me, and those, what do you call them, apartments – that's right, where you have other people just a wall away from you, yuck! How horrible!"

"I have to admit it's a different life style than this, but I love it, and found yours to be something I really never wanted. I always wanted the crush of humanity around me. The energy and movement makes me feel so much more energized and so alive."

Lauma shaking her head said, "I'll never understand that."

"Again, now that you have lived this for a while," Lauut asked, "do you still prefer the township, or is there room inside for the outback here?"

"To be truthful, I really hadn't thought about it too much. I'm learning so much about your life and work that there's been little time to contemplate which life style, I in the end, would prefer. I will say this though, it is completely different than I expected. The challenges it throws at you can make you a better person in the end. It is a continual learning experience and if you fail here, it, at times, can mean your life."

Nodding in agreement Lauut said, "You are so right. We've seen the results, as you know, with the loss of our sires. Just about the time you think you have it figured something unexpected is thrown your way."

"Okay both of you enough on that, I want to change the subject here."

All of a sudden the sister and brother knew what was coming, because Fauul started to sound a little nervous with the tone of his voice changing followed by his shifting position in his seat. "I've never been in this situation before, and as you know when we met never was expecting this to happen. Anyway Lauma, I'm formally asking for the right to pursue. And yes I do know what that means, not that you two didn't figure out that this was coming anyway. I know that it is only a few cycles before the next major gather, and if you would accept, I would love to be your mate then." The room was silent, so silent that Fauul wondered if he had done something wrong. But he looked over at Lauma and saw tears forming in her eyes. Looking at her he asked, "Did I say or do something wrong? Why are you crying?" Then looking over to her brother he shrugged helplessly.

Lauut responded by saying quietly, "No, you didn't do anything wrong, and yes I knew this day was coming. Anyone who watched you two knew it. I really think for once you have left my sister speechless, am I right Lauma?"

All she could do, being so choked up with emotion, was nod her head in the positive. She got up and motioned for Fauul to do the same and she approached and hugged him deeply and whispered, "Yes, oh yes."

They clung to each other for a few minutes, and Fauul asked Lauut, "I hope that this is acceptable to you as well?"

"Of course, I for one only want happiness for her. After all she is my sister. I really wish our sires were here to see this. I know they would definitely approve."

CHAPTER SIXTEEN

Later that day, while they were still drying out, Doube approached Jllon, and stated, "Looks like the water has pretty much left. There is only a small amount running at this moment – probably will the rest of today. I'm going out to look at the surrounding minerals – no, won't be entering into any mines, but I'm starting to develop a theory, and after this storm it will make it easier for me to keep working on it."

"You know you should take someone with you, and as you know, there's nothing happening the rest of the day. Once everything is dry, and here in the desert it will not take long, the portable shelters will be back up and then anything else that needs to be repacked will be. The morrow is when we will take a good survey of the mining and mines. So in reality you could wait."

"Thought about that, but I really feel, at this time, I need to do this on my own. Truthfully, won't be getting too far away from the camp anyway. Glad we were right here when that storm hit. It was a disaster waiting if we had been out in the flat areas. With as much water as that storm dumped, I doubt if it would have stayed within the banks of those dry channels. I suspect that the whole desert floor was briefly under water."

"Okay, just be careful, and yes you're so right. That was a strong storm, and we were very very fortunate to have been where we were. Still, even here, we might have ended up with more damage, and probably might have had someone killed if we had camped in a different location, you know, in this chosen area here, since there are a number of different places we might have chosen to set up the camp. "

"True, and there were a number of sites that were better than this one, but wouldn't have fared as well. Anyway, I'll only be gone for a couple of hours, and will be in the area. Just to let you know, I'll be walking the streambed where those floodwaters just were. Need to look at the strata, and with the washing and cutting of that water it will make it easier to see." Doube, finishing the conversation, turned away and headed out, while Jllon watched him go.

After talking with Doube, Jllon headed up to the area where the guards were. He wanted to see how they were doing and to look over the area ahead of them. Not that the skies weren't normally clear, but with the rains, it would clean whatever dust that might be hanging in the air, allowing one to see further into the distance and with sharper detail. He wanted to get a feel and a sense for what was ahead of them.

Once he reached the point that overlooked the camp he found the two guards conversing, both being from the old dig team, and both having been with him in the past. Yet, it had been the distant past because there had been no digs or planned digs in the recent turns. Both Celt Morlen and Flar Pern were very good at their chosen professions. Jllon, commenting, "Hey you two, long time since we've been on a dig, and, as you are quite aware, at least not one that has ever been so important. I know we've only been here a very short time, but looking around here do you feel we are going to find anything to help us?"

Celt replied, "Funny you should ask . . . We were both just discussing that very issue. It's hard to say, but if you didn't know this had been a mining area it would have been easy to miss. Most of what we see could pass as being part of the natural world."

"Yeah, I have to agree," Flar said, "I think, with the age of this site, and the fact that it is a common stopping point, makes it likely that anything of value would have been taken long ago."

"Right, but both of you know we have worked other sites that showed little promise only to find something of value."

"Yeah," Celt replied, "but this area seems to be much more ancient and probably more contaminated."

"True, and I really do not expect to find anything, but this is more of a chance for the new ones among us to get in some practice. So when we reach the real area where we will be working, they'll have a better understanding of what is involved. As both of you know it's not just oh look it's sitting there on the surface, let's pick it up and go get our reward." Both diggers laughed and nodded their heads at that comment since, for many who had never worked this field, thought that was exactly what one did. At this point he looked back towards the camp and saw a female heading in their direction. Even though the distance was too great to recognize her he knew immediately it was his mate.

Funny, he thought, *how is it that after a period of time with someone, one can recognize the way another moves and know immediately, even though one cannot physically identify him or her.* He excused himself and headed in her direction to meet her half way. When they met they briefly hugged and lightly kissed and then hand in hand headed back up the hill to continue viewing the land off to the south where they would be heading shortly.

Catching her breath she said, "Now that's quite a climb." Then looking for and finding a rock to sit on she sat down, leaving room for him to join her. "You know I miss our intimacy, but know that we have to play our roles here. So do you think that maybe we could sneak off like a couple of younglings?"

Smiling he said, "Now that would be fun wouldn't it? My problem by being the leader of this group is finding time, even a minute. There never seems to be a moment when someone isn't asking me for something or wants to know what is happening." Pausing a moment and staring out into the distance Jllon said wistfully, "But, it sure would be fun to try, and you surly are tempting that's for sure. Always was from the beginning. Sure glad that back then, you accepted my pursuit, as well as your sires, and then agreeing to become my mate. I'll never be sorry for that decision."

"You expect me to argue? I don't think so, after all, you were very attractive to me, and even though you were somewhat shy, I couldn't get you off of my mind. So, as you know, I set those female traps to catch you, and let you think you were doing the pursuing, and as they say the rest is history." Laughing a little seeing a joke in the statement she then continued, "History . . . get it? After all that is kind of what we do is dig up the history."

Smiling he said, "Yes I got it." Pausing and looking out to the south he said, "You know, looking out over the desert, before one becomes accustomed to it, it's easy to think that it's an ugly barren place. Yet, there is a different kind of beauty here. Of, course with this rain, most of the vegetation will start flowering, and completely change the land. We will be witness to a rare moment or event here." They were quiet for a while enjoying each other's company when they saw Doube approaching from the distance. "Now what?" Jllon asked quietly.

They could see that something was up, because Doube approached with a purpose. As both stood up to meet him he first waved to them from the distance, and then in a short time joined them. "Been looking for you, glad to see you have had some time to spend with your mate – on this type of project it can be rare, not good for the relationship, in my mind, that's for sure." Not sure where this was headed they waited for him to continue. "I have a theory I want to run by you but you need to come with me so that I can visually show while I explain it, and why don't you join us Nouma. I can present it to both of you, and maybe have the three of us discuss it."

"Okay," Jllon replied, "since this is supposed to be a quiet after-zenith with no assignments other than the normal camp and guarding duties, sure we'll come with you."

Jllon and Nouma looked at each other wondering what it was he wanted to present, and then followed him back down the hill towards camp. Once close to camp Doube changed direction and went east and carefully headed down into the ravine where the water had been a raging torrent just a few hours earlier. "I figured as much as this surprise storm was a problem, it was also an opportunity."

"How so?" Jllon asked, "I mean the break we're taking is something we probably needed, and I'm sure the rain washed some of our equipment that really needed it, but an opportunity?"

"Remember that besides being a scout I'm a geologist and it is that side that sees the opportunity." He continued leading them down into the ravine, then turned north and headed up stream. It took him about fifteen minutes to reach the point he was looking for, and at the same time isolated them completely from camp. "First off let me say I found a place right here that the two of you can spend some intimate time with each other." He could see the surprised looks on their faces, smiling he said, "Now go ahead, I'll cover so no one finds you two, and when you are finished come back here and join me, I really do have something to show or present."

Again looking at each other and then at Doube, they thanked him and headed over to the hidden area he had just shown them. In about a half an hour they returned with smiles, and thanked him again. "Funny thing, we were discussing this very thing and trying to find a way to get together . . . You definitely solved that for us, and it was very nice."

"Nothing needs to be said, since it never happened, and I brought you here for another purpose anyway. Still I'm an observer of people and I know that the two of you are close, and with you having to lead this group it means that such opportunities are rare, and not good on any relationship no matter how strong."

"So true, we have to find a way to work this out since this project will be covering a couple of turns by the time we are finished. I think once we set up at the sites and start the actual work it will become easier."

"Nouma asked, "Okay you have me, ah us curious, what could be so important?"

"As I said, I have a theory, and at first, when I was scouting for the mapping team, I didn't think much about it. But it seemed wherever water had been active and had cut down through the soil layers I would observe the same thing at approximately the same level. So it hit me today that I should look here after the storm since it would carve away soils and leave a fresh cut into the strata making it easy to see if it existed here too."

"Okay, you definitely have our attention. Can you point out what you are talking about, and why it is so important?"

"First of all let me say that if the layer that I observed turns out to be everywhere, then it had an effect on the entire planet. I haven't been on the other continents but will send out a question to others in my field that live there to confirm it is there also."

"Affect the entire planet? I'm sorry but I'm not quite following what you are saying."

"Okay, let's look at a small area where over time and in the past there was a lake, and eventually, for whatever the reason, it dries up. Then because of an earth shake or something similar the low point now gets pushed up and now is a high point."

"That really does happen?" she asked.

"Yes, as a geologist I see it all the time. In fact you can see it right here. This area at one time was below water and as soils were washed into it they settled on the bottom and formed these layers. After sufficient time these layers can become rock. Each layer is a view into the past, almost like a book. If I cut a trench then those layers would be visible to me."

"Oh I see", Nouma stated. "Kind of like when we uncover something from the past and make a judgement to as when it was made by its style and quality of workmanship."

Listening, Jllon continued to follow as his mate had asked the questions. He thought. *Just how can this relate to what we do?* "Continue please."

"So are you two with me at this point?" Both nodded agreeing. "Now if you look here you find this dark line of material. Very similar to what volcanic ash would look like, but at the same time not quite." He waited for them to agree. "So my guess is that it is a mixture of volcanic ash, probably regular ash from large fires, and something else. That something else I'm not quite sure of yet. Anyway from the size and thickness of this line it was a major event in our past.

While it isn't very close to the surface, it's not that far down either. So my guess is, this happened roughly a few thousand to maybe a hundred thousand turns ago – again that's just a guess."

"So how does this apply to us?" Jllon asked.

"Talking with your crew and looking at some of the records you have I've come to the conclusion that most of your work has been above this line. I think, and it's a long shot here, that if you are going to find anything from the *ones before*, it will be at, in, or below this line. This indicates a major disaster, and by its thickness it came close to destroying everything."

"I see, a dividing line between us and them, if they existed, or in other words the present and the past. You say that in most of the areas you have traveled that you have observed this line?"

"Pretty much so. I mean at first I wasn't looking for it, but soon realized that it was consistent. So since then, I've been actively searching for it, and it has always been there. I would say if we existed before this event, that we were probably driven close to not being here at all. So we may be climbing back from where we once were."

"That's a lot to take in and think about. I'm more than ever glad you came along now. I can see how your field of learning can benefit ours. Speaking for both of us, I'm quite happy you pointed this out. This could definitely be something of great importance! Thank you Doube, shall we head back so as not to worry the rest of the team?" Thinking a second as they started their hike back, Jllon asked, "So what made you want to become a scout anyway?"

"I love the outdoors and the outback, and found more freedom in being able to travel. Also it gave me a better chance to work my field of choice. If I had just stayed with it, most likely, I would have never seen as much as I have. That's what scouting allows me to do. Earn a living, besides, I love it, and then apply geology to the areas I travel."

"Understand that. Believe it or not, both of us love the fieldwork, and it's something we don't get to do very often, and I feel this is probably the last opportunity for us. To get approval to do a dig, any dig is nearly impossible, as understanding the past isn't high on the ones who control the coffers." As they headed back towards camp Jllon asked, "So why do you feel that this particular line of sediment says so much was destroyed?

"Good question. In many areas, including the area close to where we will be working on your one of your digs, fire is a normal thing. Most of the time they aren't large but of course, like all things, sometimes they are. Once the fire has burned through an area there is an ash layer that remains. It replenishes the soils and allows the cycles of vegetation to continue. But in the soils through the winters some of this gets washed into the streams and lakes, and then settles on the bottom as a layer. Plus as soils build a small dark line is left to show there was a fire here. The key word here is small. If you noticed, that line, back there where we just looked, was at least a hand width, while what I just described could easily be from just a hair's width to less than a finger in width. In some areas it is less, but in others it is much wider."

"I see it has to do with the material involved at the time of the incident. So if there was say a minor incident it may not show at all in the geological record. Still, if it was something major then the record would be thicker, right?"

"That's the gist of it. There is just one additional factor that needs to be looked at and that is this, is it something that shows up only in a particular region, or is it everywhere?"

"I'm beginning to see, it can get so much more complicated. By not being in one's field, it is easy for someone to oversimplify things. As in our field it takes a trained eye and mind to come to proper conclusions. So as I'm seeing it now, if the particular line you were looking at only showed up, say here, then the incident only affected this area and would have a minimal influence in other places."

"You would think that, but that's not always the case. But generally it is so."

"What do you mean by that?"

"Well, you have to figure, since this planet is a closed environment that if the incident is pretty large in a particular region, say a large volcano erupts, then it can influence the weather in the rest of the world. The record would only be in that area where the eruption took place, but if there was a way to look at the vegetation from the same time period you would probably see something in them which would identify how it influenced the rest of the world."

"Very complicated," Jllon said. I didn't know you needed to know that much just to study rocks."

"Interesting," Nouma replied, "Until now I just considered a rock, a rock. The only interest I had was, is it pretty, does it sparkle in the light, and look at all the different colors. You know, how a particular rock would look in the border for my vegetation I kept in my garden, things like that. Who would have guessed that like in our field, you could learn so much from them? Not me, that's for sure. It just goes to show how much I don't know." They had been so deep in conversation that all of a sudden they realized that they were back at the campsite, not even knowing how they had gotten back. Before they broke up and went their separate ways, Jllon again thanked Doube.

After Doube had left he turned to his mate and said, "That's one smart male. He probably could become the head of his department if he wanted, and that would be either as a geologist, or as a scout. He is one observant person, and obviously knows how to apply what he sees."

Nodding, and smiling she replied. "Yes, you are probably right, but I can see that in reality he is a loner. He prefers to observe, and that one quality makes him good at what he does. He sees things that others would overlook." Jllon couldn't disagree.

* * *

The rest of that day the team rested around the camp area, and as the equipment dried out it was repacked. Overall it was a lazy after-zenith and was welcomed and needed. On the morrow they would do a quick survey of the mining site, and then with the rising sun on the following day head on down south to their main goal. That being the first of the possible two sites, the one on the edge and in the desert, and if that first one failed to produce then they would move on to the other having one last chance to find a viable site and proof. It was fortunate that both of the prospective sites were within a few days of each other. It was one of the selling points to get this project approved, and it had worked since here they were. Still sitting here in the desert in the spring after a storm with a cool breeze and the sunlight warming one it was hard to concentrate on exactly why they were here anyway. At the moment it seemed more like a peaceful vacation from work than a respite from the storm.

When they had hiked over to the area that Doube wanted to present to them Jllon had kept looking to see if this place might have something of interest. With the amount of water that had dropped on them plus the amount of water that had run down the streambed there was a slight chance that something would have been uncovered. But it didn't happen or appear that there was anything left after all the time had passed since the mines had been worked. It would probably be a bust, but any opportunity wouldn't be passed up. Sometimes such a place would unexpectedly turn up something of value. So far, on this journey, the few places they had checked out as they had headed south, produced nothing. He hoped that this was not a sign of things to come. He really did not want his time as the Head Keeper of the Past, to be nothing more than a paper pusher, record keeper and a very brief side note in their history – not that this in itself was unimportant. Keeping the known past in the existing records was important – critical really. After all, one needed to learn from the past to be able to approach the future. The past helped one understand how the future might be approached, and why they did something a certain way in the present.

Again, he realized, that even though the information was available, it seemed each generation would forsake what the previous generation had done, saying they knew better, and then find they had to learn the same lessons their sires had learned. He wondered if it had always been that way and would always be that way. What was it that led each generation to continue to repeat the same mistakes over and over again, even when the facts showed the very thing in the records? Yet the pride and ego of youth seemed to lead one in the belief that they were better prepared and they would not repeat the past. Those same records seemed to show that trait also. So how does one make a change to a society that seems to be continually locked in a cycle of repeating what their sires did? Was there a way to get to the new generation and make them understand that unless they changed, they would be doomed to repeat? In the end if change came, would it be a good thing? Shaking his head at the thoughts, he had too many questions. Could he just not think, relax, and let the after-zenith just go by? Still his mind kept going. He found he was going to have to force himself to think of nothing if he was going to get the most benefit from this break.

* * *

The day broke clear and cool with the promise of heat that only the desert can give as the day progressed. After the night meal, he had discussed, with the team, what their assignments would be today. Again, the team would divide up into groups of three and begin to work the surrounding area where the mines were located. He, Doube, and Celt Morlen would search for the possible living area and then a dumpsite. Once again, he sensed that the overall survey would produce nothing. Yet and because there were new individuals on this team it would be the experience they gained that would come in handy when they finally set up at the team's chosen destination – any experience and knowledge gained would be a plus.

True to the prediction, the desert was coming alive with blossoms and greenery. These events always seemed accelerated in the desert, since water was the source of these events and that same water was rare. So the vegetation made the most of its short window before they became dormant again and waited patiently for the next event. The sight was pleasant to ones' eyes and momentarily hid the fact that they were truly in a desert. First the vegetation would become green and then a profusion of blossoms would come forth.

At first, in Jllon's mind, the area where they were camping was a good candidate for where the miners had been living, but found nothing to confirm this. A little to the northeast was another area that was somewhat sloped, and while it was less desirable than where they had camped, it appeared to be the only other area close to the mines that might have been used. While overall, miners were hard working, they would want their shelters somewhat close to those mines. After a day underground one would be tired and would not want to walk very far to get back to their shelters, and whatever entertainment a mining village could provide. Still by the zenith meal, they had found nothing to either prove or disprove there had been a village here – no dump, not a scrap of wood, no piled stones for the shelters, *nothing.*

He was hoping that some of the other teams had better luck, but listening to the conversations during the meal, it seemed the results were the same for all of them. Before having them return to their assignments he had each leader write up what they did and where they had searched so that the information could go into the archives for future generations. Also what they wrote provided information that would prevent duplication of the work they were doing if any future generations had a desire to work this old area.

Thinking back on what Doube had shown him, he wondered if this worldwide disaster might have wiped out any evidence that would have existed. He knew, since this was a stopping point along the interior north-south route that his own kind could have easily destroyed any evidence that would be here. Who knew how long this had been used for that purpose? It might have been generations, and if so that was plenty of time to contaminate and destroy anything of value to them as seekers of the past. While, in truth, this was not a proper survey, because it only encompassed one day, the findings, so far, gave one no faith in ever finding anything of value here. It had been picked over heavily and it was too far in the past when the site was occupied and, of course, anything found would be considered to be from the present and past known generations. Still, he had to admit to himself and the why he had the team searching, the experience gained was important.

As far as the line in the soil that Doube had shown him, it left more questions than answers – yes, what a surprise. It, after all, seemed to be the way things went. When something was discovered that was unknown, instead of answering the questions asked, it just added more to the stack. Again, if the *ones before* had existed, was it this possible worldwide disaster that destroyed them? Could it be that they destroyed themselves, and then this world event followed to remove any trace? Or was it a combination of both? Or maybe any of this didn't have anything to do with them at all, and they truly never existed. Shaking his head, as he thought about all these points, he found that he had no answers, and no possible answers so far had been found on their journey. It was looking more and more like the *ones before* had never existed and were no more than myth and legend. At least when they had finished the project, he would feel more confident in giving an educated opinion one way or the other on the subject.

* * *

The next morn they continued in the southerly direction among the many blossoms and greenery that is rarely a part of the desert. By the morrow, or probably the day after, this area would return to what it normally was. Sand, rock, the vegetation with those spines that always seemed to attack and the other vegetation that always looked like it was dead. At least the day promised to be cool. He hoped to make a great distance today and only be a few out of their destination. *It's funny*, he thought, *how when one looks at it on the maps that one is using that the distances always seem less. Then when you walk or hike it, it always seems to be a much greater distance.*

Overall he had been happy with the results from the mining area. He did not expect to find anything and as expected nothing was found, but listening around the night fire he heard the discussions from both the experienced and inexperienced showing that they had gained needed knowledge and insight. Now if only the site where they were heading would produce . . . anything really . . . he really did not want to come back with nothing. Still nothing would be something, yet . . .

Up ahead he saw Doube waving and wanting them to come in his direction. When they caught up to him he pointed out in the distance and said, "Cinder cone, an old volcano. If you look you can see the flows from it, and again if you look around you can see much of the rock is volcanic in nature. I feel we will find more of these. I think we will pass pretty close to it, but don't worry this one appears to be dead and has been for a long time." Once they arrived they saw that the cinder cone in itself was not very large, so had been short lived. Yet it spoke of a more violent past, but how old was unknown, and it wasn't his field of expertise anyway. Still it was more evidence of a major event – at least he thought so. But he would be the first to admit he had been wrong before.

Doube stated, "I believe that this precedes the event that the line shows. If you look you can see that this cinder cone has been partially covered. I suspect if we dig down we would find that line above and the base of this cone would then be below."

Subtly, the terrain had changed it was now semi desert with the vegetation making a slow change to brush mixed with sage. The desert remained to the east and south of them here, but looking west there appeared to not be much improvement in the vegetation, even though it changed somewhat – although this was definitely a dry, forbidding land.

* * *

It took them an additional seven days to finally be able to overlook the site where they were going to be doing their dig project. The area was definitely desert. It was desolate with small desert vegetation, bare mountains, and areas that could easily be called badlands. From his or her vantage point Jllon couldn't understand why anyone would have wanted to live here. There appeared to be nothing to draw anyone. This in itself was a discouragement. Yet, from the personal notes of the cartographers, at least from Doube and Fauul, their conclusions said a good-sized village or small township might have been here. As they approached, he had Doube show him where the mappers had camped, which turned out to be just outside of the badlands. They then moved off to the west where there was a better place to set up for the night – this would be a temporary camp. On the morrow they would have to find a water source, followed by setting up the permanent camp.

Jllon also wanted to see the abandoned village that was within a day's hike from this site. In fact he wanted the whole team there so he could use it as an example of what can happen, and to see how such a place looked before it returned to the natural world. It would give the new team members a better idea of what happens when a village is abandoned and how time affects what is left behind.

They had a few hours before the sun set, so setting up the camp would be easy, and once completed, if time allowed, he'd have teams out to do an initial search for water. If there was a village or township here somewhere in the past there had to be water. As the two of them waited the team caught up to where they were, Jllon said, "Believe it or not, here is where we will set up our temporary camp. Out there to the west of us is our initial project. I know it doesn't look very promising right now, but that may change as we work. Also, once we have our permanent camp set up, as a team, we will head out and view an abandoned village so all of you can see what happens when people leave. Without people to maintain their village, it, the village quickly returns to the natural world. So in a few hundred turns very little remains recognizable to one coming through the area. Okay let's get to it."

Like an army who had done this task too many times, they set to work setting up the camp. To much of the team, this site didn't look like it would support a desert beast, let alone a village. At least they knew if this one didn't produce anything, there was the second site towards the coast that should hold more promise. The question being asked: Other than spring and winter, why would anyone want to be in such a desolate area anyway?

Doube turned to Jllon and said, "There is a water source that can only be used as a last resort. The nomads control it, and from the brief look I had, they have used it for themselves and their beasts for generations. Still that was, I am guessing, a place where people once lived, and this source is a distance outside of what I thought was the main living area or township, so there has to be another source. Of course, when we were here, we needed the water before heading out to finish the mapping and you'll find no mention of it in any of our notes. I had to promise the nomad clan that there would be no mention of the water, location, or that ever existed."

It had been late in the day when they arrived at the temporary campsite location. The plan was for the team, once the camp was established, to follow Doube along the route the mappers had used so that a brief initial inspection could be made. While doing this they would also look for a secondary campsite that would be closer to the working area. Looking around, once away from the badland area, they saw that the lay of the land was flat. The area where they were located was surrounded by Desert Mountains, and like when the mapping team was here there was no obvious trail out of the area. Because they were going to be here for at least a couple of cycles before the heat of summer made it unbearable to work here, they would be able to take their time and do a proper job. So, for the team, going to the abandoned village posed no imposition on their time. With the new members it would be a lesson in the natural deterioration of an abandoned site. To the old members of the team it would be a refresher.

With the camp set up, the working team headed out to the southwest with the scout as Doube explained to the group what was happening at the time he was last here. Like before, when he headed out to find water, with the group led by Fauul attempting to find a way out of the desert, the only difference this time was that he added a change where he came upon the trail and then had headed west. The trail pointed straight towards the mountains. But just a little ways down he stopped and pointed out the unusual material that was all over the ground just off the trail to the north.

They all went over to look at this substance, a broken black-gray rock like substance that covered quite a large area. It had a beginning and an ending area, and generally formed a huge elongated rectangle. On the southwestern edge of this rectangle sat two large connecting mounds which at first glance didn't look like anything but one or two of the many sand piles or sand hills one found anywhere in the desert. Yet, when viewed in the proximity of this rectangle of broken rock, these two were also laid out and aligned in the same direction as the rectangle.

To the unpracticed eye it was just another sandy area in the desert, a little different maybe, but uninteresting. To the practiced eye it immediately stood out as something that should be investigated. It gave all the indication of having the touch of being artificial at some point. This was something Jllon easily saw. Now that he had seen the same area that Doube and Fauul had talked about in the notes he was even more excited. He had to agree with those notes. It really did appear that sometime in the past this area had people living here. Now came that question once again, why? They continued down the trail in the westerly direction all the way to the edge of the mountains where the trail took a sharp left and skirted the mountain. Looking at the surrounding terrain, Jllon wondered why the trail hadn't cut at an angle instead of going straight towards this mountain before making the direction change. It really didn't make any sense. Yet, if this had been the edge of a village or a township, with shelters to the north of it then it would make sense. He felt his excitement rising. *Yes, he* thought, *this site could really be rich in artifacts, and with it located in a desert means there is a greater chance of finding something that would have been untouched by our known people.* Also, because its location was far away from the normal travel routes and it being very isolated helped. *Such a large area,* he thought, *will have to probably create and maintain two camps and break up the group into two teams.* Even with the time they had available he was eager to get started.

The sun was setting and it was time to return to the temporary camp. Even knowing they would be working this site for a long time to come he found that he was excited and really wanted to get to it now. He had a strong feeling about this location, and that was a very positive sign. Still, as the days moved on into cycles, he hoped these initial feelings would remain. Yes to be in the field again and to have reached the first of two dig sites, he was exhilarated.

* * *

The sun rose early with the promise of a beautiful day. Of course, in the desert the sun always seemed to rise early, and at least in the present time of the turns, other than summer, promised good days. Today they would have two things to accomplish. The first was to locate a more permanent main campsite, and then proceed to that abandoned village. Of course if this part ended up requiring two days, so be it. Of the two, finding a permanent water source was the most critical. Once one was located then the main camp would be placed. The second would wait until this was accomplished.

After the morn meal he divided the team into three groups, and gave each of them areas to search. A fourth team would be organized later consisting of Doube and his protégée. They would go to the nomad's area to see if they were there and if not to come back and get the beast handlers. This was only to happen if an alternate source of water was not found, that way, at least they could replenish their water at the known waterhole. Still, because of his skills, Doube initially would assist in attempting to locate a new water source.

At the same time the camp managers and their assistants would be dividing up the supplies so they could work out of two camps – one being the main, and the other secondary. The main camp would hold most of the supplies and have the working area for anything they found as they worked the site. The secondary camp would be mostly a living and eating area. With both camps strategically placed so that any member could go to either with equal ease. Plus once set up, specific areas would have to be set up and pits dug away from the camps to take care of nature calls. Since on this dig they had females, there would have to be two, and with the female area it had to provide privacy. Generally males didn't have a big issue with such things, but to insure equal treatment the areas were to be placed on opposite sides of the camps and of course downwind and a little distance out. In both cases one of the portable shelters would be placed over the area with signs to inform one if they were in use. Just outside of the camps and next to the eating areas a bench would be set up with water and soap and toweling for the team to wash up. As far as bathing it would be just a wipe down in another shelter set up for this purpose. While it would not come close to equaling a real bath, it would help in keeping down the body odor and make it easier for the team to be around each other. While it was primitive living they would at least try to make do and be somewhat civilized.

With the camp managers and their assistants left to work the supplies and the beast masters remaining also to find fodder for their beasts, the rest of the team headed down the trail located by the mappers. The winds were picking up early and it looked like it would be very strong by early in the after-zenith. The teams that were going out would do so as a group until they reached the Desert Mountains that were directly west of them. It would give them a chance to see the size of the area they would be working when they finally began their research. These winds were out of the west and it made it difficult, at times, to be heard over the winds as they gusted. With these gusts if one was not careful it could knock one off balance, and as they approached the mountains Doube stopped and asked. "Did you smell that?"

"Smell what?" Danuld Mield responded. He was one of the experienced diggers.

Doube signaled the group to gather around him and then said, "It just was a brief whiff, but I smelled water."

One of the learners incredulously asked, "You can smell water? Come on now how is that possible?"

Looking at him, Doube replied, "Ah, one from a township is it? Used to have water available and easy to get, are we? You have much to learn, yes you can smell water, and when one gets close you can feel a difference in the air. You really need to pay attention. This learning area – this desert is such that if you fail you can die."

"Really? Come on now your joking right?" Yet, as the student looked around, he saw that all were serious and not one cracked a smile.

Jllon said, "Okay then, let's break up here into teams and search west of here, both up and down these mountains. We are down wind, so obviously the source has to be ahead of us. With all the twists and turns and multiple canyons these desert mountains provide, the wind could have brought the smell from any one of them."

In front of them were two canyons. With the team split into three groups two of the groups headed towards these two visible canyons and the third went north around a point before heading towards the mountains again. The plan was simple, proceed a short distance up the canyons to see if there were any sign of water. Things such as a change in vegetation, changes in the air and of course the smell of water. If nothing was found to return to the starting point and wait for the other teams.

Each team consisted of four members. Celt Morlen was put in charge of one, while Jllon and Doube lead the other two groups. Celt and Jllon headed towards the visible canyons while Doube took his group around the point and headed into the area not visible to the team. Doube made sure he had the learner in his group who was incredulous about smelling the water. He personally wanted to have him learn some more survival skills. Jllon and his group headed down the southwesterly drainage while Celt took his group up the drainage that was almost directly west. Doube headed north around the jutting hills to follow the lay of the land against the mountains. From a distance Doube and his team saw that once past the extension the desert went further west before coming against those same desert mountains. The three groups would either follow these courses to their ends, or if no water was found within a reasonable time come back to their starting point.

From their vantage point it appeared the one that Jllon was to explore had the greatest potential for water. The area lying before them appeared to have more areas draining into it, and the resulting delta at the base of the mountains was large. Still, until it was explored, they would not know. The area Celt's team was to explore went directly ahead and did not appear to be promising. Yet, with the desert, the water source could turn out to be a tank, and if you did not know where these were they would be easy to miss. So it had to be carefully searched. While the final area to be searched by Doube and his crew was an unknown, as none of the search area was visible to any of them. From a distance it appeared to have a number of drainages that ran from the mountains to the desert floor all having the potential of water.

The teams spread out. If water could be found rather quickly, then an evaluation could be made as to whether it would be a good source for a permanent camp. As Jllon and his group headed into the search area they found that the drainage split with two sources. While he did not want to break up the teams to less than three, here he had no choice. Putting Danuld Mield in charge of the second he sent a second team digger with him Wihl Iame. They were to search the fork on the right of them and then return to the spot where the team split. While Jllon and one of the learners Kaern Slopes continued up what appeared to be the major drainage of the two. So far there wasn't even a sign of water. It appeared that only time water had been here was during the passing rare rainstorms, and thunderstorms – meaning the only time these drainages had water in them was when it rained.

Still to be sure, they hiked to the top of the ravine, once there and looking off to their right and in the distance they saw the other members of their team coming out of theirs. Waving and yelling across to get their attention, they noticed the other two were looking at something that caused their backs to be turned towards them. He suspected the high winds would have made impossible for them to hear them yelling anyway. Curious now, they hiked across towards the other members to see what it might be that held their interest. As they approached the other two cautioned them to be quiet. Curious as to why the caution they quietly approached the other two. Danuld turned towards them and whispered and then pointed. "Look up there. Do you see them?"

"See what?" Jllon asked. Then his eye caught a brief movement and saw what they had been looking at. "What are they? Kaern can you see them?"

"No, what are you three looking at?" Trying to see where they were pointing and having no luck at all.

"Okay, kind of look north and maybe a little west. You see that line of rocks there . . . follow it back up the ridge a bit . . . you with me so far?"

"Yes, I can see that line of rock . . . oh . . . what was that?" Then excitedly, "Yes, I can see them now, what are they?"

As they watched the beasts it appeared the beasts were watching something else that was off to the north and below them. With their attention pointed away from Jllon and his group it was easy to stand and watch. Trying to determine what the beasts were looking at, just in case it was a predator, they looked in that direction also. Since their angle was different it was next to impossible to see where or what the beasts were really staring at. Kaern then caught a bit of color, and tried to see if it was something of importance or just vegetation moving in the wind. "I think I see something, but really not sure. If you look straight across from us to, oh, I believe to the north, you can see some red."

The other members looked hard and didn't see it. "Just where are you looking?" Danuld asked.

"Yes, give us some landmarks, something to let us tighten our searching." Wihl said.

"Okay, if you follow this main ridge around to the north, as you do there is a second one that drops downhill . . . then, oh let's see . . . go just a short distance down that one, and then come back to us and you will see a small hill . . . um, follow that hill back up to where it ends, and I think it's right there."

"Okay, let's see if I have this right. I can see this major ridge here, and then the one that goes off of it, does it kind of dip away from us?" Jllon asked

"Yes, yes that's the one."

"So then there is only one smaller one close to it . . . oh . . . I see it now – great directions there Kaern."

Shortly the other two members of the team had also located the red color. But the distance was too great for them to identify what it was. Then it moved and suddenly they saw that it had to be Celt with his group. And by the way they were moving they must have been observing the same beasts – although it seemed to be both ways, the beasts watching them as they watched the beasts. Jllon remarked, "Let's go quietly across the land here, and join up with Celt and his group. We will have to move carefully since we will be coming closer to these beasts, and I don't know their temperament – would hate to find them aggressive with those massive horns. You know those are the largest horns I have ever seen on a beast that size."

Fortunately for them, the land in this area was relatively easy to hike. The vegetation was sparse, but the ground itself was quite rocky. Because of this, they moved carefully. Being always aware of what the beasts were doing, and at the same time keeping their eyes on the other team. So far one of their goals of the day hadn't been accomplished, but theses beasts were something none of them had ever seen before, and this was exciting. "Wish one of the beast masters was here with us," Jllon stated, "maybe they've seen them before."

"But, if they are desert beasts, I doubt if many have ever seen them. If we hadn't been working up these washes and then the mountainside here," Danuld whispered, "I doubt that we would have ever seen them. Look at their colors, I mean if they didn't move it would be hard to even see them."

"I really don't think you need to whisper with this wind," Jllon stated, "but who knows, maybe their hearing is really good . . . which, if I think about it, would be important out here, along with good eyesight." Still watching both the other team and the beasts they continued their approach. It was obvious Celt's team hadn't seen them approaching having only eyes for these unusual beasts. Not wanting to startle the other team as they approached they made a noise that would only be heard close by. The other team turned around and was surprised, "Where'd you guys come from?!" Celt exclaimed.

Laughing a little, Jllon said, "If you hadn't been watching those beasts so closely, not that I can blame you, you would have seen us approaching from the south. There is no cover and we were plainly visible."

The third team continued heading in a northerly direction skirting the mountains that were directly west of them. It turned out to simply be a finger jutting out in their direction. Once by it, the mountain dipped sharply to the west into a shallow canyon. Here the smell of water became stronger, and even the learner had to admit he could smell water now. He began to wonder what other things he was capable of. When one lived in a township one had no need of these skills. Yet with that smell of water there still was nothing to indicate where it was located, let alone that it was here. The team headed west towards the canyon and caught a movement on one of the mountainsides that was facing them. The distance was too great to be able to identify anything, but there had been something moving. They stopped to see if anyone in the team could pinpoint where or what it was. Whatever it was had the color of the surrounding land, and if it did not move it became invisible, and it definitely wasn't moving now.

The area they were hiking was extremely rocky, and if one was not careful one could turn an ankle. Then add to the mix was the vegetation which was quite unfriendly, resulting in cuts and scrapes with a thorn or two added for effect. They continued towards the mountains, and the smell of water started teasing them by first being strong then completely disappearing. Plus whatever that beast was, the one they had seen from a distance, seemed to have completely disappeared. The mountains themselves were completely bare of any vegetation and as such completely uninviting. They kept the finger of the mountain on their left and remained close, as they continued up towards a canyon. They dropped into a wash, crossed it, and finding it was not the source of water, they continued their hike. As they continued west, as much as the ridgeline would allow, they again came into the same wash they had crossed earlier. Now by being able to follow the wash the hiking was a little easier, but still hiking in sand can tire one out quickly.

As they approached the point where the canyon narrowed considerably before disappearing back into the mountains they found it. Just ahead of them coming out of that narrow canyon was a small stream. Doube suspected that it was seasonal. Meaning that it ran through the winter and spring cycle and when the heat of summer arrived would dry up.

Before hiking up the canyon to see if they could find its source, he had them hike down and follow the water flow out into the desert. In a short distance it disappeared below the sands, and even after following the wash for a distance after the disappearance, the water never resurfaced again.

They returned to the entrance of the canyon and followed it back into the Desert Mountains. As they hiked up the canyon they came upon some of the desert trees. These things seemed to be spread throughout the canyon. Then off to the right up on top of one of the ridges they saw the beast. It stood up on top of a large boulder and looked down upon them. To the team it appeared to have been impossible to scale that boulder, but the proof was before them that it truly was. Looking closely at the beast they saw it had a large set of horns, and seemed almost as curious about them as they were about it. Doube quietly said, "Don't really know what they are, seen them a time or two, they are vegetation eaters, so at least we don't have to worry about them coming after us for food." He turned and signaled the rest of the team to follow him further up the canyon. He wanted to see if there was a source to the stream close by, or whether it kept going. After about an hour of additional hiking, no source for the stream of water was found. The stream just seemed to continue up the mountainside, besides; it was time to get back and tie in with the other teams, then head back and get the camp managers and beast masters over here to set up their permanent camp.

When they got back to the meeting point the other two teams were already there. They seemed to be excited about something from the sound of their voices. Although he was still too far away to be able to understand anything they were saying. Once close enough Jllon turned to Doube and asked, "Were you successful? We didn't find any water or a source but did run into some unusual beasts."

"So did we. Did the ones you find have large horns?" The one we saw surely did, and yes we found a small stream running out of the mountains. Funny, but in truth, if you did not know it was there, you would not be expecting to find water – no special vegetation, the mountain was bare and after a short run into the desert sands the water disappears. The area is just like thousands of others in the desert"

"Then, I guess the next question is will it fulfill our needs for this project?"

"My guess would be yes. I have a feeling it is seasonal, meaning during the hot cycles here it probably is dry, but I have no proof of that."

"Okay, let's head back to the temporary camp and move it to this new location, and then, this after-zenith, take a break after set up, and we can plan a day in that abandoned village. I know originally we were to go today, but I believe from your description that we would not get much time there if we headed back out today. I guess this will give me some more time to look over this area and do some early planning. Of course, only if time allows it today. Still I know from personal experience that it usually takes longer to do something than you originally thought it would."

True to Jllon's word, it did take longer to move the camp. Even with all the experience the team had gained on the journey to this location, of breaking down and setting up of the camp, the move and subsequent new location and setup didn't happen very fast. Part of the problem turned out to be the camp itself. This time it had to be set up more completely with thoughts of it being in its present location for more than a few days, not just part of one. So much more had to be unpacked and more had to be set up. It was leaning towards a semi-permanent status instead of a "pick up and go". Yet, as the sun began to set the camp finally had been moved to its new location and an initial setup accomplished. Over the next few quarters of a cycle it would shake itself out as to what would be the most efficient. If the truth were told, actually finding a campsite in the area of the stream turned out to be the most difficult portion. The whole area around it was relatively flat, but covered with rocks and boulders. Add to it that the whole area was crisscrossed with dry washes, and while these washes looked promising, since they had fewer problems, they were dangerous.

Originally the plan had been to set up close to the base of the mountain, but that idea turned out to be unworkable. So they had proceeded north and eventually found an "okay" location above a dry wash that tied into the stream. At least it had some elevation above the surrounding washes. Still there were obvious negatives since they now sat out in the open making them more vulnerable to these periodic winds. The portable shelters would have to be anchored well into the surrounding soil. Only time in this location would tell if this was a good choice. In the end the winds might make it too uncomfortable to stay, and once again the camp would have to be moved to a more sheltered location.

If anything was located at this proposed dig site, if it advanced into a long time dig, then over time, they would probably have to move this camp anyway. And if necessary, during the day the beast masters, camp managers, and their assistants, could clear an area closer to the Desert Mountains to get away from the winds. Until then it was hoped these winds were not a regular thing or would become a problem at their chosen site.

The morn broke bright and clear, with a gentle breeze. The team got an early start heading out to the abandoned village. Jllon was curious as to the abandonment. Was it quick, or did it show a slow abandonment over time? Only by being in that village would this be determined. The trail they were on climbed twisted and wound around and through the Desert Mountains, eventually dropping down into the abandoned village. They were to spend most of their day here researching the site. Walking into the village was unsettling. One was used to seeing people move about, the sounds of dogs and beasts, but here only silence – with a dust spirit whirl being the only greeter.

Jllon brought the team to the center of the village and stated, "In a sense this is what our passion is. Yet, this one area is a relatively new abandonment, in the scheme of time, that is. My initial guess is a minimum of . . . well . . . I'll leave it to you to determine when the last ones left. For any of you learners here, can you tell me whether this was a mass abandonment or a gradual one?" It was a good question to ask. It was one that had to be asked if they were to do their job right. This area gave them a real existing example – where on a dig, one rarely found any shelters, and sometimes only artifacts remained. Jayson spoke up saying, "I believe it was a gradual abandonment." The other learners nodding their heads in agreement turned back to Jllon.

"Why? Why do you feel it was gradual and not, say one that happened quickly, or one that may have been an emergency type of abandonment? Now before you answer that question, I want you all to wander the village, go into the abandoned shelters, and search around. Then as a group come back and give me your consensus, and back it up with facts please."

He released them to do their research, while he and the rest of the team, the ones who had worked with him before, went out and did their own research. He had sensed from the initial walk-through they had just completed that it had been a gradual abandonment. This probably was a case where over the turns the water source produced less and less. Thusly unable to support the village as a whole, people started leaving, until finally the water played out and the last die-hard members finally gave up. This type of abandonment seemed to follow a pattern that ran from village to village with only minor variations. As the resource slowly ran out, the first few would leave, and these places would be boarded up. And with most of the village still living there, these abandoned shelters would be considered off limits.

Then slowly as more and more left, the attitudes would change. You would begin to find the poorer members of the community moving into these nicer shelters and abandoning theirs. Until finally, when there was no hope of recovery, when the final diehards, the ones who held on to the end, would give up and leave. Then the only thing left were the shelters, broken dreams, and the small beasts that would roam the empty byways. Yet if it had been a quick abandonment, things would look much different. The almost predictable evidence of the slow abandonment would not be present for any to see. Instead, there would be a sign of chaos of panic, of important personal items left. Doors would be open, there would be an appearance that the owners had just stepped out for a short time and would be returning. It would look almost alive, with only the residents gone – as in a play where the curtain has been drawn with the scenery in the process of being changed for the next act and the actors yet to return to the stage.

Looking over this village it had been the former and not the latter. Dust lay heavy on everything – giving testament to the time that had passed since the last resident left. Yes, fifty turns or greater was a good estimate. Some of the poorer constructed shelters were starting to fall apart, while the better constructed were showing wear that time places on all things. Without the loving care of the residents to keep time at bay, these shelters were slowly returning to the earth from where they had originally come.

He and his members headed back towards the middle of the village to await the learners, and find out what their conclusions were. They didn't have long to wait as they saw them approaching as a group. "Okay," Jllon asked, "now that you have had time to look over this village, what are your conclusions? I will also need a 'why' to your conclusions." Jllon noticed that Jayson and Kaern were beginning to be with each other more often now. It appeared that the attraction that was there at the beginning was starting to grow.

Suzzane came forward and stated, "We feel that probably this was a slow abandonment. There is no sign of any chaos, just an organized slow reduction of the population over time."

Ehlie added, "At first we discussed the idea that it was quick, but the evidence did not support this. Then we thought maybe a little slower where it might have happened over a few cycles, but again there was nothing to support that either."

Kaern added, "Yes, that's true. Some of what we found showed that some of the less fortunate members had moved into the nicer shelters for a period of time before they too left. So with all the evidence it looks to us like it took a few turns for it to become what it is today."

Jayson followed by stating, "We guess from the shape of the shelters this village has been empty for twenty five to thirty turns."

"Great conclusions all of you. You're only off on one account and that is time. This place had been empty closer to fifty turns, still not bad. In truth we have a rare opportunity here. Most of the time, when a village is abandoned, like this one, others come later, and salvage the materials for their own uses, and all that can be is reused is, leaving little that is recognizable. This village has been untouched by being in this out of the way location since the people left, which have kept the scavengers away. It would be a great place to continue to study, as it slowly returns to the earth."

They broke for the zenith meal, and continued their discussions, what they thought the members of this community were like, and leaving them with many unanswerable questions. It, of course, was all in fun, since they had no way of knowing. Jllon added,

"You all know that once we start the digs that there will be similar evidence, just much less of it. So seeing this is important. It always seems to follow a similar pattern, as if people are no different than some of the creatures that exist." It was something he had seen in many of the digs in the past, this pattern of villages and townships. Sometimes when one was destroyed, the residents would rebuild especially if the surrounding area supported them. Yet, likely as not, the village would move and start again. Unless, like here, the reason for staying had been removed, or changes in the climate forced the move. Like all, here water was one of those critical things. It apparently had become less and less over time until finally the wells went dry. It really appeared to have taken a few turns around the sun before the water was completely gone. Evidence suggested that the attempts to find other sources were unsuccessful, and in the end the last had to finally admit it was over and they themselves would have to leave. And any who faced such a thing knew that it is always a hard decision to leave in the end.

It was time to head back to camp, so that they would be there before dark. Yet, when these abandoned villages were located and the story told, it usually left him a little depressed. All he could imagine was the hopes and dreams of the residents, their many plans, the families, the joys and sorrows, the many individual stories, and so much more gone, finished, never to be fulfilled – at least here anyway. Still it seemed to be the way of the world – one was born, grew up, tried to do what was right in their own mind, and in the end die. It appeared that even villages and townships lived by those same rules. It also seemed to include much of the wild lands, the natural world, that even there a life cycle existed, even though it covered a much greater time period. It left him wondering if it would include this world in the end. Shaking his head he thought. *Enough of this, I can and should only deal with what I can, and not attempt to take on the whole world and its problems.*

It was approaching the dark time of the evening when they finally made it back to the main camp. Much had been done while they were away to bring the camp up to better accommodations. He knew that in the passing days that each member of the team would be doing their best to make it easier to work here in the field. On the morrow they would explore the site and make decisions as to where they were going to start the dig, followed by where they would place the temporary or secondary camp. Until then, he was tired after the hike to and from the abandoned village and was looking for some good sleep.

* * *

Jayson Braylok would have never volunteered to join the team even if it meant free learning turns. He was from at least the third generation of township people. They had always been merchants, and good at what they did. He was the first to step outside of this. Yet the female he was interested in as a possible mate Kaern Slopes, did volunteer. So what could he do but do the same? He wanted to be able to win her, and if they went their separate ways because he did not join the team whom could he blame but himself? So with great trepidation he did agree to join the project. He knew he would be well outside of his element, and this could be a great disadvantage. Still, he had to admit, it was exciting to be doing something he had never done before, and as far as he knew, something that none of his family had ever done. When he had went back to the shelter and explained to his sires what he was going to do and would be gone for possibly a couple of turns they were not exactly thrilled. Still, when he stated he would be on the team with the Head Keeper of the Past, they thought it might be good. After all they, as merchants, would brag that their whelp had been on a team with the well-known and well-liked Jllon, one of the greatest to ever hold that position.

Then after he finally had started the journey and with that first night's stop when that pack beast got loose and starting running amuck, he just figured, when it started to run by him that he'd just reach out and grab those trailing lines and bring the beast under control. Of course he didn't think about the fact he had never been around a spooked beast before, and really had no idea of their strength. It was to be so easy, in his mind, and maybe just maybe, it would impress Kaern, so that he would be able to start talking to her. So with these thoughts he had reached out and grabbed the dangling line, and before he knew it, the beast dragged him a little then jerked its head, which sent him flying into the air. Now completely surprised, and completely off balance, and of all things, being thrown into the air he knew that he didn't want to hit the ground awkwardly and get hurt. So he attempted to twist himself straight. Then adding to his surprise he found himself astride the beast. The surprise seemed complete for both of them. At this point some of the older members of the team finally grabbed the dangling reigns and brought the beast under control.

Well, so much for impressing a female, at least at that moment. If anything that incident showed he had much to learn. While he might be good in a township, here he knew next to nothing. So he set his mind to learn. Those first few nights, even though being exhausted from the day's travel, he found difficult to sleep. The ground was hard and uneven, and it seemed impossible to get comfortable, plus he hurt in places he never knew existed. This led to many morns feeling tired, drug out, and his mind in a fog. Still as time continued he found his body adjusting, and now he thought that he would probably have difficulty in sleeping in his own bed. He also had found many a muscle he didn't know he had. It seemed that every muscle in his body was sore, and this contributed to those sleepless nights. Yet, now that they were setting up for the dig he felt that he had come far in his personal growth and he found himself more confident in his own abilities – something he did not even realize he lacked. He definitely was not sorry he had made the decision. And yes, even if the original idea had been because of a female, he was quite happy with the results within himself.

On the subject of that female, he found that there had been a mutual attraction, and slowly over the journey they had started talking and being together more and more. Still with Nouma in charge of the females it was not an easy thing. She protected them, and since she was the leader's mate, had the power to enforce the rules against any impropriety. So it was only over assignments and breaks they had shared that they been able to see and talk with each other.

He had to admit that Nouma was more than fair with all her charges. Since and very rarely were there females on this type of project, it was something that was quite necessary. He had learned, from experience that there was a whole different side of the world – one that was vicious and without mercy. In this world death and torture were common. Plus females who were unfortunate to have been caught by these were abused, used up and then thrown away. It was a part of reality he wished he had missed, but was important to know. It was far better to think that all were civilized and lived together well. Still he could not deny the truth when it was presented. Those dead traveling merchants and then the facts of what they faced, laid out by Jllon, had really opened his eyes. While he had been one of the learners who had griped about the training in defense and the guard duty, after the incident he realized why it is so important.

He also now knew that they had one of the best scouts that there ever was, and this was a comforting thought. He also had grown to appreciate Jllon. The leader would lead by doing, showing, and assisting in everything. He seemed to always have a good word for all of them. Even during the serious time of the escape from the area where the traveling merchants had been attacked and murdered, he was everywhere, making sure all that could be done was done. Even then it was obvious he cared for the whole team, and treated each equally. Even this visit to that abandoned village had a purpose. All the learners had learned from that visit. His hard questions forced them to look beyond just the shelters and find a pattern there. Then when they found it to have to explain why they had had come to those conclusions. One thing for sure he would now be looking at villages and townships differently. The one thing the abandoned village showed all of them was the patterns of people. It almost seemed to be predictable. He wondered if there was a special study in group patterns, not individuals, but the whole village or township, where overall patterns of life expressed themselves through the group. Again he wondered if the group had more influence over the individual and while thinking that as an individual you had free will, while in truth it was the group that directed more of your actions. Yes, it would be something to think about and observe when he returned to the township.

It was after the evening meal and Kaern who was sitting next to him asked, "What are you thinking? You seem to have a faraway look on your face."

"Oh, nothing really . . . was just looking back. You do know that you're the reason I came don't you?"

"Really? No I didn't. So how long have you been interested in me?"

"I guess that's a valid question. At first when I saw you back at the learning center I was attracted to you immediately. But I tried to put you out of my mind. I figured that I was here to learn and not to romance. After all part of the costs were being covered by my sires, and as such I didn't want to disappoint them. So as time went on, I found it impossible to do so. Something would come up and while I didn't know you well then, it would remind me of you, and then my mind would go off on a tangent. So when you volunteered for this project you left me no choice but to do the same."

"Oh, one of the reasons I volunteered was because I and my family did not have the marks necessary for me to continue. This was a way out for that. It would allow me to finish the learning I had set out to do and not burden anyone. In truth, I had seen you a few times and you kinda interested me, but since you stayed away I really didn't think anything about it or you. Then you volunteered for this project and I thought *why did he do that*? From what I had heard about you, you were just a township type of male. One who had never wanted to go into the outback or the natural world, and that left me curious. You know, as to, why the change of heart?"

Looking down at his feet Jayson continued, "Well, you kind of know why now. Anyway I'm not sorry. You've been everything I had hoped, and the learned, the Keeper of the Past, is someone worth being around. I have learned so much in so many areas. I really never realized how ignorant I was about so many things."

"Know what you mean. I really had no plans on doing this kind of thing, but when one is desperate and a good solution presents itself you generally take it. As a female the outback or natural world was never my favorite, unless it was some of the gardens close to the shelters. And that was as close as I wanted to come — at least for a while anyway. Then I met Suzzane, and she changed much of what I thought about the outback. She's from the outback and started showing me things that were much different than what I had expected. Funny thing is after a while I found I enjoyed them. So when asked to volunteer I said to myself what the heck let's give it a try. So I did."

"And then I did and here we are." With that they had a little private laugh and he continued, "While I would enjoy staying here all night with you, that trek we took today, and knowing what we will be facing on the morrow says I had better turn in. Besides I think I see Nouma looking your way which says our time is over anyway."

Looking around Kaern saw her and then looked back at Jayson nodded saying, "Know what you mean. Sitting here I can feel the waves starting to roll over me. I really think that if I sat here for any length of time I would fall asleep anyway. Okay then, will see you at the morn meal you have a good night." She rose stretched and walked over to Nouma and the two of them headed for the female area.

He watched them until they were out of sight. Like her he felt the weariness in his body, but still sat there for a while longer before rising and heading off to his own temporary shelter. The morrow would bring its own surprises.

* * *

In the morn after the meal Jllon called the team together for a brief meeting. There was a bit of excitement in the air as all knew today would begin the actual search in this area for any sign of habitation that may have existed here sometime in the distant past. He started out by saying, "This is why you all came on this little vacation." This brought a few chuckles from the group, "You see, at least for you new to these teams, that once the digging and removal of dirt begins it is tough dirty work – often times with no reward at the end. While we have no real proof, and to my mind other than the nomads, I see no reason to live in the desert – still there are signs that people actually lived here. Who knows, when they lived here it may not have been desert. First of all, I'm going to have Doube show all of us something he has discovered, and I feel it is important enough that we all know what it is. So before I continue I am going to have him explain what he showed me, and then we will go see an example in the mountains behind us here, Doube, if you would."

Doube then got up and came up next to Jllon and said, "Now I wasn't expecting this, of course I should have." This brought laughter from the team. "You're the type to use every resource you have, and not take credit for anything other than your own work."

"Thanks," Jllon responded, "but this is your specialty not mine, so enlighten us please."

Turning towards the expectant team Doube stated, "What I showed your boss while we were heading here was a line in the soil. No not one you can draw, but a layer that I first discovered when I was with the mapping team. Didn't think much about it for a time, but as we continued our mapping this line kept showing up consistently. It set me to wandering what could have caused it, and why was it everywhere.

"So far it has been everywhere I have been, and I've been looking hard. In some areas it is thicker, others just barely visible. In places where layers of soil have been laid out over time, like the bottom of a lake or a delta region, it is there also. Its depth is consistent. I feel that this represents sometime in the near past, maybe five or ten thousand turns ago . . ."

Someone in the group yelled out and said, "That's the near past, really? I would have thought maybe fifty turns would be the near past." Again this brought a chuckle to the team.

"Yes, yes in our view of things since we do not live that long. But in geologic time fifty thousand turns would be just a drop of water in the ocean. Anyway, it is the type of line that suggests a worldwide catastrophe, one that could have easily destroyed the ones from the past. An event so large it would have destroyed most of what they may have built – which leads us to your field. This is probably why nothing has ever been found to confirm or deny these early people. It may well be that we are their descendants." He turned and faced Jllon asking, "I'm assuming here that once we head out this morning I'm to lead you over to show you what I am talking about, right?"

"Exactly," Jllon responded picking it up from there. "What he has pointed out to me is that most of our work that we've accomplished in the past has been above or at this line, never into or below. So it is something we are going to concentrate on here. Anything above that line is tied to our civilization. So we are going to use it as a dividing line. Anything we discover above it or on top of it we will say is of our civilization. Then hopefully, if we are successful here, and we do find items in and below this line, it will be from the *ones before*. Once we have observed this layer we will break into two teams. Each will have a beast master with them, because anytime we make these treks you must have at least two skills, and their secondary skills are as artists. So when the real work begins they will sketch our progress. Once the two sites for the initial digs are located we will start. Good luck and good hunting everyone. Now let's gather what we need and Doube will lead us out. Just one last thing and that is this, as we begin the dig all will assist. As you know we have to move the soil away from the site, then as we approach the layer we are most interested in we will break down into the diggers, haulers, sifters, and whatever might be found will then be taken to either the temporary camp or the permanent camp whichever is closer. When we do make the break down I want the females working as the sifters. It has been shown they are much better at detail work than we males."

They left the equipment at the camp and followed Doube towards the mountains, since this was the opposite direction to where the initial work was to be performed. Once they actually started digging and by the end of the day they would all be dirty and exhausted anyway. Because the camp was as close to the mountains as it was, it only took a short period of time to reach them. Doube led them up into the canyon where the stream came from and up to a split in the canyon. At this point, sometime in the past, there had been a small earth slide – one that had most likely been caused by either one of the flash floods or an earth shake. It was new enough to still have sharp edges to it. What it revealed was visible layers of soil. One of the layers that stood out was a dark thick layer, which was only a little distance from the surface. To be as thick as it was, said that something in this area, had once had a large impact here.

Doube said, "As you can see this dark layer here is quite thick. In other areas it isn't so pronounced. I discussed this with Jllon and he agreed that almost all the work that has been done by his group or past teams over the turns worked at or above this layer. The dark layer was pretty much ignored since nothing has ever been found within it. I believe this layer represents something that affected the whole planet. And as such, anything that would have existed during this episode would probably be destroyed, and if not destroyed, so close to it that there would be little evidences it ever existed. If the *ones before* lived during this time, this kind of catastrophe would have most certainly come close to completely wiping them out. Any shelters, monuments, just about everything would have been destroyed or eliminated. So as the flow of time continued to us, it would be nearly impossible to prove they ever existed or that we might be their descendants."

Ehlie asked, "So this layer we are looking at here, it's large in comparison to the others, what do you think it is, and what caused it?"

"I believe that this is some major volcanic event. As to what set it off I have no idea at this moment. If it was volcanic, by the size of this layer it was huge, and most of what would have fallen from the sky or came down the sides of the volcano or many of them would have buried or burned up most everything." For a few moments they all were silent as they realized the magnitude of what they were hearing and seeing. If they had been here at the time of this event it had to be overwhelming and terrifying. It would have been a time of great and unexpected chaos. One day your life is normal and all is well, then out of the sky would be this stuff falling on you and destroying all you had, all you had even known. It really did not take much imagination to see what this could have done to their possible ancestors from the past.

504 · F. D. BRANT

The team headed back to camp to pick up the equipment needed to start the dig. Jllon had studied the area earlier and had determined where he wanted the test digs to begin. The first site had been really determined before they had even reached the area. It had been decided from the notes on the area from the mapping team, especially Doube. It was far enough away from their permanent camp to warrant a secondary, smaller camp. The second site was along the trail that led out of the area. When they had been looking to locate their permanent camp Jllon had seen a hill that sat right next to the trail that appeared to be out of place. The hill had even intruded on the trail, which had led to a jog required to go around the hill. This said to him that at some time in the past that this trail had been straight at this point and then the hill at a later time had covered part of the trail leading to this detour around it.

On the site closest to the main camp, he had placed Celt Morlen in charge. His team consisted of Juri Symons, Payle Evyrs, Celt himself as the diggers. Rasti Abs, who was the beast master, would do the sketching. And for the sifters he had his mate Nouma and one of the learners Kaern Slopes assigned to this task. Ehlie Mattie and one of the camp assistants Jahy Delb would rotate with the diggers as part of the hauling team bringing debris to the sifters.

That left him in charge of the second dig site. He placed Flar Pern as a second in charge since Jllon knew that he would be traveling between sites to keep up with any progress that had been made. That left Suzzane Karnes as the lone sifter for this site. He would assist her as needed. The diggers at this site consisted of Flar Pern, Danuld Mield, and Wihl Iame. Wahlter Waeters was the other beast master who would sketch this dig site. Jayson Braylok the remaining learner would assist in the hauling of debris to the one sifter here. Jahnsyn Lytle, a camp manager would be in charge of the secondary camp. With him would be Mihls Bacr as his assistant. That left Mealoh Forsby to cover for the beast masters, while Bayleh Pands operated the permanent camp. Metchy Fellsen, who was a camp manager, would assist him, but would also be in charge of inventorying any of the incoming artifacts.

Of the two teams the one close to the secondary camp was the smaller. Partly because the area they were to work was smaller, and partially because it put a less of a burden on the secondary camp for support. Since there was no water source near its location it would have to be hauled in by the pack beasts every day. Doube would assist by surveying the total area. His expertise in rocks and lay of the land made him an excellent choice for finding places that did not fit. The two artists would also document, in writing, a "rough out" of the day-to-day work. So between the sketches and written descriptions an accurate record would be kept.

With everything in place it was time to start the physical work. For the next few days it would be nothing but removal of the top layers of soil until they reached the top of that dark layer. Once there then the work of attempting to locate anything of value would begin. Value here did not mean something monetary, but more towards a value of learning from the past. How did these ones from their distant past live? How was it for the common everyday person? What was the society like? On and on, the questions could continue for, well, it seemed forever – since many times when one question was answered it created so many more.

As Jllon hiked, with the second group to the chosen site on the eastern portion of the trail, not far from where the mappers had camped, he looked around at the surrounding desert. He thought that in a harsh way this place was beautiful. He could see how some would prefer such a location – such a life. Yet he had to admit that he preferred a wetter area or climate, a place where there was a profusion of color, and the wonderful smells of the natural world on the winds, especially the fresh smells after a new rain. Here there was little of that. Most of the area was somewhat barren. Still the vegetation that clung to this part of the world could, for brief periods, bloom and show similar beauty. Yet, again, this vegetation was very unfriendly. It protected both itself with wicked thorns and needles, and its turf for the precious water that seemed to show itself rarely.

Yet he had to admit the sunrises and sunsets were spectacular. It seemed that at times the very ground took on the shades of the sunrises and sunsets. When it happened the results were breathtaking. This led to his thoughts about his initial survey of the area that it seemed to have supported a relatively large population, one the size of a small township. If it proved out to be so, he was left was another larger question or two. Why live here in the desert, and where did they get their water? Again he thought there was another harder question and that was, was it desert when the people lived here? Without realizing it he reached the site with the team, looked around at the team who were looking at him expectantly, and said, "Oh, sorry I was lost in thought – didn't realize we were here already."

Flar returned a comment, with a smile. "Really, would not want to be lost out here, Jllon. That would be dangerous."

"Now, now you know what I mean."

"Do I?" Flar asked innocently.

From the look on Jllon's face the rest of the team started laughing, and, of course, he had to join in. "Okay you all, the joke's on me. Jahnsyn, you can set up over there at the edge of that weird looking broken rock. It is pretty flat and by being there you are out of the way, and still close enough to make it easy for both us, and the daily supply deliveries."

"Okay boss, and once I'm set up I'll send back my assistant to let them know the location for the first trip. Of course, once that is completed, they'll know where the camp is anyway."

"True, but it's only right that this team will help you set up. That way it won't take you all day, and the one thing I know is we will be here longer than one day. So taking time out to help in the set up isn't going to affect us that much." Turning around to the team he said, "Okay, I'm sure you heard me, and if not let's get this camp set up, that way when we do break for the zenith meal there actually might be one." He knew that as time went on the work they would be doing would become almost routine. But for now, with a new camp, and a new site, there would be some disorganization. With the team assisting Jahnsyn and Mihls, the camp setup took just a short time. The idea of having food when they broke for the zenith meal was all the motivation the team needed to do a thorough job of it.

While this was being accomplished Jllon located a site for the removed soil, and next to that a place for the sifter to set up. Then he and the team walked the small hill, the one that intruded on the trail, to get a feel for the size and type of soils they would be dealing with. Once on the top of the hill it appeared to be much larger in size and volume than first imagined. The soils appeared to be semi solid, which meant the digging would not be easy. So, from this initial survey, it was obvious they would be spending the whole season here and probably at the other dig site just down from the main camp. The second proposed site closer to the coast and to the far west would have to wait.

As they worked this site, he would send messages to and receive them from this and the other location by runners if necessary. Still, because of their isolated location runners would be rare if any showed in the area at all, so any messages would have to be sent from that trading post. At this point he knew the closest re-supply was a couple of days from their location. It would have been nice if the abandoned village had still been there and active, then it would have been a simple thing to get needed supplies. As such, the small trading post on the other side of the mountains to the west was the closest. He knew he would have to send someone there soon so the owner could bring in the supplies to his post that they would require. If the trader couldn't meet their needs, the next place was the village where the other possible site was located. This would entail almost half a cycle to accomplish. So he was hoping it wouldn't be necessary. Still it was something that would only be known when one of the camp managers with an assistant made the trip across. Doube, of course, would be with them. Never would send out a team with less than three members, and in the case of the supply run one additional member from each of the dig site would also go to provide a reasonable number for both assistance and safety.

* * *

The following quarter cycle went by fast. At both sites they had removed two body lengths of soil, and had yet to reduce the size of the hills by much. It was obvious, not that it wasn't before, that they would be here for the entire spring and into early summer before they would find anything, *if* there was anything to find.

It was time to check with the trader. Doube, Jllon, with Metchy, headed out one morn to go to the trader's location to see what he could provide. The morn that they left it was a cool day with a nice westerly breeze helping to keep the desert cool. Since

Jllon had never made this portion of the trip he wanted to do so. By making it himself, he could judge conditions, the time necessary to make the round trip, and if additional pack beasts would be necessary.

They passed back through the abandoned village before heading down canyon to the south. There, as the mappers had done, they cut across to the southwest and headed up the narrow canyon into the mountains. Once they reached the top they headed in a westerly direction. Here they found that the village that had been burned out was still mostly in the same condition, although there was much re-growth from the returning vegetation. So far only a few had returned and rebuilt their shelters. When he saw that there had been some rebuilding he thought that maybe they would only have to come this far for their supplies, but on closer inspection he knew, at this time, it would be impossible. *Never seems to be an easy way,* he thought.

From that village they began dropping down in altitude as they headed west. As they continued, every once in a while the trees cleared allowing them to see the area ahead of them. Yet, in the area where the trees had been undamaged, their ability to see ahead was quite restricted. At least the trail was in good shape and easy to travel. Eventually they reached their destination, and Jllon looked around noticing the change in the land. Here it was flat for quite a distance in all directions except for the mountains behind them. In the distance he could see hills, but none had the height of the mountains they had just crossed. He could see why the trader had picked this location. There were two major trails crossing at this point, and it was far enough inland from any of the townships and villages to be a natural stopping point.

Jllon looked around the shelter and found overall this merchant was neat and tighty in his operation. He even had pack beasts that could either be purchased or rented as the need arose. With the discussion concluded the merchant said he would accept the marks, and notes of payment. He stated that he worked with some of the traveling merchants who passed through the area each cycle who covered the gathers to the west. He further stated he would contract with them for the delivery of supplies to his location here at his shelter, and he would need plenty of lead time since it was just about a cycle round trip for these traveling merchants. He also stated that the runners stopped here regularly.

Finding that out, Jllon decided to go ahead and leave an order with the merchant since he was told that shortly these traveling merchants would be arriving. Finalizing the arrangements and advancing payment they headed outside to enjoy the weather, and some ale the merchant kept on hand. The trader said that the ale came from Rancho, much further to the west.

The merchant came out to join them as they idled around. Jllon turned to him and asked, "If we head out of here going north what's it like?"

"Well, the land remains what you see here. Those mountains you came out of remains on your east side. As you travel further up the westerly hills start drawing towards you narrowing these meadows. Eventually the mountains drop down and there is a canyon that you can pick up that will take you south. If you take that canyon it will eventually take you to the abandoned village. If you continue north, eventually, and not far past that side canyon, the meadows narrow further and turn to the west."

Listening carefully Jllon then asked, "You mean there is another way into that abandoned village, one that doesn't require going over the mountains?"

"Yes, it's easier travel. The only problem is the canyon that you will travel down becomes narrow in a couple of locations. No problem as far as travel goes, but if one ran into trouble from bandits or such, it would be a problem. Of course I haven't heard of any working this far out since generally there are too few travelers to interest them let alone to attack. Of course if you continue to order this amount, I'm sure the word would eventually get out and then the situation could change sometime in the future."

Turning towards Doube, Jllon stated, "I think I really want to explore this other option. We've just traveled the same route that you and the mappers did; I want to see how this other one fares in comparison."

"Okay with me, I like to know an area as well as I can, and a second route is always important. Never like to limit myself to one if it can be avoided."

"Okay then, first thing in the morn we'll head off in that direction and see what we find."

The morn broke bright and clear, with a soft down-canyon breeze. After a quick meal they headed north staying on the existing trail. The travel was easy and slightly downhill. As they continued to travel north and as they had been advised, the mountains to the west started closing in on them. They saw, in the distance, a point of where the area narrowed down and became a canyon. From the conversation they had with the trader they knew that they still had some distance to travel once they reached this point. The direction change would be towards the west as the canyon continued northward. Once through this it would again turn north and open up. Once it opened up and off to the west there would be a dry lake bed. Once they saw the dry lake bed the trail would split at that point. Here, just to the northwest of them, would be a large peak and this split in the trail, if they took the left branch would lead them up that peak, and eventually down the other side. By staying on the right branch they would pass the dry lake bed, which would remain to the west of the mountains they had crossed. Once past this dry lake bed they would be close to the canyon trail that they needed to find to head back towards the abandoned village.

Because this was the first time they had traveled in this direction knowing they had to pass this dry lake bed was important. They had been informed there was another canyon branch with a trail that headed in the direction they wanted to go. It branched off the trail they were on when the canyons narrowed in on them. If they took that trail instead, eventually they would find themselves heading more to the south than planned, then the trail would simply peter out and disappear. Why it existed or why it was there no one knew.

Their plan, as they saw it, was to get past this first branch and then set up a camp for the night. This would give them a little exploring time, and would also mean they would not have to push as hard to return to their permanent camp. Again the weather was cooperating. It was a really beautiful day with soft breezes coming out of the southwest. It would be easy to simply ignore things and watch the day drift by. It was spring and while the vegetation was green, it was obvious that water, even here, was an issue.

It gave the appearance that sometime in the past this area was much wetter than it was now. If it continued in the direction it was presently heading, then in the future, this would be desert like where they were presently researching. That would be a sad day to lose such a mild land. Yet the signs were everywhere. Reading the notes from the mapping team, even in the desert, there had been a large body of water that was no more. Eventually as they traveled this route they would be passing that dry lake bed mentioned by the merchant, again a sign of wetter times.

When they reached the area where they planned on spending the night, it was just past the canyon entrance where the other trail branched off. They found the area crisscrossed with wild beast trails. Looking them over they picked an area that was clear of them. From studying the tracks on these trails they found some trails were old and not used much anymore while others showed much activity. They decided to camp above one of the washes in the area. Here they had good views in all directions, and it was far enough away from any of the unknown wild beasts to be safe.

Jllon turned to the others and said, "You know this is a beautiful land in its way. My thought would be that when one quits their occupation, somewhere near the end of one's life, this would be a great place to finish one's time."

Doube agreed, "Know what you mean. When we came through here, the mapping team of course, we found it easy just to sit and let the day go by. It is a wonder that anyone that lives here gets anything done at all. Again, with it being like this, it's probably easier to do things since most days are like this."

"Bet it gets hot in the summer." Metchy said.

"Don't know really," Doube answered, "but you're probably right."

"True," Jllon responded. If this is as close to paradise that we can get, then there has to be a down side somewhere, and the summers are probably hot. But I bet along the coast it wouldn't be that way, since the ocean would help keep it cool."

With camp set up Jllon and Doube headed down the side canyon to see where it led and if the information passed on was accurate and if the trail was a dead end. Metchy, being a camp manager, stayed to prepare a meal for the evening, and waited their return. He found as he waited that as the evening approached that the area was still, and very quiet. With a fire going, and being careful about that, and the camp arranged he didn't have much to do until Jllon and Doube returned. Sighing, he didn't really have any idea how long they would be away.

As the two of them proceeded down the side canyon they found that it headed in a southeasterly direction and seemed to be easy to travel. Once through the opening of the canyon it widened out. Then, after a while, the trail they were following split, with one portion continuing down canyon and the other heading out of the canyon. They decided to stay with the main trail heading down canyon. In truth the canyon itself was shallow, more like a deep and wide ravine really, and if they so decided they could climb out of it at any time.

Jllon quietly said, "You know this is kind of a nice area. If one wanted to live isolated but still be somewhat close to supplies this area would be one you could do that. I admit the views aren't the best, but most likely since you would not be visible, you would be left alone."

"True, these trees here would provide shade during the hot times, and from the indications I see here there isn't a great amount of winter runoff. Yes, if you had a good water source, it would easily be that kind of place. So, is that your plan sometime in the future? You know locate to something like this?"

"No, no, not really. But it just kind of hit me that one could do that here. And if the weather we've seen so far is any indicator, it would be a great place to live and enjoy the quiet."

"Yeah, must agree with that. I myself have to leave those townships after a while . . . just too noisy and chaotic for me. Give me the natural world and its challenges any day over a township life."

"I understand that feeling completely. That's why my mate and I love to come out on these digs. It gets us out of that noisy world. The change does us a world of good. Still I know many who would think we were crazy for thinking that way."

"Right, I've seen some who were all positive and looking forward to the outback style only after a few cycles, leave, and running back to the townships stating that they didn't understand how anyone could live out here."

"I've seen that. You wonder why it is so, where some embrace it and others run from it." As they were talking they had continued their hike down the canyon and found that eventually the trail they were on climbed out of the shallow canyon and abruptly ended. The one thing they noticed was that there were smaller older trails heading out to the north and east. These appeared to have been little used in the recent past. They may have been wild beast trails, but at this time they did not have time to explore any of them so it was time to head back to camp. It was good that they had been warned earlier about these trails.

The next day went without incident and they found the trail that would take them back towards the abandoned village. On the way they went over to the lake bed to see if only recently had it become dry, but from the growth in the bed and the lay of the soil, it said that it had been dry for a very long time. While it was only a quick study, it left them wondering how much water, lakes, streams and such had once existed in this area. Eventually towards late after-zenith they were overlooking the main camp and the two sites they were working. Yet, from a distance it appeared that no one was working either site. Wondering what was going on they studied the surrounding area and found activity to the south of the sites. Doube stated, "Looks like the nomads have returned. This time it looks to be a larger group than when the mapping team was in this area. Probably the reason your team pulled back."

"You're right, I left a standing order that if they did return to stop and wait for further instructions. I didn't want to cause any problems. Of course, the team knew not to go over to that area as I had placed it off limits after you explained what we'd face with them." As dusk approached they entered the permanent camp, and found the rest of the team there. Once there he could sense the tension and nervousness of the team. Walking over to Celt he asked, "Is everything okay?"

"Yeah, so far anyway. They haven't made any attempt to come this way, but I sensed they were unhappy that we were here. So, as you so stated, I brought everyone back to this camp, and we are waiting to see what transpires."

Nodding, Jllon turned to Doube and asked, "With you having a bit more experience with these nomads, do you feel that since we did not encroach on their area we will be okay?"

"Never know really. They can be real notional in truth. I think the last thing they expected was to have this many outsiders show up in what they consider a secret or protected area. Yet, since we have not approached their water, or camp, I think we will be okay. As far as how long they will be here . . . I don't have an answer. So I would give it a day or two, and then start your work again slowly, but keep someone on watch at both sites. I have found them to be curious people so we may get visitors, and if that happens you and I will have to deal with them."

"Okay then, we will remain in camp on the morrow, and on the following day we will continue, and we will need to maintain a presence in our secondary camp to keep from losing anything. So on the morrow the team that was assigned to the second dig site will spend the day there." Turning to the team he explained what was planned, and said, "On the team that will be at the second site, we will rotate throughout the day with the main camp. We have to maintain a presence there to show it is occupied and is off limits to the nomads as their site is to us."

* * *

Throughout the next day they stayed in both camps. Everyone was nervous and continued to look out in the direction of the nomads. They were well aware of what could happen if the nomads decided that they had infringed upon their sacred or secret area, and while they had been trained in self-defense, they knew they were no match for the nomads. For the nomads protection of both their perceived lands and of their herd beasts was learned from the time of birth and practiced to the time of their death. As the day progressed nothing happened and there were no visits by the nomads. It appeared that as long as they stayed away from the nomad's watering place they would be left alone. Jllon was quite glad that Doube had warned him, and he had followed up by placing the nomad area off limits to any, including himself. Because he was a learned of the past he could appreciate the nomad's position and would respect it. Even though it was obvious this site had been occupied somewhere in the past and would have been a draw to any of his team.

On the following day they returned to their digging, but at a slower pace since one team member had to keep watch. This was rotated as the day progressed to give each an opportunity for a break and to keep a new set up eyes watching. After the zenith meal the whelps of the nomads finally broke the impasse. Whelps, being infinitely curious, started showing up at the sites, but keeping their distance, showing some shyness, but from observing their body language it showed that they wanted to get closer. He was sure the elders had told them to stay away from outsiders, but that was like an open invitation to the whelps to go see what the elders did not want them to see, and to push the restriction placed on them.

Finally after a good amount of time had passed one of the whelps approached one of the team members and then stood politely waiting to be recognized. He had approached one of the females, while not yet sifting, was taking a break close to the area where the sifters had been set up. The one on guard had followed the whelp around and kept a comfortable distance. Close enough to be assistance if necessary but far enough away to allow the whelp to answer his curiosity.

Bowing to her, he asked, "I do not understand what it is you are doing here?"

Turning and facing the male whelp that was approaching the time of being a youngling, and appeared to be around ten to twelve turns old Suzzane responded, "We are seekers of the past."

"You mean you do not have story tellers that keep your past and tell it to you in stories so it is not lost?"

Smiling she said, "Yes we do have our own story tellers, and we have the written word to assist us, but here we try to find what is not written or spoken. We try to find the part of the past that is before. We try to find a time of myth, to either prove the myth is false, or maybe true."

"But why is it so important to you? Does it help you find food? Does it help you take care of your beasts? Does it show you the way of your people?"

"Those are good questions that you ask. Let me see if I can explain. You see we all originally came from somewhere – kind of like when you and your people travel. To get here you traveled from somewhere else, so in a sense this search is the same.

For us to get here and to be what we are is what our ancestors created in the past. So to understand why we are who we are requires knowing and understanding the past. The times these ancestors lived, and what made them do what they did – which in the end, leads to us and the way we are today."

She looked and saw one of the elders from the nomads approaching, most likely attempting to locate the whelps, she warned the whelp saying, "I think one of your elders may be looking for you."

Turning around the whelp saw him, bowed to her and started to leave. He then turned back around and said. "If I get permission from the elders, do you think that I can come and watch? I will stay out of the way; I want to see this trail you are trying to find."

"Tell you what, I will ask the elder of our clan if that is okay, and if it is okay with yours then I see no problem. Still I think it would be better if the two of them got together and made arrangements so there would be no misunderstandings. You can return with your elder and the two, your elder and ours, can decide what needs to be done."

"I will ask, and then let you know the answer." He turned around and ran over to the elder who was waiting for him – he being the last of the whelps to join the elder. Together they headed back to the nomad camp.

The next day, as if ordained, the whelp from the nomads returned with an elder. Jllon being the boss of the group represented his team. The night before the possible meeting, he had talked with Doube, to become familiar with the nomads and their ways, since he did not want to offend accidentally, or cause some misunderstanding that might lead to trouble. When the nomad group arrived they came to the larger dig, and Jllon, of course, was at the smaller. The same whelp with an elder went to the female he had talked to the day before, and she directed them down to the other dig. Both of the nomads bowed and headed off to the smaller dig.

Jllon expecting them, continued to watch as they worked the site, and as is usually the case, it was another member of the team that actually saw them approaching. Jllon signaled for Doube, who was in the area, to come to him in case he needed to correct something. He began walking in the direction of the approaching nomads. When they met Jllon and Doube bowed to them, which they immediately returned. "I'm Jllon the leader of this clan. We have honored your people and have remained from your sacred site."

"That is good . . . JAYllon? Have I pronounced it correctly?"

"Yes, that is correct and this one here is Doube."

"Of him we know well. He is always welcome at our fires and camps. I'm the sire of the whelp that has asked to watch what you do. I am Soolonge the keeper of knowledge for our tribe."

Doube turned towards Jllon and said softly, "He is their wise one, the one who keeps all that is important to them and their culture."

"As you are aware, we have a verbal history, and the story tellers are responsible for the accuracy of that record. The ones who do this study long and hard and must be perfect in their recital. They are not allowed to add anything unless the leaders and myself approve. We are only allowed to add what we know from our individual clans. In the great gathers the additions are judged by the other clan leaders, and knowledge keepers. As a group they have a final say in any changes that is made. By doing it this way we are able to keep our history strong and accurate."

Nodding, Jllon responded. "I understand, yet our ways are somewhat different. We have much of what we know as written text, and we have many who study this."

"Since this that you do here is for knowledge, I do not understand. If you have all written, why is this search necessary?"

"As in all things our written history can only go so far. We search for knowledge before the written word. It is of a time deep in the past. A time of myth, where only the verbal exists, and that in itself leaves no proof that it is real other than what is said in the story."

"So by digging here in the desert you hope to find what is only told as stories? Yet, as I have said, we use such to confirm our past and who we are now. So you still leave me puzzled."

"I understand what you say, yet I feel that even your story tellers only cover so much of your history."

"We can go back at least one hundred generations of our people."

"If you think about it, in real time one hundred generations is roughly six thousand turns around our sun, which is a great amount of time. But we are looking even further back to either confirm or deny these myths – Myths that have been with us from the beginning."

"Ahhh, I understand. Still what is the importance in such a great amount of time?"

"We are what our past is. Still by not knowing what our beginnings really are, we are unable to understand much of what it is that makes us. So we search to find those answers."

"It is always important to search for answers. Still the questions that seem the most important can be the most difficult to solve."

"This is true and this one has proven to be so. We are learning that by putting different learnings together that it assists in problem solving." About this time Jllon noticed one of the team members from the large dig approaching quickly with excitement showing on his face. When he arrived he waited, since he did not want to disturb the three who were talking. Jllon turned to him and asked, "Do you have something you need to speak to me about?"

"Jllon! We've found something and would like you to come and see it."

"Okay." Then turning to the wise one of the nomads he asked, "Would you like to join us to see what this is?"

"Of course, I am always interested in knowledge."

As they hiked back from the smaller site to the larger, the person who had brought the information brought Jllon up to speed as to what had been happening. "Celt decided that maybe it would be a good idea to move the digging to that jog in the trail. Since digging there to get down to the original soil level would be easier. And he was right. After digging only about a half body length down we found something. They are clearing it now."

As they approached the site Jllon felt the excitement in the energy the team was displaying. When they reached the site he approached Celt and let him show the three of them what they had found. While they had yet to completely uncover it, there was enough to know it was not from the natural world. It apparently was a trail, but unlike anything they had seen. Jllon turned to the one who had given him the message and said, "Go get the other team; I want them to assist on uncovering this for a distance in both directions."

"Okay, I'll head over there now."

Turning back to Celt he asked, "Have you found the edges of this yet? What I'm seeing so far appears to follow where the trail now exists. So most likely the original direction that this goes is where the present trail heads."

Soolonge turned towards Jllon and stated, "We have seen this before deep in the desert. There are places where this surface runs for a distance, and places where this surface comes to a wash, and then actually goes over it. We always attributed it to the great ones or others we do not know of. These just appear and disappear into the sands, having no real beginning or end."

"Really, do they also have these yellow lines I am seeing here? And is the surface this gray-black color?"

"Some do and some do not. We have seen broken white lines and also the long continuous lines that are yellow. Although both were much faded and worn from time. Many places where this surface is found, the surface is broken and falling apart. I believe these areas have been exposed to our sun for a long time. While the surfaces we see like this we feel were uncovered by the winds and the rain – when the rains come to the desert. The sands shift continually here."

Finally as the day progressed and the full team worked on the area both edges were exposed showing the width of the surface. It was close to four body lengths. It had double yellow lines with a black line between the two running down its center. Then the team started to dig along its length to see if it was just a short piece that was not a trail but maybe part of a living area.

The wise one turned to Jllon and stated that he had to return, but his whelp would stay and watch. Later he would return to watch the progress and report back to the leader of the nomads. Then he was gone leaving the whelp who watched and remained out of the way.

In the next few days as the digging continued along the surface, it became clear that it was not a living area, but part of an actual trail – if you wanted to call it that. Since in their time there had never been anything like this. What required such a large path? There definitely was nothing in this world, at this time that required it. Even the two wheeled carts had no use of something this wide. Still the questions came – how was it built, and what was this stuff it was made of? Jllon was finding, surprise of surprises; he was ending with more questions than answers.

The hill they were now working, while the edge had covered this revealed strange surface, which lay mostly to the south, became their focus. So with this surface as an anchor point they proceeded to dig into it, and remove the sand and soil. So far they had not brought the level of the hill down to the trail's level.

As they continued to dig along this trail, they found that they were getting well into that dark layer that Doube suspected of being part of a worldwide event.

In the second quarter of the present cycle, at the main dig site another discovery was made. The object found was built of native rock and had a rectangular object attached to it. Once it was completely uncovered, they discovered more of this surface material that came into the main uncovered trail at a perpendicular angle. This object sat just to the west of this new surface. This new surface was smaller, but was definitely of the same material.

On closer examination of the object, very faintly, there appeared to be letters. It took some time, since it was obvious that heat had damaged it. With work, slowly the letters were recovered, read, and recorded. There were two lines that could be read, but the third, which was much smaller, was completely unreadable. The first line's letters were D E S E R T, and the second line was, S A N D S. Now that was an obvious statement. Since they were in a desert, and there was sand everywhere. This, of course, led to another question, why state the obvious? The other item on the object was a simple drawing that depicted some female in an unknown outfit of clothing. Against this object on the trailside was a pole that had some black sticky type of material on it. This pole had also shown some of the same heat damage. Well, maybe as the dig continued some answers would be provided. Still the sign cleared up one question. When this surface was placed the area was a desert and it was nice to finally find the base of the desert trees that seemed to line the trail at this point. It had been one of the clues that led them to dig here. It had been obvious that from what was visible of the trees they had to be partially buried.

As is always the case, when one starts a project of any kind, it seems that it takes much longer to complete than originally guessed or planned. As the digging continued the dark soil had become harder slowing down the progress. But eventually they reached the original ground level. This trail that had taken off from the main one, and after a short distance, had turned to gravel. On both sides of this trail were the remains of what they guessed were shelters, although it was something to be debated. Before these had been buried there had been an intense fire destroying almost everything. There was very little left, so careful work would be needed to recover anything from this site. It was decided, now that the major digging had been completed at this location that they would leave a quarter of the crew here to do the delicate final work, and to survey the site further. The rest would move on to the secondary site to see if anything was at that location.

The one thing that was strange to him was the way these shelters seemed to be laid out. They were in a straight line – lined up on both sides of this side trail. So different from how settlements were organized today. Almost all in this present time were set in a circle radiating out from the center. Why were these shelters setup this way? Another question added to the growing list of questions, instead of answers to all the questions they had before coming here. Another oddity, the shelters seemed to have been constructed using metal. It was lying all around in solidified puddles. Where, with the intense heat of the fires, the metal had melted and ran into pools of liquid metal that had eventually cooled. The bases of these shelters had large metal frames, and weirder yet, in the center of these frames running across them were what appeared to be axles. Did this mean that these shelters moved? Were they a part of a caravan, and if so, what beast would be able to move something so massive? Did these people have much larger beasts or did they have some other means to move these things around?

In the present to use metal for a shelter was unheard of. In this time it was expensive and used for tools and axles and such, but not for the shelters. The material of choice was almost exclusively wood. With such an extensive use of metal could it have been that these people were rich? Again, so many questions, and no ready answers. At least he could say that the chosen site was producing results, and while nothing had been found yet to establish a time period, it was quite obvious, from what little had been found, that these people were quite different from them. Just by studying the layout of the area showed a different mentality. Once everything the site would produce was cataloged and studied then maybe a better picture would emerge – at least he could hope.

It was time to move back to the secondary dig site and let the team do its work. Maybe later he would have some of the answers. At least he knew the area was important. In all the other digs he had done in his career nothing like this had ever been found. Plus, in studying the archives, any discovery that had been made in the past did not resemble this site either.

* * *

The second site turned out to be quite different from the first, which, in the end, was no surprise – because the hints about what might be here were quite different from the first site. At first they abandoned the initial dig to dig up the existing trail to see if maybe that same surface existed here also.

As the days passed the whelps from the nomad camp came and went, but remained completely out of the way. Every once in a while an elder would come to see what was happening but they too kept their distance. The wise one would come rarely, but would ask questions before returning back to their camp. Then one day the team realized that none of the whelps were around. Curious, they looked in the direction where the nomads had been camping and where their beasts grazed and found that they were gone. It was a surprise since they had come to expect them and to answer the questions of the wise one. Now they were quite alone. Other than the trips to pick up supplies at the outpost they had no contact with anyone. At the outpost they left messages and sent letters home for the runners to deliver, and of course receive return correspondence, but other than that there were just these digs.

On the main dig much research was being preformed, but few answers as of yet. The fires had been so intense that there was very little left, still small things were being found. On the secondary dig site the removing of soil and sand continued. They had found that the surface of the trail that they had been located at the first dig site existed here also. They ended up digging approximately fifty body lengths to confirm it continued. It still left them wondering what was it traveled these surfaces.

If the overall site began to show more promise they would have to get more workers here. Still as the season progressed, he knew that soon the hotter part of the turn would be here and it would probably be almost impossible to work. After all this is a desert, and the desert in the summer cycles is quite hot, and of course dry. It was unknown whether the water by the main camp would remain throughout the summer or whether, as the temperatures rose, would dry up and go away.

As the work continued on the second site, Doube continued to survey the existing area and had come up with additional promising areas to work. Once most of the work had been completed on the first two areas, Jllon would begin to send out small teams to test dig these newly surveyed areas, but all of that was in the future. The results of the present sites, plus what these test digs revealed would determine if he would be able to request additional help, or even have such a chance. Anyway, once it became too warm to work here, they'd head over the mountains and look at the area close to the remote village where that object had been found. But, again that was all in the future, and they still had time here before the desert became unbearable.

Fortunately this site was located in an isolated area. Once the temperatures raised enough to become unsafe, they would have to abandon the area. If the water did indeed disappear, then one wouldn't be able to stay and guard the sites. So if they could keep the worksite a secret they would keep out anyone who would come in trying to find something of value. After all, if it was discovered before they finished, then these outsiders would destroy what was of value to them, contaminating the site, and making the site completely useless. It was a loss they could not afford.

Jllon continued to work with the two sites, the first site to see what had been located or found, and the second to see the progress of the digging. One of the first things that were found at the first site was something that they had overlooked. In truth it was not small – just about two and a half body lengths long and one body length wide. It was originally dismissed as maybe a small shelter. Yet on closer examination, they realized that it was much too small for that kind of use. Still it was easy mistake to make and think it had to be a shelter as it had four doors, plenty of places for windows, and the remains inside of what appeared to be seating. In the front the structure extended out, but there was no obvious way to enter this area. In truth it was too small to place a person. So it was speculated that this area and the area in the back was used for storage – thusly the mistaken identity of a shelter. As it was uncovered, eventually it revealed its true purpose, there appeared to be wheels at the four corners. This meant that this thing was to be mobile, and yet there seemed to be no way to hitch a beast to the thing to be able to make it move. Of course such a hitch may have been lost in the fires. Yet a closer inspection revealed no place for a hitch. Again this unknown unit was partially made of metal.

As the site continued to be worked a second one was found. Yet again, it was completely different from the first. It was larger, but only had two doors, and the back area reminded them of a wagon or cart that would be used to haul materials. It had locations for four wheels, although in both discoveries there were only metal rims where these wheels would have been. It was obvious that at some time there had to be something on those metal rims since these rims were much too small to allow these discoveries to move. On the second they found the same problem. There were no hitches or places to place a hitch. *How do these things move* – yes, of course, adding another question. Here he thought he would be answering the many questions, but instead he was ending up with infinitely more than what he had started with. These two units were too large to be moved presently. Once the second site was finished then with the many they might successfully relocate them.

As in most digs they had completed in the past, they were finding broken dishes, and some cooking utensils. Most had shown major damage from the heat of the fires. It was while he was looking over recovered items that he was approached by one of the members on the second dig team. He was informed that they had found the top of a partially collapsed shelter, and would he come back to the site. Dropping what he had been doing, he immediately headed out with the team member and returned to the second site. He found, when he arrived, something unexpected. Again, this area or site overall, had been doing nothing if not providing surprise after surprise. Expecting something along the lines of what they had uncovered at the earlier site, he was immediately taken back by the sheer size of this one. And once again, to his chagrin, it seemed to have been constructed of metal. Turning to Celt Jllon commented, "Wow, this thing his huge, and the roof appears to be metal also. What is it with these people? They seem to have used it everywhere, and were able to form it however they wanted as it shows here, what skills they must have had."

"Yes, I agree and I must admit at this moment I'm in awe of what I'm seeing. It seems that they used this stuff as if it was easy and plentiful. I mean it appears that it was a common building material. And looking at the size of the roof alone there was a lot used."

"I'm going back and bring the rest of the team up here. They need to see this as we uncover it. I can see that this shelter has partially collapsed; maybe whatever was inside is still there. So I want everyone to concentrate on uncovering this. (And yes they were below that dark line that had been pointed out by Doube.) This might end up being the answer to our big question for us."

* * *

With the complete team the work went much faster, and in the end it turned out to be two shelters. The one on the east side had partially collapsed into the west shelter. When it had collapsed it was of good fortune for the team, as it ended up adding additional support to the west shelter. So while there was some collapse where the two met it was not as great as it might have been. Yet, the teams had a ways to go before the shelters were completely uncovered. One of the questions added that had yet to be answered was; why did these shelters not burn, while the others discovered earlier had burned intensely? As the digging continued they noticed that these had no windows, and the sides were again made of metal – it left them wondering if these people had constructed all their shelters this way. Another factor may have protected them from the fires, was that these two seemed to be somewhat isolated – they had found nothing else, just these two. No promising sand hills close and no sign of anything artificial. Like at the other dig it showed the same soil type progression, the regular desert soil on top, and as they had progressed down the dark volcanic ash type soil, then these shelters below that.

* * *

As it was revealed it became obvious that this dark layer had not been cool when it was deposited here. These shelters had shown some signs of scorching, and probably it was a miracle that these two had not burned – burned . . . something that they had never applied to metal before. Yet the first uncovered site had shown them that metal would burn. The other surprise was their size. In the present time there was nothing to compare to these ancient shelters. What they would have considered large would probably fit at least twice over in any one of the two shelters.

What were they used for, and why was something this size needed? It became obvious to Jllon that adding builders to their team would become a necessity. They could study the construction methods and maybe help identify these shelters. Adding such a skill to the team had never entered his mind. Since, other than recent abandoned areas, there had never been uncovered or located, a standing, or a partially standing shelter for any to study. This large site was creating all sorts of challenges and changes to the methods they were presently using. It was unprecedented that was for sure. This site would make history for what was being learned here, and if nothing else, the methods used in this time would be changed forever once they finished, and never would a site be studied in the same way again.

CHAPTER EIGHTEEN

Eventually they uncovered the shelters all the way down to the same material that existed on the recently uncovered trail. Again it was a substance they were unfamiliar with, and these ancients seemed to use it everywhere. In places where it had been exposed to the elements for the eons of time it was mostly destroyed, looking more like areas of rock than a solid surface. Yet in the areas where it had been buried, then uncovered, it was whole, although showing wear that time laid on everything, and heavily cracked. Yet one could see that at one time this was smooth without the cracks and breaks.

Again, this dig site was one surprise after another, and these shelters did not disappoint either. Once the north side of the shelters had been exposed they saw what they assumed was a huge door or doors, and off to each side there were additional doors the size they could use. These smaller doors were not that much different from the ones they presently used. Yet even here, there were things they had never seen. On the doors that they used in this present day, the door was of wood with leather hinges using a simple latch system that would be pinned from the inside to lock it. Here again they ran into silver like metal hinges and a knob like handle that was probably used to enter, and it was locked or seemed to be. How, they had no idea, although that slot in the middle of the nob might be the solution. It appeared that the large doors were also locked, and on the outside there was nothing to even grab on to, so it was assumed they were locked from the inside like the doors they would use every day.

On the east end of the eastern shelter they had left the soil in contact with partially collapsed shelter to help support it and at the same time this allowed them to climb up on top of it – even though it appeared to have partially collapsed under the weight of the soil. Yet once the soil had been removed it still appeared to be solid enough to support them. Since the partial collapse had been into the western shelter they thought they might be able to make entrance into the other that way. But on closer inspection they found that it had made no real penetration into the western shelter. When it had fallen into the western shelter, it had warped the wall of that western shelter, followed by slipping under the roof, adding a double support to the western shelter and preventing a total collapse of the eastern one.

The next thought was to dig down below the foundation on the south side and then come up through that way. Again, when tried, it failed. It seemed the foundation was of some type of stone, thick and smooth. It appeared unbreakable. The team, standing outside these massive shelters, frustrated, and tantalized, was at an impasse. "Tell me, how are we going to get into these things?" Ehlie, one of the learners asked.

"I don't know . . . I really don't know as of yet." Jllon replied as he shook his head. "I really don't want to break down that door, but it may come to that. Still, by looking at it, it does look pretty substantial. Not wood that's for sure."

"Not only that, did you look at the frame it's sitting in?" Juri asked.

Celt replied, "Yeah, as stated, none of it is wood – which makes even more difficult, if not impossible."

"At least it's not going anywhere," Jllon stated. "Let's head back to camp and think about it for a while. Maybe we can come up with a solution. The two artists need additional time anyway to finish the sketches and to put them to scale. It's getting late after-the-zenith so let's just call it done for today, have a discussion tonight after the meal and tackle it fresh on the morrow." Turning towards the artists he said, "When you finish here come back to the main camp. We are going to want to look at these drawings tonight, and make sure you get a good sketch of those possible entry points." With that said the team headed back to camp, with feelings of elation and at the same time frustration. Here they were on the verge of one of the greatest discoveries of their or any generation, but for a door, and that same door continued to deny entry.

The camp managers and their assistants had not been able to see the massive shelters, and after listening to the rest of the team discuss what they had been working on wanted an opportunity to see something so massive. Jllon gave them permission to join the team after the morn meal. After all, maybe they would come up with a solution that had yet to be tried. He also knew that the drawings would never give the actual shelters justice as to size. There just wasn't anything to compare them to in their world.

That night around the campfire there was much discussion, and a few ideas thrown around as to how to gain entry. Since this was again something that had never been encountered, it was all speculation. Earlier, a close inspection of that handle had revealed a clever anti-break-in device. So by attempting to jimmy or slide the interior latch back had failed. The large entry had doors that were massive and had no obvious hinges on the outside, and still appeared to be as solid as the smaller entry. And on closer inspection these large entry doors, even though partially recessed, were solid against the shelter so they weren't on the type of roller system that would allow them to slide to the side. With the large size of those doors verses the length of the walls there just wasn't room for them to slide in either direction anyway. Nor was there a split down the center that would allow them to open in both directions. That left only up. Even in that direction the door appeared to be solid, *how could something so massive move up?* They had to admit there was more room for it to move in that direction than in any other, still with the suspected weight, how would such a door be lifted?

Again, as things had been uncovered, there were more questions being added with few answers. Jllon was beginning to feel that if he had two life times he would never be able to scratch the surface of what was being discovered here. As far as finding answers it might take generations. It left him feeling somewhat inadequate. Not just for him, but for where their people were, in comparison to these finds. Whoever these people were, their skills and abilities were well beyond anything they presently, as a culture, could produce, and that led to the question, are there more such places in the desert? In the end it still came down to questions as to what had destroyed a culture that was definitely far ahead of where they were presently. And if, in the end of these discoveries, they found that they were the descendants of this possibly advanced culture, why were they so far behind presently?

With the drawings passed around and everyone having a close look at them, the group fell silent, in deep thought, as they attempted to find some way to gain passage into those mysterious shelters, and whatever secrets they might hold. It was kind of like the anticipation of opening those birthday presents one would receive from their sires. Hoping for something special, but unable to really know since it was hidden inside the wrapping – trying to use the shape, the density, and weight as a tool for identifying the gift, and in the end, being mostly wrong. Except in this case, there could only be speculation, but with nothing to base their thoughts and suppositions on, there were no real answers, none at all. In the end when everyone turned in except the ones who were on watch they were no closer to a solution than when they found their way blocked by those sealed and locked doors. Hopefully, when they returned to the shelters on the morrow, a solution would present itself. The damage to the eastern shelter had been great, and with its subsequent collapse, had then damaged the western shelter. So if anything had survived it would be in the western shelter. It appeared the only way into the other would be finding a way to cut through the metal, and those kinds of tools were only available to a blacksmith.

The next morn after the meal, the whole team headed back out to the site to study it first-hand. Once again they tried the locked door, they walked around the whole shelter, they studied the foundation, and once again they found no real weak point. Then one of the team noticed that on the bottom of that large entryway there appeared to have been something that acted as a seal, which confirmed this huge door would open in the "up" direction, and not left and right. Jllon looked at the whole team and said, "I need the strongest members of the team to get up to that door and see if you can get your fingers to slide between the door and the foundation, then together see if you can lift it up any distance at all."

Excited they all volunteered, but there was not room for all so he picked the ones who appeared to have strength – which of course were the diggers, since they did most of the physical work. With care they slid their hands under the seal, which scraped their knuckles because the seal had hardened with time. Then they attempted to lift carefully. The results were positive if not a little disappointing. The large door had moved up, but ever so slightly. It seemed as if it had some type of latch or lock on the inside to prevent this type of entry. Still the slight movement was a good sign if not a surprise. Here was a promise of possible entry. They knew that they would not be able to break the foundation but with that movement the diggers tried again and was rewarded with a little more movement, with a groaning and slight rattling from the door. In this attempt some of the seal started to disintegrate and break apart.

"Wait, wait," Jllon exclaimed. "Can someone go find something we can prop under that slight opening? I think if we remove that seal material there might be enough room for the smallest female to slide underneath, and then with a torch she may be able to see a way to gain entrance for the rest of us."

And that is what they did. It took half a day to prop and then break off the old sealing material. It was obvious that sometime in the past that it had been flexible, and probably had provided good protection against wind and rain. Now it was worn, hard, and somewhat brittle. Again whatever it was made of was unknown to them. After all the prep they had an opening approximately two fists wide. Not much room, and there was no male who would fit through that small of an opening – only the smallest female had a chance, and here on site that would only be Kaern Slopes, and even for her it would be a tight fit.

All of the team could at least look inside by lying down. Since the only light entering the shelter was from this opening nothing could really be seen – tantalizing but unsatisfying that was for sure. Almost there, but the secrets it held, if there were any, still were well beyond their reach . . . but probably not for long.

"Kaern are you ready?" Jllon asked.

"Yeah I guess so. You know, for once my size is an advantage. I get to be the first one inside of this shelter in who knows how long, and this is definitely special."

"You're so right. Once you're inside we'll pass you a torch, and then see if you can find a way to open the door so we can come in. Once we are inside we can work out how this big one works and get it open. Once open we should have plenty of light to see what is in there."

As she approached the small opening she lay on her back and started to slide under the opening. The diggers added additional effort in trying to give her as much a space as they could. Even with their effort it was very tight, even for her. Still, with some work she made progress, but felt that most likely she was leaving a little of her skin from her backside in the process. It took some squirming and sliding, letting out her breath, and with the diggers continuing their effort to add additional lift she finally slid through, while she continued to hold her breath. Coming out of the bright sunlight into the darkness left her momentarily blind. She remained lying down for a second. Then sitting by the entrance she waited for her eyes to adjust to the darkness, and was surprised to find that at this moment the interior was cool, and floor was actually cold. Outside the team waited for some response from Kaern, and when none was forthcoming asked what she saw.

"Nothing yet," she replied, "still waiting for my eyes to adjust. Can you go ahead and pass me the torch? That will probably help." She turned back to the opening got on her knees and stuck her hand outside. She knew that once they handed her the torch, they would ignite it and she would pull it inside. She knew the one reason that a torch had not been thrown in earlier was the fear and possibility that they would accidentally burn something that would be irreplaceable. It had been decided that the torch needed to be in someone's hand to prevent that kind of accident.

When they handed the torch to her, once lit, and with a word she carefully brought it inside. Now with some light she stood up. At first she was disappointed, as there didn't appear to be much in here – mostly empty space, but the floor was smooth cool and solid. *Just what is it made of?* She walked deeper inside the shelter and then realized that one of the items in here looked like the flyers. *No, that can't be right, since we've never been able to do that.* Still this thing had wings on it, and a tail – well sort of. It was kind of different than the flyers, still when the flyers caught the wind currents they didn't look that much different than this thing.

Momentarily lost in thought she then heard Jllon asking a question.

"What? Sorry didn't hear you."

There was a little impatience in the voice, but at the same time envy. "Have figured out how to open the door yet?"

"No, actually I haven't gotten to the door yet, was distracted by what I found here."

"What do you mean – found here?"

"It would be better for the rest of to see it first, and see if your conclusions are the same as mine. Okay, I'm heading for the door now and will see what I can find out." She turned around and walked over to the door and tried the handle, which was more of a lever, and to her surprise it easily moved in her hand. When it moved to the end of its range she pushed and the door opened – it was surprisingly simple. For a moment she was blinded by the bright sunlight and covered her eyes. When she opened them she could see all of the team members standing there in expectation, waiting for her to say something. Not sure what to say she said, "Would someone please block this door open. I don't want to have to crawl under the other one again." That brought a nervous laugh from the group.

"Sure, sure a great idea," Jllon replied. Once it had been blocked all of them entered the shelter in single file and then with the light from the torch went to work on trying to open the large entrance. On both sides they found metal pins that slid into holes on a metal rail, which the large door was attached. Attached to the door were metal rollers that rode inside the rail and on top of the door attached to both sides appeared to be small metal ropes, which disappeared somewhere in the darkness towards the ceiling. It took some manipulating to figure how the pins worked as they had locking levers. Once the levers were released the diggers gave a heave upwards and to their surprise the door rose with less effort than they expected considering the size, and once it reached a certain point in its upward travel, continued on its own until it stopped. As it raised it was obvious to the team that the door consisted of many hinged sections, and with the light they then could see where the metal ropes went. Hanging down next to this large entrance was a pull rope, probably meant as a way to close this large door.

With the additional light the whole interior became visible to them, and like her when they saw mostly empty space they were disappointed. Still this was probably why this hadn't burned. With so little to burn what was here would remain unharmed except what damage time had laid upon the items. What was there stopped them in their tracks. If ever there was proof of the *ones before*, it was here before them.

"That looks like a flyer!" Celt blurted out, then he continued a little sheepishly, "Well, sort of anyway."

"That was my reaction," Kaern said.

As they looked it over it was the only conclusion they could make. What else could it be? It had wings in both the front and back, and a tail that stood straight up – and doors. There was a funny shaped wood blade in front. While different from the construction of blades used in windmills it was similar enough to be considered one.

The other thing in here was an unburned unit similar to the two that was found at the other site, the ones originally thought to have been small moveable shelters. Both the possible flyer and the moveable unit located here had some type of semi flexible material on what they would have called wheels. Apparently the ancients had a way to put something inside of them to keep them round, but whatever that had been was gone, and this material was flat on the bottom. Again time had made the substance hard and not flexible. The good news was that since this had been buried these two discoveries were in pretty good shape considering how long they probably had been here. One of the team members wandered over to the west wall and found a desk. Again the desk itself was metal, but the surface was made of some softer unknown substance.

Jllon, doing a quick study, realized that this had been a quick abandonment. When the people left, it had been fast, and it was obvious they had planned on returning later, yet for whatever the reasons were unable to do so. He realized that they were the first to see this since the owners had left. At this point the team spread out and did an initial inventory. Jllon stated he wanted nothing touched until the artists had finished sketching a detailed drawing of what was here and how it positioned. He also wanted the shelter to air out as it had a "closed in" smell, and a little fresh air would correct that. As the rest of the team left the shelter Jllon thought. *So they could fly. Of course this is just an impression at this moment. We really don't have any proof. Still, what a thought, if they flew why couldn't they avoid this disaster? Yet, maybe it was something that happened without warning and because of this couldn't, who knows?* Shaking his head, he knew too little and so it was all speculation.

Flar walked over the Jllon shaking his head and said, "You know looking at this thing I think that it will fit on one side of the trail we uncovered. So I wonder if that's why the trail is so large." Jllon nodded as he thought about it. While they had no proof it did make sense.

The temporary camp was just a short distance, and he had, once the shelter had been opened, sent the camp managers over to it so they could prepare the zenith meal. The team now went there to eat, giving time to the artists who would shortly join them, for the meal, and let them know how their work had progressed. Everyone was exhilarated from the finds. Not in their wildest dreams did they feel that they would be part of the team that would find definite proof of the ancients, the elusive *ones before.* Confirmation would take time. Still, if the evidence held up, and at this moment it appeared that it would, here at this site was the actual proof.

What they had uncovered here was obviously a different culture, a different way of life. These people were well advanced and much further along than they themselves were presently. The little bits that were being found were not enough to jump-start the present world. Still it was possible that their existing society was better than the one they were discovering. Yes, at this time, at this very moment, there was no way to know – too little had been found to be able to even identify a way of life for these ancients. And still the questions continued to flow. If these ancients had conquered flight, what other things had they accomplished? Were the present people descendants or something entirely different? So far no burial sites had been located so even remains could not be compared. It was humbling to see what these ancients had accomplished, and apparently with ease, and to see how far they, in the present, were from them.

Still there was a positive thought out of all this, and it was this; they were here and thriving, while the ones from the past with all their accomplishments and advancements, were not. Jllon knew from what had been found so far, that this overall area should continue to reveal much. So what he had originally thought would be a couple of turns of work probably would most likely take the rest of his time, and whoever replaced him. He also realized that soon he would have to return for a short period of time back to the halls and write up an initial report on the findings, and then present them to the counsel. And he knew in the end that he would have to bring some of the leaders here so that they could see for themselves. It always seemed to be that way. He wondered if it had been that way back when these ancients lived.

Still, sitting here with his mate and the team around him, he couldn't help but smile. He and the team had accomplished the impossible. They had found those elusive *ones before* and had proved they were real. So the myths were myths no more. These myths were now fact. And while the stories told to the young ones were probably fiction, the ones they talked about were not and had actually lived sometime in the very distant past.

After the meal he would return to the large shelter and see what other fantastic finds awaited him and them. He remembered seeing other closed doors inside and a cart of some kind that looked as if it may have tools for some kind of work. If he remembered correctly he had seen a name on its front and it said C R A F T S M A N. So his initial thought placed these tools to a specialist, a craftsman in some unknown area. One of the females curiously had opened one of the doors and then stated "Hey look, this sort of looks like the necessary space." And everybody had to agree that it did. Yet so much of it that was in there was strange and different. The biggest surprise was the looking glass. It seemed to be almost perfect. Something that even the best produced now could not match. And there had been what appeared to be a drawn picture on the wall showing one of these flyers in the air. In fact there was a second picture with a view from high in the sky looking down on these shelters. Still, whoever the artist was who created them, these images were more realistic than any could create in today's world.

He knew that soon they would bring in a second smaller team to continue here, and he and his present team would move on to the other area over the mountains where that object or objects had been found. He was of the hope that this other area would be just as revealing as this one.

Yes, at this very moment, he considered this the greatest find of his generation – a discovery that probably would put him and his team into the history books. Yet, and to be honest, little did he know that what the future held for he and his team . . . and what they would possibly discover would make this first great find, this initial proof seem small and insignificant in comparison. But that would be for the future, one that might not happen, yet for now, what had been found here, and knowing that there was still much to find, left them all excited and at the same time humbled. For here before their eyes was a hidden past now for the first time revealed. Doube had been correct all along. Their true past was hidden below that dark line. Just a little deeper and further down into those ancient soils than any had worked in the past.

Sitting with his mate Jllon stared out into the distance. Would his initial exhilaration turn to disappointment? It was always a possibility, but he suspected that it would not. So much that had been found here was foreign to the way of things – strange and different, yet at the same time familiar. With those thoughts he turned to his mate and smiled. Yet it was a sad smile because he could almost see those desperate moments when the ones who had lived here in the past and in their present had left hoping to return, but never got the chance . . . Leading, for him and his team, to a discovery that put truth to those myths that refused to die. *The Ones Before* existed, and patiently waited for their time, while lost deep into the unknown and unwritten past, to be rediscovered and be written into history.

The *ones before* were moving from fantasy and myth, to reality where they truly belonged, all because of a lost township long buried in the desert. Not only the physical desert, but the endless desert of time . . .

TO BE CONTINUED

ABOUT THE AUTHOR

Storytelling and writing has always been F.D. Brant's
passion, but responsibilities took preference. And
because of those responsibilities it took retiring to
allow those passions to come to fruition. Since
retiring he has written 9 books, and maintains a
weekly eclectic blog, Words in the Wind.

Growing up in the backcountry he learned the
appreciation of "doing things for yourself". Because it
was impossible to call in someone to repair anything

one either did it themselves or went without. This led to the appreciation of the natural world, and the daily struggles that one faced as nature threw problems at the family that had to be overcome, leading to confidence and self-sufficiency. This led to the strong characters that populate his stories and books. And his female protagonists are strong willed and confident – something that he saw in both in his mother and sister.